A QUESTION OF BOUNTY:
THE SHADOW OF DOUBT

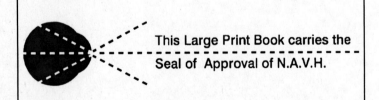

A QUESTION
OF BOUNTY:
THE SHADOW OF DOUBT

PAUL COLT

WHEELER PUBLISHING
A part of Gale, Cengage Learning

GALE
CENGAGE Learning·

Farmington Hills, Mich • San Francisco • New York • Waterville, Maine
Meriden, Conn • Mason, Ohio • Chicago

GALE
CENGAGE Learning®

LIBRARY OF CONGRESS CATALOGING-IN-PUBLICATION DATA

Colt, Paul.
    A question of bounty : the shadow of doubt / by Paul Colt. — Large print edition.
        pages ; cm. — (Wheeler Publishing large print western)
        ISBN 978-1-4104-7336-3 (softcover) — ISBN 1-4104-7336-8 (softcover)
        1. Billy, the Kid—Death and burial—Fiction. 2. Outlaws—Southwest, New—Biography—Fiction. 3. Garrett, Pat F. (Pat Floyd), 1850-1908—Fiction. 4. Large type books. I. Title.
    PS3603.O4673Q47 2015
    813'.6—dc23   2014039238

Published in 2015 by arrangement with Paul Colt

Printed in the United States of America
1 2 3 4 5   19 18 17 16 15

A QUESTION OF BOUNTY: THE SHADOW OF DOUBT

FOREWORD

Las Vegas, New Mexico
September 23, 2010
The familiar brown delivery truck wound its way up a quiet, hilly suburban street. The driver carefully ticked off the house numbers until he found his address. He turned into the drive of a modest, neatly kept ranch house done in the Southwestern architecture suggestive of traditional adobe. He grabbed a thick manila envelope off the passenger seat and stepped out of the air-conditioned cab into the late afternoon heat. He crunched up a stone walkway to the portico shaded front entrance and rang the bell.

Moments later retired police detective Rick Ledger opened the door. He signed for the delivery, thanked the driver and took the envelope to the small office he maintained in a back bedroom looking out on a small backyard pool. He laid the envelope

7

on the desk, took his seat and gazed out the window.

This was it. After all the years of mystery and controversy, could it be he now held in his hands another important piece to the puzzle? Had it been worth it? Had it been worth the lawyers, the courts, the public outcry, the ridicule? Soon he would have his answer. In the end they'd prevailed. Not in the quest to exhume the grave reported to be the victim's. Their opponents argued successfully that flood damage to the cemetery had so disturbed the remains of those buried there as to render the task of identification impossible. Still they'd found another way. They obtained the necessary samples. Blood from a bench believed to be the one from the carpenter's shop in Pete Maxwell's home. The second sample came from an old hat they found stuffed in a box of discarded clothing and personal effects in a back room of the Pioneer Nursing Home in Prescott, Arizona. The hatband inside was inscribed J. Miller. They'd found a hair sample sufficient enough to analyze. Matching the DNA would end at least part of the mystery.

The controversy had raged for nearly a hundred and thirty years. Did Pat Garrett really kill Billy the Kid on July 14, 1881?

The question gained notoriety in the 1930s, when a man in Texas, "Brushy" Bill Roberts, claimed he was Billy the Kid. Roberts' claim on the Kid's identity was subsequently discredited.

Rick's grandfather, Brock Ledger wasn't surprised. He'd heard a different story from his grandpa Ty, a rancher and deputy US marshal in the New Mexico Territory at the time of the Lincoln County War. For Rick, the controversy always centered on the story he'd heard from his grandfather.

He closed his eyes and remembered a summer night, sitting on a creaky porch step at his grandfather's knee. He must have been eleven, maybe twelve. Summer vacations on Grandpa's ranch in those carefree childhood years happily ran together. Those days were almost like rolling back the calendar to the last century and a time when rugged men rode these hills, taming a raw land to a new way of life. He felt a part of it back then, joining in the cowboy work by day and riding the past by night in his grandfather's stories. This story had stayed with him. The story he heard on magical nights more than fifty years ago.

He could almost taste the chilled Coca-Cola in the little green bottle. He saw insects swarm around the bare bulb porch light. He smelled sweet hay and horse scents drift up from the corral. He listened to quiet night sounds, as he waited for Grandpa to begin his yarn. Grandpa Brock gazed into the darkness as he brought the story back from another long-ago time. He recalled the words of the tall handsome cowboy in the faded tintype, framed in filigree on a parlor end table. It was a story Great-grandpa Ty told his grandson. A story that happened some eighty years before the night he first heard . . .

ONE

Blazer's Mill
New Mexico Territory
August 5, 1878

The Lincoln County War was over, the legend making had only just begun. John Tunstall and Alexander McSween were dead. John Chisum's men had withdrawn to his South Spring ranch in the Pecos valley. The Dolan faction had won. The Tunstall Regulators were mostly scattered, gone back to peaceful pursuits. The last remnant of the Tunstall McSween faction, the so-called Ironclad Regulators remained. They were Tunstall loyalists; men who fought to the last. They'd left more than a few of their friends dead at the hands of Jimmy Dolan and his men. Then again, they'd taken their share of the boys who rode for the Dolan faction, known as the House. William Bonney, now better known as Billy the Kid, had informally taken over for the last official

Regulator captain. The gang included Doc Scurlock, Charlie Bowdre and Tom O'Folliard. They drifted toward the Mescalaro Apache agency at Blazer's Mill accompanied by a gang of no-account Mexican toughs, curious to see what the gringos would do now that the fighting was over.

Blazer's Mill appeared out of the distant sun shimmers, ragged shapes climbing a low hill. Billy winced at the memory. The Regulators caught Dolan man Buckshot Roberts in the tiny settlement during the height of the war. The old gunman had put up a hell of a fight. Badly outnumbered, he'd shot up a handful of them including the Kid. Roberts died, gut shot in the encounter, but not before killing the Regulator captain Dick Brewer. The bad memory stood out fresh as a bloodstain on that old hill.

The sprawling Mescalaro agency building sat atop the hill beside Dr. Blazer's fine two-story home. Further down the slope, a sawmill powered by Tularosa Creek stood beside a small general store and post office. Across the dusty ruts that passed for a street, two small adobe homes sprawled up the side of the hill to a blacksmith shop, barn and corral below the crest. Doc signaled a halt. He stepped down followed by Billy and the rest of the Ironclads.

Antanacio Martinez, leader of the Mexicans, leaned down from his saddle. "Why stop here, amigo?" He pointed with his thinly whiskered chin. "There is a hot meal in sight."

Scurlock spat. "These horses is about played out. We need to figure how to replace them."

The Mexican laughed. "Nothing could be easier compadre. There you can see the corral for yourself. Where they have a corral, they have horses, fresh for the taking." He turned to his men. *"Vaminos muchachos!"* He spurred off at a lope.

Josiah "Doc" Scurlock watched them go. He might have been mistaken for a school teacher. Clean shaven and sober of expression, he had a prominent nose, chiseled cheekbones, square jaw and neatly trimmed brown hair. He wore a dark frock coat he had a habit of pushing open behind the butts of his guns.

"I know you get on with Mexicans, Billy, but it might be best if we didn't hang so close with them bastards. They're trouble sure as sin."

William "Billy the Kid" Bonney patted his big roan and nodded. A boyish-looking young man ladies found fetching, he had light brown hair, a gap-toothed grin, cherub

13

cheeks and eyes a-glint, somewhere between mischief and murder. His attempt at a beard amounted to patches of fuzz on his lip and chin. He wore a battered sombrero perched on his head at a jaunty angle. Plain spun britches, shirt and a stained canvas vest hung on a slight frame of average height. He wore a .41 Colt self-cocker known as the Thunderer slung low on his hip.

"Where do we go from here, Billy?" Bowdre said. "I'm feelin' like it's time to go home."

Billy understood. Charlie had a wife, Doc's half-sister Manuela. Average height and plain featured, Charlie Bowdre had a broad forehead and questioning eyes. Drooping mustaches accentuated a weak chin. He wore a double-breasted shirt, baggy canvas britches and a Colt .44 holstered butt forward on his hip.

"Old Fort Sumner might make as good a hideout as any." Charlie called the old fort home. Manuela lived there.

"Get out of Lincoln County and the heat will simmer down," O'Folliard said. A pudgy, ruddy Irishman, Tom O'Folliard had a ready laugh. He had red hair, green eyes and a splash of freckles across the bridge of his nose. He looked more like a mischievous schoolboy than a hardened gunfighter. Like

14

the Kid, his appearance might lead a man to dangerous misestimation. He took gleeful pleasure in pulling pranks all right, often at the business end of a gun.

Shots sounded softly in the distance. All eyes cut toward Blazer's Mill.

"Sounds like trouble," Charlie said.

"Maybe them folks objected to givin' up their horses," Tom said.

"I had a hunch," Scurlock said. "Mount up."

The Ironclads rode into Blazer's Mill to find the Indian agent dead, the corral cleaned out and the Mexicans gone. They fed and watered their horses. Laid in a few supplies and rode northeast bound for Old Fort Sumner.

The postmaster ambled across the rutted dirt street to the blacksmith shop.

"That looked like Billy the Kid."

The blacksmith spat a tobacco stream. "Sure 'nuf."

Lincoln

They camped in the hills northwest of town. No point in riding in there at the risk of stirring up trouble. The war might be over, but there were plenty of gunmen on both sides still around, nursing long memories

15

and vengeful tempers. Billy sent Bowdre into town for supplies and to find out how things had settled out.

He sat cross-legged in front of a small fire, just enough to heat coffee. The air was still. The day's heat lingered. Heat lightning winked out of a dark cloud bank off to the northwest. His stomach growled. Supper had to wait until Charlie got back. Doc had gone off on one of his walks down their back trail. He smelled trouble creeping up behind them like spooks in the night. Billy guessed the precaution couldn't hurt. It gave Doc something to do. Tom lounged beyond the circle of firelight cleaning his guns.

The Kid shook his head. How had it come to this? He hadn't been party to the bad blood between Mr. Tunstall and Dolan. At least not until Mr. Tunstall gave him a job. The man treated him better than most anyone ever had. He took it real bad when Dolan men, posing as a sheriff's posse, killed his benefactor in cold blood. It was Dolan's doing. Everybody knew it. You could never prove it, though, not that anybody tried. Dolan owned Sheriff Brady. Brady might have worn the star, but Dolan was the law in Lincoln County. Brady wouldn't shit unless Dolan said he could. So Dolan had Mr. Tunstall killed over his mercantile and bank. Dolan probably figured that would be the end of it. He didn't count on Mr. McSween and the Regulators.

The Regulators went after the murderers and got most of them. Once the shooting started, blood spilled on both sides, including that rat-bastard Brady. Things kind of ran together for a while until the big shootout in Lincoln a month ago. McSween and the Regulators figured to force a showdown in town. Dolan found a way to call in the army. Dolan men, backed by the army, shot the shit out of McSween and the Regulators.

Mr. McSween died in the five-day battle. The Kid and the Ironclads escaped. Escaped to what? They had no jobs. They'd never even gotten their last pay. Dolan still had the law in his pocket. George Peppin was his new puppet with the star.

The sound of an approaching horse drew the Kid back from his thoughts. Bowdre rode in. He handed O'Folliard two flour sacks of supplies and stepped down. O'Folliard followed his nose into the sack with the fatback and set about slicing long strips into a frying pan. Scurlock crunched out of the shadows into the firelight, drawn back to camp by Bowdre's arrival.

"What news from town?" Doc asked.

Charlie poured himself a cup of coffee. "Well in case you didn't know, we're now Billy the Kid's gang. We shot up Blazer's Mill, killed the Indian agent and run off their stock."

"Don't s'pose we can get by claimin' it wasn't us," Doc said.

They all laughed.

"Well if we'd done all that, at least we'd have money to show for the horses them Mexicans stole," Billy said.

Tom put a smoky pan of fatback to sizzling on the fire and stirred a little water into a pot of beans. He pulled a bottle of whiskey out of the sack with the beans. "Hey, Charlie, you been holdin' out on us." He poured some in his cup and passed it along.

Bowdre shook his head. "Looks like we cain't keep out of trouble for not gettin' in any."

Doc took a swallow of his drink and poured another. "It's Dolan's doin'. He wants us on the run and out of his way."

"I cain't figure what he's got to gain by that. Hell, he won," Billy said.

"Well, I'm goin' home," Charlie said. "I ain't goin' back to Lincoln anytime soon."

Heads nodded around.

Patrick Floyd Garrett tended bar at Beaver Smith's Sumner Saloon. Old Fort Sumner was a two-saloon town. Bob Hargove's place set the standard for modest. The Sumner made a measure of shabby. The air smelled of stale tobacco smoke, sweat and beer. Late afternoon sun fought its way through dirt streaked windows giving the room a muddy yellow glow. A few scarred tables dotted a stained rough cut plank floor. The bar Garrett served had a once polished top, blistered and cracked by the abuse of harsh climate and harder use. At that, it was the only finished surface in the Sumner.

Tall and lean, Garrett carried himself with a quiet competence despite his humble circumstances. He wore his brown hair and mustache neatly trimmed. He had alert brown eyes that missed little. He knew trouble when he saw it and he knew how to handle it. Old Beaver Smith kept a baseball bat and sawed-off shotgun under the bar in case of trouble, not that much of that happened with Pat on duty.

The Ironclads looked the part when they came in. Garrett had heard Bowdre was home. He wasn't with the other three. Word was they'd come to Sumner to lie low. He doubted they'd cause any trouble, unless somebody caused trouble for them. They sidled up to the bar. He put on his best welcome and moved down the bar.

"What'll it be, gents?"

"Whiskey," the redhead said.

"Same." The cool quiet one nodded.

"Make it three." The gap-toothed kid grinned.

Garrett set out glasses and poured. He set down the bottle. "You boys new in town?"

"Rode in yesterday," the Kid said.

The redhead took the bottle. He and the quiet one took themselves off to a corner table.

"Billy Bonney." The Kid stuck out his hand.

"Pat Garrett, Billy. Welcome to Fort Sumner."

"Pleased to meet you, Pat. Seems like a real nice little town."

"It is. We like to keep it that way."

The Kid's eyes twinkled. "We surely do appreciate that."

"Good. Then we understand one another." Garrett moved down the bar and went back to polishing glasses.

"Say, you're Billy the Kid, ain't you?"

He glanced over his shoulder at the slight young man who'd quietly come up to the bar. "What's it to you?"

"My name's Billy too." He stuck out his hand. "Billy Barlow, pleased to meet you."

He eyed the young man. Apart from dark hair and dark skin, he might have been looking at a slope-shouldered, gap-toothed brother.

"Is it true what they're sayin', Billy?"

"Is what true?"

"That you killed that reservation agent over to Blazer's Mill."

He shook his head. "Ain't true. Mexicans shot him. He was dead by the time me and the boys rode in."

"I know'd it weren't true. Hell, Billy the Kid wouldn't waste his time on a feller like that. Can I buy you a drink?"

"Sure. Why not?"

Barlow puffed his chest and bellied up to the bar. "Set 'em up, Pat."

Garrett set down another glass and poured. He stepped back to his endless polishing.

"How long you figure to be in Fort Sumner, Billy?"

The Kid shrugged. "Hard to say."

"Well, if you ever figure you could use another gun, I'd be right proud to ride with you boys."

He arched a brow and glanced down at

the .44 strapped to Barlow's hip. He smiled to himself. "That's still mostly up to Doc, these days."

"If you was to put in a good word, he'd sure take me on."

The Kid turned toward Barlow and leaned against the bar with a lazy smile. "He might, if I had a good word to give." In a blink, the Kid's gun appeared in his hand. "But then you'd be dead, Billy Barlow, just for bein' slow."

Barlow reddened. He touched the brim of his hat. "Good day then." He hurried out the door followed by the Kid's laughter.

Two

South Spring Ranch
September 1878
The long striding, big boned buckskin ate up the last mile home at a slow lope. John Simpson Chisum sat an easy saddle at the end of an uneventful ride down from Lincoln. The trail spilled out of hills dotted in juniper and thatched in greens burnished old gold by the sun. A faultless blue sky soared overhead in the waning light of late afternoon, setting a perfect stage for the ascent of the evening star in the east. Average height and rangy strong, Chisum had a presence about him. He tucked wavy brown hair salted gray at the temples under a sweat-stained hat. Intense blue-gray eyes flickered under a rack of bushy brows set in lean sun-weathered features. His mustache was neatly trimmed and waxed with a whisker patch at his lower lip. He wore a plain spun shirt and britches. A Winchester

rifle rode in his saddle boot on the trail. Past that, he found no need to carry a gun. Others did that for him.

South Spring Ranch was home to Chisum's Long Rail brand. His herds ranged up and down the Pecos Valley, numbering near one hundred thousand head. The ranch sat on a low rise, a half day's ride west of the river near the north end of the valley. He loped through a weathered split rail arch bearing the Long Rail brand and let the buckskin turn his nose up the rise to the bunkhouse, corral and stable beyond. A large adobe hacienda sprawled across the crest of a rise backed up to hill country to the north and west. A creek ran out of the hills from the north along the back of the house and corral, providing fresh water for the ranch house and stock.

He drew up to the stable and stepped down. A bright white smile lit the shadows beyond the open stable doors. Deacon Swain's shiny broad features resolved out of the shadows.

"Welcome home, Mr. John. Here, let me put up that horse for you." A bear of a man, the former South Carolina slave came to South Spring with Wade Caneris, the Long Rail foreman. Deac had proven himself a

24

capable hand and Dawn Sky's closest friend until Johnny Roth came along.

"Thanks, Deac." He pulled the Winchester from the saddle boot, rested the long barrel on his right shoulder and handed over the reins. He set off up the hill to the house. His eyes drifted northeast to the house Roth built for Dawn Sky. He'd given them the section for a wedding present. He could see the beginnings of a second house further down the slope. Johnny took Ty Ledger on as a partner after the battle for Lincoln. Ty and his new bride Lucy settled right into South Spring's extended family. They'd all be interested in the news from Lincoln.

He clumped up the porch to a massive front door. The door opened to a sprawling adobe hacienda furnished in heavy rustic wood and leather covered furniture. The smell of fresh baked bread greeted him. Dawn Sky stepped out of the kitchen into the dining room.

"Sure smells good in here," he said.

She smiled. The girl was the closest thing to a daughter a man could have without being blood kin. Her mother had been his housekeeper until the fever took her, leaving the little girl to no one's care but his. He'd raised her like his own. In time, she kept house for him too. She was a young woman now, married he reminded himself. She carried her lean frame with the proud bearing of her Navajo people. Wide-set dark eyes atop high cheekbones gave lively expression to the serious set of full lips. Those eyes might flash like summer lightning or turn soft and liquid like a river eddy with the mood of the moment. She'd grown up easy on the eye. Easy to see why she'd dropped a loop on a man like Johnny Roth. Likely the first thing that ever held him in one place.

"You got enough supper fixin's in there for the five of us?"

She nodded.

He knew she would. Dawn saw things or felt things or dreamed things in ways he never understood. He just came to accept the fact she was always a step ahead of him.

They gathered around the dining room table just after sunset. Dawn and Lucy served a steaming platter of roast beef, baked potatoes, gravy, and green beans fresh picked from the garden Dawn kept along the creek at the back of the house.

Johnny Roth had already started to feel like something of a son to Chisum. Tall and muscled, Roth came with a history. His eyes, the color of mountain ice told some of it along with a small scar that split his lower lip. He wore a pair of black leather rigged Colts that marked him a competent man. He'd worn them in his days as a bounty hunter, a part of his past Chisum feared might haunt him. Still, Dawn loved him and he loved her, plain to see. In the end, that had to be enough.

He felt better for having Ty Ledger around. He and Lucy hadn't married yet. They planned to once the house was finished. For the time bein' she was bunkin' at Dawn and Johnny's place while Ty stayed down in the bunkhouse with the hands. That arrangement probably accounted for the noticeable rate of progress on the house. Ty and Lucy had their stories too. Chisum didn't know them near as well.

Ledger was a tall wiry rough shaved Texan who'd worked as a drover before turnin' to lawman. He'd been sheriff up in Cheyenne and a deputy US marshal for a time. He and Roth came to New Mexico on the trail of a man who'd murdered Ty's wife. They'd nearly got their hair lifted by renegade C'manch in the bargain. It made for a special bond between the two men.

Lucy Sample showed up in Lincoln about the same time as Roth and Ledger. A wisp of a girl, she was almost childlike, taking her woman's figure from a tiny waist. She had a rich fall of sable hair and large brown eyes that said they knew more than the rest of her let on. She'd worked for John Tunstall before he got killed. Ty managed to get her out of the store before the battle for Lincoln started. Somewhere along that way the romance must have gotten started was all Chisum could figure.

The ladies took their seats and started passing platters of food. Roth helped himself to a slice of beef and passed the platter to Chisum.

"So what's the news up in Lincoln?"

"Well, things has quieted down some since you three left."

They laughed.

"Dolan's fixin' to get back in business. They say he's makin' a deal to turn the House over to the county for a new courthouse. He'll take over Tunstall's old store and fix up the damage."

"John's turnin' over in his grave," Lucy said, passing the potatoes.

Roth cut a bite of beef. "What's Evans up to?"

"Nothin' I've heard."

"Likely we'll know next time Dolan needs cattle for the fort or the reservation."

Chisum shook his head. "Don't look like

28

we accomplished much does it?"

Conversation fell silent for a time. "There's more news out of Santa Fe." All eyes fixed on Chisum. "President Hays has replaced Governor Axtel. He's appointed General Lew Wallace governor. He's also removed T. B. Catron as US attorney."

Ty knit his brow. "What do you suppose that means?"

Chisum paused, a forkful of beans halfway to his mouth. "For one thing it puts a big hole in the Santa Fe Ring. They say General Wallace is honest."

"Santa Fe won't know what to do with an honest governor," Roth said.

"A man like that might have answered my call for martial law," Ty said.

Roth cut his eyes to Ty. "A lot of people might still be alive if he had."

Chisum gave a wry nod. "The president is a day late and a buck short. Just like government, tryin' to catch up with what's already happened."

Sumner Saloon
September 1878
Oil lamps flickered along the walls and behind the bar, the beacons shrouded in a fog of tobacco smoke. Conversation set out a low hum, punctuated by an occasional

peel of laughter or outburst of profanity.
Garrett filled the Kid's glass.

"They say this new governor might grant
them as fought in the war am . . . am . . .
nasty . . ."

"Amnesty."

"That's right. It's kind of like a pardon,
ain't it?"

"It is."

"You think he will, Pat?"

Garrett shrugged. "He might. It'd be a
quick way to settle things down."

"If I could get me one of them pardons,
I'd start over fresh. I wouldn't be no trouble
to nobody. I'd be the same Billy Bonney
Mr. Tunstall saw fit to hire. I'd get me an
honest job. Maybe even settle down."

Garrett refilled his glass. "Write a letter to
Governor Wallace and ask him for one."

"You think that would help?"

"Couldn't hurt."

"Aw shucks, I wouldn't know the first
thing to say."

"Give it a try. I'll help if I can."

"Would you, Pat? Would you really? I'd be
much obliged."

"Sure, Kid."

"Evenin', Billy."

The Kid glanced over his shoulder.

"Remember me? Billy Barlow. I been

workin' on my draw. It's comin' along real good. Someday I'll show you I'd be a good man to ride with."

The Kid turned back to the bar. Barlow slid off to the far end. Garrett's gaze lifted toward the batwings. The Kid followed his eyes in the mirror behind the bar.

A stern-looking, bespectacled man of average height stood framed in the doors. He wore a shabby coat, plain shirt and baggy britches. He had a prominent forehead, courtesy of a receded hairline, and a drooping mustache. He blinked behind spectacles reflecting the low light. He seemed to settle on Garrett and crossed to the end of the bar near Barlow.

"Excuse me." Garrett sidled down the bar to his new customer. "What'll it be, Pete?"

"Whiskey."

Garrett set down a glass and poured.

"Nice to see you honestly employed."

Garrett shook his head. "How many times do I have to tell you? I didn't have nothin' to do with them cattle of yours."

"So you say. Leave the bottle."

Garrett returned to the Kid.

"Nice feller," the Kid said.

"Pete? Oh he's all right. I used to work for him. He lost some cattle and blamed it on me."

"Did you take 'em?"

He shook his head. "He got it wrong."

The Kid tossed off his drink. "I know how that works."

Pete Maxwell eyed Garrett and the Kid.

"You know who that is talkin' to Pat?" asked Billy Barlow.

Maxwell glanced at young Barlow and shrugged.

His eyes glittered. "That there's Billy the Kid."

Pete took a second look.

"He's the fastest gun around these parts."

Maxwell studied his drink. "You'd do well to find someone else to admire, Barlow. His kind ain't nothin' but trouble."

THREE

Old Fort Sumner

Pretty as one of them peaches. Billy watched the girl stretch to reach the ripe fruit. Bright sun filtered through the trees catching the lights in her dark chestnut hair. She dropped one peach after another into her apron until she deemed the makeshift handbasket full. She emptied the apron into a basket at her feet and reached to pick more. He eased the roan into the orchard.

She looked up at the sound of a horse approaching, her dark eyes wide, instinctively wary. He smiled his crooked boyish grin to reassure her.

"Mind if I help?"

She looked uncertain.

He stood in his stirrups and plucked a ripe peach well beyond her reach. He bent down and handed it to her. She smiled, reassured. Her delicate fingers felt soft and light to the touch. A little something kind of prickly passed between them. She wore a long full skirt and white cotton blouse gathered at her shoulders. Her dark skin looked as though she might be Mexican.

"My name's Billy, Billy Bonney."

"I'm Paulita, Paulita Maxwell."

The name registered. "You Pete's girl?"

"Sister. Do you know my brother?"

"I've seen him around. Cain't say we've been formally introduced. Hold the basket and I'll give you a hand with some more of these."

He filled the basket and stepped down, looping his reins around the saddle horn. She was no bigger than a minute except for those big eyes and handsome swells where a girl was supposed to have them. Standing beside her his breath caught in his throat. She had a pleasant scent too, like good earth in the spring.

"Here, that looks heavy. Let me carry it for you."

"What about your horse?"

"Ol' Red? He'll follow along." And he did, just like a dog, padding at his master's heels.

She started back toward town.

"These peaches sure smell good. Sweet too I'll bet."

"Take one if you like," she said.

"I surely will, once my hands ain't so full."

They walked down Roswell Road into town from the orchard. The Maxwell house was the former officer's quarters, a large rambling one-story affair with a covered porch across the front that wrapped around the north side.

"Where can I put these for you?"

"I'll show you." She started up the porch steps. "Say, he won't follow you inside will he?" She tossed her head at the horse.

He laughed and shook his head. "Not Red, he'll mind his manners."

She led the way inside. The dark wood interior gave off a warm golden glow. He followed the sway of her hips down a long hall dimly lit by a large sunlit kitchen at the back of the house. A young Indian girl, somewhat older than Paulita, glanced over her shoulder from the batch of bread dough she was kneading and smiled.

"You can put 'em on the counter," Paulita said.

Billy set the peach basket on the counter and tipped his hat to the smiling girl. "Ma'am."

"Deluvina, this is Mr. Bonney. He helped me pick peaches."

She smiled again, showing even white teeth. She had wide-set black eyes. The chiseled copper features of her Navajo people

35

composed a plain appearance she carried on a sturdy frame.

"My friends call me Billy."

She nodded. Said nothing and went back to her dough.

Paulita selected a juicy ripe peach and handed it to Billy.

"You fixin' to can these for the winter?"

"Mostly, but I'll make up a pie with some."

"Peach pie, that sounds mighty good."

"You've been such a help, Mr. Bonney, I expect you've earned yourself a piece of pie. Come by after supper and I'll have one for you."

"Why that's most kind of you, Miss Maxwell. Please, call me Billy."

"Very well, Billy. Then you must call me Paulita."

" 'Til this evenin' then." He smiled his crooked smile and took a bite of his peach. A dribble of juice trickled down his chin. He wiped it away with a finger and a sheepish grin. He doffed his hat, made a silly little bow and went back outside to his horse.

Paulita watched him go with a half smile.

"He very nice boy," Deluvina said as she turned her dough.

"He is, but don't you think he's a bit more grown than a boy?"

Deluvina turned to the girl who might be her pretty younger sister. "You think so, little Paulita?"

"Yes, I do. And I'm not little anymore." She stomped a foot to her point.

Deluvina suppressed a giggle at the girl's determination.

"I do think he's nice." Something about him disturbed her in a curiously pleasant sort of way.

Sumner Saloon

The Kid strolled up to the bar just before sunset. Garrett greeted him with a smile.

"What'll it be, Billy?"

"That help you promised me."

"What help was that?"

He slid a folded sheet of paper across the bar. "A letter to the governor. You said you'd help me with it."

The barkeep picked it up.

"I'll take a whiskey while you look it over."

He poured the Kid a drink and opened the letter.

Dear Governor Lew Wallace,

I read in the papers you plan to grant pardon to those involved in the Lincoln County War. I hope you will consider my case for pardon. I fought with the Tunstall

Regulators after the Dolan men murdered Mr. Tunstall. We was duly swored deputy US marshals with legal warrants on the men we pursued. Those warrants included Deputy Sheriff Billy Mathews.

When we Regulators sought to arrest Mathews he was in the company of Sheriff William Brady and Deputy George Hindmann.

Sheriff Brady drew his gun to resist our arrest order and was killt in the gunfight that followed as was Deputy Hindmann. This was done in self-defense as I am sure you will agree by your pardon of amnesty. With grateful appreciation for your hearing
of this matter
I remain,
Your faithful servant,
William Bonney

PS Them stories about me killing the Indian agent and steeling them horses up to Blazer's Mill ain't true. A bunch of Mexicans led by Antanacio Martinez done that. They was already dead when we got there. WB

Garrett slid the letter back across the bar. "Well?"

"Not bad. You need to address him as

Honorable." He fingered the paper.

"What?"

"The Honorable Lew Wallace, Governor, Dear Governor."

"Oh."

"You believe you were duly sworn deputies, not swored."

"We did too swore, I mean swear."

"I know, but once you did you were sworn."

"If you say so."

"And it's killed, not killt."

"What the hell, he's dead either way."

"You asked me to help."

He nodded. "I did. And I appreciate it, Pat. If Honorable Ole Lew gives me animosity, I'll have you to thank."

Pete greeted the knock at the door. The only thing more unexpected than an evening caller was this particular caller.

"What do you want?"

"Evenin' Mr. Maxwell. We ain't met yet. My name's William Bonney. Paulita invited me to come by for a piece of peach pie."

"I invited him, Pete." Paulita appeared in the hallway behind her brother. "Billy helped me pick peaches this afternoon and was kind enough to carry them home for me. I thought such kindness at least de-

39

served a slice of pie."

Maxwell scowled at his sister.

"Come along, Billy. Pie's in the kitchen."

Maxwell let him pass. Billy could feel her older brother's eyes burn his back as he followed her down the hall to the kitchen.

She cut two pieces of pie, arranged them on plates and handed one to Billy with a fork. "Let's go out to the porch. It's cooler out there." She led the way back down the hall. The rough cut planks of the top step made as good a place to sit as there was. The roan stood in the yard splashed in moonlight, watching them with one shiny dark eye.

Billy took a forkful of pie. "Mmm, this is good. You always make pie this good?"

Her cheeks blushed hot in the dark. "Hard not to with good peaches."

"Well I declare these is the best I ever tasted."

She blushed again.

The pie got the better of conversation, leaving the evening to night sounds. Crickets chirped. Somewhere down the street toward town a dog yapped. A lonely owl called to its mate. Billy cleaned the last of the pie from his plate with his fork. He felt her eyes and met them in his.

"Your brother don't like me."

"Pete? He doesn't like any man that pays attention to his little sister."

"Cain't blame him for that, I reckon. He must go around not likin' a lot of men."

Her cheeks burned in the moonlight. She liked the notion he might think it. "Not so many."

"I don't believe that."

She pursed her lips in mock surprise. "Who'd ever figure Billy Bonney for a sweet talker?"

"Me? I ain't no sweet talker. It must be the company."

"Mind now I don't believe a word, but I do like the sound of it. Care for more pie?"

"If I don't eat it all, maybe you'll invite me back another time."

Her eyes caught the moon, white light reflected in black pools. "I'd like that."

Her voice sounded like music. "Well I guess I best be on my way whilst I'm still in your brother's good graces."

"Don't pay no mind to Pete. You come back soon. Please?"

"I'd like that." He rose.

She stood on the porch. Moonlight frosted the bow of her lips. He felt a powerful urge to kiss her. Too soon he thought and smiled his crooked smile. He stepped away to collect the roan.

She picked up the plates and took them back to the kitchen. Pete followed her down the hall.

"Paulita, do you know who that is?"

She sighed. "A boy named Billy who was real nice to me."

"Nice boy." Pete folded his arms across his chest. "That there's Billy the Kid. Hired his gun out to Tunstall in the war down in Lincoln he did. He's got blood on his hands and lots of it. His kind ain't nothin' but trouble. You stay away from him, you hear me?"

"I'm a grown woman, Pete. I'll see who I want, when I want."

"Grown woman! Paulita, you're fifteen. You ain't growed up by a long sight. You best listen to your elders before you get hurt."

"Sure Pete, I'll listen."

He turned on his heel and trudged down the hall toward his room near the front door.

Deluvina appeared in the pantry doorway. "You know Señor Pedro speaks only for your good, *muchacha.*"

"I don't need Pete to think for me and I am not a little girl anymore."

The serving girl's bare feet padded across the plank floor. She placed her hands on Paulita's shoulders and turned her around.

She stroked the girl's hair with a half smile and a twinkle in her eye. "He is muy guapo."

Paulita matched her smile and shook her head. "No, he's not cute. He is . . ." She groped for the words. "He makes me feel . . ." She looked down, inspecting the budding young woman she'd nearly become.

"Ah, muchacha, the boy makes you feel a woman. This is good. It happens sometimes before you have the summers to know what it means. Be patient. Summer will come." She put her arms around the girl and hugged her.

Lincoln
October 1878
Sharp northwest wind howled out of the mountains under a rumpled blanket of low running cloud. Lincoln sprawled along a ridge on the south bank of the Rio Bonito surrounded by tree-covered hills. Adobe and frame buildings lined a single shaded street. The west end of town was dominated by a large two-story clapboard building that housed the Murphy & Dolan mercantile known as the House. It stood across the street from the Wortley Hotel, a symbol of Dolan's power and a stark reminder of the war that followed from it. The House was

being converted into a county courthouse. J. J. Dolan sold it to the county in exchange for cash and the former Tunstall bank and mercantile down the street. Dolan's repairs to the damage done the Tunstall store in the battle for Lincoln were nearing completion. At a distance it all looked familiar to Lucy.

They had the South Spring house down the hill from Johnny and Dawn's under roof. Under roof didn't mean finished, but as far as she and Ty were concerned it was finished enough. The prospect of living through winter under the bunkhouse arrangement persuaded them they could put up with some inconvenience while they lived through finishing the work inside.

They decided to keep the wedding small. Johnny rode into town with them. He'd stand as witness for Ty. Lucy planned to ask Susan McSween to stand for her. They'd arranged to meet the circuit judge at the Wortley. They planned a simple ceremony, supper in the dining room and a wedding night in the hotel. What they hadn't planned was the strange brew of emotion each felt riding through town.

The war was over. The shooting had stopped. Still the scars lay bare for all to see. Dolan's repairs on the Tunstall bank and store remained incomplete. The front windows were boarded and the storefront pockmarked and bullet riddled. The burned out McSween house remained a charred cinder beside the store. Memories of the dead lurked in the devastation. The names rang hollow in the soft clop of the horses' hooves: John Tunstall, Alex McSween, Dolan men, William Brady, George Hindmann. Flawed men, some right, some wrong, all rendered equal in death.

They drew rein at the Wortley hitch rack and stepped down. No one spoke for a time. Roth collected the reins.

"I'll put up the horses."

"I'll get us rooms," Ty said.

"I'm going over to Mrs. O'Hara's and talk to Susan," Lucy said. She crossed the street away from the battleground, squared her shoulders and headed back down the street to the widow's house. Wind whipped her riding dress and stung her eyes as she passed the burnt out ruins of the McSween house. Poor Susan, she thought. It must be terrible living with these constant reminders of her home and the place where her husband died.

The familiar creak of Mrs. O'Hara's gate brought her back home. She'd taken a room with the widow after arriving in Lincoln. It seemed a long time ago now. In truth it was not much more than a year. Was that possible? She'd followed Ty to New Mexico, hoping he might turn to her after the loss of his wife. When that hadn't happened she'd allowed herself to be wooed by John Tunstall. Her heart had never really been in it. John offered a safe haven away from her old life. Lord knows what might have become of her after he was killed if it hadn't been for Ty. He'd come back to her after all. And now they were to marry. Maybe fairy tales did come true. She climbed the front step and rapped on the familiar green door.

A stout woman with strands of gray hair strayed from a severe bun opened the door and blinked behind her spectacles. "Lucy, dear, come in, come in. What a pleasant surprise."

The welcome warmed her. The house smelled of furniture polish and fresh baked bread. It came with a big affectionate hug.

"What brings you back to Lincoln?"

"Ty and I've come back to get married."

"I'm so pleased for you, dear. He's such a handsome catch."

"I guess I best get him quick before you lure him away."

She laughed.

"I was hoping Susan might be here."

"Of course, my dear." She inclined her head to the stairway. "Susan! Look who's here to see you."

Susan McSween appeared at the top of the stairs. She smiled weakly. "Lucy, it's so nice to see you." She descended the stairs slowly. "Ranch life must agree with you. You look positively radiant."

"Blushing bride," Mrs. O'Hara said.

"Of course, I'm so pleased. Congratulations." She hugged Lucy.

Lucy couldn't help but notice how thin she'd become, positively skin and bone. The luster seemed to have gone out of her green eyes along with the dampened fire in her hair. Lucy could only imagine the loss of a husband under such tragic circumstances. She banished the chill feeling.

"Go along now you two. No need to stand here in the hall." Mrs. O'Hara sent them off to the parlor. "I'll put on a pot of tea," trailed over her shoulder as she headed down the hall to the kitchen.

Susan led the way to the settee. She looked pale and wan in the parlor lamplight. Strains of the summer's ordeal had plainly taken a toll.

"How have you been, Susan?"

She resigned a smile. "Well enough all things considered."

Lucy patted her hand. "I know it must be difficult for you."

A tear welled in her eye. She shook it aside. "I'm leaving Lincoln, Lucy. There is nothing to hold me here. I can't even walk up town without being reminded of those terrible days."

"Where will you go?"

"North, Las Vegas I think. I have to settle the estate. It's all tangled up with Tunstall's holdings and Dick Brewer's too. I don't have to be here to do that. But enough of such dreary reflection, tell me about your new life."

"Ty spent the last couple of months building us a house. It's not quite done but with winter comin' on we figure it's done enough. We came to town to catch Judge Bristol tomorrow and get married."

"What a lovely beginning."

"I was wonderin' if you could stop by the Wortley tomorrow and stand up for the wedding?"

"Oh, Lucy, I'd be honored."

"It'll be small, you and Johnny, Mrs. O'Hara if she can come. We'll have some supper in the dining room afterward."

"We'll be there." Mrs. O'Hara smiled and set down the tea service. "Wild horses couldn't keep us away."

FOUR

Sumner Saloon
November 13, 1878

Billy slammed a fist on the bar. The low hum of conversation quieted in the smoky yellow haze, the crowd's attention drawn to the young man at the end of the bar. "Dolan, Evans, Mathews and all the rest of them sons a bitches got blood on their hands. Wallace pardons them. Me, Doc, Tom, Charlie, do we get a pardon? Hell no! We get warrants issued for our arrest. Where's the justice in that?"

Garrett topped up the Kid's glass. The hum returned to conversation, games and laughter with the Kid's outburst quieted.

"Don't seem fair when you put it like that," Garrett said. "Then again, you gotta face the fact Brady and Hindmann were law officers. The law don't take kindly to them kind a killin's."

Billy tossed off his drink and set his glass

on the bar for another. "Law, hell. Brady might just as well have put guns in the hands of them responsible for killin' Mr. Tunstall. We had warrants for their arrests. We was law officers too."

"If you'd arrested 'em, you wouldn't be havin' this trouble."

"They drew on us."

"If you've got witnesses to that, provin' self-defense should be a simple matter. Turn yourself in. If you're acquitted, you don't need a pardon."

"Ain't never that simple when the law gets around to me. I'm the only one got a bounty on his head. Five hundred dollars, fancy that. Hell, if I'm guilty, I'm worth way more than that. It's a damn insult."

"I don't know as I'd go off complainin' about that if I was you. The bigger the bounty, the more hunters will try to collect. Reason enough to turn yourself in."

"And trust I'd get a fair shake from them bastards? I'd have to be loco." The doors creaked behind them. The Kid glanced in the looking glass behind the bar. Pete Maxwell stood in the doorframe. He noticed the Kid right off and stepped up to the bar.

"What'll it be, Pete?" Sober warmth passed for Garrett's good humor.

"Whiskey."

"Let me buy," the Kid said.

Maxwell arched a bushy brow. "I'll take care of my own drinks, thanks just the same."

"Aw, Pete, I was just tryin' to be neighborly."

"Be neighborly enough for me if you quit sniffin' around my sister."

"Paulita don't seem to mind. We's just friends. That ain't no reason to get all sore on me."

"Look Bonney, I don't figure you for a good influence on a young girl. She's only fifteen. She don't know no better than the likes of you."

"I don't mean her no harm. Some girls is pretty growed up by fifteen."

"Not Paulita."

The Kid eased around to face Maxwell, freeing his gun hand. "Are you forbiddin' me to see your sister?"

He heard the edge in the Kid's voice. His hand trembled as he tossed back his drink.

"Just askin'."

"Fair enough. I'll let Paulita decide."

Maxwell tossed two bits on the bar and left.

The Kid watched him go. He shook his head and turned back to his whiskey, still saddled with a murder indictment and a bounty on his head.

"Maybe if I talk with the governor . . ."

Las Vegas, New Mexico Territory
December 1878

The office was small and sparsely furnished. The scent of fresh stain and wood polish hung in the air. The young man who greeted her in the outer office struck her as quiet, thoughtful and not terribly imposing for the loss of one arm. Still, he came with the reputation for a terror in the courtroom. Just the sort of advocate she needed.

"Mrs. McSween, Houston Chapman. Please have a seat." He gestured to a side chair as he rounded the desk to his chair. He smiled. "Now, how may I be of service?"

She arranged her dress around the stylish — though bothersome — bustle and took the offered seat. Maintaining the appearance of fashion annoyed her at times like these. "I'm in need of a solicitor to settle my husband's estate and see to the prosecution of those responsible for his murder."

"I see. Estates are usually rather routine. Murder prosecution is a matter for law enforcement."

"You assume the law is being enforced. In this case, it is not. My husband was gunned down defending our home in Lincoln against an unlawful assault by surrogates of James J. Dolan and troops under the command of Colonel Nathan Dudley."

"Lincoln." Chapman rocked back in his chair. "I heard something about that. The papers said it was a war."

"I guess you could call it that when the military attacks citizens in their homes."

"Didn't Governor Wallace recently issue a rather sweeping amnesty for those involved in the Lincoln County disputes?"

"He did. But I'm not willing to accept the legality of actions taken by Colonel Dudley and Mr. Dolan. I believe there may be civil if not criminal remedies available to satisfy my complaint."

"It sounds as though you have some knowledge of the law Mrs. McSween."

"My husband was a lawyer."

"I see." He took pen in hand to a stack of notepaper. "Let's start with the estates in question. Real property?"

"There is a ranch, the Flying H, and the remains of my husband's mercantile and bank and lastly the ruins of our home. The ranch stock is subject of a spurious lien allegedly owed James Dolan by the previous owner. The county has taken possession of the mercantile and the bank for purposes of transferring ownership to Mr. Dolan in

53

exchange for his former mercantile."

Chapman paused his writing and bit the tip of his pen. "That seems a rather odd transaction."

"The county wants to use the Dolan property for a courthouse. Dolan gets my husband's store, the bank and, I suspect, all of it free of mortgage obligations."

"Hmm, rather convenient all around I must say."

"Convenient? Criminal, I'd say."

"Is that the extent of the estate?"

She nodded.

"Now about the prosecution, then."

"The root of the dispute began with my husband's former business partner, John Tunstall. He opened the mercantile and the bank in competition with Jimmy Dolan. My husband provided Mr. Tunstall legal services in return for a minority partnership. Mr. Tunstall was quite successful in bettering Dolan's mercantile business at first. So much so, I believe Dolan turned the law on John in hopes of a violent confrontation."

"John?"

"John Tunstall."

"And just how might this Jimmy Dolan turn the law on him?"

"John owned the Flying H. Dolan placed a lien on the stock."

"I thought your husband owned the Flying H."

"He inherited it along with the rest of the partnership after John's murder."

"He was murdered?"

"For all intents and purposes. Sheriff Brady sent a posse to the Flying H to impound the stock. They confronted John and killed him."

"I see, but what does all this have to do with your husband's death?"

"That's what started the war."

Lincoln
February 2, 1879
Bright winter sun did little to blunt the sharp wind rattling the window panes. The visitor bell rang over the clatter. Jimmy Dolan glanced up from his ledger. *Jesse Evans, now what?* He'd already had more than enough troubling news for one morning. A man of medium stature and lean build, Dolan projected a confident dashing demeanor women found dangerously attractive. In matters of business he could be cold eyed and ruthless. He wore his dark wavy hair and mustache neatly barbered. Not your typical shopkeeper, he carried a nickel-plated .44 short barrel shoulder rigged under his frock coat.

"Mornin', Jesse. What's on your mind?"

Short of stature, Evans was solidly built. He presented a serious demeanor that bordered belligerent. He had cropped dark hair, a square jaw, generous mouth and a slightly crooked nose courtesy of a saloon brawl over a soiled dove. He had a distant look to his eye as though he might be observing something unseen from afar. He wore a bibbed shirt, bracers and woolen britches. A .44 Colt rode butt forward on his left hip. He blinked at Dolan, his eyes adjusting to the light.

"Mornin', Jimmy. You ain't never gonna believe this."

"Try me. It's been that kind of morning."

"The Bonney kid came to see me."

"You're here so I'm guessin' he's dead. I'm impressed, Jesse. I didn't think you were that good."

"He didn't come lookin' for gunplay. He wants a peace treaty."

"A what?"

"A peace treaty."

"Why?"

"He's the only one didn't get a pardon. He figures it will help his case with the governor. I didn't see much in it for us, but I said I'd talk to you."

Dolan scratched his chin in thought.

"There may be something to the idea at that."

"What?"

"Sheriff Kimbrell came by this morning. He tells me Susan McSween has a lawyer diggin' around the courthouse lookin' at the record filings on the Flying H and my lien on the Tunstall stock."

"A lawyer?"

"Yeah, some feller name of Chapman down from Las Vegas. He's askin' questions about Colonel Dudley and the five-day battle too. He's been out to see George Peppin."

"So what's that got to do with a treaty?"

"Susan McSween is fixin' to make legal trouble. Probably try to prove there was some sort of a conspiracy to kill her husband and Tunstall."

"So?"

"So part of the treaty is nobody testifies against anybody."

Lincoln
February 18, 1879
The Kid figured a peace treaty would cut down on the number of people gunnin' for him and the bounty on his head. He hoped the gesture would put a good light on his bid to meet with the governor. Dolan had

57

agreed. They arranged to meet on neutral ground in the back room at the cantina.

The Kid rode into town under a cold billowed blanket of afternoon cloud. The air smelled heavy with snow. Tom O'Folliard and Doc Scurlock rode with him. They drew rein at the cantina hitch rack. A gaunt Eugenio Salazar met them, still suffering the effects of near-fatal gunshot wounds seven months after the five-day battle for Lincoln. The Kid greeted his friend with a warm clap on the shoulder and led the way into the cantina.

A hush fell over the small crowd at the sight of the Regulators. Those who braved the cantina that day knew who waited in the back room. Most of the regular crowd knew the meeting had been called to make peace. They didn't believe a peace treaty was possible and stayed away from a meeting they fully expected to end in gunplay. Only the brash and uncontrollably curious risked a drink that afternoon for the privilege of gawking. The Regulators crossed the stained plank floor, the room near silent save the clatter of boot heels and the jangle of spurs. Eyes straight ahead, none gave a glance to the left or the right.

The door to the back room creaked open. Jimmy Dolan sat at a lone round table flanked by Evans and Billy Mathews. Billy Campbell lounged in the back corner leaning against the wall. Seeing Mathews tested the Kid's resolve. Brady's former deputy had a fowl temper and a hair trigger you couldn't hide behind a badge. He had dull vacant eyes below a brow knit in a perpetual bunch. His crooked mouth twisted in an apparant sneer. He wore a plain spun gray shirt, wool pants, and a gray hat with a silver concho band. A brace of double-rigged Colts slung on his hips. He'd suited Sheriff Brady's purposes when the situation called for a violent conclusion. He was the lone survivor among those who had a hand in killing John Tunstall. The Kid had sworn to kill them all. Mathews was unfinished business.

"Billy, Doc, Tom, Salazar." Dolan nodded to each man.

The Kid spoke for his side. "Jimmy, Jesse, Mathews." They took seats.

Dolan glanced around the table. "We're all agreed to make peace here once and for all. Is that right?"

"We are," the Kid said. "We best make it a bit more understood than that."

Dolan nodded. This was headed where he wanted to go. "First off, we stop the killin'."

"Agreed," the Kid said. "No revenge,

either, and that includes friends."

"Agreed." Dolan cut his eyes from the Kid to Doc and Tom. "And nobody testifies against anybody."

"Agreed." The table fell silent. The Kid looked around. "That about it?"

Mathews and Evans nodded. Dolan hunched forward. "Death to anyone breaks the treaty."

"Agreed." The Kid stuck out his hand. Dolan took it. "Let's drink on it."

Later that night they stumbled out of the cantina, soaked in whiskey, tequila and goodwill. None of them noticed the cold. Starlight frosted the air. They stood in the street joshing good-byes in liquid good humor. A lone stranger walked up the street headed for the Wortley.

Houston Chapman noticed the knot of unsteady drunks outside the cantina. The fact they might be trouble briefly entered his mind. Common sense said cross the street and give these men a wide birth. He didn't know them, but the town was abuzz with talk of a peace parley between the formerly warring factions. He had a strong suspicion one or more of the men he was interested in might be part of such a group. Curiosity and a righteous bravado born of the law overcame the dictates of common sense.

Mathews noticed the one-armed stranger first.

"Hey, Jimmy, look there. You see what I see?"

He nodded. "It has to be him. Kimbrell said he had one arm."

"Not many men like that wanderin' around Lincoln." Mathews stepped away from the group followed by Campbell. "Hey stranger, you wouldn't be that lawyer feller the widow McSween sent down from Las Vegas?"

"Why, yes, I am. Houston Chapman." He touched the brim of his hat.

Campbell blocked his way.

Low light from the cantina reflected on the lawyer's spectacles hiding his eyes. "You wouldn't be James Dolan by any chance would you?"

"Not me." Campbell laughed. "Just a real good friend."

"Then do give Mr. Dolan my regards. I'm sure I shall have the opportunity to meet him quite soon."

Campbell drew his gun and stuck the muzzle in the lawyer's chest. "I believe I'd enjoy seein' you dance your way to the answers to all them questions you been askin'."

"Put that gun away before someone gets hurt."

"Hear that? The man says I should put my gun away before somebody gets hurt. Any of you boys afraid of gettin' hurt?"

Dolan eased his gun out of his shoulder rig and pointed it at the ground. He figured to scare the shit out of McSween's dude lawyer. He fired.

Campbell flinched. His gun exploded into the lawyer's chest.

Chapman staggered back, his vest aflame from the muzzle flash.

"My, God!" He beat at the flames, owl-eyed in disbelief. "I'm killed." He slumped to the frozen ruts.

Sobriety dawned like a slap of cold night air with the realization of what had happened. "Remember the treaty," Campbell called as they started for their horses.

FIVE

Las Vegas
March 1, 1879
Chapman dead, Susan McSween closed her eyes to the threat tears burned in harsh lamplight. She didn't know the man that well, but she couldn't help feeling responsible. He'd gone to that hellhole on her business. It cost him his life, yet another victim of senseless violence. When would it end?

The news accounts coming out of Lincoln were vague. An unarmed man gunned down in the street. A man named Campbell had been charged. Dolan was named an accessory and released. The *Santa Fe New Mexican* reported that Governor Wallace would travel to Lincoln to personally investigate the situation. What good would a politician do? People said he was honest. He was also Republican. If the Santa Fe Ring hadn't gotten to him yet, they soon would. More than likely his purpose was to reassure Dolan that he still had the support of his friends in Santa Fe.

Lincoln needed honest law enforcement. It looked as though the new sheriff was in Dolan's pocket like Brady and Peppin before him. Marshal Sherman had given Lincoln Marshal Rob Widenmann. He couldn't beat Dolan by himself, but at least he was honest. She felt the need to do something, but what could she do? She'd invested what little she had in Chapman. Now that was gone. Dolan seemed to have the better of it at every turn. His hold on the county had to be broken. Alex died on account of it. She couldn't let it go. She owed his memory at least that much.

Ty Ledger had proven honest for the short time he'd acted as sheriff. Perhaps he would serve again. She'd start with Marshal Sherman. She'd point out the continued miscarriage of justice in Lincoln. She'd ask him to appoint a special deputy for Lincoln County. She would remind him of the honest service given by Ledger during the war as Widenmann's deputy and temporary sheriff. If Governor Wallace were indeed as honest as people said, how could he oppose such an appointment? Nothing might come of it, but it was all she could think of. She crossed the small parlor to her desk. She took a sheet of vellum and composed her thoughts. *Dear Marshal Sherman,* she scratched in even hand.

Sumner Saloon
March 3, 1879
The Kid sat at a window table, his shadow haloed in afternoon sunlight. Garrett watched him scratch and scribble, struggling with the words. The governor was on his way to Lincoln. The Kid had decided to plead his own case. He hoped to arrange a meeting with a letter that would greet the governor on his arrival. Eugenio Salazar had agreed to deliver it by virtue of his pardon. He dozed at a corner table, his siesta soothed along by a stout measure of tequila, an expression of the Kid's gratitude. Billy scraped his chair away from the table and approached the bar. Garrett wiped a place for him.

"How's it comin'?"

He fingered the fuzz on his chin as he ran his eyes over the page. His head bobbed approval. "I think maybe. Whiskey, Pat. Have a look." The Kid laid the letter on the bar.

Garrett set down a glass and poured. He picked up the letter, squinted and read.

Most Honorable Governor Lew Wallace,
  I was in Lincoln the day Mr. Chapman was murdered. I was there to meet Mr. J. J. Dolan and certain of his associates to lay down our arms and take up peace as friends. I witnessed Mr. Chapman's murder and know who done it. If I came to court as a witness, I could give the needed truthful information. As you know I have indictments against me, owed to the war in Lincoln County. I cannot present myself at court if I am to be arrested and my enemies perchance to kill me. It is in your power to set those indictments aside so that I might serve my duty as a citizen. I hope you will do so. Please send me your answer that I might know what to do. You can send your answer by the bearer of this letter. My only wish is to right the grievances against me. I am in good favor with the citizens of Lincoln County, many of whom are my friends. I am sometimes called William Antrim. Antrim is my stepfather's name. Grateful for your answer, I am your obedient servant. W. H. Bonney

He slid the letter back to the Kid. "Makes your case square enough."

"Think he'll go for it?"

"Hard to say. You won't know until you

try. If you testify against Campbell and Dolan won't they consider it a violation of the treaty?"

"What do you think they done when they killed Chapman? He was workin' for Mrs. McSween. That puts him on our side. Far as I can see the treaty didn't last no longer than the whiskey we drunk."

Garrett shook his head. "I don't know, Billy, I'd say you could count on Dolan's boys comin' after you."

"Wouldn't be no worse off than I am now would I? No, if I got me a pardon, I'd clear out of New Mexico for good. You can count on that." He folded the letter.

"Eugenio!"

Lincoln County Courthouse
Dolan climbed the familiar steps to the House, buffeted by a strong northwest wind and lacy wet snowflakes that showed up for spring. He stepped into transformed surroundings. The county made quick work of converting his former mercantile into a courthouse. They turned the store into a courtroom and converted storage area on the first floor into a sheriff's office and judge's chambers. The second floor housed the jail and an armory. He paused in the

entry, allowing his eyes to adjust to the dim light. He started down the hall past Sheriff Kimbrell's office. His boots tapped the plank floor, leaving a trail of muddy wet prints. At the far end of the hall he stopped at the door to the judge's chambers and knocked.

"Come in."

Judge Warren Bristol sat at his desk in the small office he used on his monthly circuit. He sat in a halo of lamplight, a concession to the scant morning light afforded by a single window. He looked up from his reading stack, blinked behind his spectacles and nodded.

"Jimmy, good to see you." He rose to shake Dolan's hand. A gray-haired gentleman somewhere in the later part of his fifties, Bristol wore a rumpled black suit and a stained linen shirt mindful of some recent meal. The clothing needed the dignity provided by his usual black robe.

"Pull up a chair. I thought I might see you this trip. What's on your mind?"

"A couple of things, Judge."

"A couple, is it? I'm pretty sure I can guess one."

"Actually they're related. I had nothin' to do with the Chapman shooting, other than having the misfortune of being there."

68

"According to some of the witnesses you fired the first shot."

"Not exactly, my gun went off accidentally. Damn near shot my toe off when it did. Campbell was the one who fired on Chapman. Charging me as an accessory makes no sense."

"You got witnesses to that?"

"Hell, yes, all of 'em. Even Campbell admits my gun fired into the ground."

"He says it startled him."

"Maybe so, but he's the one with a cocked gun stuck in the deceased's chest. I didn't pull the trigger."

"Hmm, I see your point. I'll give it some thought. What's the other matter?"

"I've got this lien here." He drew the papers out of his coat pocket and handed it across the desk. "It was issued on Tunstall's Flying H stock. Tunstall's boys run 'em off before Sheriff Brady could serve it."

"Wasn't that the occasion of Tunstall's death?"

"So they say. I wasn't there. The lien's never been satisfied. I want it transferred to the Flying H."

Bristol scratched his whiskered chin. "Hmm, stock lien comes round to the whole place."

"There ain't nothin' else there to lien on."

"I s'pose not. How's that relate to the Chapman killin'?"

"Chapman represented Susan McSween. He was in Lincoln to settle Tunstall's estate. Her husband was Tunstall's partner. When Tunstall died, McSween became sole owner. She inherited it from her husband. All I want is my money, either that or the ranch."

"I see. Well that seems easy enough. Your other little problem may not be so easy. The governor's coming to town to look into Chapman's death. I can dismiss the accessory charge for lack of evidence if the witnesses back up your statement."

"They will."

"That don't mean that further investigation or testimony at trial won't result in the charge bein' reinstated."

"I'll take my chances."

His eyes crinkled at the corners. "You always do, Jimmy. You always do."

Lincoln
March 20, 1879
New Mexico Territorial Governor Lew Wallace felt a keen anticipation reminiscent of the nervous edge he'd felt as a field commander the night before a battle. He didn't expect trouble. The negotiations, though cautious, had been altogether cordial. Still

70

the Kid had a reputation. His penchant for violence should not to be taken lightly. They'd agreed to meet alone and unarmed. Finding a location for the meeting had proven the most challenging part of the negotiation. In the end they'd settled on the small store owned by Juan Patron, a Mexican friend of the Kid. The Kid felt comfortable there. It was located on the east end of town. The governor's security stood watch across the street in the old jail. That gave him some comfort, though in truth, if he needed help, they'd never reach him in time.

At fifty-one, Wallace stood tall and lean with the crisp austerity of a military bearing little softened by the comforts of civilian life. He had coarse, steel-gray hair, bushy brows, full mustache and goatee. His eyes bore an intensity amplified behind wire fitted spectacles.

He waited alone in a small lamp-lit back storeroom. The room was lined with wooden shelves stacked with canned peaches and tomatoes, jars of pickled eggs, sacks of beans, coffee, sugar, potatoes and flour. The scent of coffee and tobacco mingled with smoked hams and sausages hung from the rafters. Juan Patron and the governor's administrative aide waited outside in the darkened store near the unlocked front

71

door. They would verify the conditions unarmed and alone for the two sides. Wallace's stomach growled. The clock crawled toward the appointed hour, late enough to be dark, early enough for the evening crowd to be off the street, occupied at supper. He thought he heard the faint step of a horse beyond the darkness. Perhaps he was hearing things. The clump of a boot on the boardwalk came clearer. The visitor bell confirmed the arrival. The sounds of a muffled conversation announced approaching footsteps. His administrative assistant appeared in the doorway.

"Everything is in order, Governor."

The Kid stepped out of the darkness behind him and removed a battered sombrero from a mop of shaggy brown hair.

"Governor Wallace, thank you for seeing me." He smiled a crooked boyish grin that bore none of the menace foretold by his reputation.

"Come in, William. Have ah, a seat." He gestured to a box beside the barrel that served as a lamp stand. Wallace squatted on a second box in the halo of lamplight. "That will be all." The aide closed the storeroom door and disappeared into the gloom.

"I've read your appeal for pardon in return for your testimony in the matter of

Mr. Chapman's death. I can't say I'm persuaded, given the circumstances surrounding the deaths of Sheriff Brady and Deputy Hindmann. Still I thought it only fair to give you a hearing."

"I'm mighty grateful of that, sir. There's two sides to the war. Santa Fe had a habit of only hearin' one of 'em. Where would you like to begin?"

Straightforward, no pretense, no bravado, not at all what he'd expected. "Let's start with the Chapman murder. That way I know what I'm bargaining for."

He nodded. "Like I put in my letter, I come to town to make a peace treaty with James Dolan and members of his side. We met over at the cantina."

"Who was there?"

"Dolan, Billy Mathews, Jesse Evans and Billy Campbell from their side. Me, Tom O'Folliard, Doc Scurlock and Eugenio Salazar from ours."

"Go on."

"We agreed to stop the killin' and back each other up. Once we made peace we had a drink to celebrate."

"A drink?"

The Kid made a sheepish smile. "No, sir. More like a few."

"You got drunk."

73

"I s'pect most folks would think so. It was late by the time we went outside to go our own ways. That's when he come up the street."

"He? You mean Mr. Chapman."

"Yup, that's him. There'd been talk about him bein' in town, pokin' into stuff."

"What sort of stuff?"

"Dolan's claim on Mr. Tunstall's Flying H stock, Colonel Dudley's bein' involved in the five-day battle, that sort of thing."

"Hmm, so Dolan had reason to resent Chapman's inquiry."

"I guess maybe. Anyway Campbell blocked Mr. Chapman's way. They argued some. Billy pulled his gun, fixin' to make Chapman dance up the street."

"Did he mean to kill him?"

He shook his head. "I don't think so. I took it for joshin', until the first shot was fired."

"Who fired that shot?"

"Dolan."

"Did he fire at Mr. Chapman?"

"Nah, that shot went into the ground. That's when Campbell fired. I think the first shot might a startled him. Anyway that's what killt Mr. Chapman."

"You're sure Dolan fired first."

"Sure am."

74

Wallace sat back on his box and stroked his beard. "Tell me about the killings of Sheriff Brady and Deputy Hindmann."

The Kid took a deep breath. Now they were getting down to the part that might get him pardoned. "The Regulators come to town with arrest warrants for Billy Mathews and some others wanted for the murder of Mr. Tunstall."

"Warrants?"

"Yes, sir. We was all duly swored deputy US marshals. The warrants was issued up to Santa Fe on the say-so of Marshal Widenmann. He deputized Dick Brewer. Brewer deputized the Regulators to help him arrest the suspects on account a Sheriff Brady wouldn't do nothin' about Mr. Tunstall's murder."

"And why was that?"

"It was Brady sent the posse that killt Mr. Tunstall down to the Flyin' H."

"Why did he send a posse?"

"They was to serve some kind of court order in favor of Dolan."

"How did that result in Tunstall's death?"

He shrugged. "Me and the boys got there just after it happened. We didn't see exactly what happened, we only heard the shots."

"What made Marshal Widenmann believe Mr. Tunstall was murdered?"

"Mathews, Evans and the rest claimed Mr. Tunstall fired on them whilst resisting arrest."

"So it was justifiable homicide."

"No, sir."

"Why not?"

"We only heard two shots. One was fired from Mr. Tunstall's gun and one from some other gun."

"So how does that justify suspicion of murder?"

"Mr. Tunstall was shot twice."

"I see. So you rode into Lincoln to serve an arrest warrant on Deputy Mathews. The same Deputy Mathews that was present at the murder of Mr. Chapman?"

"That's right."

"Then what happened?"

"We caught Mathews on the street with Sheriff Brady and Deputy Hindmann. When we tried to arrest Mathews, Sheriff Brady pulled his gun on us. That's when the shooting started. Brady and Hindmann was killt. Mathews got away. The war got worse after that."

"Did you kill Sheriff Brady?"

He shrugged. "I fired my gun. So did several others who was back of that wall."

Wallace made a thoughtful steeple of his fingers.

"Most of the rest of the boys that was there that day got pardoned along with everyone else. Everyone but me, all I'm askin' for is the same shake everybody else got." He sat back, silent.

"I'll consider it on the following conditions. One, you testify against Dolan and Campbell and two, you turn yourself over to Sheriff Kimbrell to await trial."

"I ain't goin' to Kimbrell's jail. He belongs to Dolan every bit as much as Brady and Peppin before him. That'll get me killt."

"What if we hold you here?"

He thought. "I'd think on that."

"Good. Then I'll consider your pardon request."

Six

Patron House
April 30, 1879

Tortillas and frijoles, frijoles and tortillas, Billy sopped up the last of the gravy with a bite of tortilla. The days ran long confined to the small room they'd given him. He'd been stuck there over a month. The grand jury wasn't scheduled for another two weeks. No one knew how long the proceedings might take. If they got the indictments as expected, who knew when Dolan would actually go to trial? Hell, he might just as well have gone to prison for his crimes at this rate. Well, not exactly. If he went to trial for his crimes, he'd end up hanging. That was the point of all this.

He set the tin plate on the small table beside the bed and stretched out on the lumpy mattress. He stared at the ceiling. A crooked little crack in the plaster came as close to amusement as you could drum up in this place. His thoughts drifted to one of those soft nights in the peach orchard. Paulita smiled up at him in his mind's eye. He could almost feel the soft warm possibilities of her body pressed against his. She tasted sweet. She smelled of good earth and spring blossoms.

What the hell was he doing sitting here? It was jail without bars. Oh, there was a guard outside, more for his protection than for any expectation they could keep him in if he decided to walk away. Why not walk away? He could be in that orchard with her in little more than two days' time if he did. It was all for the promise of a pardon, the governor's promise. He hadn't heard from the son of a bitch since they met downstairs more than a month ago. Could he trust the man? No telling. So here he sat, waiting for a piece of paper that said he could stop running. He could get lost in Arizona or California and live in peace without the paper. Paulita would likely come with him. What was the point of all this, just to make things right?

Well things wouldn't be right until he got pardoned like everybody else. That was the point. He hadn't done more or worse than the others. Why was he singled out? Wallace didn't have no ax to grind against him. That

was true enough. Why wouldn't the governor give him his pardon? He had no reason
not to if he testified against Dolan. If he did
testify, the man best get locked up for a
good long time They'd made that treaty.
Dolan had been the one to make the point
about testifying against one another. Break
the treaty, you die. That's what they'd all
said. Pardon or no, he'd have a different
kind of sentence hanging over his head after
the trial. Damn. There just wasn't a clean
way out. Was it all worth it? Things just
wouldn't be right until he got his pardon.

He rolled over on his dreams of Paulita.
The bed springs groaned.

Lincoln County Courthouse
May 15, 1879
"All rise." The hum of subdued conversation faded into the muffled sounds of scraping chairs, creaking benches and the rustle
of those fortunate enough to have a seat. A
cloud of dust motes rose with the drab
mottled crowd, floating into the afternoon
sun pouring through the courthouse windows. "The grand jury is now in session,
the Honorable Warren Bristol presiding."

The black-robed Bristol took his seat at
the bench and rapped his gavel. The rustling, creaking and scraping reversed itself.

He ran his bespectacled gaze over the standing-room-only crowd on his way to the jury box. Bushy gray mustaches and beard revealed little of his expression. "Has the jury concluded its deliberations?"

The foreman rose. "We have, Your Honor."

"Very well, then proceed."

"With respect to the death of Alexander McSween, the jury finds probable cause to charge James Dolan and George Peppin with arson and murder."

A low buzz erupted in the courtroom. Bristol rapped his gavel, calling for order. The crowd quieted. "Proceed."

"With respect to the death of Houston Chapman, the jury finds probable cause to charge William Campbell and James Dolan with murder. We further find cause to charge Jesse Evans with accessory to murder."

Again the crowd murmured. Again Bristol banged his gavel. The foreman handed the verdict to the bailiff. "The bailiff will enter the jury's findings in the record of these proceedings. The court orders the issuance of indictments consistent with the jury's findings." The gavel rang. "This court is adjourned."

Patron House

The Kid sat on the bed, staring into the golden light on the fresh-air side of the window. The sparsely furnished bedroom they used for his incarceration looked out on the dusty street at the south end of town. He chewed on the news. O'Folliard sat in the small room's only chair. He'd come with the verdict before the courtroom had even cleared. Dolan charged with McSween's murder and Chapman's. It wasn't Mr. Tunstall's, but for all that followed from his death, it came pretty close. It'd go to trial all right. He'd have his chance to testify. Then it was up to Wallace. Tom intruded on his thoughts.

"You gon'na testify, Billy?"

"If I don't lose my mind, sittin' here waitin'. Protective custody, the governor calls it. Protective my ass, it's a sentence to everlasting boredom."

"You may need protection if Dolan finds out you're plannin' to testify. He'll sure enough take that for breakin' the treaty."

"Likely. Then again, there ain't much he can do about it, swingin' from the end of a rope."

"You're that sure they'll convict him?"

"They will if I testify." That wasn't the question that bothered him though. The question was Wallace. Could he trust the man to keep his word?

J. J. Dolan & Company
June 16, 1879
Charged with murder Dolan couldn't believe it. He sat at his desk in fading light, his fury blackened in shadow. He drummed his fingers on the desk as if the wood might tell him what to do next. He'd need a good lawyer. T. B. Catron, he nodded to himself. Wallace had replaced him as attorney general. T. B. could get a change of venue. Get the trial out of Lincoln. Someplace where his Santa Fe friends could help. A venue where Bill Rynerson served as prosecutor should do it. He felt his calm return as he formulated his plan. One detail still troubled him.

"They're holding the Bonney kid, but not in the jail. Why?"

Jesse Evans, lost in his own indictment, blinked at the question. Dolan answered for him.

"They're hiding him for a reason."

"Maybe he made a deal."

"Maybe he did."

"That violates the treaty. You want me to kill him?"

"No. I want you to help him escape."

"Why?"

"The treaty says we help each other."

"He sold us out."

"We don't know that. If he goes, he ain't done no harm. If he don't, we know he sold us out."

"Then we kill him."

"Then we kill him."

Patron House
June 17, 1879
The Kid pushed a bit of egg around his breakfast plate with the remains of a biscuit. The room was warm already, promising yet another hot day. He might never have agreed to this if he'd known how long it would take. Still the question gnawed at him, could he trust Wallace? The governor left Lincoln before the indictments were handed down. He hadn't heard a word from him since their meeting. The trial was fixing to start. Once he took the stand, the cat would be out of the bag. He had the uncomfortable feeling of a sitting duck in a shooting gallery. He'd bet a lot on Wallace. The deputy who passed for his guard appeared at the door.

"You got a visitor, Bonney." He let O'Folliard in.

Billy waited for the door to close and the

footfalls to die away down the hall.

"What's up Tom?"

"Evans come to see me."

"Evans? What the hell did he want?"

"He wants me to help bust you out of here."

"Why would he want to do that?"

"He says it's on account of the treaty. We agreed to help each other."

Billy rubbed the bridge of his nose. "Dolan knows."

"Don't see how he could."

"Maybe he's guessin', but I don't think so. This town ain't big enough to hide much."

"Well, either way, you got a choice."

"Yeah." He bit his lower lip in thought. "I'd feel better about this if I trusted Wallace. I ain't heard a word from the son of a bitch in nearly two months. I go into that courtroom and testify, he could just as easy leave me stand trial for the Brady murder as give up my pardon. He'd probably have fewer questions to answer if he did."

"That and you got a bunch of boys sworn to kill you."

"It don't look good either way right now, does it? When's Evans plan to do this?"

"Tonight."

"Damn. I want that pardon."

"Two chances out of three, it's a death warrant."

He pressed his lips in a tight line of resignation. "Guess I best take my chances on the outside. Tell Evans I'll be ready."

SEVEN

Old Fort Sumner
July 1879

Billy stepped out on the porch of the old Indian hospital. He'd taken a room near the rooms occupied by Charlie Bowdre and his wife Manuela. Charlie sat on the porch, smoking his pipe, the chair propped against the wall. Pale moonlight frosted the porch steps. Shadows masked Bowdre's expression, his head wreathed in a cloud of fragrant smoke. He smiled, teasing.

"Headed out, Billy?"

The Kid felt his cheeks flush, thankful for the cover of shadow. Charlie knew good and well where he was headed.

"Nice evenin' for a walk."

"You wouldn't be goin' to the peach orchard would you?"

"I might. What's it to you?"

"Oh, nothin', less a course I was lookin' for Paulita Maxwell."

"That wouldn't be good, Charlie, you bein' a married man and all. Evenin' Manuela." He tipped his hat as she appeared in the doorway behind her husband. "Best keep an eye on him. He's keepin' real close account of Paulita Maxwell's whereabouts."

"Only as a favor to my good friend Pete. He's worried over his little sister spendin' time with such a disreputable sort as the likes of you."

The Kid flashed a moonlit smile over his shoulder. "I wouldn't know nothin' about that. Evenin', Charlie. Manuela." He touched his hat brim and set off west along the Stinking Springs Road to the peach orchard north of town.

He ambled into the shadows among the trees. A light breeze, tinted with the scent of young fruit and good earth rustled the leaves. It softened the warm evening air. Moonlight frosted the treetops and fluttered blue-white through the leaves. She stood beside an old gnarled trunk deep among the trees. The shadow of a night sprite, she fixed her eyes on him and waited, expectantly rocking from heel to toe.

He smiled his crooked grin. The last step between them closed in a rush. He covered her lips with his. She melted against him, hungrily open to his kiss. Time froze. The world around the grove dissolved. He held her tight, lost in the soft possibilities of her embrace. She pressed her head to his chest with a small sigh.

"Did you have trouble getting away?"

She lifted her eyes to his and shook her head. "Oh, Billy, I wish we didn't have to go sneakin' around like this."

"We won't, soon as your brother decides to like me."

"It's not his place to say who I see and who I don't."

"He thinks it is and I don't plan on makin' any trouble."

She stiffened in a pout. "You would if you loved me."

"Make trouble? I don't make trouble 'cause I love you."

She tipped up on her toes and kissed him softly. "Do you mean it?"

"Shucks, I wouldn't say so if I didn't. I'm the most honest thief you'll ever know."

She giggled and pulled him to the ground, resting his back against the tree. She snuggled up beside him. He cradled her in his arms across his lap. She felt soft and light, warm and willing. Moonlight glistened at the surface of her eyes, large, dark, liquid pools. Her lips parted moist, her teeth bright white against her copper skin. He plucked the petals of her lips with his. A small pulse throbbed in her throat. Her breast swelled. Oh, Lordy it did. She sighed into his kiss and threw her arms around his neck. She kissed him with all the breathless ardor of young love. The kiss tasted of need. The air hung thick with promise. The ache burned. She seemed to sense it. So sweet, so warm he couldn't get enough, not yet, though, he told himself, not now, but soon. That's a promise.

She tiptoed into the darkened house in her stocking feet, carrying her shoes. Off to her left the heavy rhythm of Pete's breathing gave her comfort. The man could sleep in a sawmill. He was a sawmill. She hurried down the hall, slipped into her room and closed the door. She stood there feeling her heartbeat. Pale moonlight splashed through the window staining the bedclothes. She felt a quiet presence before she heard it.

"It is late."

"Deluvina!" she whispered. "What are you doing here?"

"Waiting for you."

"Why?"

"Someone must look out for you."

Paulita relaxed. She sat on the bed beside the shadow that concealed her friend.

"You were with the boy."

"He's not a boy. He's a man."

"Maybe so, but this does not make you a woman."

"Not yet."

"But it may?"

She turned to face the darkness that shrouded the question. "I, I don't know."

"Do you love him?"

"Oh yes, Deluvina! I do. I think."

"How do you know this?"

"He makes me. He makes me feel."

"He makes you want to feel like a woman."

"Yes! Oh, yes. That's it. He does."

"Does this make you feel like a wife and a mother?"

"I, I don't know."

Deluvina reached out of the darkness and drew her close. "Paulita, you feel a woman's wants, but you still think like a girl."

Paulita rested her head against the older woman's warmth. A crystal tear moistened her eye. "What makes you know so much? You ain't that much older than me."

"Not much, but enough."

Las Vegas

Susan McSween stood by the window of the small room she'd taken at the rooming house. A light breeze ruffled the yellowed lace curtain, providing some slight relief from the oppressive heat. Her unseeing eyes fixed on the court order. The words swam liquid in the lamplight. Her hand trembled. She wanted to cry. She wouldn't give him the satisfaction. That was all she had left. The thought of James Dolan winning yet again sickened her stomach. She'd failed Alex.

There was nothing she could do about it. With the stock gone, Dolan had refiled the lien, this time on the whole ranch. The court order pronounced her defeat in the flowery legal way Alex once practiced. It said she either paid the amount due or forfeit the Flying H in satisfaction of the debt. Tunstall denied any debt was ever owed. She put more store in John than anything Dolan said or did. For all she knew he made the whole thing up.

Then there was the missing stock. It would have galled her to settle the matter on principle, but she would have done it if she'd had the means. Unfortunately the stock had gone missing. Convenient for Dolan, too convenient her intuition told her. He knew where the stock went and likely who took the herd. She could file a complaint for the recovery of the herd, but Kimbrell wouldn't lift a finger. She could challenge the legitimacy of Dolan's claim, but that took money. Money she didn't have. Besides, what good would that do? Judge Bristol did whatever Dolan and his Santa Fe friends wanted done. She couldn't pay the lien. She had nowhere to turn. Dolan had won again. Her meager fortunes would grow ever more meager.

She tossed the court order on the scarred dresser top. She hung her head and massaged the throb in her temples. She wiped her eyes. She wouldn't cry. She wouldn't give him the satisfaction. She didn't.

Sumner Saloon
July 1879

The room swam in a blue yellow fog of kerosene-lamp-lit tobacco smoke. Stale beer and sweat seeped through the haze. The Kid sat across a dark corner table from Scurlock, flanked by Bowdre and O'Folliard. The ever-present Billy Barlow sat ignored at the next table, hanging on their every word. News of the White Oaks gold strike had the town abuzz.

"I ain't got much more than drinkin' money rattlin' in my jeans," Tom said. "Maybe we ought to ride on up that way and pick a little gold off the ground."

93

The Kid shook his head. "Best claims is gone by the time the word gets out. The rest is gone soon after. I got a better way to cash in on that strike."

Doc cocked his head. "How's that?"

"Beef. All them miners need to eat. Fresh beef on the hoof will be in short supply and high demand."

Bowdre looked from Doc to Tom to the Kid. "Last I checked we didn't have no cattle to sell."

"That's just 'cause we ain't rounded 'em up yet. There's lots of cattle to be had round these parts."

"You sayin' rustle 'em," Tom said.

"Don't know no easier way. Hell it'll be quicker and easier than lookin' for gold and the profits is certain sure."

Bowdre, the experienced cowman, chewed on the notion. "How many head you figure on?"

The Kid hadn't thought about that. "As many as we can handle I reckon."

"That ain't many without at least one more drover."

"So we get somebody. Hell, Jesse Evans knows some about rustlin'."

"He's likely back down to Seven Rivers since the war's over," Doc said.

O'Folliard bunched his lips. "Long ride

for an extra hand."

"What about me?"

The Kid glanced at Barlow. The others followed. They'd all but forgotten, the youngster's hanging on had gotten so regular. The Kid started to shake his head.

"Hell," Bowdre said. "He can sit a horse. He can ride drag. That way none of us has to eat dust."

"I can drag cows real good."

Billy threw up his hands in mock surrender.

Barlow beamed. "When do we ride?"

Pecos Valley

Caneris didn't need a head count to know they were missing more than the usual strays. All his years as a cattleman had given him an eye for it. You couldn't fool him even with the size of Chisum's Long Rail herds. They were missing fifty to seventy-five head, maybe more. He eased the buckskin cow pony down the sage dappled valley wall, weaving among the mesquite and creosote bush. Hot wind blew dust and dried sage balls down toward the river. River bottom grass and water held the herd. They'd not wander off unless given purposeful encouragement to do so. So who took them? Where'd they go and how long ago? He needed sign for that. No point reporting the loss to Mr. Chisum until he could fill in the particulars.

A big rawboned Texan with an unruly shock of sandy hair, Wade Caneris was a seasoned cowman. He'd started young, driving herds to the Kansas railheads. It didn't take long for his abilities to make him a foreman. He proved himself capable of handling storms, stampedes, river crossings and anything else the trail threw at his herd. Cowboys followed the quiet leader with the drooping mustache and intense blue eyes, knowing he'd pull them and their herd through to payday.

Instinct told him to start at the north end of the valley and circle west to south. It didn't take long to find the sign. They'd taken at least seventy-five head, lined out northwest. Five of them by the look of it, three, maybe four days ago by the horse sign. Pushing a herd, they might still catch them. It'd be close. He wheeled the buckskin and kneed up a lope for South Spring.

EIGHT

South Spring
"Son of a bitch!" Chisum slammed fist to palm. Caneris stood by, turning his hat in his hands. Roth and Ledger followed the Long Rail foreman into the hacienda to hear the news. It came as a surprise. Rustling had quieted some since the end of the war.

"You suppose Dolan is up to his old tricks?" Roth asked.

Chisum thought for a moment. "Hard to say, I wouldn't put it past him, though. If it is Dolan, he must have some new hands. Evan's Seven Rivers bunch got pretty much shot to hell in the run-up to the war. The timing doesn't fit a delivery to Fort Stanton or the Mescalaro reservation either." He turned to Caneris. "You think we can catch 'em, Wade?"

"Maybe, pushin' a herd is slow. It depends on how far they're takin' 'em."

Chisum turned to Roth and Ledger. "Get

the boys ready. We ride in the morning."

Shafts of pink dawn lit the underside of a heavy blanket of dark cloud streaming out of the northwest. Chisum, Roth, Ledger, Caneris and Deacon Swain rode west out of South Spring, hoping to cut the rustlers' trail at the Rio Hondo crossing. If they succeeded, they'd save backtracking to the Pecos Valley to pick up the rustlers' trail. It made sense. If it was Dolan up to his old tricks, the herd was eventually headed for Fort Stanton or the Mescalaro agency at Blazer's Mill. If it wasn't Dolan's work, the herd might be headed for Lincoln or possibly the mining camps up around White Oaks. All the possibilities had one thing in common, Rio Hondo.

They struck the river just before dark as the mountain clouds boiled up a wind-driven storm. As the first spatters of rain started to fall, they cut the herd's trail, tracking northwest toward Fort Stanton. They made camp in a dry wash north of the river under a sheltering overhang that permitted a fire and relief from the rain. The big ex-slave, Swain, laid a fire while Caneris and the boys watered and bedded the horses. Deac had coffee boiled and a pot of beans bubbling beside the fire by the time the men came in out of the rain. He bent over a skillet sizzling smoky fatback.

Roth's mouth watered. "That smells mighty good, Deac."

"Be ready pretty quick, now." He forked over a slice of fatback to crackle in its own grease.

Ledger passed cups around and poured coffee. Wind whipped silver sheets of rain across the mouth of the overhang, lashing the wash in the darkness beyond the firelight.

"Looks like we found us a home just in time," Roth said.

Caneris took a sip of coffee. "Hardly ever happens that way."

Ledger tossed his head at Roth. "It's likely his fault. When it comes to luck, he's got pockets full."

"Be worth bringin' him along then I reckon." Swain straightened up. "Grab your plates. Vittles is fixed."

They filled plates and cups and settled around the fire.

Roth swabbed a bite of hardtack in his beans with an eye on Chisum. "You figure Dolan's back to fillin' his government contracts at our expense?"

"Sure looks like it," Caneris said.

"I'm surprised he'd risk restartin' the

war," Ledger said. "You'd think he had enough problems what with the murder charges and all."

Roth eyed him over the rim of his coffee cup. "Probably figures he kicked all the fight out of us the last time."

Chisum furrowed his brow, his face a mask of firelight and dark etched lines. "Won't be no more war." His voice barely rose above the howl of the wind. "If it is him, he's a dead man, simple as that."

White Oaks

Billy called a halt at the base of a hill southeast of the tent-top cluster that passed for a town. Bowdre turned the bawling, plodding herd in on itself from his position on right swing. Scurlock and O'Folliard took his lead. Barlow pushed the stragglers from drag as he had all the way from the Pecos, cloaked in the river of dust trailing the lined out herd.

"Hold 'em here, Charlie, whilst I make arrangements to sell 'em." The Kid wheeled away at a lope toward the only permanent structures in hailing distance of the mining camp. A ranch house, stable and stock pens stood at the east end of the camp. He pulled the roan down to a jog as he passed an arched gate. A crude sign proclaimed

Dedrick Brothers Livery and Ranch. He drew rein at the house and stepped down.

A gnarled rancher in dusty boots, worn canvas britches, bracers and plain spun shirt in need of a washtub stepped out to the covered porch. He squinted beneath the brim of a battered black hat, his dark eyes darting up one side of the Kid and down the other. He fingered the buckle of a rough worn cross-draw rigged Army Colt he couldn't have jerked on the Kid if his life depended on it. It would have, had he been so foolish.

"What can I do for you, stranger?" His voice cracked like a dry corn husk.

The Kid smiled his crooked smile as he did when disarming distrust. "Afternoon, sir, William Antrim's the name. I got some cattle to sell. I heard you supply the miners."

He glanced over the Kid's shoulder toward the bellowing herd and spat a tobacco stream. "How many head?"

"Seventy-five. You interested, Mr. . . . ?"

"Moses Dedrick. You got a bill of sale?"

"Don't need one. I got my brand registration from the Texas Stock Growers Association right here." He patted his vest pocket.

"That so?"

"See." He drew the folded paper out of

the inside pocket, spread it open and handed it up the step.

Dedrick studied the document and wrinkled his brow. "Rockin' H, don't know that brand and I ain't never seen a registration like this before."

The Kid smiled again. "You don't need to know the brand. You seen the registration plain enough. Folks told me that'd be more than enough to satisfy your need."

"They did, did they? What folks is that?"

He scratched behind his ear and shook his head. "Danged if I can remember the feller's name exactly. Just folks I reckon will have to do."

Dedrick handed the registration back. "Ten dollars a head."

The Kid's jaw dropped. "You know the market's closer to forty."

"I said ten dollars a head."

"Ten dollars? Why that's robbery!"

"So's rustlin'. You want to sell 'em or not?"

He clenched his jaw. Empty pockets was empty pockets. "All right, I guess. It's been a long dry trail."

"I'll need a bill of sale. You can make it out for ten cents a pound."

"Why that's more like forty or fifty dollars a head."

Moses smiled. "I reckon it is."

Rio Hondo

The storm cleared through over night. The sun rose bright and hot, bleaching the sky white. At midday the stolen herd's trail passed east of Fort Stanton and continued north. Chisum drew a halt.

Caneris shook his head. "What do you make of this?"

"Well they ain't headed for either of Dolan's usual haunts," Chisum said. "It looks like they're headed for White Oaks."

Caneris nodded. "Them miners gotta eat."

"You still think it's Dolan?" Roth asked.

"Could be. Then again, a new market could be anybody. One way to find out."

Roth, Caneris and Ledger turned inquisitive.

"We'll find them cattle at the Dedrick place."

"How do you figure?" Ledger asked for all of them.

"They got a spread right near the mining camp. Ain't never been too particular where their stock comes from. The Cattle Growers Association's got more than a few complaints about them." He squeezed up a lope north.

White Oaks

The sun hung low, flaming the hill rise west

of the ranch. Moses Dedrick stood on the porch as the long shadows of early evening crawled across the ranch yard. He watched the riders come. Five heavily armed men, setting a purposeful pace. His crusty chin whiskers parted in a hint of a smile. He'd half expected them. Most of the herd milled around in the holding pens under a light dun dust haze. His younger brothers, Sam and Dan, had already butchered a few for sale in town. No trouble. He had all the paperwork a man could want.

They rode through the gate, slowed to a trot and circled the yard past the stock pens on the way to the house. He recognized Chisum and made the connection. Chisum would too soon enough, even if he couldn't prove it. The riders drew rein at the house and stepped down.

"John."

"Moses."

"What brings you all the way up here?"

"Them cattle." He jacked a thumb at the pens.

Dedrick pulled a puzzled look. "I don't know what you're talkin' about."

"Where'd you get 'em?"

"Bought 'em from a feller named Antrim a few days ago. Real nice young feller he was."

"Rustler you mean."

"Nah. Showed me his brand registration from the Texas Stock Growers Association and wrote me a bill of sale for the lot of 'em."

"Mind if I have a look at it?"

"Nope. Hold on a minute. I don't carry that sort of thing around on my person." He ducked inside the house. He returned moments later and handed Chisum the receipt. "There. You see, every bit in order."

Chisum held up the paper to catch the last light over his shoulder. "Ten cents a pound," he raised an eyebrow. "Generous price for stolen beef."

"Fair market price and you know it."

"And you saw the registration for this Rocking H brand?"

"With my own two eyes standin' right here on this very porch."

"I've no doubt."

"Like I said, every bit in order."

"I'll tell you what's in order, Moses. I could run an iron over a Long Rail brand and have myself a Rocking H with no more than an hour's work by a good smithy. Where is this Antrim feller now?"

He shrugged. "He and his boys rode west."

"Straight back to Texas."

Dedrick looked down the bridge of his

nose from his perch on the porch. "A man comes off a long drive like that is due for a little rest."

"Long drive with seventy-five head of cattle, my ass." He stepped into his saddle. The boys followed his lead. "I'll tell you something else, Moses. You got a new business here feedin' these miners. If I have to come back here again chasin' Long Rail beef, I'll burn this claptrap of yours to the ground and hang you and your brothers from that gate over yonder."

"I'll bear that in mind."

"See you do."

The Long Rail crew lit out and swung west. "Where we headed?" Roth asked.

"Whiskey Jim's."

Whiskey Jim's

It started as a trading post that expanded into lodging for traders and travelers. The proprietor, James Greathouse, better known as Whiskey Jim, had a nose for business. Trading was easy when you started with whiskey. The clientele followed along with the rest of the merchandise. Many of those who frequented Whiskey Jim's found they could use a hot meal and a comfortable place to spend the night or a few days. The rooming house most called the Greathouse was a rambling two-story clapboard affair perched on a low hill beside the adobe trading post and cantina. Business boomed with the discovery of gold at White Oaks, forty miles to the east. If a man wanted a little civilized relief from the rugged conditions of a tent-top mining camp, Whiskey Jim had the place.

Bowdre had had enough cards for a spell. He sat at a rough hewn table in the shade of a thatched roof patio that served the cantina as a porch. The breeze was hot, but the air was fresh. He needed it. Good thing too. If he hadn't, they'd never have seen the riders coming. They didn't amount to much more than a dust cloud at first. Soon enough he made out riders, stirrup to stirrup in a tight knot. He didn't recognize them at a distance, but five hard-riding men was enough to rouse the suspicion of a man on lookout for law trouble. He slipped out of his chair and retreated into the stuffy cantina. A stale haze of tobacco smoke dulled the mid-afternoon glow. He spotted Billy at a back corner table with O'Folliard, Scurlock and Whiskey Jim. He crossed the packed earthen floor on long strides.

"Riders comin'."

All eyes turned. "Trouble?" the Kid asked.

"Won't know 'til they get here."

"How many?"

"Five."

Chairs scraped back. They followed Bowdre out to the patio.

"Recognize 'em?" Greathouse asked.

The Kid squinted. "Maybe. I can't be sure. If I'm right, we ain't here."

Greathouse nodded. "You boys slip out the back. Get over to the rooming house and lay low." He lifted his chin. "Leave them jaspers to me."

Billy and the boys disappeared back into the cantina and out the back way. By the time Chisum and his men rode up to the cantina, Whiskey Jim sat on the patio nursing a drink.

"Afternoon, gents. Jim Greathouse is the name. Light down and make yourselves to home. We can take care of most whatever you need."

They swung down. The tall one and the big black man took the horses. The older man strode onto the patio, flanked by a pair of young guns.

"Greathouse, John Chisum." He extended his hand. "This here's Johnny Roth and Ty Ledger."

"Mr. Chisum, your reputation precedes you. Welcome to Whiskey Jim's. What can we do for you gentlemen?"

"We're lookin' for some men."

Greathouse chuckled. "Well we see lots of 'em. Do these men have names or something they look like?"

"The leader goes by the name Antrim."

He scratched the brushy beard on his chin. "Antrim, Antrim." He shook his head. "Cain't say that rings any bells. What do you want with him?"

"He run off some of my cattle."

"That's a serious charge."

"Dead serious."

"Sorry I cain't be more help. We can sure fix you up with a hot meal or a room, though."

"No thanks. We'll water our horses and be on our way."

"Corral and watering trough are yonder past the rooming house."

Chisum touched the brim of his alkali-stained hat. "Much obliged." He led Roth and Ledger back to collect their horses.

"Where to now?" Roth asked.

"Lincoln."

NINE

Lincoln

They rode out of the hills into town under a hot, dusty midday sun. Chisum led the way at a jog flanked by Roth and Ledger. Caneris and Swain trailed behind. He wheeled into the hitch rack at the new courthouse and stepped down. Down the street Dolan had the Tunstall store refurbished and reopened for business. Chisum handed his rein to Swain.

"Wade, you and Deac put the horses up over at the Wortley. Get us rooms for the night. We'll start back to South Spring in the morning. Johnny, you and Ty come along. We'll see what Kimbrell has to say about our rustling problem."

Caneris and Swain collected the horses and started across the street. Chisum squared his shoulders and led the way up the courthouse steps. They found Kimbrell in a stuffy, small first floor office. He glanced at the clock on the wall, wiping his brow with a bandanna.

"I guess it's good afternoon, Mr. Chisum. What can I do for you?"

"Afternoon, Sheriff. We've come to report a cattle rustlin'."

"I see. What happened?"

"They hit us last week, took seventy-five head or so from our river valley herd. Near as we can tell they changed the brands and drove 'em up to White Oaks. Sold 'em to Moses Dedrick and his brothers."

"Any idea who done it?"

"Trail sign says five of 'em. Dedrick claims he bought the herd from a man named Antrim. That mean anything to you?"

He shrugged. "Cain't say it does. That don't mean much though. Men dealin' in stolen cattle ain't given to usin' real names that often. Dedrick have any idea where this Antrim went?"

"Sounded like they headed for Whiskey Jim's. We rode over there to have a look. Greathouse says he never saw 'em."

"You say they changed the brands."

"Yeah, took a runnin' iron to Long Rail and come up with a Rocking H."

"Rockin' H. They could use that on a Flying H too. Mr. Dolan will want to be on the lookout for that."

"What's Dolan got to do with the Flying H?"

"I guess you haven't heard. The court awarded it to him in payment of Mrs. McSween's debt."

"So Dolan's in the cattle business."

"Well I don't know what to tell you, Mr. Chisum. We'll keep an eye out for this Antrim feller and any stock runnin' a Rockin' H brand. I don't know what more we can do unless we manage to catch 'em in the act somehow."

"That's it?"

"I reckon so."

Chisum reddened. A vein throbbed in his neck. "You be sure to warn Jimmy Dolan like a good little soldier, Kimbrell."

The sheriff blinked a watery eyed question. "I'm sure Mr. Dolan will appreciate the warning if that's what you mean."

Chisum turned on his heel and led the boys out the door.

The supper crowd at the Wortley dining room arrived with Chisum and the boys. Cooking smells mingled with the scents of coal oil, beeswax and furniture polish, though the exact sources of the last two didn't appear obvious. Table lamps gave the room a muted glow. Caneris and Roth pushed two tables together to make seating for all of them. The cook, waiter, bartender came around to take drink orders. Chisum brooded at the head of the table, plainly unhappy at Kimbrell's treatment of the rustling report. It felt like the same old problem all over again. They'd never fix it until they got the sheriff's office out from under Dolan's thumb. He could see only one way to do that, but how?

The bartender returned with a bottle and glasses. The boys passed them around. Caneris poured. Chisum tossed off his drink and poured another. At the other end of the table Roth tilted his chin in Chisum's direction. "He's thinkin' pretty hard on somethin', Ty. What do you make of it?"

"Rustlin', I'd guess. That was most of his stake in the war. It don't look like much has changed from here."

"You think it's Dolan up to his old tricks after all?"

"No way to tell for sure. Kimbrell acts about the way Brady used to back when it was Evans' Seven Rivers boys doin' Dolan's dirty work. If it is Dolan, this Antrim feller must be somebody new. I ain't heard of him before."

Roth shook his head. "Me, neither."

"It don't matter much anyway. The prob-

113

lem is Kimbrell won't do nothin' about it. Without real law, we're right back where we started."

The waiter served steak, potatoes, biscuits and beans. The hungry men fell on their food. Conversation went still. By the time the apple cobbler came along, Chisum looked as though he come to some decision.

"Johnny, you, Wade and Deac head back to South Spring in the mornin'. Ty you come with me."

"Where we goin'?" Ty asked.

"Fort Sumner."

Old Fort Sumner

By the time they rode into Fort Sumner Ty understood Chisum's thinking on what to do about the rustler problem or more particularly about the sheriff problem. They needed to get control of the sheriff's office away from Dolan. Somebody needed to run against Kimbrell in the next election. The first night out, Ty had the uncomfortable feeling John thought he might be the man for that job. He'd made his decision on that. He was a rancher now with a wife. He wasn't going back to bein' a law dog. Chisum seemed to understand that. It turned out they were on their way to Fort

Sumner with a second candidate in mind.

Blue shadow followed the last spears of sunlight over the western peaks as they jogged into town. Chisum led them up Roswell Road to Beaver Smith's Sumner Saloon. He wheeled his big buckskin into the hitch rack. Business came first. They could worry about a place to stay later. He needed to have this conversation before the saloon crowd picked up for the evening. He stepped down and looped a rein over the rail. He trod the boardwalk to the batwings with Ty at his heel.

Garrett held his usual place at the end of the bar, polishing an endless parade of glasses in need of a wash and dry polish. The place was all but deserted. Faint rays of sun fought back shadow in a faded blue light that beckoned the unlit lamps. He nodded in greeting as Chisum and Ledger sidled up to the bar.

"Mr. Chisum, Ty, what brings you up to Old Sumner?"

Chisum smiled. "Evenin', Pat. Just a little friendly conversation."

Garrett cut his eyes around the empty saloon with a shrug. "Hell of a long ride for a little conversation. Sorry there ain't much of it here this early."

"It'll do. Bring us a bottle and a glass for

yourself. I've got something I'd like to discuss with you."

Garrett looked puzzled. He collected a bottle and three glasses. He followed Chisum and Ledger to a back table. He set the bottle and glasses down and scratched a lucifer to light. He lifted the chimney of a nearby wall sconce, lit the lamp, snapped out the match and trimmed the wick. He poured three drinks and pulled up a chair across from the two ranchers.

"What's on your mind, Mr. Chisum?"

"John, please." He lifted his glass and knocked back a swallow. The others followed. "The Lincoln War may be over Pat, but the problems ain't. Rustlers still have free run of the range. Law enforcement is left up to a sheriff who dances to Dolan's tune. Dolan's been known to turn a profit on rustled beef, maybe still does. He don't give a shit about the ranchers' complaints, so nothin' gets done."

"What does that have to do with me?"

Chisum's smile crinkled the corners of his eyes. "Right to the point, I like that. Pat, some of us been talkin'. We think you're the man to run for sheriff against Kimbrell next year."

"Me? Why me?"

"You got the grit to do the job. You're hon-

116

est. We can trust you."

"Who's we?"

He leaned back in his chair and smiled. "You do get to the nub of things. The Cattle Growers Association has the worst of the problem. Those of us who've been talkin' can deliver the backing of the rest of the members. That ought to be enough to get you elected." Garrett wrinkled his brow.

"You'll have to move to Lincoln to establish residency." He poured another round. "We'll see to it you get work and enough campaign contributions to make it worth your while."

Garrett turned the idea over. Sheriff was a plum job what with tax collection and all. If the Cattle Growers Association backed his candidacy, that'd likely get him elected.

"Dolan ain't likely to take kindly to the idea."

"That bother you?"

He shook his head.

"Good. Then you're just the man we thought you were. Shall we drink to it?"

Garrett shifted his gaze from Ledger to Chisum. He lifted his glass. "Looks like you got yourself a candidate."

TEN

Wallace clasped his hands behind his back and paced the sun splashed tiled office floor. Without the Kid's testimony the case against Dolan had fallen apart. The Santa Fe Ring's roots ran deep. You could smell it from here. The Kid broke out of protective custody the night before the trial was to begin. Dolan must have seen it coming and gotten to him somehow. Either that or the Kid figured out he'd never get the promised pardon. Either way Dolan got off. Wallace shook his head. He should have paid more attention to his star witness, kept his trust at least until the verdict was in.

The war may be over but the situation in Lincoln was far from settled. Now there were new reports of rustling troubles. That old problem had contributed to the start of the war in the first place. He'd seen enough of Sheriff Kimbrell to know he couldn't be counted on for serious law enforcement. Dolan and his friends could easily manipulate the man. He might even be sympathetic to the Dolan faction. Brady was reported to have such sympathies. So was Peppin. He needed to do something about law enforcement in Lincoln. He'd soon enough see what he had in Marshal Sherman. As though completing his thought, a rap sounded at the office door.

"Marshal Sherman to see you, sir."

Wallace motioned to his aide. "Send him in."

The door swung open. US Marshal for New Mexico Territory John E. Sherman stepped past the aide.

"You sent for me, Governor?"

"I did, Marshal. Thank you for coming. Please have a seat." He motioned to a pair of leather upholstered chairs drawn up before his desk.

Nephew to the Civil War hero William Tecumseh Sherman, the marshal may have owed his lean wiry frame to family resemblance, but little more than that. He had nowhere near the fiery disposition of his famous uncle, tending instead to a more considered demeanor, sensitive to the winds of political power and influence.

"How may I be of service, Governor?"

"It's the situation in Lincoln. The war may be over, but the trouble is not."

"So I understand. What would you like me to do?"

"I recently returned from Lincoln. I went to look into the Chapman murder personally. The opposing sides have made some sort of treaty, but that doesn't mean law and order has come to Lincoln. We had a solid case against the two men responsible for the murder with an eyewitness in protective custody. The witness broke custody the night before the trial and the case fell apart. I don't think Sheriff Kimbrell is capable of standing up to the lawless elements. He may just be next in the line of Lincoln sheriffs who do James Dolan's bidding."

"How can I help, Governor?"

"I want you to appoint a special deputy for Lincoln County, someone who will actually enforce the law."

"You understand the limits of federal jurisdiction I'm sure. Much of what happens in Lincoln County falls under local jurisdiction."

"Yes and that would be the aforementioned Sheriff Kimbrell. I am also aware that federal officers have been known to make, shall we say, creative interpretations of their jurisdiction in times of need. These are needy times, Marshal. In this case, I'll take half a loaf. It is decidedly better than none."

Sherman nodded. "In that case, I know just the man we need, if he'll take the job."

"Who do you have in mind?"

"Name's Ty Ledger. Rob Widenmann used him as a deputy when he worked down there. McSween got him appointed sheriff to serve out Brady's term. He resigned when Peppin took over the five-day war. He must have done a pretty good job. I got a letter from Susan McSween recommending him for a similar appointment shortly after Chapman's murder. For what it's worth she agrees with your opinion of Kimbrell."

"McSween, doesn't that put this Ledger chap on their side of the war?"

"I don't think so. Even Dolan admitted Ledger stood up to McSween's Regulators when they assaulted his store. Ledger tried to head off the battle for Lincoln. He called for the army. Governor Axtel chose to answer a later call."

"Let me guess. From the Dolan side."

Sherman nodded. "That put the army on the side of the Dolan faction. If that didn't cause the five-day battle, it sure settled it."

"Will Ledger take the job?"

"I don't know. I hear he took to ranchin' after he resigned as sheriff. The only way to find out is to ask."

"Then ask."

Fort Sumner

Autumn turned golden. Late afternoons turned to long blue shadow before sunset and a sharp chill blew out of the mountains. Paulita sat at the kitchen table peeling potatos for the stew pot. Deluvina cut meat at the counter. She'd watched the girl go about in sadness for weeks. She knew the problem. It was the boy. So often it was the way with men. A woman had one thing in her heart while the man had another somewhere else. Life must go on. This could not.

"Paulita."

"Si."

"What is the matter with you? Are you sick?"

"No."

Deluvina set down her knife and wiped her hands on her apron. She went to the table and sat across from the girl. "Will you mourn your life away?"

"Mourn? What are you talking about?"

"I'm talking about him. Billy."

"Why would I mourn over him?"

122

"Because he has been away these last months without word. He comes, you love him. He goes away, you love him. But does he love you?"

"He does."

"How do you know?"

"He says he does."

"Does he do as he says?"

"Sometimes."

"Do you love him sometimes?"

"No. I mean all the time."

"That is your problem. You are not in love the same. You will hurt until your love is the same. This is what your brother tried to protect you from. Give him up, muchacha. I love him too, but he has no feelings for me. Deluvina knows you cannot draw water from a stone. You would be wise to consider the truth of this."

South Spring
October 1879

Harness buckles announced Caneris and Swain as the big black man drew the buckboard up at the hacienda porch. He climbed down to the squeak of the unburdened spring seat. He swung around the back wheel and began sorting bundles in the heavily loaded flatbed. The front door swung open to Chisum followed by Dawn

123

Sky. She stepped into the waning afternoon light to help Swain with the weekly supply order.

Caneris climbed the porch step with a small bundle of mail and handed it to Chisum. He flipped through the stack of envelopes, pausing at one official-looking letter from Santa Fe.

"Wade, you headin' down to the bunkhouse?"

The ramrod nodded. "We got supplies to unload."

"Ty and Johnny are shoein' a horse in the barn. Tell Ty to come by, he's got mail."

Minutes later Ty knocked at the hacienda. "Come in," Chisum called from the parlor. The door creaked. "Wade said I had mail."

Chisum crossed the spacious room muted in golden light. He handed Ty the letter. "This one's for you. It looks important."

The return address read *US Marshal's Office, New Mexico Territory, Santa Fe.* Ty tore it open. His eyes ran down the page. "It's from Marshal Sherman. He wants me to take a special deputy appointment." He handed the letter to Chisum.

He read for himself. Finished, he passed it back and scratched his chin. "What do you think?"

Ty shrugged. "I gave up lawin'. I'm a

rancher now, thanks to you and Johnny."

"A rancher whose range is open season for rustlers."

"Rustlin' ain't a federal crime. It's the sheriff's job," Ty said.

"And you saw how much help you can expect from Kimbrell. Look Ty, the war changed nothing. Dolan still controls the county and that includes the sheriff's office. We need to change that."

"That's why the Cattle Growers are backin' Garrett for sheriff next year."

"That's right, but Garrett ain't won yet and you never know when a little extra jurisdiction might come in handy."

"I got a wife to support. I cain't be runnin' off chasin' mail robbers and such."

"Special deputies deputize men to do that sort of thing."

"I don't know. I'd have to talk to Lucy."

"Just think it over. The election's not until next fall. We got nowhere to turn until then. The Cattle Growers Association is going to elect the next sheriff. I plan on seein' to that. Partnered up with a US marshal appointment we'd have an edge on enforcin' the law we don't have now."

Ty nodded. The suggestion stirred a sense of unfinished business he had going back to the battle for Lincoln in the last days of the war. That had him thinking. It might be worth going along with the idea at that, as long as Lucy agreed.

"I gotta think it over, John. I'll talk to Lucy."

The fire crackled, shooting sparks up the stone chimney to the cool night air. Lucy liked the onset of colder weather and the cozy feeling that came at the end of the day. She snuggled closer to Ty on the wooden settee drawn up before the fireplace. She rested her head on his chest, his arm close around her shoulders.

Life as a rancher's wife had come easy. She'd surprised herself by that. All the long hard nights, working the saloon trade in places like Dodge and Deadwood seemed another lifetime ago, a different person's lifetime. Ty seemed to feel it too.

"Lucy."

"Hmm?"

"A letter come for me from Santa Fe."

She put aside her dreamy musings. Official letters came from Santa Fe. "What sort of letter?"

"From Marshal Sherman. He wants to appoint me special deputy for Lincoln County."

"Oh. Are you interested?"

"John says I should take it."

"Why? What about the ranch?"

"The Cattle Growers Association is going to back Pat Garrett for sheriff next year. They're fed up with the rustling and Kimbrell's excuses for doin' nothin' about it. They want to get the sheriff out from under Dolan's thumb."

"So what does that have to do with you and a US marshal's job."

"Jurisdiction mostly. Garrett's gonna need help. Between the two of us we'd have the authority to go after most any situation."

She pulled a pout. "I thought we were through with gunplay once we moved down here."

"We won't be completely through until Lincoln gets law and order and New Mexico gets statehood. John knows that. The Cattle Growers know it. That's why they picked Garrett. The appointment letter from Marshal Sherman just happens to fit the plan."

"Have you talked to Johnny about it?"

He shook his head. "No point to it, unless you agree first."

She knit her brow that funny way she did when she was thinking. "It'll take you away."

"From time to time."

"I don't like that part." She thought some

more. "Dolan's unfinished business isn't he?"

"He is."

All the bloodshed and tears from the war washed back through her mind. John Tunstall, Alex McSween, so many others killed. She saw Colonel Dudley's soldiers and Dolan's men surround the McSween house and store. She heard the cannon roar that shattered the storefront. The store she worked to build. She smelled smoke and saw the McSween house burn. She felt the pain in her heart Susan McSween must have felt at the death of her husband. Would it never end? She turned misty-eyed to her husband.

"You do what you think best, Ty. Just be careful. I love you."

Eleven

Whiskey Jim's
November 1879

As long as the money held out, the Kid, Tom and Doc were in no particular hurry to leave Whiskey Jim's. Barlow was content to hang out wherever the Kid did. Bowdre pulled out first and went home to Manuela. After a spell the Kid got to thinkin' about Paulita. The girl held a fascination for him like no other in his youthful experience. Fort Sumner tugged at a restlessness it seemed only she could satisfy. He wanted no part of a winter without her. It was time to go home. Funny he thought of it that way, but it seemed to fit. It didn't matter to Doc or Tom. And Barlow? Hell the boy might as well have been his shadow.

They rode north into town along Roswell Road as night fell, cold and cloudy. Snow scented a sharp breeze. The Kid gave a longing look to the Maxwell place as they passed, hoping for a glimpse of her. He wheeled the roan east at the orchard and followed Stinking Springs Road to the old Indian hospital. Barlow bid his good-byes at Bob Hargrove's saloon. He peeled away and drew up at his old haunt. They put up their horses in the corral across the road and humped their saddlebags over to the abandoned hospital. They stowed their gear in vacant rooms down from Bowdre's place.

Tom nudged Doc playfully in the ribs. "You goin' over to Maxwell's tonight, Billy?"

The Kid flushed in the dim light of a single candle. "Maybe. First things first though."

"How's that?"

"A drink and some supper." He led the way out the door.

They clumped along the boardwalk and across the road to Beaver Smith's Sumner Saloon. Frosted glass doors, closed to the night chill, glowed in warm welcome. Inside, the smell of burning coal lamps mingled with tobacco smoke, wet wool and beer. The Kid blinked in the hazy yellow glow. He glanced at the bar looking for Garrett's familiar figure. The heavyset bartender in the stained apron wasn't his friend. They sidled up to the bar.

"What'll it be, gents?"

"Whiskey," the Kid said.

"Two," said O'Folliard.

"Taos lighting." Doc grinned.

"Where's Garrett?" Billy asked.

"Moved to Lincoln."

"Lincoln? What for?"

"Some say he's fixin' to run for sheriff."

"Sheriff?" The Kid tossed back his drink. "Well I'll be. Fancy that, boys, our ole pal Pat Garrett, sheriff of Lincoln County."

"He's got to get elected first. The election don't come around until next fall," the barkeep said.

"Oh he'll get elected all right." He poured himself another drink. "Pat Garrett's a good man. Smart too. Folks couldn't do much better than elect him sheriff. He won't knuckle under to Dolan either, that's for sure." He turned to Tom and Doc with his crooked, boyish grin. "We'd best get our outlawin' done before he gets elected. We don't want that hombre takin' up our trail." He turned back to the bartender. "What's for supper?"

Scurlock thought about the taciturn steel-eyed Garrett. He was a competent man all right. He'd make for a no-nonsense sheriff. Like the Kid said, maybe it was time to get done with outlawin' before serious law enforcement got elected.

■ ■ ■ ■

An hour later, Billy crunched up the street to the Maxwell place. The night had turned cold on a biting wind. Light snow swirled in the air. He clumped up the porch and rapped on the door. Heavy boots sounded inside. Pete, he thought. Swell. The door cracked open, faint light behind the shadowed figure.

"You."

"Evenin', Pete." He smiled. "Nice to see you too."

"What do you want?"

"Well I just got back to town and thought I'd drop by and say hello to Miss . . ."

"Billy!" She ran down the hall past her startled brother and into his arms.

Pete slammed the door, leaving them to the cold porch. For the moment neither noticed.

"I've missed you so." She breathed, snuggling against him. "I didn't know if you was ever comin' back."

"Shucks, sweet girl, I couldn't stay gone long from you. It was just business."

"You mean it?"

He took her lips in his and felt the chill melt clear through to the bone. She sighed into his mouth, a small pulse racing in her throat.

"Come in," she said. "It's cold out here."

"What about Pete?"

"I got a fresh pot of coffee in the kitchen." Her eye twinkled. "He'll be gone to bed directly." She took him by the hand and led him inside. They followed a dimly lit hall past the parlor and Pete's front bedroom to the kitchen at the back of the house. Paulita sat him at the kitchen table. She took two cups from the cupboard and went to the stove where the coffeepot warmed.

It felt good just watching her. She wore a plain skirt, a simple blouse and a shawl against the chill. Her long black hair fell past her shoulders. The young girl he remembered from fleeting encounters in the peach orchard had ripened some in the months he'd been gone. Ripened in ways even the shawl couldn't hide. She carried the steaming cups to the table. She moved in a quiet catlike way that drew a man's attentions to her womanly places. Her dark skin flushed with the echoes of their kissing. He guessed she'd come by the coloring on her Mexican mother's side. Her dark eyes glistened, fixed on him as though he were something more than he was. Something out of one of those romantic dreams young girls were known to have. He didn't quite know where he fit, but he sure liked the feeling of fittin' there.

"Where have you been all this while?" She sipped her coffee.

"Up to White Oaks." He kept it vague.

"Did you find gold?" She giggled.

He shook his head. "Just sold them miners some beef."

"Did you find yourself a pretty girl to keep you company while you was gone?"

"Aw Paulita, you know I'm sweet on you."

"That's not what I asked."

"Heck, no."

"I don't believe you for a minute."

He reddened. "What about you? Am I supposed to believe you been sittin' around here pinin' for me all the while I been gone? I don't believe you, either." She smiled a teasing little smile. Gawd she was pretty.

"Boys come and boys go." She pulled herself up straight and looked him in the eye. Her breast swelled. "But they don't mean nothin' to me."

"I'd like to believe that."

"Believe it."

She had a little starch when she said it. He liked that too. "So what's been goin' on around here whilst I been gone?"

She prattled along with local news and

gossip for a time. The Kid contented himself with the melody of her voice and all the ripe promise that seemed to go with it. She ran out of steam sometime after the coffee ran out. He realized they'd lost track of the hour.

"Gee, it's gettin' late. I best be goin'."

She pulled a pretty pout. "It's cold out there."

"Might get too warm if Pete finds me here much longer."

She scraped back her chair, resigned to his leaving. She led the way to the hall.

The Kid followed the sway of her hips. She paused halfway down the hall. Deep snoring rumbled toward them from the front bedroom. She cocked her head, listening. A mischievous glint lit her eye. She grabbed his hand and ducked through the door to a room at her side.

Deluvina stepped into the kitchen from her room off a hall at the back of the house. She folded her arms across her breast and listened as they paused on the way to the front door. She heard the door latch softly. She lowered her eyes. A tear gathered at the corner of one eye. She turned back to her room.

■ ■ ■ ■

The room was dark, save the silver light from a single window that fell across the dark shape of a bed. Her room, he realized. The thought flooded him with an odd mixture of excitement, danger and want. She drew him to her kiss. The shawl slipped from her shoulders. She shuddered against him. The air grew heavy and moist. He needed air.

"But, Pete . . ." His voice cracked.

She smiled up at him. Pale window light lit her eyes. Shadow veiled her expression. "Once he gets into the sawmill he don't never wake up." She moistened her lip with the tip of her tongue, teasing. Something somewhere nudged the door closed. She stepped back. Her fingers moved slowly up the front of her blouse, dark fingers fluttered over tiny buttons.

His mind screamed some meaningless warning. He paid no heed, his will rooted in anticipation. His senses tingled, vision slowed. The blouse slipped from her shoulders. His breath caught in his throat. She wriggled her skirt over her hips. It slipped past her thighs. Copper cream gleamed in the frosty light. Soft waves of black hair spread before him, pricking the darkness in points of reflected light. She unbuckled his gun belt and laid it on a small table beside the bed. She lifted her eyes to his and drew him to her. He went lost in a fever.

He snapped awake. The sky beyond the window pane turned gray. He found himself holding the most beautiful creature ever to grace nature. He remembered the fever and shook his head in disbelief. Reason reared its ugly head. He needed to get out of there before Pete and the rest woke up. She stirred against him with a soft sigh.

"Paulita," he whispered. "It's mornin'. I gotta get out of here."

She looked into the shadow covering his face through the tangled curtain of her hair. "It is, isn't it?" She pinched his nipple and bit his lip playfully.

It was morning all right. Hell he might have to shoot his way out of here before all was said and done. He'd done that before. Just then something else struck him as more important than his gun.

She snuck him out the back way after Pete went off to see to his ranch chores. The walk up Stinking Springs Road to the hospital felt bright and airy despite a cold wind and gray flannel clouds laden with the promise of more snow. He'd said he was sweet on her. Gals liked to hear that sort of thing. He'd never got the meaning of it before. That little Mex miss had his head fogged good'n proper for a fact in one night. He didn't know what to make of it. He'd need more time to figure that out, a lot more time. He smiled to himself as he climbed the steps to the old hospital.

Tom sat on his bunk, cleaning his gun by the light of a coal oil lamp. He glanced up and grinned when Billy came through the door.

"Where you been?" He didn't expect an answer.

"None of your business."

"I'm sure it ain't."

"Where's Doc?"

He tossed his head toward the back room. "Inside packin'."

"Packin', packin' for what?"

"You talk to him. I tried."

He found Doc, rolling his blanket in the back room. "Where do you think you're goin'?"

Scurlock straightened up. "Dunno for sure, back to Texas maybe."

"Why, Doc?"

"It's time, Billy. The war's over. We lost.

138

Them as hired us ain't payin' no more."

"We're gettin' by."

"Outlawin'."

"So?"

"Look, after you ah, left last night, me and Tom stayed around and talked to some of the boys. Garrett went to Lincoln to run for sheriff all right, with the backin' of John Chisum and the Cattle Growers Association."

"Yeah, so?"

"Don't you see, Billy? Folks is ready for law and order. They get honest law up to Lincoln, and you know Garrett'll be honest law, they'll all turn against the outlaws. It's only a matter of time 'til they get us."

"How can you be so sure?"

"Statehood's comin'. Just like it did in Kansas. Law and order comes with it. The owl hoot trail ends up at a gallows or the wrong end of a bullet. I ain't done with life yet."

"You'll die of boredom, Doc."

"Yeah, I might try that. Sounds better than havin' my neck stretched or my gut shot."

Billy shook his head. "Well, good luck to you, pal. It's been a good run. We'll miss you around here."

"It has been a good run. We've had some

fun, haven't we?"

He nodded.

"Think about it, Billy. Wouldn't you rather live long enough to tell your grandkids about all the fun we had?"

Grandkids? Hell, I just figured out I might be in love.

Twelve

Winter wind howled out of the high desert, buffeting Hargrove's Saloon. The rafters groaned in protest to the drafty chill. Lamplight flickered in a gray haze of tobacco smoke. Oily black wisps climbed to the darkened planks overhead, trailing the smell of kerosene. Potbelly stoves in the back and front corners crackled, pushing a thin halo of heat toward the card tables and bar. The suggestions of warmth faded to chill at the middle of the bar. Whiskey warmed patrons bundled in heavy coats, the low hum of conversation turned visible in whispers of steam.

Billy stood at the bar with O'Folliard, nursing his drink. Barlow stood off a pace, eager to join the party uninvited. Tom blew on his fingers and rubbed his hands together.

"Why in hell did we stay up here for the winter? We ought to be warmin' our backsides on senoritas and tequila down in Mexico." He tossed off his drink and poured another. He glanced at Billy. "Oh that's right. One of us is warmin' his backside. It's me who's freezin' his ass off. You know you was more fun when you wasn't so ground tied."

"Who's ground tied?"

"You, that's who. Ground tied for a fact."

"Well, maybe a little."

"A little! You ain't slept up to the hospital in so long I rented your room to a coyote. The critter's more company than you."

Billy's eye twinkled. "There's your problem, Tom."

"What?"

"You rented the room to a coyote. You should have taken in a girl."

"Say, ain't you Billy the Kid?"

The Kid cut his eyes up the bar. The cold-eyed questioner stared back at him. Not much more than his own age, the young tough had an edge to him. Billy smiled his disarming crooked smile.

"Some folks call me that. I don't believe we've met. What's your name?"

The stranger sidled down the bar. Nothing special about his baggy britches, plain spun shirt, heavy coat, boots and slouch hat.

"Joe Grant," he said. "I heard of you. You as good as they say?"

"As good?"

"With one of these." He drew a pearl-handled Colt from beneath his coat and laid it on the bar.

The Kid snatched it up in a blink. He tested the balance. "Say this is a real beauty." He opened the gate and spun the cylinder, counting three rounds. He set the gun back on the bar. He nodded to Hargrove. "Bob, pour our friend Joe Grant here a drink."

Grant holstered his gun. "I'd as soon shoot a man as drink with him."

"Who'd want to shoot a man when there's drinkin' to be done?" Billy smiled again, a little forced this time. "If I was you, Joe Grant, I'd appreciate my good humor. Have yourself a nice sociable drink before you find out just how good I am." He lifted his glass.

A shadow of doubt passed over Grant's eyes.

The door cracked open with a gusty blast. The muffled newcomer squeezed the door closed. He turned to the bar, brushed snow from his coat and hat. He unwound a muffler from his face and blinked, adjusting his eyes to the light.

"Billy, Tom, what the hell are you boys doin' here?"

Billy smiled, Grant forgotten. "Drinkin', Mr. Chisum, come along and have one. It'll take the chill out of your bones."

"That'll take some doin' about now." Jim Chisum, John's brother, elbowed his way to the bar between Grant and the Kid.

"Hey, you're takin' up my place." Grant crowded the newcomer. "Just 'cause you're the great John Chisum don't give you call to push folks around."

Chisum glanced to his left. "Sorry stranger, it's just this here's an old friend. Guess I forgot my manners. Besides you've got me confused. I'm Jim Chisum, John's my brother."

"You'd do well to mind your manners when you don't know who you're pushin' around."

"I said I'm sorry."

"Don't draw no water with me."

The Kid stepped between Chisum and Grant. "Shut up, Grant! My friend said he was sorry. Now why don't you go crawl back to wherever it is you came from while you still can?"

Grant's face reddened. "I've had enough of your meddlin' Bonney." He drew his gun and fired point-blank.

Click, the hammer fell on an empty chamber. He blinked in disbelief.

The Kid's gun appeared cocked before Grant could thumb the hammer a second time. "See, I am that good."

Grant dry fired again.

The Kid smiled his crooked grin and shook his head. "Didn't nobody never tell you not to let another man load your gun?" The muzzle flash bloomed powder smoke. Grant's eyes went wide. The back of his head blew off in his hat. He dropped to the floor like a half-filled potato sack.

Barlow stood at the Kid's side and stared at the body in awe. "You got him sure, Billy."

"Get the body out of here and you can join us for a drink. Com'on, Jim, there's a table over yonder."

Barlow grabbed the would-be gunman under his arms and dragged a bloody smear across the floor to the door.

Snow crunched under his boots as he fought the wind. Cold cleared the whiskey haze. Sweet warmth beckoned. It gathered a ball of desire in the pit of his belly. The storm deserted the streets. He eased up beside the Maxwell house and scratched the frosted windowpane. A gauzy shadow tapped the glass. He turned to the back of the house. He waited at the back door with a shiver, part cold, part anticipation. The door creaked.

He stepped into the darkness. Her dark eyes glistened. She closed the door and touched his cold cheek with a warm finger. He bent to her kiss, soft and sweet, her body tender beneath her nightdress. He slipped his boots off. She led him across the kitchen dimly lit by bright snow beyond the windows. Her gown floated spectral as she led him into the blackened hallway.

Somewhere down the passage Pete snored slow and steady, sleeping soundly comfortable in the appearance of ignorance. He'd said his piece with Paulita to no good effect. She'd stood up to her brother. Billy smiled. Pete had to know of his nightly visits. He simply chose to ignore the fact. Billy figured that left him with no need to do anything about it. Not that he could do anything that wouldn't end badly.

Paulita stepped into her room and softly closed the door. She peeled the heavy coat off his shoulders, hung it on a peg beside the door and slipped into his arms. He held her close. She shuddered, tipped up on her toes and bit his bottom lip, her nibble sugary. She tugged at his buttons, shirt, britches, long handles. Chill air prickled his skin. She eased him onto the pale island of light pooled on the bedsheets. He drew her night shift over her head, her smile white and even against dark copper skin. He took her in his arms, and wriggled her under the covers.

Blazer's Mill
February 1880
The Kid eased forward in the saddle, peering through a gray curtain of light snow, swirling out of the hills to the valley below. "There they is just like I said." The herd, close to fifty head, browsed winter grass in a pasture west of the stable. Snow caught in patches on grass clumped at the horses' hooves.

"Looks like a fine herd of range stock. You say they belong to Dolan?" Bowdre asked.

Billy glanced from Charlie to Tom to Barlow. They needed the tagalong for what they were about to do. "Not exactly. Dolan had Evans push 'em up here when they found 'em."

"Found 'em?"

"Yeah, found 'em where we hid 'em for Mr. Tunstall."

"Those the horses Dolan holds a lien on?"

"Yup."

147

"Well looks like he's about to get what's comin' to him."

"Yeah it does, even though that wasn't really what he wanted."

Tom shook his head. "You're talkin' in riddles, Billy."

"Dolan wanted the Flying H. He took the horses so Mrs. McSween couldn't pay off the lien. He got it transferred to the ranch. Now he's got that."

"Leave it to Dolan to get himself paid comin' and goin'."

"That's about it."

"Somehow it don't seem right."

"It don't. We can do somethin' about that, though."

"What?"

"We take them rustled horses off Dolan's hands."

"Dolan ain't gonna take kindly to that."

"Probably not. Then again, I don't expect he'll even complain."

"How's that?"

"He's got the ranch. Them horses ain't his. They's stolen. He said so himself."

Tom smiled. "You said we was gonna steal some horses. Hell, I thought it was just for money. I didn't know we was gonna have fun doin' it too."

"It is for the money. Seems like a fair

settlement for our part in the war. I been thinkin' about it ever since we saw Jim Chisum. The Regulators never saw our pay after the war. McSween owed us. John Chisum owed us. We never got paid. Mrs. McSween ain't got the money to pay us. Well, these horses is kind of a way for her to pay us what's due. Then we pay Chisum a visit to get what he owes us."

They ran off the herd after midnight and drove it to White Oaks.

Dedrick Brothers Ranch

Moses Dedrick stood on the ranch house porch bundled in his greatcoat against the cold. He gazed across snow-covered hills clotted in clumps of white crusted juniper and pinon. Four riders pushed a horse herd down the face of the nearest slope. The mottled blanket of plunging animals rippled bay and black, buckskin and gray, sparkling in snow showers caught by the midday sun. Steam from his breath frosted his beard. Odd time of the year for anyone to bring in a herd, he thought. That is unless someone had a reason to move a herd fast.

The herd slowed, approaching the frozen creek below the ranch yard. The riders let them stomp the ice open to drink. It suited their purpose. A lone rider astride a big roan broke away and short loped up the rise to the ranch yard. Dedrick had a recollection of the roan. Likely he'd done business with these boys before. The rider checked the roan to a trot at the gate and rode in. The boyish pink cheeks under the battered sombrero had a familiar look about them too. He drew rein with a friendly grin.

"Afternoon, Mr. Dedrick. Remember me, William Antrim?"

"Now that you mention it, matter of fact, I do. I bought some cattle from you last year, off a Texas brand registration as I recall."

"Yup that's me. You got a good memory."

"I tend to remember trouble."

"Trouble? Why I have no idea what you mean." He flashed that grin again.

"John Chisum thought that Rockin' H might have been run over his Long Rail brand."

The Kid shook his head. "Don't know the feller. Don't know nothin' about no Long Rails neither."

"I s'pect not. What's on your mind?"

"Them horses. You interested?"

"They ain't Long Rail or Rockin' H stock are they?"

"Nope. Free and clear range stock, every last one."

"Odd time of the year to be roundin' up range stock."

"We didn't round 'em up. We just sort a stumbled on 'em."

The old man guffawed.

The Kid let him shake himself off. "You interested or not?"

"Five dollars a head."

"Five! Hell you'll get twenty green broke come spring. Them horses is worth at least ten."

Dedrick shrugged. "Then take 'em along to somebody who thinks so."

"Five dollars is robbery!"

"Seems like we had this conversation once before. As I recall, it was robbery. This here's the slow season. I gotta feed them horses until spring, before I can even think about breakin' 'em. Five dollars is my offer."

The Kid spit. It was enough to make a man resort to honest labor. "Where do you want 'em?"

THIRTEEN

Pecos River Valley
March 1880

They found the yearling heifer mired in a sinkhole. Fortunately the spring thaw hadn't progressed far enough for her thrashing to swallow her above the chest. They'd been lucky to find her, though. The hole had her good. Chisum felt the sun warm the back of his heavy coat. The thaw was well under way despite a chill wind on his cheek. He sat his big buckskin uphill of the hole and watched Caneris and Swain do their work.

The foreman let out a loop, gave it a lazy turn and dropped it over the heifer's head. He dallied the rope around his saddle horn and nudged the sturdy piebald back to take up the slack. That secured her while Swain collected a bundle of dry mesquite. The black man arranged the branches in front of her with a soothing word to her round-eyed terror. Satisfied he had enough to give her footing he remounted his chestnut gelding and added his loop to Caneris' hold. He took up the slack in his rope and nodded to Caneris. Both men eased their mounts back, dragging the young cow through the sucking muck until her knees and front hooves found purchase on the mud meshed mesquite. She got her forequarters into the effort and with the tug of the cowponies, slogged out of the hole onto firm footing. The men slacked their loops. She shook them off along with clots of mud, lifted her tail and trotted off in the direction of the rest of the herd.

"Nice work."

The call echoed down the ridge. Chisum turned in the saddle. They'd been so busy rescuing the heifer they hadn't noticed the three riders, resting on the crest above. One waved. Chisum didn't recognize any of them at that distance. They eased on down the slope. He recognized the big roan first, followed by the crooked grin. Billy Bonney. He had Tom O'Folliard and Charlie Bowdre along with him. Men like them had been useful during the war. Now, short of rustling, he couldn't imagine what the three young guns found worth doing down this way. They'd had their part in the war, but the war was over. The Kid touched his sombrero brim as he drew rein.

"Afternoon, Mr. Chisum. Wade, Deac, nice to see you."

"Last I heard, Billy, you boys was up to Fort Sumner. What brings you down this way?"

"Business. Old business I guess you could call it."

"What sort of business?"

The Kid hooked a leg over his saddle horn. "Well you see, Mr. Chisum, after the war ended me and the boys here never got paid."

"I'm sorry to hear that. Seems like you ought to take that up with Mrs. McSween."

"No point to that, she's lost everything."

Chisum shook his head. "Looks like a bad run of luck all around then. I wish you better luck next time."

"There won't be no next time, Mr. Chisum. This is about the last time. The way we figure it you owe us four hundred fifty dollars in back pay."

"Me? How do you figure that? I paid my Regulators, McSween paid his."

"We was all fightin' on the same side. I'm tellin' you, we been shorted three months' pay."

"That's not my problem, Bonney. Now if you'll excuse me, I got a ranch to run." He laid a rein to his horse's neck.

"Not so fast, Chisum." The Kid leveled his Colt Thunderer. "You ain't goin' nowhere until we get paid."

Chisum slouched in his saddle with a small head shake. "Put that thing away, Bonney. You ain't gonna shoot an unarmed man. It'd ruin your reputation. And you ain't gonna get paid, either." He wheeled his horse away, leaving the gap-toothed Kid agog.

"We ain't finished, Chisum."

He glanced over his shoulder. "I say we are." He squeezed up a lope.

"We'll see next time." Billy called to his back.

"There ain't gonna be a next time. You said so yourself."

He was gone, leaving the Kid to mutter.

"There'll be a next time, old man. There'll be a next time for sure. Count on it. What you don't pay in cash, you'll pay in cattle and more. You can figure that last bunch we took for your first payment."

Fort Sumner
May 1880
Billy sat on the old Indian hospital front porch outside the Bowdres' place, passing a bottle with Charlie and Tom. The town

quieted in early evening before things got going in the saloons. The evening star twinkled in a steel blue sky not yet turned black.

"The gang's breakin' up," Billy said, passing the bottle to Tom.

"You still sour about Doc quittin'?"

"Yeah, I reckon. We ain't got enough of us left to do a job unless we drag the Barlow kid along for what he's worth. I'm broke. We got to do somethin' about that."

"We could turn a hand to honest work," Bowdre said. "Doc did. So did Fred, Henry, the Coes, they's all turned to honest work."

"Where's the fun in that?" Tom offered the bottle to Bowdre.

He shook his head.

The bottle passed back to Billy. "I figure we can still make us a livin' runnin' cattle and horses up to White Oaks. Hell, Chisum's got plenty of cattle. He'll never miss a few head."

"Make a good living until you get your neck stretched," Bowdre said.

"You're so married, Charlie. It's makin' you soft." He passed the bottle to Tom.

"Maybe so, then again, maybe I'll live to tell my grandkids how I knew the great Billy the Kid before he got hung."

"How about it, Tom, you still with me?"

"Damn right. Why not?"

"Good then all we got to do is find us some boys that still got some sand."

Bowdre grimaced at the jibe.

As if conjured up by the mere suggestion, three horsemen jogged up the street shrouded in evening shadow.

"Know 'em?" Tom asked.

The Kid shook his head.

The riders drew rein, searching the street up one side and down the other. After a moment they eased their horses over to where Billy and the boys sat on Bowdre's porch. The big one waved.

"Charlie, where can a man slack his thirst and get a bite to eat in this town?"

"That you, Dave?"

The big man with a dark unshaved beard showed teeth so yellow they couln't get close to white in the dark.

"I thought so. I can smell you from here."

"I've killt men for less than that, Bowdre. If I wasn't so hungry and thirsty I would. I'll overlook it this time if you'll tell us where to get a drink and some supper."

Billy stood. "I'll show you down to Hargrove's."

"Who might you be?"

"William Bonney, my friends call me Billy."

157

The stranger wrinkled a crusty black brow. "The one they call the Kid?"

"Some do. This here's Tom O'Folliard."

"Dave Rudabaugh." He tossed his head at Bowdre. "Them as call me Dirty Dave like him most times end up dead."

Billy crooked a grin. "I'll keep that in mind. Who are these gents?"

"This here's Tom Pickett and that there's Billy Wilson."

"Tom and Billy, Billy and Tom, least we won't strain nothin' rememberin' names. Follow us." The Kid, O'Folliard, Rudabaugh and his boys started down the street toward Hargrove's. "Good night, Charlie. Say good night to the missus for us."

Rudabaugh, Pickett and Wilson stepped down at Bob Hargrove's rack. The Kid led the way inside. Smoky yellow light and bar smells greeted them along with a suggestion of warmth to push back the evening chill. He sidled up to the bar with O'Folliard. Rudabaugh and his boys bellied up down the line.

"Bob these boys is hungry and thirsty. You can probably hold 'em off with a drink long enough to fill their plates with whatever you're cookin'."

Hargrove set out glasses, put the bottle in front of the Kid and headed off to the kitchen to see about food.

Billy got a good look at Rudabaugh and his partners. *Dirty Dave* fit his moniker. The man was filthy. His nondescript dark trousers and shirt were mud spattered and stained. A tattered coat so large it might have fit a buffalo hung loose on his hulking frame. His skin was coarse and crusted. He wore a bushy dark mustache little distinguished from the heavy stubble of beard on his chin. Besides yellow, his teeth were cracked and stained. A fringe of matted hair fell to his shoulders from a shapeless slouch hat. Dirty fit the bill all right, but two things about him gave the Kid pause, his dark eyes blazed menace that said he could go off like a hair trigger. The .44 Colt butt forward on his left hip looked like it went off with a trigger that suited its owner's temper. Dave Rudabaugh looked like a man worth givin' a wide birth, upwind to be certain.

The other two didn't appear any more prosperous. Tom Pickett was younger, with watery blue eyes, a dull-witted expression and greasy blond hair. Billy Wilson had a wild ferret-like cast to his eyes. A scruffy, red-patched attempt at a beard framed a mouth locked in perpetual sneer. Neither of the two looked good for much more than killing on command.

"Looks like Bob's got us a table and some grub." The Kid nodded to a back corner. He picked up the bottle and led the way. They fanned out around the table. Rudabaugh and his two henchmen scraped their chairs, hunched over their plates and wolfed their food like they hadn't eaten in a month. Billy and Tom drank quietly until Rudabaugh sat back, ripped a lusty fart and poured another drink.

"That's some better."

"What brings you boys to Fort Sumner?" Billy asked.

He took in the Kid suspiciously. "Clear air. What's it to you?"

He shrugged. "Nothin'. I just thought we might do some business."

"What sort of business?"

"Does it matter?"

"Does it pay?"

"See, Dave, we do understand each other."

"What you got in mind?"

"Before we go into business together, I'd like to know a little more than you come to the old fort for 'clear air.' I ain't never heard of you boys. Should I?"

Rudabaugh scowled. He measured the Kid, weighing his answer. He'd heard of him all right. Made a name for himself in the Lincoln County War. He didn't look like much, but he found it best not to let such things get in the way of respecting a man's reputation. Reputations didn't come easy. Even if they was taller than truth most of the time, it never hurt to stay cautious until you figured out for sure.

"Some folks up north called us the Dodge City Gang."

The Kid nodded. He'd never heard of the Dodge City Gang, but the admission told him which side of the law came with clear air.

"Then you'll likely have an interest in our kind a business."

"You ain't told me what that is yet."

"Cattle. There's a good market for 'em up to White Oaks."

"Cattle always sound like work."

Billy shook his head. "Not so bad. We pick 'em up, change the brands a little and sell 'em right nearby. The buyer takes 'em to White Oaks. Care to ride along and see what I mean?"

He nodded, tossed off his drink and poured another. "Never hurts to look."

FOURTEEN

Lincoln

Jimmy Dolan sat at his desk counting the day's receipts. Business picked up again with the elimination of Tunstall's mercantile. If you needed something in Lincoln, once again you had to deal with Jimmy Dolan. He owed Tunstall for the bank. The Englishman was smart about that one. The ranch would come in handy too. It gave him the appearance of a cattle operation to cover his army and reservation contracts. Let Chisum and the rest wonder how he could sell so cheap. They probably knew, but knowing and proving were two different things. Yup, life was good again. It had been a bloody mess getting rid of Tunstall and McSween, but he'd done it. Nobody would take him on again anytime soon.

The old store clerk, Jasper, was about to flip over the closed sign when the visitor bell rang.

"We're closed."

"Dolan in?"

"He's busy."

Dolan heard the old man's muffled protest. The visitor ignored the old man.

"He'll see me."

Who in hell? He pushed back his chair and went to the office door. The slope-shouldered Bonney kid stood silhouetted in the late afternoon light, spilling through the storefront window. He had a hulking stranger Dolan didn't recognize with him. *What the hell does he want?*

"It's all right, Jasper. Let him in."

The Kid brightened his crooked smile. "See, old-timer, I told you he'd see me." The old man went back to straightening shelves. Billy crossed the store glancing around at the tidy shelves and new furnishings. Battling army artillery had taken a toll on the store. Dolan had put some work into fixing it up. He presented himself at the office door followed by the stranger.

"I'm a busy man, Kid. What's on your mind?"

"A bit of business, Jimmy, a fine bit of business."

They stepped into the office.

"Who's this?"

"A friend of mine, Dave Rudabaugh."

Rudabaugh nodded.

Dolan turned back to the Kid. "What's on your mind?"

"The Flying H."

"What about it?"

"I understand you own it."

"I do. What's it to you?"

"There's a premium market for beef in the mining camps up to White Oaks."

"Tell me something I don't already know."

"Them Dedrick brothers own the market for now. How'd you like a supply of low-cost beef to sell up there?"

He pursed his lips. "Low cost? Have a seat. I'm listenin'."

Dolan sat down at his desk. The Kid and the stranger took the visitor chairs beside the desk. Billy took a piece of paper out of his shirt pocket and spread it on the desktop.

"May I?" He gestured to Dolan's pencil. Dolan handed it to him. He drew a line.

"What's that?"

Dolan wrinkled his nose and shrugged.

"Chisum's Long Rail brand, now watch."

Dolan hunched forward suddenly interested. The Kid drew a second line matching the first and a third between the two. He added Flying H wing checks to the top and bottom of each rail.

"We can supply all the beef you want at twenty dollars a head. Twenty dollars that'll fetch forty by the time they get to White Oaks."

Dolan sat back and smiled. South Spring to the Flying H for twenty dollars a head. Twenty dollars a head for a couple days' drive up to White Oaks. He thought about the reservation and Fort Stanton contracts. That price wouldn't work quite as well.

"I got reservation and Fort Stanton contracts to think about. Twenty dollars a head won't serve them. Now at fifteen dollars, I'll take all you can deliver. You just need to keep that runnin' iron off Flying H range."

Billy cut his eyes to Rudabaugh, thinking about where to change the brands. It came easy. He chuckled to himself.

"What's so funny?" Dolan asked.

"Just thinkin' about where to change them brands."

"What's funny about that?"

"Keepin' 'em off Flying H range that's all. Dave, what do you think? More cattle at fifteen dollars?"

He nodded.

"Fifteen dollars it is then."

"Kid, you got yourself a deal," Dolan said.

"I thought so. Say a hundred fifty head to start?"

The herd spread across the valley below, grazing the lush spring grass along the river bottom. Gray dawn rendered their backs a fluid muddle, bawling here and there where a cow summoned an errant calf.

Billy stuck out his chin. "Look there. Old Chisum got himself a watch on this herd."

"Must have heard we was comin'," O'Folliard said. "Now what do we do?"

Billy paused to consider the options.

Rudabaugh drew his Winchester from the saddle boot, jacked a round into the chamber, shouldered the weapon and fired in one fluid motion. The drover pitched from the saddle, hit the ground hard and lay still. "No trouble there." He rebooted the rifle.

The Kid pulled a scowl. "Now why'd you go and do that? Stealin' a few cows is one thing. Kill one of his men and Chisum is likely to take it personal."

Rudabaugh returned the scowl, a hand resting beside his gun butt. "Hell, he ain't nothin' but a drover and black at that. You got a problem with that, Kid?" Poison washed the killer's eye.

Billy shrugged.

"I didn't think so. Now let's get them cattle and get the hell out of here before Chisum gets on to us personal or otherwise.

Where we takin' 'em?"

"South," Billy said. "Down towards Seven Rivers. We'll change the brands on Evans' range before we move 'em west to the Flying H."

O'Folliard laughed.

"Now what's so funny?" Rudabaugh demanded.

"Jesse Evans and his Seven Rivers boys rustled for Dolan back before the war. That's what got Chisum into the war in the first place. We're gonna make it look like he's back in business."

Rudabaugh shook his head, annoyed. "To hell with the damn jokes, let's just move the damn cows and get paid."

Bright light, red orange and hot intruded on the darkness. Bright might mean the pearly gates. That'd be good. Red hot might mean something altogether different. Things started to clear some. His shoulder burned like that altogether different place. The sun blinded his eyes. He had a powerful headache. He remembered hearing a shot before he hit the ground and everything went black. A looming shadow snorted at his cheek. Peaches, she'd waited up for him. Damn good horse. He tried to right himself. His head went all light and fuzzy, like he'd taken to too much whiskey. Judging by the muddy stain beside him, he'd lost a fair amount of blood. Somebody'd bushwacked him good. *Why? Rustlers, it had to be.*

He reached up with his good arm and caught a stirrup. He hauled himself up to his knees and rested, letting his head settle down. He wretched. Not much left of supper. He struggled to a knee and pushed himself to his feet on the stirrup, dragging his hellfire right arm. He leaned against the horse. She held still. At least something did. He grabbed the saddle horn and took a deep breath. Just the shoulder, no innerd trouble best he could reckon. He measured the distance between the toe of his boot and the stirrup. He took a stab. Not even close. The shoulder mocked him near to unconscious.

"All right, girl, I get my butt in this saddle, you go on home and don't pay no mind to my complainin' or prayin'." The boot toe caught. He heaved. His butt hit leather. The sun went dark.

South Spring
"Uh-oh." Caneris tipped his hat back and wiped sweat on his shirtsleeve.

"What?" Roth dropped the heavy brush back in the grease bucket and straightened

168

up from the wagon axle. Caneris pointed with his chin. A lone horse jogged through the gate and headed for the barn, its rider slumped over the neck.

"It's Deac," the ramrod said, starting for the horse.

"Dawn Sky!" Roth called across the yard to the house.

Caneris met the horse halfway to the barn and caught the bridle. Her wounded rider's blood bathed her right shoulder. He led her up to the barn. Roth helped him ease the big man down as Dawn came running from the hacienda with Chisum huffing along behind.

"He's been shot," Johnny said.

Dawn skidded to a stop. "Get him up to the house." She turned and ran back to the kitchen.

"Get a blanket to stretcher him on and a couple more boys," Chisum ordered.

They got him up to the house. Dawn cleaned the wound. Chisum, Roth and Caneris hovered nearby. "Is he gonna make it?" Chisum asked.

"He has lost much blood." She applied a clean hot dressing to the entry wound.

His eyes fluttered open. "That you, Miss Dawn?" The familiar chest deep voice had withered to a dry husk.

She put her finger to her lips.

"For a minute there I thought you was the angel of mercy."

"What happened, Deac?" Chisum asked.

"Rustlers hit the herd."

Dawn turned on the men. Summer lightning flashed in her dark eyes. She shooed them all out of the room.

They clumped out to the porch just as Ledger rode up. He swung down from the steel dust and bounded up the porch step to Roth. "What happened?"

"Rustlers hit the river herd. They shot Deac."

"He all right?"

"Dawn's with him now. He's lost a lot of blood. He's tough. I reckon he'll pull through."

"Any idea who done it?"

"I know."

All eyes cut to Chisum. Roth wrinkled his brow. "How?"

"I got a strong hunch here." He tapped his gut. "It's the Kid takin' his Regulator pay, sure as God made little green apples."

Ty nodded. "When do we go after 'em?"

Chisum looked at the slanting sun. "First thing in the morning. They can't get too far pushing cattle."

FIFTEEN

Pecos Valley

The sun had climbed to midday by the time Ledger, Roth, Caneris and a handful of South Spring hands reached the river herd. It didn't take long to pick up the trail of a hundred fifty head driven south. They pushed hard along the trail to a shallow draw along the bank of a creek northeast of the old Seven Rivers Ranch. Roth drew rein, signaling a halt.

"Looks like John may have got his hunch about the Kid wrong."

"Sure has the look of Evans' gettin' back to his old tricks, don't it?" Caneris said.

They circled the draw. The herd had been held there for a time. Fire sign said the cattle were likely all wearing new brands. From there the trail lined out west just south of Flying H range. The sign dwindled as it seemingly disappeared among the meanderings of Flying H stock. Roth called a halt in frustration.

"Where'd they go?"

Caneris shrugged and spit.

Ledger shook his head. "Something stinks."

"Dolan couldn't be that stupid, could he?" Roth said.

"You wouldn't think so, but those cows didn't float away on thin air either."

"Might be some pretty smart rustlers," Caneris said. "What better place to hide a herd of stolen cattle than in the middle of a bigger herd of cattle. We might pick up their trail if we circle some."

Roth shook his head. "I'm bettin' on Dolan."

Ledger wheeled away taking the lead to the ranch house.

Flying H

Billy hunched across the table watching as Dolan drew a stack of gold certificates from his saddlebags. Rudabaugh lounged near the door, watching the Kid and Dolan finish their business. O'Folliard stood by the window, keeping an eye out for trouble. The ranch hadn't changed much since the day Tunstall died. Dolan either hadn't had time or hadn't bothered to spruce things up any. Still it struck Billy as odd. Here he was doing business with the man most likely responsible for Mr. Tunstall's death. Not so long ago, he'd sworn to kill anyone who had a hand in that. Times had a way of changing.

"Two thousand two hundred fifty," Dolan said as he passed a stack of gold certificates across the table to the Kid. "Pleasure doin' business with you."

Billy gave him one of his crooked smiles. "It's a start. We'll lay low a spell and let you know when we're ready to bring in another delivery."

"Rider comin'," O'Folliard said. The distant sound of fast hoofbeats broke the moment.

Rudabaugh joined Tom at the window. "That's Pickett comin' up our back trail. Likely we got company comin'."

Dolan nodded. "Best we get out of here and let my foreman handle whoever it is."

Billy scooped up the bills. "Com'on, boys." He led the way out the front door to the horses hitched at the rail. He tugged the roan's rein free and swung into the saddle. The others followed. He touched the brim of his sombrero to Dolan and wheeled out southwest.

Dolan watched them go. He stepped into the saddle. If Chisum had discovered his loss so soon he was certain to be in no humor Dolan aspired to meet up with. He swung his bay northwest toward Lincoln and squeezed up a lope.

By the time the South Spring riders reached the Flying H all they got for their trouble was the foreman's thanks for the warning. Rustlers were operating in the area.

South Spring

Chisum paced the parlor, fuming in the late spring promise of summer heat. Roth, Ledger and Caneris stood hats in hand watching the old man. The Seven Rivers boys got shot to hell during the war. He couldn't believe Evans would dare rustle Long Rail stock again. Jesse'd been quiet as a mouse since the battle for Lincoln. He shook his head.

"It's the Kid, I tell you. I can't shake the notion."

Roth pulled a frown. "Trail sign went straight to Seven Rivers."

"I heard you. I just don't believe Evans would be fool enough to try rustlin' Long Rail stock again, let alone top it off by drivin' it on his own range to change brands."

"Then what makes you think it was the Kid?" Ty asked.

"Like I said, he's mad over that back pay he says I owe him. He and Dolan made peace. Dolan owns the Flying H. You can run that brand and he's still got a ready market for rustled cattle. The war didn't change nothin'."

"So what do we do now?" Roth's question hung in the air.

Chisum paced. What to do was a damn good question. Kimbrell was a waste of time. The election wasn't until fall. Until then the law belonged to the most likely culprit behind the scheme. He'd lost a hundred fifty head of prime stock and damn near a good man in Swain. The rustlers' trail had gone up in smoke. He clenched his jaw in frustration.

"We ain't got many options. I'm goin' up to Lincoln in a few days. Maybe I can bluff Dolan. Ty, polish up that badge of yours and ride along."

Ty tightened his jaw. John knows rustling isn't a federal offense. What can a deputy US marshal say that would bother Dolan even a little bit if he is guilty? And that was nothing more than Chisum's hunch.

Lincoln
June 1880
Storm clouds gathered in the hills west of

town. Black towers boiled up like giant boulders thrown into the sky against the laws of nature. The cloud banks turned green and purple around the thunderheads. Jagged white streaks slashed the ground. The promise of hard rain picked up with the wind, holding out hope the day's oppressive heat might give way to a cooler evening.

The steel dust danced up the street, stirrup to stirrup with Chisum's long striding buckskin. Wind-whipped dust swirled across the street, lashing man and animal with stinging sheets of sand. The storm agitated both animals, filling their nostrils with unstable charged air.

Chisum cocked an eye to the sky. "Let's put these horses up at the Wortley before we go see Dolan." They jogged past the old Tunstall mercantile now home to Dolan's operation. They wheeled into the stable yard behind the Wortley and swung down. They led the horses into the stable and felt them begin to calm with the break from the wind. They turned the horses into two vacant stalls and went to work on the saddles.

"Looks to be a hell of a blow comin'," Ty said. "Maybe we should hole up in the hotel before we go see Dolan."

"I expect the worst will blow through

Union West Regional Library
704-821-7475

Customer ID: **********0118

Items that you checked out

Title: Loyalty /
ID: 871091008487885
Due: Saturday, October 7, 2023

Title: A question of bounty :
ID: 871091005257798
Due: Saturday, October 14, 2023

Title: Robert B. Parker's buckskin /
ID: 871091006638343
Due: Saturday, October 14, 2023

Title: The woman with the blue star /
ID: 871091007936092
Due: Saturday, October 14, 2023

Total items: 4
Account balance: $0.00
9/23/2023 9:03 AM
Checked out: 7
Overdue: 0
Hold requests: 0
Ready for pickup: 0

pretty fast. I ain't about to let a little rain put me off of what needs doin'." He stripped the latigos and hauled his saddle and blanket to a rack at the back wall of the stable. He scooped grain into buckets while Ty fetched water. They added a forkful of hay to each stall and headed for the hotel just as fat raindrops began to splatter the stable yard. By the time they grabbed their saddlebags and reached the shelter of the back porch, sheets of rain swept across the yard behind them. Chisum led the way down the back hall to the lobby.

The mousy desk clerk blinked behind smudged spectacles. "Afternoon, Mr. Chisum. I see you brought rain with you."

"Afternoon, Hiram. Looks like we made it just before things got interesting. We need a couple of rooms for the night and we've got two horses out back."

"Sign here." He spun the register. "That'll be three dollars."

Ty stood at the front window, watching wind-whipped torrents splatter the street to a brown slurry. Chisum came up behind him.

"Look there." Gray light built in behind the fast-running thunderheads. "The worst will be through in no time. Let's get our gear stowed and head on down to Dolan's place."

Twenty minutes later the visitor bell clanged over the door. Dolan stood behind the teller window preparing the bank for its three o'clock closing.

"Chisum, Ledger." He nodded. "What can we do for you?"

"I come to make a withdrawal," Chisum said.

"How much do you need?"

"All of it, I'm closin' the account."

Dolan's eyes went wide. He knew the account, though he couldn't recall the exact figure. "Why would you want to do that, John?"

Chisum squinted, boring a hole in the smaller man. "I've suffered some unexpected losses recently. A hundred fifty head of unexpected losses to be exact. Course you wouldn't know nothin' about that."

Dolan met the glare. "Sorry to hear that. Let me check the account record." He thumbed through the tub of account cards, his mind racing. He knew he didn't keep that kind of cash on hand. "Ah yes, here it is, five thousand two hundred twenty-nine dollars. That's a rather substantial sum. Are you sure it's wise to go around carrying that much cash?"

"Afraid I might get robbed Dolan? I s'pect you might know somethin' about that."

"What are you trying to say, Chisum?"

"You know damn well what I mean. My stock went missing right near Flying H range. That's why I've got Marshal Ledger here with me."

Dolan flicked his gaze to Ty, noticing the badge for the first time. "Marshal? I thought you'd taken up ranching."

"Marshal Sherman asked me to serve as special deputy."

"I see."

"That'll come in right handy once we have an honest sheriff after the next election, don't you think, Dolan?" Chisum's voice barely rose above the rain spattering the front window. "Now about my money."

"Why would you close your account? It's been here since the bank opened."

"John Tunstall opened this bank. Let's just say I'm not sure I approve of the change in ownership."

Dolan clenched his jaw. "I don't keep that kind of cash on hand. You'll have to give me a few days to have it shipped in from Kansas City."

"You don't have it on hand, you mean it's all busy runnin' this little empire of yours? All this and you need to go back in the business of dealin' in stolen cattle. So whose idea was it Dolan, yours or the Bonney Kid?"

"I don't know what you're talkin' about."

He said it, but Chisum's hunch cut too close to the truth to hide.

"I, ah, I'll arrange for the cash."

"Have it sent to the Roswell Bank. I ain't ridin' back up here to make my point again."

"What point is that?"

"I lose any more stock, Dolan, and you and me are gonna settle this once and for all."

"You're talking nonsense."

"Am I? Billy the Kid runs off one more head of Long Rail stock and you'll both pay for it." He turned on his heel. "Com'on, Ty."

Dolan watched the big rancher go. *Time for the Kid to get lost for a spell.*

They sat at a back corner table in the Wortley dining room, waiting on steak and potatoes. The storm had cleared through, leaving the air freshened and cool. Golden sunset painted the western peaks purple. Lamplight chased gathering shadows as Chisum recounted his story. Garrett scratched his chin. "You sure, Mr. Chisum? That's a powerful lot of hunch. The Kid may be a lot of things, but I've never known him to be a rustler."

"It was writ all over Dolan's face. Ty saw it."

He nodded.

"The Kid threatened he'd get even for the back pay he says I owe him. He went out of his way to make it look like Jesse Evans done it. Evans ain't that stupid, even if his gang weren't all shot to hell from the war. Nope. The Kid's got an ax to grind and Dolan's more than willin' to profit by his doin's."

"What about Sheriff Kimbrell?"

"That's why you're here, Pat. You know as well as me that son of a bitch won't do nothin'. We got no law in Lincoln until you beat him in the fall. All we got is Ty here with a deputy marshal's badge to fill in a federal crack any chance we find one."

Garrett shook his head. "I just hope we beat him."

"You will. The Cattle Growers will see to it. In a way Dolan and the Kid done us a favor. Every honest man in the county knows the trouble rustlin' brings on."

The waiter arrived with sizzling plates of fried steak and potatoes.

When Billy got word from Dolan, it wasn't

an order for more cattle. Somehow Chisum had caught on to their deal. He and Garrett were using rustling to drum up support for Garrett's campaign for sheriff. Billy was being blamed for the latest rash of stolen cattle and horses, but rumors pointed an accusing finger at Dolan, and the lack of arrests created a shadow of suspicion that hung over Sheriff Kimbrell. Dolan warned Billy to clear out for a spell. They rode southwest out of Whiskey Jim's.

Sixteen

Calico
Arizona Territory

Calico was nothing more than a wide spot in the road just south of Fort Grant. The town consisted of a cluster of adobe and clapboard buildings loosely arranged around a small central plaza. A narrow rut road ran into one end and out the other. Calico's claim to fame was a spring-fed well that got some help from mountain snowmelt, courtesy of a stream that ran south out of the Gila River before it petered out in summer. Most days, commerce consisted of a freighter or maybe a bone wagon, a couple of hipshot horses at a hitch rack, and a campesino or two taking siesta in the shade by counting sage balls blowing down the street. The town consisted of a blacksmith, livery, mercantile, a café that rented cots in the back and Calico Cait's cantina.

When it came to good times in Calico,

men came to Cait's Dusty Rose Cantina. The squat adobe sprawled in the middle of town behind a thatched roof that created a shaded outdoor patio and small relief from the worst summer heat. Inside the Rose had a scattering of worn wooden tables, a hard packed dirt floor and a rough cut bar top stacked on stout adobe pillars. The mirrored back bar held an array of bottles of uncertain origin, decorated by colorful serapes and an old guitar that hadn't been played in years.

Cait ran cards, whores, whiskey and a piano man . . . all the ingredients for a hell-raising good time. She understood men and money. A tall flaxen-haired beauty with alabaster skin somehow preserved from sun-hardened conditions, she might have made a sportin' gal herself if she had a mind to. She had all the right curves, sloe eyes and a teasing smile. She learned early those charms were better spent distracting players fool enough to sit down at her game. Oh she knew the worth of a soiled dove all right. She employed them, and that's where the Kid came in.

Once they hit town, it didn't take long for the Kid and his gang to find their way to the Dusty Rose. Most men did. They might have moved on if it had been up to Rudabaugh and his two stiffs. That wouldn't have bothered Cait. The best she could say about the one they called Dirty Dave behind his back was that he had money. The rest of the man was rattlesnake mean, stinking filth and downright disgusting. She wasn't going to get rid of him easily either on account of the fact the Kid wasn't going anywhere. The red-haired Irishman, O'Folliard, would stay where the Kid did. And that kept the rest of the gang around too.

The Kid fell in love with dark-eyed Rosa Diaz. Well not exactly in love, more like lust. His heart belonged to another dark-eyed beauty back in Fort Sumner, but the old fort was a long way off and Rosa's considerable charms most nights were right under his nose. She had classic Castilian beauty, skin the color of creamed coffee and long black hair that hung in waves around proud cheekbones. She had stormy eyes and full lips turned down at the corners in a pretty pout. She wore a simple white cotton blouse off her shoulders rendered stunning by the swell of firm breasts. A red and white flowered skirt cinched to a tiny waist hugged the round of her hips. Her beauty was marred by a dirty smear on one cheek, a sign of hard work in the dusty cantina.

Cait didn't mind the Kid hangin' round

all moonfaced and cow-eyed. He was pleasant enough and sort of cute. So long as he paid for Rosa's company and kept his gun where it belonged, he was just business. Cait kept a pearl-handled derringer in each garter, just in case the Kid, or anyone else, got confused.

Things went along pretty much the way things usually went at the Dusty Rose. The Kid passed his time and money with Rosa. The boys got drunk and Cait took their money at cards. Business as usual, until the dusky evening that citified dude showed up for a drink. He was smooth all right, dressed in a black frock coat suit with a brocade vest, starched linen, paper collar and ribbon bowtie. He had the look of a gambler with a waxed mustache and lively gray eyes, but he never sat down to play. He sat down at a table and ordered a bottle of Cait's best bourbon. Rosa served him. The way he eyed her hips sashay it was pretty sure he'd order up a helping of her to go along with the bottle.

"Care to fetch a glass for yourself and join me?" he said.

She set down the bottle and glanced around the Dusty Rose. No sign of Billy at this hour. She smiled and fetched a glass from the bar. When opportunity knocked, a girl might as well make a little extra on the side. They'd settled down to civil preliminaries over a drink or two when the Kid and his gang came in.

A keen sense for trouble tugged Cait's attention away from her game. The Kid had it bad for Rosa. He wasn't going to take kindly to the handsome stranger. She eased her hand below the table, found the hem of her dress and followed a silk stocking up her shapely calf to the butt of a derringer tucked in the garter at her thigh. The little pistol wasn't much good outdoors, but in here at close range it packed a .41-caliber wallop that had a way of nipping nastiness in the bud. She kept a close eye on the situation as things developed.

Billy found Rosa's back at the corner table with the handsome stranger like a divining rod draws to water. His eyes registered something unpleasant. He sauntered across the cantina while the boys headed for the bar. The stranger looked up with a flicker of recognition in his eye and eased back in his chair. Rosa sensed him.

"Who's your new friend?" Billy asked.

She pulled a frown as if to say none of your damn business. The stranger spoke up.

"Royal Cage at your service." He smiled.

"William Bonney." He glared.

"Yes, I expected as much. The one they call Billy the Kid, unless I miss my guess."

"Expected, how'd you know?"

"I heard you were in town. I decided Rosa here would be the fastest way to a friendly introduction."

She pulled another frown, realizing she'd been used though not in the paying kind of way. She'd been irritated before, but now her Latin blood got up a wet cat fury for sure.

"So you got your introduction, Royal Cage. Rosa's keepin' company with me."

Her eyes flashed anger at the suggested possession.

Cage held up his hands palms open. "No offense. I just want to discuss a bit of business."

"What sort of business?"

"Perhaps you'll excuse us Rosa. Be a good girl now and go fetch Mr. Bonney a fresh glass."

She stood. Billy looped an arm around her shoulders.

"Don't go and stray too far now darlin'."

She shrugged him off with a look fit for a scorpion and stalked off to the bar.

Cait eased off her weapon. "Sorry boys." She smiled and returned to her game.

Billy took Rosa's chair.

"I say, you must like them feisty."

"She's a she-cat all right. Might just about have her claws put away by the time we get done. Now what's on your mind, Mr. Cage?"

He paused while Rosa set down the glass. She brushed Billy with a hip as she turned to the bar.

He grinned his crooked grin. "See, she's forgive me already. Where were we? Oh yeah, you were about to tell me about your business."

Cage reached in his coat pocket and drew out a stack of crisp new hundred-dollar gold certificates. Billy's eyes bugged. He peeled one off and handed it to the Kid.

"I like your business already. How do you come by these?"

Cage glanced around and hunched across the scarred table, his voice barely above a whisper. "I print them."

Billy's eyes went wide with sudden comprehension. He turned the note over in his fingers. "No shit!" He breathed.

Cage nodded.

"Where do I come in?"

"Distribution."

He wrinkled his brow.

"You and your boys pass the bills around."

"What's the split?"

"Fifty for me, fifty for you."

Billy nodded. "This is way better than rustlin'. Where do you figure to pass 'em?"

"I'm open to suggestion."

He thought for a moment. A lonely part of him brightened. "The gold camps up to White Oaks."

Cage sat back with a half smile and a nod. "Perfect."

Billy stuck out his hand. "You got yourself distribution, Mr. Cage." *And I got a reason to go back to Fort Sumner.* He offered Cage the hundred-dollar note.

"Keep it." Cage chuckled. "There's plenty more where that came from." He nodded at Rosa with a twinkle in his eye. "It may help mend your tattered romance."

They both laughed.

She forgave him. And forgave him, and forgave him and forgave him again. They tossed the bedclothes in her crib to a fury. In the dark small hours they lay spent, a tangled jumble of arms, legs, rumpled sheets and discarded clothes. Billy stared at the ceiling, his body slick with sweat. His nose filled with the scent of her, his mind adrift on the echoes of sex. Rosa lifted her chin from his chest, her eyes a black gleam beneath tangled curls.

"You're leaving."

He came back to the moment. "What makes you say that?"

"You think about her."

"What?"

"You think about the girl back there, wherever it is you come from."

"What makes you think that?"

"Rosa knows. You want to own me for a time, like tonight. But your heart is not here."

"Rosa, I . . ."

"Don't lie. There is no need. You pay me good money. You show a girl a good time. Sometimes it is nice to be owned for a while."

"I do mean that part."

"I know. I feel it."

"Forgive me?"

"Four give you?" She lifted the sheet. "I think I give you five." She laughed thick and smoky.

He woke to the gray light of predawn. She slept beside him, snoring softly. Something about her tugged at him, just not that hard. She was right. His heart belonged to Paulita. It was long past time to get back to her. There wasn't any reason not to go back. As long as they stayed away from cattle rustling,

Chisum and his friends wouldn't be no trouble. Hell the counterfeits were good enough he figured they'd hand out a lot of them before anyone figured out they weren't any good. A man couldn't come up with a better way to get rich. Time to get to it.

He eased himself out of bed. Rosa turned over and resumed her rhythmic breathing. He dressed quietly, picked up his boots and tiptoed out the door of her small room at the back to the Dusty Rose. He padded across the dirt floor into the dawning light. He pulled a chair up under the outdoor canopy. The air felt light and warm, not yet heated by full daylight. He pulled on his boots. Down the street the boys were saddling their horses. A mule drawn freight wagon waited, its canvas cover securely lashed down. Royal Cage stood by the team dressed for the trail. Billy put aside the rumble in his stomach. They were about to make some serious money.

Rosa awoke to an empty bed as she most often did. The Kid was gone. She roused herself, searching the rumpled sheets for her nightdress. Her eyes went wide. A hundred-dollar gold certificate lay on the bedside table. She smiled. What a sweet boy.

Cait took the note in exchange for small bills.

SEVENTEEN

White Oaks
August 1880

The ride up to White Oaks took time owing to the wagon. You couldn't haul a printing press on a horse. It wasn't all that big or heavy, but it was bulky and awkward. Then there was the supply of special paper, so the first leg of this easy money trail turned out to be the slow slogging job of a freighter. It gave Billy time to mull the problem of where and how to set up the printing operation. Cage needed a quiet place to work in secret. The Dedrick ranch at Bosque Grande fit the bill nicely, if the brothers would go along. Billy had a hunch they would for a small slice of the pie.

The Dedrick ranch finally wound its way into view one hot dusty afternoon. Billy eased the roan back alongside Cage seated on the wagon box and drew rein. He popped the cork on his canteen and took a long pull.

"That there's the place," he said with a nod, wiping his mouth on the back of his hand.

"Don't look like much."

"That's the beauty of it. Nobody will bother us there."

"You're sure."

"I'm sure. Now give me one of them crisp hundreds."

Cage fished in his coat pocket and peeled off a bill.

"Let me do the talkin'. I'll have us set up in no time. Oh and just to keep things straight, these boys think my name is William Antrim." He squeezed up a lope ahead of the wagon. He led the way through the gate and across the yard to the ranch house. He drew rein and stepped down. A dust boil swirled across the yard toward the corral as Moses Dedrick stepped off the porch to greet them.

"Antrim ain't it?"

"It is, Mr. Dedrick. You have a good memory."

"Sometimes its good and sometimes its bad. It depends on the pay." He glanced at the wagon and riders coming along his back trail. "That don't look like another herd. What's up this time?"

"Nope, no herd. My pards and me need a

quiet place to do some work."

"What's that got to do with me?"

"We'd like to rent that shed behind the barn over yonder."

"Hell I ain't in the property rental business. Take yourself on over to Whiskey Jim's. He'll be more'n happy to fix you up."

The Kid shook his head. "Too many nosey folks hang around Jim's, if you know what I mean. We'll make it worth your while." The Kid held up the hundred-dollar note.

The rancher arched a doubtful bushy brow.

"How long you fixin' to stay?"

"Not long, a month, maybe two."

"That's a lot of money. Looks new too. Where'd you get it?"

The Kid smiled his crooked smile. "We printed it."

Dedrick took the bill and turned it over in his hand. "Antrim, looks like you rented yourself a shed. This should cover the first week."

"Damned expensive shed."

"It's worth what you pay for it." He pocketed the note.

They cleared out the shed and set up the press. A week later the boys hit the trails for Whiskey Jim's, Lincoln and the tent-top saloons around the mining camps in White Oaks. Rudabaugh took Whiskey Jim's. O'Folliard and Pickett set up shop in White Oaks. Wilson rode into Lincoln. Cash was easier to trade or gamble in than gold. As long as they offered a fair price there was no shortage of miners willing to turn dust or nuggets into cash. Every few days Billy rode the circuit between the Dedrick ranch and the boys, trading currency for gold. Even Dedrick got into the game when he figured out he could buy cattle and horses using his rent money, or buying more bogus bills when the need arose.

The Kid stuck him for fifty cents on the dollar for those bills. He counted it the first time he'd ever gotten the better of the Dedricks. They'd been at it for a month before the first bogus bill found its way to a suspicious banker in Santa Fe.

Lincoln
September 1880
The Kid rode into town with the sun firing the hills and peaks in the west at his back. He drew rein amid long purple shadows, spilling across the street in front of the cantina. He figured to find Wilson buying, selling or gambling the skim. Honor among this gang of thieves owed to the fact they all

197

knew they were thieves. In this river of profits nobody begrudged anybody a little walking around money out of the paper profits. The boys were all living high up the hog, except for the Kid who filled his days riding circuit on the take. He reckoned Cage had the worst of it, sitting in that stuffy shed printing money all day. Then of course half the gold was his. He'd be soaking up sunshine, senoritas and tequila for the rest of his life one day soon enough.

As he climbed the boardwalk he noticed the circulars. Up and down the street, they were tacked to most everything that didn't move. In fact he saw a couple of them tacked on wagon gates that did move.

Garrett for Sheriff.

Cattle Growers for Garrett.

He actually saw one or two that said *Kimbrell for Sheriff.*

It looked like one hell of a race. He'd forgotten they'd talked old Pat into running. He shook his head. Inside the cantina the lamps glimmered to light, tinting a light haze of tobacco smoke yellow. He glanced around the room, no sign of Wilson. It was early. He stepped up to the bar. The early crowd stood at the rail. A few afternoon card games appeared to be winding down for a supper break. He ordered a whiskey.

He'd finished his first glass and ordered a second when a familiar figure swung through the bat wings and started around of the room greeting patrons one by one. Billy motioned the bartender for another glass and the bottle. He took it to a corner table and watched him work the crowd, meeting each man with a smile and a hand-shake. He worked his way down the bar. As he drew closer, Billy could hear.

"Pat Garrett. I'm running for sheriff. I'd sure appreciate your vote come election day."

Again and again the message was mostly the same. Now and again he'd recognize some feller and address him by name. At the end of the bar he turned to the corner table. He recognized the Kid with a half smile and came over to the table. Billy held up his hand.

"I know you're runnin' for sheriff and you'd appreciate my vote. Sit down, Pat. Let me buy you a drink."

He pulled out a chair. Billy poured three fingers and slid the glass across the table. Garrett lifted the glass.

"Billy, it's been a while."

"It has. I'd forgotten they'd put you up for sheriff." He shook his head. "Why'd you want to go and let 'em make a sheriff out of an honest bartender?"

Garrett laughed. "Somebody's got to do it, besides it pays better than pourin' whiskey."

"Lots of things pay better than that."

"So I hear. Some folks think rustling might be one of 'em. But you wouldn't know anything about that would you?"

"Rustlin', me? Pshaw, no."

"I hope so Billy. For your sake, if I win this thing, I hope so."

Billy lifted his hands in mock surrender. "Not me, Pat. I'm clean as the wind-driven snow. You figure you're gonna win?"

"Hope so. The Cattle Growers Association backing should count for some."

The Kid nodded. "Chisum's doin' ain't it?"

He met the Kid's eyes. "They want the rustlin' stopped."

"You figure you can do that?"

"I can sure try. That's more than Kimbrell can bring himself to do."

He grinned. "You can try."

"I hope you're as clean as you say, Billy."

"Me? Com'on Pat, you know me."

"I do. I also hear the rumors."

He shrugged. "People talk. Can't do nothin' 'bout that."

"Sure Billy. It's just talk. It better be.

'Cause if it ain't and I win, we both know what that means." He tossed off his drink. "Well, I got more work to do."

"The election's not 'til November."

"It takes work to win, Billy. I plan on winnin'. If I do, the rustlin' will stop. Let's make sure the next time we meet it's over a nice friendly drink." The words hung in the air. Garrett scraped back his chair.

"Sure, Pat, sure thing."

Santa Fe
October 1880

The outer office door swung open. US Marshal for New Mexico Territory John Sherman glanced up from a stack of mail. His stomach growled a lunch hour reminder. His caller, a pinch-faced man in a tweed jacket and derby hat blinked behind smudged spectacles. He carried a small travel-worn valise.

"Marshal Sherman?"

"Yes."

He reached into his vest pocket and produced a card. "Special Agent Azariah Wild, Treasury Department."

Recognition registered in Sherman's eye. He extended his hand. "We've been expecting someone. John Sherman."

The agent took his hand. Sherman read

the card.

"New Orleans. You're a long way from home."

"Fortunately, counterfeit isn't a common crime. Unfortunately, that means those few of us who investigate it have to cover some pretty large territories."

"What can I do for you?"

"I'm told you have samples of the suspected counterfeit notes."

He nodded. "Step into my office."

Wild followed him into his cramped office.

"Have a seat." He gestured to a side chair and took his seat at the desk. He drew an envelope from a side drawer and handed it to the Treasury man.

Wild withdrew three bills from the envelope. He held one up to the bright afternoon sunlight, streaming through the office window. He produced a small magnifying glass from his coat pocket, adjusted the focus and moved it back and forth across the printed surface. He nodded.

"Quite good actually, I'm surprised your banker caught these."

"He might not have, if there'd just been one. He got suspicious when he found three of them. It seems we don't see that much new currency around these parts. Even then he couldn't be sure. Since then we've had other reports."

"Treasury has seen them show up in Kansas and as far west as Arizona. Do you have any idea where they are coming from?"

"We've had reports from several places down south. The mining camps around White Oaks seem to have more than their share."

The Treasury man scratched his chin. "Where is that?"

Sherman turned to the territory map on the wall behind his desk. He traced a line two hundred fifty miles south of Santa Fe. "About here."

"I see. And the nearest local law?"

"There's a town constable. He doesn't do much more than arrest drunks and break up fights. Past that." He drew another line southeast fifty miles or so to Lincoln.

"Lincoln's got a sheriff. I suggest you start in Lincoln. I'm told they've taken some of it there. Sheriff Kimbrell is likely to figure counterfeit for a federal crime. He's facing a tough reelection. I doubt he'll make much time for you. I've got a deputy down there. I'll have my man meet you there in two weeks. His name is Ty Ledger. He'll be staying at the Wortley Hotel."

"Don't tell me, let me guess. The Southern

Pacific doesn't go to Lincoln."

"Very perceptive, Mr. Wild."

The agent's eye glittered at his own scarcasm. "And the best way to get to Lincoln?"

"A good horse and a guide. I can help you with both."

"A good horse, you're too kind."

EIGHTEEN

Lincoln
November 2, 1880

The Western Union messenger from Roswell delivered Sherman's telegram to South Spring. The order to meet a Treasury agent in Lincoln suited their plans. Ty and Roth accompanied Chisum into town on a brisk fall afternoon, sharpened by the prospect of early snow. The election was held the next day. They cast their votes at the courthouse and that evening joined Garrett and other members of the Cattle Growers Association in the Wortley dining room to await the results.

Cigar smoke and whiskey fueled a festive mood that anticipated victory. The atmosphere among the Kimbrell backers down the street at the cantina was a bit more subdued. Around nine o'clock, County Clerk Ben Curtis hobbled across the street from the courthouse. The room fell silent at the appearance of his bent scarecrow frame. He adjusted his spectacles and held up a crumpled tally sheet.

"Kimbrell, one hundred twenty-three; Garrett, one hundred eighty-six."

The room exploded in cheers and clinking glasses. The clerk limped out to finish his thankless job down the street. Likely the news preceded him on a chorus of raucous hoots driven by the night wind.

Garrett accepted the congratulations of his supporters with the sober half smile he passed off for mirth. Ledger and Roth stood near the lobby door watching the festivities.

"What do you think?" Roth asked.

Ty shrugged. "These boys think the rustlin' problem is done for. Pat's a good man, but them's high expectations."

Roth nodded. "He'll need help all right, but at least we got a fightin' chance with Dolan's influence out of the way."

A slight man in a tweed jacket and bowler hat appeared in the lobby doorway. He surveyed the room.

"I say do you know which one of these gentlemen is Marshal Ledger?"

Ty looked past Roth. "That would be me. Special Agent Wild?"

He nodded.

"I've been expecting you. Marshal Sherman asked me to assist you with the investigation of a counterfeit ring believed to be operating in the area."

"Indeed, is there someplace we can talk?"

Ty tilted his chin to a corner table. "It's pretty quiet over there."

He nodded.

"Can I buy you a drink?"

"That would sit well. It's a damn long ride down here from Santa Fe."

"Mind if my partner sits in?"

Wild eyed Roth.

"We work cattle together mostly, but sometimes in law."

"Suit yourself."

"I'll get the drinks," Roth said.

Ty led the Treasury man through the jubilant crowd to the corner table. Chair scrapes drowned in laughter and back slapping.

"What's the celebration about?" Wild asked.

"Election results, Pat Garrett over there was just elected sheriff."

"Likely we'll bring him into this at some point."

"George Kimbrell still holds the office until the end of the year. I doubt we can expect much help from him."

Roth arrived with glasses and a bottle. He

pulled up a chair and poured.

Ty lifted his glass. "Now Mr. Wild, how can I help?"

He drew a crisp hundred-dollar note from his pocket and passed it across the table. "We need to find the source of these."

Ty rubbed it between his fingers, held it up to the lamp, shrugged and passed it to Roth. "Other than bein' new, it looks pretty good to me."

"That's the problem. They are good. The flaws are small. You need a magnifying glass and a trained eye to be sure. A territorial banker got suspicious when a couple of them showed up in his deposits."

"What makes you think they're coming from around here?"

"The deposits all had links to the goldfields around White Oaks."

Roth nodded. "That would be a logical place to peddle 'em. Sellin' gold for currency makes walkin' around a good bit easier."

"That's the way I figure it." Wild tossed off his drink. Ty poured another.

"So when do you want to ride up to White Oaks?"

"Give me a day or two to get the sore out of my backside. We can use the time to poke around town to see if any of the funny money has turned up here."

"That won't take long," Ty said. "Dolan's store, the Wortley here, maybe the cantina, that's about it."

Wild drained his glass. "Let's get to it in the morning. Just now I need some sleep."

The visitor bell broke the afternoon siesta. Dolan roused himself from his ciphers. With Jasper gone to lunch he had to mind the store and the books. A young tough with a patchy scruff of red beard stood at the counter picking over the cigar selection. He paused over the higher end of the selection.

"A man couldn't enjoy a finer smoke," Dolan said.

He glanced at the shopkeeper. His sour expression never changed. He laid five cigars on the counter.

"That'll be two bits."

He tossed a coin on the counter, stuffed four smokes in his shirt pocket and bit the tip off the fifth. He started for the door, fishing in his vest pocket for a lucifer.

Ty Ledger clumped up the boardwalk to the door accompanied by a slight man in a tweed jacket and bowler. They stepped inside past the young man scratching a match to light.

"Ledger. What do you want?" Dolan asked.

Ty picked up on Dolan's icy demeanor. Likely as not he was still plenty sour over the election. Garrett's successful campaign was clearly the doing of Chisum and the Cattle Growers Association. The way Dolan saw it, he and Chisum must be some of the same. The handwriting on the wall had been clear from the moment Dolan took over the Flying H. That made him a cattle grower. It didn't make him a welcome member of the association. The man should have figured that out. Then again, maybe he did.

"Need to ask you a couple of questions, Dolan. This here's Treasury Agent Azariah Wild."

At the mention of Treasury, Billy Wilson paused at the door to inspect the tip of his cigar.

"Treasury Agent?" Dolan extended his hand. "James Dolan at your service."

"Pleased to meet you, Mr. Dolan. We won't take but a moment of your time. Marshal Ledger and I are investigating a counterfeit ring believed to be operating in the region. Might you have taken in any notes similar to this recently?" He slid a hundred-dollar note across the counter.

A flicker of recognition crossed Dolan's

eye. "I did see one about a week ago."

"Might you recall who passed it?" Wild said.

"I didn't take it. My clerk, Jasper, did. He'd likely remember. New hundreds ain't that common."

"May we speak to him?"

"He's out to lunch. He should be back directly."

The visitor bell rang. The door clicked closed.

The sheriff's office occupied a small part of the courthouse first floor, next to the county clerk's office and across from the courtroom and a judge's chamber. The second floor of the former Murphy and Dolan Mercantile known as the House had been converted to a jail once the county took over. Chisum and Roth accompanied Garrett when he paid a call on Sheriff Kimbrell the day after the election. They found the sheriff in something of a surly mood.

"Good afternoon, Sheriff," Garrett said.

"Garrett. Come to size up the place so soon?"

"I thought we should talk things over. Just to make sure we have a smooth changeover the next couple of months."

"Sure, sure thing. Just let me know what

you need."

The office door swung open. Ty and Agent Wild stepped inside.

"Sheriff Kimbrell? Treasury Agent Azariah Wild." The government man extended his hand.

Kimbrell scowled, unused to drawing a crowd let alone on the heels of an election loss. He took the agent's hand. "What can I do for you?"

"I've just arrived in town to take up investigation of a counterfeit ring known to be operating in the area. I was hoping to enlist your support in continuing the investigation up in White Oaks."

"I don't see I can do much to help with that. My jurisdiction's here in Lincoln. I don't have the deputies to go ridin' off all over the county." He glanced at Garrett. "You'll find that out soon enough."

Chisum glanced at Roth with a twinkle in his eye. "For now, maybe you could deputize sheriff-elect Garrett here. I'm sure he'd be only too pleased to help Agent Wild."

"And who might you be?" Wild asked.

"John Chisum. This here's our newly elected sheriff, Pat Garrett."

"Sheriff Garrett, congratulations. It seems I may have crashed your victory celebration over at the Wortley last night."

"Sheriff-elect, Mr. Wild. George is still in charge here until the first of the year."

"What about it, Kimbrell?" Chisum pressed. "Deputize Pat. It'll make for a smooth changeover."

"Sure, why not. If he wants to go traipsin' all over the county it suits me just fine." He jerked open a desk drawer and tossed Garrett a deputy's badge. "Raise your right hand. Do you solemnly swear to uphold the law to the best of your ability?"

"I do."

"Done."

"Ty, why don't you add deputy US marshal to Pat's authority?" Chisum said. "That'll give him all the jurisdiction he needs to help Agent Wild here."

"Sure thing, John."

"Ain't that cozy," Kimbrell mumbled.

Chisum smiled. "There, Mr. Wild, it appears you've got everything you need."

NINETEEN

Fort Sumner
November 1880

Deluvina floated across the kitchen floor in silent darkness. The sound intruded so softly, had it not been for a pause between wind gusts and a break in Pete's snoring, she might never have heard it. Even at that she couldn't be sure. She felt her way to the front hallway. She pressed her lips in resignation. She knew the sound. It came from Paulita's room. It came as no surprise. In a way, she'd been expecting it. She shivered. A chill draft prickled goose flesh beneath her thin nightdress. Her first thought was to return to the warmth of her bed. The child made her own misery when it came to the boy. Still she was no more than a child. She'd been one herself not so very long ago. She followed the sound to Paulita's door. She tapped softly. The sobbing paused. She took it for permission and let herself enter the silence.

Paulita lay wrapped in a blanket of thin darkness below the window. Deluvina went to the bed and sat beside her. She found her tear streaked cheek under a mass of black curls and gently wiped her tears away.

"What is it, muchacha?" she whispered without needing a reply. The girl lifted the covers, inviting her friend to the warmth of her bed. Deluvina lay down beside her. Paulita covered her with the blankets and curled up in her arms, her head resting in the comfort of her friend's embrace. They lay there for a time, letting warmth join their bodies, listening to the mysteries of breathing and heartbeat. Deluvina felt hot tears moisten her breast. "What is it, child?" She didn't flinch defiant at the diminutive.

"He's gone. It's been five months. What if he doesn't come back before winter? What if he doesn't come back?"

"He is a man."

"But I love him."

She let that be enough for a time, stroking Paulita's back. The girl made no attempt to hold her tears back or the silent sobs her body shuddered.

"Will he come back?"

"Si, if he loves you."

She lifted her head, her eyes liquid fire

215

behind a tangle of curl. "He must. He must love me."

The servant girl's expression softened in the dark. She touched Paulita's cheek with tender concern. "You gave him your greatest gift to hold him. Sometimes even this is not enough." She felt more than saw the girl's jaw quiver.

"How did you know?"

"Women know these things."

"You don't think he's coming back." Anguish tasted bitter on her tongue.

"I didn't say that. I said only sometimes."

"Oh, Deluvina." She fell to her breast sobbing again. Time passed. Her sobs slowed. Her breathing grew more regular. The servant girl smoothed away hair from her mistress' cheek. The girl sighed softly and cuddled close. Deluvina held her. She wondered how much longer she would. Not much. A knowing formed in her mind. Sleep little one. This one will come back. What man with blood in his veins would not? Life comes for one, even as it slips away for another. She lightly kissed the cheek enfolded in her embrace.

White Oaks

It wasn't much as law practices go, even by frontier standards. A tent for an office, a

216

practice that handled the routine work of helping miners secure their claims. Once the field played out, the work would too. But for the time being the clientele paid in gold and that kept Ira Leonard in whiskey, tobacco and vittles. Apart from soiled linen and a halfhearted attempt at a tie, his scruffy unkempt appearance had more in common with his clients than a barrister at law. This afternoon like most, he dozed on his cot wrapped in a blanket still a bit fuzzy from the prior evening's consumption. Somewhere nearby boots crunched dry scrabble close enough to rise above the wind. Somebody tapped the tent pole, setting the canvas off in an annoying flap.

"S'cuse me, Mr. Leonard."

He cracked a red-rimmed eye. The kid had a dull-looking gap-toothed grin, sloped shoulders and an utterly disreputable appearance, nearly the equal of his own, should he get out of bed, which he had little intention to do.

"I'm in need of a little lawyerin'."

"What the hell, can't you see I'm busy here?"

"I can pay."

"Course you can. Your claim won't get up and walk away. Come back later."

"I don't got a claim. I need help with a letter."

"A letter?" He propped himself on one elbow and blinked against the offending sunlight. "What sort of letter?"

"A letter to Governor Wallace."

He shook his head and rubbed his eyes. He discovered himself awake in spite of his best intentions. *Damn it.* Well at least it wasn't another damn claim filing. He belched, relieving a measure of last night's dyspepsia. "What do you want with the governor, boy?"

"A pardon, old man. Now are you gonna help me or not?"

"A pardon?" He sat on the edge of the cot and shook his head to clear it. At least this interruption made for more interest than his run-of-the-mill inconveniences. "What do you need a pardon for?"

"Murder."

He pulled a sour expression. "You guilty?"

"If I wasn't, what the hell would I need a pardon for?"

"Honest felon, I like that. What's your name, son?"

"William Bonney."

"Billy the Kid."

"Some call me that."

"You're askin' for one hell of a letter."

218

"Ain't that why lawyers get paid? Now you gonna lawyer me or not?"

Leonard scratched the stubble on his chin. He shrugged. "Hell, it's only pen and ink. You think Governor Wallace will pay any heed?"

"He owes me a pardon. He promised one if I testified again' Jimmy Dolan."

"As I recall that case, you never testified."

"No, but I would have."

"Well there you have it. That should make all the difference a man could imagine. Why do you need a lawyer to write your letter?"

He shook his head. "I tried writin' him a couple of times. I didn't get no pardon. Everyone else what fought in the war got pardoned. Why not me? I got one comin'. Maybe you can find the words to convince him."

He scratched his head again, squinted at the Kid, grimaced and twisted up the gumption to stand. "All right, I'll try, but no guarantees."

The Kid smiled crooked.

Leonard stumbled out of the tent. He pulled a chair up to a camp desk set under a canvas top, drew a sheet of paper from a leather case and dipped a pen in an ink pot. "Have a seat." He pointed to a second chair. "I need the particulars. Who'd you kill?"

"Sheriff William Brady."

He arched a bushy brow over a watery red eye. "This story gets better by the minute." He scratched a note.

"Him and Buckshot Roberts."

"A double murder." He made another note.

"Nah, there was others. I just ain't been charged with none of them."

"I see. Well at least we have that to be grateful for. And why is it that, in your opinion, you deserve to be pardoned?"

"Like I told you, everyone else was."

"Yes, I recall that now. Any other pertinent facts I should consider?"

"Yeah, the governor promised me a pardon."

"In the matter of your testimony that didn't happen."

"That's right."

Leonard scratched the bristles on his chin. He shook his head. "Don't know as that helps the case."

"Hell's bells, t'wouldn't a made no difference. You know Dolan got off."

"Ah yes, I'd forgotten that subtlety. No chance the prosecutor might see that differently."

"Huh?"

He waved the question aside with his pen.

"Nothing. Anything else?"

The Kid thought a moment. "Nope, that's about it."

"Come back tomorrow."

Billy liked the legal letter. It had plenty of *to wits* and *wherefores.* He paid Ira Leonard twenty dollars for it. Governor Wallace tore it up.

Billy Wilson thundered into the Dedrick brothers' ranch yard hell for leather on a lathered horse. He swung out of the saddle and dropped his reins faster than the blown horse dropped its head. He never broke stride as he ran to the shed. He burst through the door. Paper and ink smelled of currency, salted with the scents of kerosene and grease. The effect said dirty money if anyone considered it. No one did. The Kid lounged on a three-leg stool. Cage stood at the press, wiping his hands on an ink-stained apron.

"What the hell is all the fuss?"

Wilson caught his breath. "I'll tell you what the fuss is. There's a Treasury agent in Lincoln, sent to investigate us counterfeitin'."

"Hmm." Cage scratched his chin. "A bit sooner than I'd expected."

"He'll be headed this way before you know it," Wilson said.

The Kid wrinkled his nose. "Sheriff Kimbrell won't do shit and Sheriff Carlyle up here has already showed he wouldn't know a counterfeit if he wiped his ass with it."

"Maybe so, but the government man's got a deputy US marshal with him and Kimbrell won't be sheriff much longer."

The Kid's eye drifted south. "Garrett won then."

"He did."

"Ol' Pat won't fool around. Cage, I think it might be best if we lay low for a spell. Me and the boys has been out there passin' the stuff. They'll know who they're lookin' for pretty quick."

"Suit yourself, Billy."

"We'll take our half of the gold." He turned to Wilson. "Go into White Oaks. Find Pickett and O'Folliard. We'll ride out to Whiskey Jim's and collect Dave."

"My horse is blown," Wilson said.

"Take a fresh one out of the corral." Moses Dedrick had stepped inside unnoticed.

Wilson headed off to the corral. Billy followed him out of the shed. Dedrick watched them go. He turned to Cage.

"You really gonna shut down?"

"Looks like it, for a time at least."

"You don't have to, you know."

"I print the stuff. I don't pass it."

"My brothers and I can pass it."

Cage smiled. "You can."

"Same deal?"

"Fifty-fifty."

"Keep printin'."

"Aren't you worried about the Treasury man?"

"Keep printing. We'll take our chances for a bit longer."

Twenty

White Oaks

The heavily armed posse rode into the tent-town mining camp. Ledger and Roth had the lead, the steel dust and black danced to a chill autumn wind. Wild and Garrett trailed along. Garrett's bay matched the mood of the lead horses. Wild's docile livery mare, chosen for the comfort of her ride, held up at a quiet steady pace.

The saloon tents stood near empty just past midday. The whores were beginning to stir, searching for a cup of coffee or something stronger and a bite to eat. Midway up the muddy ruts that passed for a central street Ledger picked out a hand-lettered sign — *Sheriff.* He wheeled the steel dust over to the tent flap and stepped down.

Sheriff Jim Carlyle replaced the coffeepot on the small stove in the center of the tent he made his office and sleeping quarters. He'd drifted into White Oaks, looking for a card game. His gambling ended when he stopped a dustup in the Sassy Nugget that was about to turn into gunplay. The next thing he knew, a delegation of saloon owners, a shopkeeper and blacksmith that passed for city fathers handed him a sheriff's star. It didn't pay much, but the work was steadier than a sometimes good run of cards. He blew steam off his coffee cup, sized up the four horsemen dismounting out front, and stepped out to meet them. The dark rough shave dressed in black stuck out his hand.

"Deputy Marshal, Ty Ledger."

"Jim Carlyle, Marshal."

"This here is Treasury Agent Azariah Wild." He pointed to the tweed coat and bowler. "Lincoln County Sheriff-elect Pat Garrett." The sober feller packed a .41 Thunderer and a twelve-inch Winchester he touched to the brim of his hat. "And my deputy, Johnny Roth."

"Pleased to meet you boys. Must be important business to call out a posse as highfalutin as this."

Wild reached in his coat pocket and handed over one of the bogus bills. "Seen any of these?"

He shook his head. "Not personally. If Treasury's interested, I take it they ain't all they appear to be."

"They're counterfeit all right. I suspect you've got some of them floating around town. We've reason to believe the gang printing them might be somewhere in the area."

"You don't say. Well the best way to find out is to talk with a couple of our saloon keepers and maybe an influential lady or two."

Two hours later they had a handful of bills and stories about scores of others passed on in the normal course of commerce. They had a like number of irate miners, saloon owners, shopkeepers and whores. The most recent cases involved the Dedrick brothers who ran a livery stable and ranch not far out of town. Ty and Roth's interest perked up at the first mention of the brothers. Counterfeiting made a suprising addition to suspicion of dealing in stolen cattle. Counterfeit brands were about all you'd expect from an outfit like that. They'd tracked one herd to the Dedrick ranch, but were put off by a Texas brand registration, claiming ownership of the cattle in question. Counterfeit currency struck Ty as a step up in criminal things. Carlyle agreed to accompany the posse out to the ranch.

An hour later Ledger called a halt on a low hill a half mile from the ranch. The wind picked up a chill, gusting away from the late afternoon sun sinking toward the horizon. Roth tugged his collar up. Ty snugged his hat.

"Don't look like much," Garrett said.

"These boys do a good business in cattle and horses," Carlyle said.

"They ain't always too particular about where the stock comes from," Roth said.

"Why do you say that, Johnny?" Garrett asked.

"We lost a small herd last year. Followed 'em here. Dedrick claimed he had a bill of sale from some Texas outfit. The bill of sale was signed by a William Antrim. I figured it wasn't worth the paper it was written on, but we couldn't prove nothin' either."

"Rustled stock and counterfeit currency don't exactly go hand in hand," Wild said.

"Same thought crossed my mind," Ty said. "Then easy money is easy money. How do you want to play this, Mr. Wild?"

"We know the brothers have passed some bills."

"Lots of folks have," Carlyle said.

"One or two maybe, but these boys had a hand in more than a few. What we don't know is if they're the ones doing the printing. That's the big fish. I say we ride on in and arrest them on suspicion. We can search the place and maybe squeeze more information out of them."

"All right, let's ride," Carlyle said.

Ty held up a hand. "Hold on a minute. It might be best to cover the back in case anybody tries to make a run for it. Give me and Johnny twenty minutes or so. We'll circle around back and keep an eye peeled."

Thirty minutes later Carlyle led Wild and Garrett through the Dedrick brothers' gate. Moses came out to the porch to greet them, wrapped in a buffalo coat that had taken hard wear since the buffalo gave it up.

"Afternoon, Sheriff. What can I do for you?"

"Afternoon, Moses," Carlyle said. "Dan and Sam around?"

"Down to the corral." He tossed his head toward the barn suddenly uneasy.

"I'll fetch 'em." Garrett shifted the double action on his hip and stepped down. He set off for the corral.

"Who's he?"

"Next Lincoln County sheriff, Pat Garrett."

"What do you want with me and my brothers?"

"Perhaps I should answer that. Sheriff

Carlyle, I suggest you go along with Sheriff Garrett while Mr. Dedrick here and I have a little chat."

"Who are you?"

"Azariah Wild, Treasury agent. Ever see one of these?" He held out a hand full of notes.

Moses blinked. Beads of perspiration popped out on his brow. "Hundreds? Cain't say we see many of them."

"Hmm, according to the reports we have, you and your brothers have seen quite a few."

"Maybe a couple, we buy and sell livestock you know."

"With counterfeit currency?"

"I don't know what you're talking about."

"Oh, I think you do, Mr. Dedrick. In fact I'm so convinced." He drew a pocket pistol from a shoulder holster concealed inside his coat. "You're under arrest."

Cage unlocked the press and inspected the impression, another good one. He added the sheet to the stack. He was about to place another sheet between the plates when he heard muffled voices coming from the direction of the barn. Something about the tone didn't sound like casual conversation. He cracked the door to the barn and peered into the gloom. The barn was empty. The voices came from the corral beyond.

He stepped inside and made his way down the dirt aisle between the stalls to the stable door. He pressed an eye to a chink in the rough wood. Two heavily armed men he didn't recognize were talking to Dan and Sam Dedrick. The tall one with the rifle jerked his head toward the house like it was an order. A metallic shield peeked out from behind his vest. Sam shook his head. Dan led the way. The two lawmen followed.

Cage ran back to the shed. He pulled off his apron and wiped his hands. He filled a flour sack with his stash of gold. He unlocked the plates from the printing press, wrapped them in rags and stuffed them into his saddlebags. No time for the press. The plates were what counted. He threw the saddlebags over his shoulder and hefted the sack full of gold into the stable. He saddled a sturdy gelding and tied the saddlebags and flour sack on the back. He led the horse through the shed. He paused at the outer door, opened it a crack and looked out. The lawmen must have the Dedrick brothers in the house. The yard was quiet. He led the horse around back of the shed, out of sight of the house and toed a stirrup.

"Hold it right there."

Cage froze.

"Ease on back down and step away from the horse. Keep your hands where we can see 'em."

"What's the meaning of this?"

"Let's see what's in that sack and those saddlebags first. My guess is this means you're under arrest. Have a look, Johnny."

Roth stepped past the counterfeiter. He patted a saddlebag, unbuckled the flap and drew out an ink-stained bundle. He pulled back the covering. "Well, look what we have here." He held up the printer's plate. "I don't know much about counterfeiting, but that sure looks like the back of a hundred-dollar bill."

"Then that would make this jasper Agent Wild's big fish." Ledger stepped in front of the printer and waved his gun at the house. "Bring the horse along, Johnny."

They crossed the yard to the house and clumped up the steps to the porch. They found Wild in the parlor with a talkative Dan Dedrick. The Treasury man looked up when Ledger and Roth came in with their prisoner.

"Looks like we got the big fish. We caught him slippin' out the back of the shed with a sack full of gold and hundred-dollar printing plates."

"Royal Cage."

"You know him?"

"Not exactly. We've been tryin' to land him for a good long time. Put him in the room over there with the other two. This one's kind of chatty."

"Shut up, Dan," Cage said.

"Piss off, Cage."

"Ty, you and Johnny help Carlyle keep an eye on the rest of the bunch. We were just getting to a part of the story Sheriff Garrett might want to hear."

Ty and Johnny moved Cage into the back room. Garrett stepped out to join Wild and the talkative Dedrick brother.

"What's so interesting?"

"Old Dan here says he and his brothers just pushed a few bills for Cage. Most of it was done by some others."

"That's right. Me and my brothers hardly did nothin'. It was mostly that Billy kid and his friends."

"Billy kid?" Garrett perked up. "He got a last name?"

"I'd say. Sold us some cattle goin' by the name Antrim. Cage calls him Bonney sometimes."

"Bonney?" Garrett connected Roth's rustlin' story. It hadn't meant anything at the time.

"That's right. All them boys ridin' with him call him Billy or the Kid."

Clean as the wind-driven snow. "Did them boys have names?"

Dedrick nodded. "One they called Tom. He was pretty tight with the Kid."

O'Folliard.

"One they called Dave, mean son of a bitch. Another Billy, Wilson I think he said and another Tom."

O'Folliard.

"Help any?" Wild asked.

Garrett nodded. "I know Billy Bonney, Doc Scurlock and Tom O'Folliard. I don't know them others, but it's a start. More'n I had when I rode out here."

"Good," Wild said.

"Where do we go from here?"

"We take these boys down to Fort Stanton to wait for the prison wagon to Santa Fe."

TWENTY-ONE

Whiskey Jim's
November 27, 1880

Last light gathered shadows in the golden glow at the day's end. The Kid sat at a table with O'Folliard, nursing whiskeys, while they watched Wilson and Pickett hoot and holler over a dice game in a dusty corner across the room. The rest of the saloon was deserted. Tables scattered around the large room stood idle, surrounded by the skeletons of empty chairs. Hiding out at Whiskey Jim's served a purpose what with that Treasury agent having arrested Cage and the Dedricks. They'd sure as hell gotten out just in time. His thoughts drifted to Fort Sumner and Paulita. He'd been away too long. He missed the comforts of the young Maxwell girl. She had a sweet scent about her. He could almost taste it. It got his britches all anxious. He tossed off his drink and poured another.

"Time we get out of here, Tom."

He cocked his head. "Where you figure we should go, Billy?"

"Fort Sumner's more like home."

O'Folliard smiled. "For some."

"We been here a spell. Hang around too long and word just naturally gets out."

"Won't never get out of Fort Sumner." He couldn't resist joshing his friend.

"We got friends there."

He smiled mischievously. "Some do."

"Aw, don't give me none of your sass."

Tom held up his hands in mock surrender. "I'm just sayin'. No offense intended."

"I know your intended. I'm just lookin' out for them as ain't smart enough to look out for theirself."

"Yo, Whiskey Jim's!"

The muffled shout from the yard silenced the game. Who'd bother to call out to a saloon when you could just as easily walk in? Somebody expectin' trouble that's who.

Greathouse set the glass he was polishing down on the bar, pulled his apron off and came around to the front door.

The Kid and Tom exchanged glances and followed Whiskey Jim's portly frame to the door.

"Who's there?" the innkeeper called. He didn't need a reply to recognize a dozen heavily armed men.

"Sheriff Carlyle, Jim. You've got some guests in there we've got business with."

"What guests?"

"Billy the Kid and his boys."

Billy stepped up behind Greathouse and put a gun to his head. "Best act like a hostage, Jim. It'll likely go easier that way."

"Much obliged," he said over his shoulder. "Glad you're here, Sheriff. They've been holdin' me hostage for days now."

Carlyle said something inaudible to his deputies. They spread out in the gathering shadows, surrounding the house. He turned back to Whiskey Jim. "Let me talk to the Kid."

"I'm here."

"How about letting me come in for a talk?"

"Alone and unarmed."

"Sure, as long as you let Jim go."

Billy thought. "Hostage exchange, what do you say Dave?"

Rudabaugh had roused himself from a whiskey haze to stand at the front window. He spat. "Jim's likely a better cook."

"Maybe so, but them posse men is less likely to do somethin' rash so long as we got the sheriff."

He grunted assent to the logic, nodded to

Pickett and tossed his head to the back room. "Tom, you and O'Folliard take the back." He motioned Wilson to the far side of the front window while he took the other.

Billy nodded. "All right, Sheriff, shuck your iron and com'on in."

Carlyle unbuckled his gun belt and handed his shotgun to a nearby deputy. He crossed the yard to the porch step, alone and unarmed. "You all right, Jim?"

"I'm fine."

"Let him go, Kid."

"He's free to go."

Jim lumbered out the door and waddled through the blue shadows as fast as his stubby legs would carry his bulk.

Carlyle stepped inside under cover of the Kid's gun. He waved to a nearby table.

"Have a seat, Sheriff."

Carlyle scowled at the gun. "Put that thing away, Billy. I'm unarmed."

"We're surrounded."

"That's the point. You are surrounded. You boys need to put down your guns and surrender. You ain't leavin' here alive any other way."

"We'll see about that. I figure if you don't lead us out of here, I'll be recitin' them same verses for you."

Carlyle shook his head. "Shoot me and

you've got no hostage, you're still sur-rounded and outnumbered. You're whipped, Kid. Face it."

"Tough talk, Sheriff. You sound like a man with no thought of dyin'." He thumbed the self-cocker's hammer to press the point.

A shot sounded somewhere in the yard. Billy turned to the door. Carlyle bolted from his chair overturning it with a clatter as he dove through the nearest front window. Early evening purple erupted in a ring of muzzle flashes, gun reports and powder plumes. Rudabaugh and the boys returned fire. Carlyle rolled across the front porch. His body jinked and jerked, peppered in lead hail. He crawled off the front porch and fell still in the yard.

Billy saw opportunity in Carlyle's death throes. "Hold your fire!"

The shooting fell silent, revealing the dead man's identity to the horrified posse. They'd killed their own, or so it seemed with no ac-counting for the bullets belonging to Ruda-baugh and Wilson. Time passed. The posse drifted back to the front of the guesthouse, leaderless and uncertain, they talked among themselves. After a time, Whiskey Jim came forward.

"They want to claim the body and be on their way."

The Kid grinned. "Truce," he said.

Fort Sumner
December 1, 1880
The Kid's back. The news stuck in Maxwell's craw as his boots crunched snow crust on the way home from Hargrove's. Cold moonlight made a ghostly cast of his breath. The young gun had been gone long enough he'd begun to hope they might be shut of him. Well he hadn't come nosin' around Paulita yet. Maybe there was still some hope.

He clumped up the porch step, stomped the snow from his boots and stepped into the warm glow inside. He closed the door and shrugged out of his heavy coat. He clenched his jaw at the sound a familiar laugh coming from the kitchen. *So much for hope.*

He hung his coat on a peg beside the door and paused. Now what? His objections to her seeing the Kid had done no good. In fact they brought out a defiant streak in the girl that likely made things worse. It might be best just to let nature take its course. She was young. He was wild. Neither one had the makings of a future together. He didn't like the idea, but he didn't know what more to do about it, short of playin' the Kid at his own game. He'd as soon kiss a rattler.

The floorboards creaked as he paced the dark passage back to the kitchen. He found Billy and Paulita having a cup of coffee. She tossed a charged glance his way, challenging him not to say anything. The Kid leaned back in his chair and smiled that crooked smile of his.

"Pete."

"Billy. I heard you was back in town. When did you get in?"

"Late this afternoon."

"We hadn't seen you in so long I was beginnin' to think you'd got lost."

"Heck no, Pete, I'm like that bad penny that turns up sooner or later."

Bad penny. "I expect so. You plan on stayin' long?"

He cut his gaze to Paulita. "Yeah."

She blushed.

Pete nodded. He stepped to the sideboard and picked up a tin plate and fork. He took a biscuit from a basket on the counter. He ladled fragrant fatback and beans from a pot bubbling on the stove. Supper in hand he headed back down the hall to his room.

"See you around, Billy."

"See ya', Pete." He tossed his head toward the hall passage. "He's mellowed some."

Paulita shrugged. Her eyes turned dreamy. "Maybe he knows."

"Knows what?"

She took his hand. "It's bigger than he is."

He twisted a grin. "How'd you know?"

Her eyes drifted beneath half lids. "Them buttons is under a frightful strain."

He followed her eyes. " 'Pears so."

"Here, have some more coffee. He'll be sawin' logs before you know it."

Twenty-Two

Lincoln
December 6, 1880

A dull gray blanket of snow-laden cloud billowed out of the northwest. The expectant scent of snow rode a cutting wind as Ledger and Roth jogged through town stirrup to stirrup. They wheeled over at the courthouse and dropped rein. They found Deputy Garrett in the sheriff's office. One advantage to a small office is that the potbelly stove actually kept it warm. They passed greetings around. Kimbrell was nowhere in sight.

"Where's Sheriff Kimbrell?" Ty asked.

Garrett shrugged. "Drunk I s'pose. He'll cash his last check the end of the month. He's been pretty much done since I swore in."

"Not surprising."

"He's been pretty much done since he swore in," Johnny said.

Garrett tilted his chin at the stove. "Coffee's hot if you've a mind to take off the chill."

"Sounds good," Ty said, fetching a cup. "Johnny?"

"Sure."

Ty poured two cups, steaming strong. He handed one to Roth. "We heard about Jim Carlyle. Damn shame. Seemed like a stand-up lawman."

Garrett shook his head. "He got a line on the Kid and his gang. Rode out after 'em with a big posse, mostly inexperienced. Got himself in a hostage situation. Somebody made a mistake. Jim made a break for it. His own men shot him in the commotion is the way the story comes out. No way to know who shot him for sure. For all their trouble they let the gang get away."

Ty shook his head. "They'll get theirs one of these days. That kind always does."

Garrett refilled his cup. "I hear the Kid is hidin' out at old Fort Sumner. I've been tryin' to figure a way to go after 'em. I got a couple of good men in John Poe and Kip McKinney, but I didn't figure three of us for enough to go after that bunch. I'm sure not gonna try it with green men. I'd try it if you two boys was to come along. How long you in town for?"

243

"We just come in for supplies," Roth said.
"Could you spare me a couple of days?"

Ty cocked an eye at Johnny.

"It'd be all right with John."

"I'd say. We could telegraph Roswell and let the women know we'll be a few days." Johnny nodded. "Looks like you got yourself a couple of deputies, Pat."

"Good. I'll let Poe and McKinney know. We'll pull out in the morning."

Light snow fell gently at first. Thick cloud cover held the temperature warm by winter standards. They made good progress the first day and again the second. The real trouble blew in the third day out. Heavy snow pushed out of the mountains driven by gusty winds. Drifting snow slowed their progress. By midday the horses blew gouts of steam and lathered at their labors. Garrett drew a halt, his voice muffled behind a snow covered bandanna.

"Maybe we should find a place to fort up and ride this one out."

"There ain't much shelter out here," Ty said.

Roth squinted into gray light and white whorls. "It's getting' hard to hold the trail."

"Fort Sumner can't be that much farther," Ty said. "I say we keep goin'. If we come

244

across a place that offers some shelter, fine, but Fort Sumner still may be the closest option."

"All right, let's see where this takes us." Garrett wheeled his big bay and took the lead. The others lined out behind, holding their horses nose to tail.

December 10, 1880
O'Folliard could hardly see beyond the next bend in the trail. He started out that morning thinking the worst of the storm had passed. Now he wasn't so sure. Sure they needed some idea of what the law was fixing to do about the shoot-out at Whiskey Jim's, but maybe that could wait until after this storm cleared. No law dog in his right mind would come looking for them in this weather. He about had himself convinced to turn back when the dark shape of a rider resolved out of the snow up the trail. It looked like he wasn't the only damn fool out on a day like this. Then he saw the second rider and a third. His gut turned icy and not from the snow. He didn't like the look of this one bit. He slipped his rifle from the saddle boot. Heads down against the wind-driven snow, they hadn't seen him yet. He jacked a round into the chamber.

"That's far enough! State your business."

The rifle cock snapped Garrett's head up. The challenge came down the trail ahead, maybe off to the left some but no telling for sure in near blinding conditions.

"Sheriff Pat Garrett out of Lincoln. We're on our way to Fort Sumner." He waited. No answer came, only the sound of a horse hightailing it in the opposite direction. Only one thing made a man run from a posse.

"Com'on, boys!" He put his heels to the bay and plunged up the trail.

They made a ghostly sight. Dark shadows, billowing dusters, horses lunging up the trail, foundering in clouds of snow. The rider ahead must have had a fresh mount. The sound of his horse faded into the wind as he pulled away. Garrett clenched his jaw. They'd never catch him. No sense killing the horses in a failed pursuit. He checked his mount down to a lope, a trot and a walk, allowing those behind him to match his pace. All totaled he made it a draw. It looked like his information about the gang's where-abouts was right. Unfortunately the gang would soon know they were coming. Then again, whoever the rider was, he'd cut a trail, following his own, straight back where he'd come.

Whatever O'Folliard's horse had left when he met the posse was long past spent by the time he pounded up to the old Indian hospital, slid the horse to a stop in a cloud of snow and jumped down. The horse dropped his head in a great billow of steam. Snow melted on the animal's steaming sweat-soaked hide. The animal had likely given his life for his master's hard ride.

Tom leaped up the plank porch to the dark rooms where the gang slept. He scratched a match, found a lamp and lit the wick. Rudabaugh and the others grumbled awake.

"What the hell's goin' on? It's the middle of the damn night."

"Shut up, Dave. Where's Billy."

"Don't shush me you pissant pup. I shut you up it'll be lead poison."

"There ain't no time. Where's Billy?"

"Where do you think?"

"Maxwell's."

"Well if you know'd the answer why'd you come bustin' in here wakin' us up in the middle of the night you dumb son of a bitch."

"Garrett's comin' with a posse. Get the horses saddled, one for Billy and a fresh one for me. You'll find mine out front if he ain't dead. Bring 'em over to Maxwell's. I'll go roust Billy."

"Where the hell we going in the middle of a damn snowstorm?" Pickett asked.

"Stinking Springs? I don't know. Any-where but here, now get a move on. They can't be far behind." Tom scrambled out the door and ran down the road toward the Maxwell place. He squinted against the swirling snow, slipping and sliding in the slush filled muddy ruts.

Maxwell awoke to darkness. A pounding at the front door beat back the curtain of sleep. A muffled voice added to the disturbance, kicking in his irritation.

"Billy, Billy, it's me, Tom!"

The Kid pulled a pillow over his head and nuzzled against Paulita's firm round warmth.

She sat up. "Billy, what's that?"

"It'll go away."

"It's Tom. He'll wake Pete."

He sat up. "I'll kill him first." He climbed out of bed and fumbled in the dark for his gun.

"You're naked."

"Shit!" He rummaged some more. "Where are them long handles?"

Billy, Tom, the noise resolved in Pete's

sleep-fuzzed brain. O'Folliard was lookin' for the Kid in the middle of the night, in the middle of a storm, at his house. The son of a bitch was probably with Paulita again. How the hell was he supposed to ignore this? As long as everybody thought nobody knew he could sleep through the disgrace. Now what was he supposed to do? He pulled on his britches and stumbled into the hall.

"Comin'," Pete said.

"No time for that," the voice said.

Pete opened the door to a shadowy figure and a gust of snow.

"Where's Billy?"

"What makes you think he's here?"

"Com'on, Pete, I ain't got time to waste."

"I'm here." Billy padded out of the dark hall into the gray snow light coming in the open door. He made a sight dressed in his union suit, holding a gun.

Pete scowled. "Close the damn door before you let all the heat out." He stomped back to his bed, stripped of decent pretense.

"What the hell's all the fuss about, Tom?"

"Garrett's comin' with a posse."

"How do you know?"

"I kind of ran into 'em on the trail. Now get dressed. Dave'll be here with your horse directly."

He padded back down the hall. Paulita sat in the bed, a dark-skinned shadow wrapped in a white sheet. Snow-reflected light lit the wide black pools filled with question.

"What is it?"

"Tom. Garrett's comin'. We got to get out of here." He pulled on his britches and bent to his boots.

She pulled a pout. "When will you be back?"

He sat on the edge of the bed and lifted her chin, her lips silhouetted moist against the light from the frosted window. He kissed her sweetly. "Soon, girl, soon as I can."

The door slammed, cutting off the icy blast. Pete fumed his breath a light fog in the drafty old barracks. He padded down the hall to Paulita's room and knocked on the door.

"What?"

"It's Pete."

"What do you want?"

He cracked the door open. She sat on the bed still wrapped in the sheet. Tears streaked her cheeks in the reflected window light.

"What do I want? That's not the question, Paulita. The question is what do you want? Is this it? He's an outlaw. He runs from the law in the middle of the night. Is that the

250

life you want?"

"I love him."

"Love? You're no more than a child, girl. Don't you see what you are doing to your life?"

"It's my life, Pete. I'll thank you to leave me to it."

He clenched his jaw in frustration. "Don't say I didn't warn you." The door clicked shut. *She won't do for herself. I reckon I'll have to do for her.*

Three hours later Garrett and his posse rode into the old fort. They put their horses up at the old stables and found shelter across the road at the old Indian hospital. The storm cleared out at sunrise, leaving a fresh white blanket and no trace of a trail. Garrett led the way next door to Hargrove's for breakfast. They ordered bacon, eggs, biscuits and a pot of coffee.

Garrett lifted his cup. "Sorry for chasin' you boys all the way up here in the middle of winter for nothin'."

Ty shrugged. "We got close. Sooner or later we'll get 'em. That's why they elected you, Pat. Hell, you ain't even officially taken office yet."

"Maybe so, but I got one job to do and that's stop the rustlin'. That means stoppin'

Billy the Kid. I won't rest until I get that done."

"You'll get him. Me and Johnny will be more than happy to help when you need it. Sooner or later the Kid'll make a mistake. They all do. When that happens, you'll get him."

"I expect you're right. I maybe got ahead of myself when I heard he was here. He likes it in these parts for some reason. I know that from my bar keepin' days. If a man could figure out why, the Kid might become predictable. If that happens, we'll get him sure."

Ty glanced at Roth. The marshal and the bounty hunter nodded.

Twenty-Three

Fort Sumner
December 14, 1880

The Kid drummed his fingers on the scarred tabletop lost in thought. He'd taken his usual table in Hargrove's near the stove. It wasn't the heat so much as the smell of wood smoke. It covered the less agreeable odors Dirty Dave gave off across the table. Experience had taught him you couldn't wholly cover the man's aroma with tobacco smoke and coal oil. He couldn't shake the feeling of being trapped. The longer they stayed around the more likely the law would catch up with them. Still he couldn't abide the thought of leaving Paulita. That left one undeniable problem.

O'Folliard nudged his reverie back to the table. "What's on your mind, Billy?"

"He's countin' the minutes until he can sneak back into that Maxwell girl's bed," Rudabaugh said.

Billy blinked. "I'm thinkin' about money."

"Good," Dave said. "We could use some. What're you thinkin'?"

Tom and young Barlow leaned in to listen. Only Charlie Bowdre seemed disinterested.

"Horses."

"Where we gonna get 'em?" Barlow asked with hero worship in his eyes.

The Kid raised a brow at the hanger-on. "We're gonna slip across the border into the panhandle and run a remuda up to Gerhart's Ranch. 'We' don't include you." He shrugged to the rest. "Shouldn't be too troublesome even this time of year."

Bowdre eased back. "You may not want to throw the boy out too quick, Billy, on account a you're gonna have to leave me out of it."

"What are you talkin' like that for Charlie? Manuela givin' you a hard time again?"

They all had a chuckle at Bowdre's marital predicament.

"Well, she's got a point. Sooner or later outlawin's gonna get a man shot or hung."

Billy flashed his crooked grin. "Hell, you can't go straight before spring. Ain't no ranch work this time of year. One more job and you'll have enough money to see you through to spring. You can turn honest then if you want."

"I'll go," Barlow said.

"I said no. What'll it be, Charlie?"

"Just this once, then I quit."

"Set up the drinks, Tom."

Lincoln
December 16, 1880

Pete Maxwell drew rein at the courthouse. He cast a long afternoon shadow across the frozen muddy ruts. Stepping down from his sturdy piebald mare, he looped a rein over the iron fence, and then crunched through the snow to the courthouse steps. He stamped his boots clean on the porch and went in. He found Garrett in his office, feeding wood to the corner stove.

Garrett glanced over his shoulder and closed the grate. "Pete, what can I do for you?"

"More like what I can do for you, Sheriff. The Kid's back."

"He must like the scenery in Fort Sumner."

Pete set his jaw, knotting the muscles beneath his rough shave. "Something like that. They're stayin' in the old Indian hospital. They rode out a couple of days ago. Something about horses Bob Hargrove told me. They'll be back, though."

"How can you be so sure?"

Pete swallowed his humiliation. "The Kid's been seein' Paulita."

"How's that sit?"

"Not good. I don't like it one bit. That's why I'm here. You get him, you solve your problem and mine."

"Then I guess we should be there waitin' when they come back."

"That's the way I figure it."

Fort Sumner
December 19, 1880

Snowstorms come in waves sometimes. This one howled out of the mountains from the northwest. Gauzy veils of blowing snow sculpted a barren seascape of drifts. Garrett waited in the old Indian hospital with deputies John Poe and Kip McKinney. One lamp burned low at the back of the rooms so as not to give their presence away. McKinney crouched beside one front window, an awkward posture for a man of his gangly frame. He peered into the storm on lookout for movement. Reflected snow light cast a mask of lean features cut off in shadow beneath a drooping mustache.

Poe dozed with his back propped against the wall near the door. Big and strong, he was an excellent shot with the Henry rifle resting on his outstretched legs. The some-

256

time cattle grower's agent was a quiet thoughtful man with the reputation for a competent lawman. An intelligent enterprising man, he staked his way West as a young man hunting buffalo. When the buffalo trade played out, he parlayed his size and gun hand into tracking rustlers. He and Garrett first met over rustling problems that spilled across the New Mexico border from Texas. He was just the sort of deputy Garrett needed to take down the Kid's gang. He wore his dark hair and mustache neatly trimmed along with a dark suit. The effect marked him a man destined for greater things.

Garrett was a little uneasy. They'd be outnumbered if the gang returned now. He'd wired Ty before they left Lincoln. He hoped Ledger and Roth would be here by now. The storm likely had a hand in slowing them down. For now he'd have to count on surprise along with experienced hands in Poe and McKinney.

Darkness came early this time of year. The storm hastened its arrival. They hadn't ordered any supper. The fewer people who knew they were here the better. They gnawed a little jerky and hardtack, though it did little to quell the rumblings of hunger. As the evening hours wore on, Garrett began to doubt the outlaws would return this night. Even a rascal as reckless as the Kid knew enough to respect a New Mexico winter storm. He tipped his hat over his eyes. "Wake me in a couple of hours, Kip, and I'll take the watch."

"Someone's comin'!"

Garrett snapped awake. He'd been asleep long enough to lose track of time. He shook the fog from his head. "My watch already, Kip?"

"Someone's comin'," he hissed.

Garrett scrambled to the window behind McKinney. Poe was already at the other. He jacked a round into the Henry's chamber. Dark shadows resolved out of the snow into riders and horses. Three, make it five, no six, headed for the old hospital.

"Is it them?" Poe whispered.

"Could be," Garrett said. "I figured 'em for five. Somebody else is ridin' with 'em."

The howling wind nearly drowned out Manuela Bowdre's warning scream from the hospital rooms to the east.

"Damn! Give 'em hell, boys." Garrett knocked his gun through a front window and cracked a shot into the swirling snow.

Poe threw the front door open to the storm. He drew aim in a practiced motion

258

and fired. The big rifle spit flash and smoke. The heavy slug knocked the lead rider on the right off his horse and into the snow. Poe ducked back from the door as the gang returned fire. Muzzle flashes blossomed in the darkness, lighting plumes of swirling snow. Hot lead shattered glass and chewed at the windows and door frame.

McKinney jammed a 10-gauge shotgun through his window. Both barrels exploded like cannon in the night. A horse on the left squealed, twisting too late from the lead storm. Its rider crashed into a drift in a shower of snow.

"Com'on, boys," someone shouted in the wind.

Garrett ducked behind the wall as the four mounted outlaws blazed away at their hideout.

Rudabaugh picked himself out of the snow-drift where he'd fallen from his wounded horse and ran as best he could under covering fire. O'Folliard struggled to his feet. Red stain imprinted the snow marking his fall. He staggered instinctively toward the hospital his eyes glazed. He nearly reached the shelter of the porch.

"I'm killt, Sheriff." His voice cracked. "Adios." He coughed blood and pitched face-first into the snow.

Rudabaugh caught O'Folliard's horse. He swung into the saddle and spurred into the storm hightailing out of town after the Kid and the rest of the gang.

Stinking Springs
December 20, 1880

Frosty gray morning light seeped into the one-room rock house. They'd managed to find the cabin in the storm more by luck than dead reckoning. Men sprawled across the dirt floor wrapped in their blankets. Dirty Dave snored like an oncoming train along the far wall. Billy sat with his back to the wall near a small stove, giving out the last of its heat. The stove needed tending. That meant leaving his blanket for the wood stack they'd found in the cabin.

Not much given to thinking too long on things, the Kid's mind worked in fits. Tom's death had given him a fit. Old Tom was his closest friend. He had been for some time. Oh he'd had other friends among the Regulators, especially the Ironclads, but they'd mostly gone off after the war. He picked Bowdre's sleeping form out of the shadowy bundles. Charlie was the only one left and he wanted out. He'd said so plain enough. This was his last job. That left Tom. Tom stuck, or would have if they hadn't killed him.

How the hell did this happen? The war explained some of it. They'd all vowed to do right by Mr. Tunstall and the McSweens. When the fighting ended everybody got a pardon, everybody except Billy Bonney. Rustling was no more than a way to make a living. He didn't mean anything by it, other than taking what Chisum owed him. Counterfeiting paid some bills too, but he wouldn't have done any of it if he'd gotten a pardon like everybody else. And now Tom was dead.

Who killed him? Who was laying for them in the old Indian hospital? Chisum men? No. It was Garrett. Chisum's handpicked sheriff got the job of putting him and his boys out of business. Old Pat was no fool. Having him on their trail would only lead to trouble. Garrett had a job to do and he'd dog it until he got it done or got done in the trying. Billy had killed one sheriff already back in the war. Sheriff Brady was a Dolan man. That was different. Pat had been a friend up until Chisum got to him. It struck him funny in a way. They'd probably have left him alone over the Brady killing if it hadn't been for the rustling. Horses and cattle counted more than a man gunned down in the midst of a war. Wind whined through the rafters with a low moan. Nope, with Garrett on his trail it might be time to get shut of Lincoln County, soon as the weather got better.

Then there was Paulita. What about her? Lord a'mighty he loved her. She'd come with him sure if he asked her. He'd quit the outlaw trail before he came to no good like poor Tom. He'd find a way to make her a proper wife, like Charlie and Manuela meant to do. Yup that's it. It's time to quit, time to grow up some, soon as the weather gets better.

Twenty-Four

Fort Sumner
December 20, 1880

The storm blew out leaving a white blanket of fresh snow under a cold blue sky. Ledger and Roth made Fort Sumner at midday. They found Garrett and his posse at the old Indian hospital. The boarded-up windows and bullet-pocked front wall told them they might be late to the festivities. Garrett stepped out on the porch at the sound of their horses.

Ty swung down from the steel dust. "What the hell happened here?"

"We had us a little lead swap with the Kid and his gang." The words formed white wisps of steam. "Com'on in and take the chill off."

Ty and Johnny stomped up the step and into the dimly lit room. Oily lamp smoke scented the air, a concession to the boarded windows.

"Coffee's on." Garrett lifted his chin to the stove.

They exchanged nods with Poe and McKinney. Roth headed for the stove to warm his hands and pour two steaming cups.

"Did you get 'em?" Ty asked.

"John got O'Folliard. The rest got away."

"Billy and Tom been together since the war. Who's all ridin' with him these days?"

Garrett shrugged. "Not sure. There's five of 'em not countin' O'Folliard. I heard he partnered up with Dirty Dave Rudabaugh, but no way to know for sure."

"Rudabaugh, now there's one mean-ass son of a bitch," Roth said.

"You know him?"

"Just his paper trail from my bounty huntin' days."

"Where do you suppose they went?" Ty asked.

"Not far in that storm. Rumor is they're hid out at Stinking Springs. That sounds about right. It was plenty bad that night. I been waitin' for you boys to ride out there and have a look-see. If they're there, maybe we can take 'em. If they've moved on, there'll be tracks. Get a hot meal and freshen your supplies. We'll head up there as soon as you're ready to ride."

Dusk doesn't last long in winter. All they had was gray light when Garrett drew a halt.

"Look there." He pointed through the tops of the trees. A thin column of smoke rose against the pale evening sky. The faint smell of mesquite colored the still air. "The old rock house is up yonder. Looks like the ghosts got company."

"How do you want to play it?" Ty asked.

He cut his eyes to the others. "You boys settle back here for a spell with the horses. Com'on Ty, let's you and me go in on foot and have us a look."

They stepped down. Garrett drew his Winchester from the saddle boot. Ty took his lead. "We'll be back directly, boys. You hear any trouble, come fast. Hear?" He took nods all around and crunched up the trail, climbing a slow rise. A half mile further on the rise crested. Garrett led the way off the trail into the tree line. The low ridge overlooked a shallow valley. The dark smudge of a small stone house with sod roof squatted beside a frozen creek bed. Starlight reflected off an undisturbed blanket of snow. Smoke from the stovepipe drifted toward them. Yellow light spilled from small frosty windows, pooling in patches on top of the snow.

"Looks right peaceful don't it?"

Ty nodded. "You s'pose it's them?"

"Sure could be."

"You plan on takin' 'em tonight?"

Garrett watched the smoke rise with a head shake. "We'd likely have us a night shoot. Then if we got 'em, we'd have to guard 'em until morning. They ain't goin' nowhere in the dark unless we give 'em a reason to run. We'll just keep an eye on 'em for the night. We can surround the place at dawn, maybe take somebody's nature call for a way to tilt the odds in our favor and take it from there. You take the first watch, Ty."

"It's gonna be damn cold waitin' out here tonight."

"Yeah, but the wind's right and they got a fire so we can have one too. We'll get up some supper and I'll send someone to relieve you."

Garrett gathered his men at the top of the ridge in the gray light before dawn. He studied the scene below. The rock house showed little more than a black block on a stark white field of snow. A shallow arroyo climbed up close to the front of the cabin. Tree lines circled north, west and east of the cabin. He turned to his deputies, his

266

breath a thin vapor.

"Here's how we play it, boys. Ty, you and me will take that arroyo below the cabin. Johnny, you swing west through the tree line. John, you and Kip take the east. Make sure one of you is far enough north to cover the back of the cabin. They'll start stirrin' around daybreak. The Kid's the one we want. Bring him down and the rest will likely fold up and quit. He wears a sombrero. Be on the lookout for it. Once we get the odds narrowed some we'll try to talk 'em into surrenderin'." He looked from one man to the next. "Any questions?" They held silent. "Then let's go."

Bowdre's eyes fluttered. Nature's call intruded uncomfortably on his sleep. The pale lit window told him dawn had come. The frosted pane reminded him it was cold. The potbelly stove had given off the last of its heat. It probably held no more than hot embers. His breath drifted into the darkness in streamers. He needed to piss. Damn. The thought of going out in the cold reminded him he was a long way from the comforts of Manuela's bed. He'd agreed to one last job and what had it gotten him? Ambushed by a posse on the steps of his home, forced to run through a blizzard only to wind up stuck in a one-room cabin with the likes of Dirty Dave Rudabaugh. Time to go home, he decided.

He threw back his blanket, pulled on his boots and got to his feet. He stepped over Tom Pickett to get to the wood box. Rusty hinges complained as he opened the stove gate. He stirred the embers with a stout stick and added several others to the flame. He closed the gate and held his hands to the promise of heat.

Billy lifted his head from the rolled coat he used as a pillow. "You're up kind a early."

"Gotta pee."

"Thanks for stirrin' the fire."

He started for the door and paused. "I'm goin' home today, Billy."

"You figure it's safe?"

"Nobody knows I was with you boys. I done my part. I done what I said I'd do. I'm finished now."

"You done your part, Charlie. Good luck."

The door creaked. A blast of cold gray light blew in. Bowdre closed the door and crunched through the snow toward the tree line they'd marked out for a privy.

"Hold it there and lift your hands easy."

Bowdre froze. The order sounded behind him.

"You're surrounded, Charlie. Give it up."

The Kid heard someone outside say something he couldn't make out. He snapped back his blanket and grabbed his cartridge belt and holster. He pulled the Thunderer and thumbed the hammer to a loaded chamber.

"Boys! Sounds like we got company." All around him the others awoke and pulled guns. Billy got to a window and scraped at the frost. Bowdre stood in the yard, hands held in plain sight. He studied the trees and brush beyond the yard. Somebody was out there. How many? Where? Nothing but gray light and dark shadow returned to his gaze.

"Drop your gun!"

He heard it clearly this time.

Rudabaugh jerked the door open and fired at the sound. Muzzle flashes popped around the clearing. He slammed the door as a hale of bullets chewed wood, shattered glass, chipped stone and whined away.

Billy pressed an eye to the corner of his window. Charlie stood unsteadily, bright blossoms of blood spread across his back from exit wounds. He sank to his knees, fighting to steady himself. He got back to his feet and turned to the cabin. He staggered toward the door, one unsteady step after another, his face a twisted mask of pain.

"Open the door for him, damn it!" Billy hissed.

The door creaked. Charlie slumped to his knees. He turned glazed eyes to Billy. "I was goin' home." He choked. "I, I almost made it."

Billy crouched beside him. He put an arm around his shoulders. "You'll make it, Charlie. I swear you'll make it."

"Manuela ain't never gonna forgive me."

"She will. Sure she will." Something wet caught in his eye.

"Billy, it's Pat Garrett. You're surrounded. Throw down your guns and come out with your hands high."

"Go to hell, Garrett!" Rudabaugh fired through a crack in the door. Another salvo raked the cabin.

"Get that son of a bitch under control, Kid."

"Hold your fire, Dave." He turned to the open door.

Bowdre coughed blood. "I gotta go, Billy. Gotta get back." He winced, racked in pain, his voice a gritty rasp. "Gotta get back to Manuela."

"Charlie's hit bad, Pat. He's comin' out." He helped his old friend struggle to his feet. It seemed like the icy blast outside revived him. He planted one boot in front of the

270

other, two steps, three steps, four. His knees buckled. He pitched face forward into the snow.

"Charlie! Damn it, get up, Charlie!"

The bloodstains didn't move. Ice cold fingers clamped the Kid's chest. He strained to breathe. *He almost made it.*

"Listen to reason, Billy. We done enough killin' today. You got no chance. Give it up. No point in dyin' here. Seems like an easy enough choice."

"Not that easy, Pat. You're talkin' a bullet or a rope."

"It'll get damn cold and hungry in there."

"You boys might get cold and hungry too."

The standoff fell silent. Minutes passed, then an hour.

Roth crawled into the bottom of the arroyo. "Sheriff, I ain't plannin' to spend Christmas out here. I had me a situation like this back when I was huntin' bounty. I put it over pretty quick. There ain't no back way out of that cabin."

"So?"

"Just keep a watch on the door." Roth disappeared into the trees. He circled back east around to the back of the cabin. One small window overlooked a corral where the gang's horses were penned. He counted five.

With Bowdre down that left four. The eaves at the back of the sod roof rose only a few feet above the corral top rail. Perfect. He cut across to the corner of the building, offering the single window the shortest sight line and shooting angle to his approach. He rushed the back of the cabin unnoticed except for the nervous whicker his presence caused a couple of the horses. They began to prance and circle as he climbed the corral fence to the roof.

"Somethin's riled the horses," Billy Wilson said.

"See what it is." The Kid never let his eyes off the mouth of the arroyo where he'd seen muzzle flashes.

Wilson scrabbled across the dirt floor to the back window.

"See anything?"

"No, but they're stirred up all right, all bunched up at this end of the corral."

Thump. The back corner rafters shook loose a spray of dirt.

The Kid whirled around. "Somebody's on the roof."

"What the hell!" Rudabaugh jacked a round into his rifle and fired into the ceiling.

The charge in the small cabin was deafening. The powder burn only added to what the Kid suddenly knew was coming.

"Roth's on the roof." Garrett pointed.

"He sure is," Ty said.

A shot sounded inside the cabin. A geyser of dirt sprouted in the air behind Roth. He shucked his heavy coat, dropped it over the stovepipe and jumped off the roof into a snowdrift as two more shots exploded behind his boot heels.

"It won't be long now," Ty said.

Garrett nodded. "Get ready boys! They'll come out soon enough. They may be shootin'."

Smoke poured out of the stove grate, adding to the trapped powder smoke. It filled the small cabin with blinding, choking clouds. Visions of the burning McSween house flared in Billy's mind. A familiar trapped feeling closed his throat along with the smoke.

"Pickett, throw some water on that fire." Rudabaugh coughed.

The Kid's eyes burned. Tears stained his cheeks, hiding those Charlie started. "That'll only make it worse." He gasped.

"Then bust out." Rudabaugh's order went unfinished in a choking fit.

The Kid stumbled to the door. "I ain't chokin' to death in here. You boys is welcome to stay if that's your pleasure." He threw open the door. "I'm comin' out, Pat!" He threw his Thunderer into the snow and stepped out with his hands in the air. One by one, Dirty Dave and his boys came along.

TWENTY-FIVE

Fort Sumner

The prisoners made a sullen lot, hands shackled behind their backs, their horses strung out in file on a lead behind Poe. Garrett led them into town with Roth and Ledger flanking the prisoners. McKinney trailed behind in a wagon borrowed from a nearby ranch that bore Bowdre's body. His shotgun rested easily at his side, a ready presence in case of trouble.

Word spread through town. People had begun to gather by the time they drew up at the old Indian hospital. Manuela Bowdre recognized Charlie's horse tied to the back of the wagon before Garrett had a chance to dismount with the news. She ran to the back of the wagon, threw back the blanket covering the ashen features that had been her husband and wailed in keening sobs. Mexican women tried in vain to comfort her. She fought them. Her tear-streaked

275

eyes fell on the Kid.

"You! You did this. You killed my Charlie. I tried to tell him. He said he would quit. But no, you had to kill him." She broke down sobbing uncontrollably until the women were able to coax her back to her rooms.

Pete Maxwell arrived moments later. He fixed Billy with a knowing gaze. This would break Paulita's heart as he'd feared all along. *So be it.* He'd done the right thing. He had no other choice.

"Pete," Garrett said. "We're gonna need a wagon to haul these boys up to Las Vegas. This one's got to go back to the rancher who loaned it to us. Can you get us a team? The county will pay you rental expense."

"I'll see to it, Sheriff. When do you want it?"

"We'll leave in the morning."

Maxwell hurried off.

Garrett turned to Poe and McKinney. "Get 'em down, boys. We'll hold 'em inside tonight." He extended a hand to Ledger. "Much obliged for your help, Ty. You too, Johnny. We'll take it from here."

"You sure, Pat?" Ty said.

He nodded. "One of them birds so much as wiggles Ole' Kip'll give 'em a double helping of ten-gauge lead poison." He said

276

it loud enough for the prisoners to hear. "No you boys go along. With a little luck and good weather, you should make it home for Christmas. We'll run these boys up to Santa Fe. According to the circulars I got, most of 'em have federal warrants outstanding. That's the shortest trip to a fair trial. I'm guessin' they got hemp ties that come in all the right sizes. You boys can pass word of the Kid's capture to Mr. Chisum with my compliments. I'm sure he'll be pleased to let the Cattle Growers Association know they got their election result."

"No doubt about it." Ty tipped his hat and toed a stirrup. He swung up to his saddle as Roth mounted the black. "You know where to find us if you need anything, Pat."

"I do." He nodded. "Merry Christmas to the missus and Mr. Chisum."

Pete clumped up the steps, stamped snow off his boots and let himself inside. He strolled down the hall toward the kitchen. He heard soft sobs as he passed Paulita's room. He paused and rapped on the door.

"Yes." The voice sounded small.

"I s'pose you heard."

"I heard." She sobbed.

"You OK?"

"No. I s'pose you're happy."

"Paulita I only ever wanted what's best for you. I didn't want you to bear sorrow like this, but it had to come. Don't you see? He's an outlaw. Sooner or later the law catches up with them. Look at Manuela. They brought Charlie home in a wagon bed. Is that what you want? It may not seem like it now, but believe me it's for the best. Time heals. You will too."

They shackled them in pairs, Wilson chained to Pickett and Rudabaugh with the Kid. It was cold. The little stove purely didn't give up enough heat for the room. Rudabaugh fouled the air. None of it did anything to help Billy's mood. They'd brought in biscuits and beans for supper, but between Rudabaugh and brooding over the way things turned out he had no appetite. Manuela's grieving hit him hard. He should have expected that. Charlie wanted out. He should have let him go. He didn't. Instead he talked him into one last deal. A deal that killed old Charlie. Now here he sat, chained to Dirty Dave Rudabaugh. Likely on his way to a gallows and not much more than a stone's throw from Paulita. Sweet Paulita deserved better. He could almost taste her kiss. What he wouldn't give to say a proper good-bye. He wanted her to know. He was ready to give it up for her. He'd planned to. He'd just run out of time. Damn it. He had to try.

"Pat?"

"What is it, Billy?"

"Can we talk?"

"Sure. What's on your mind?"

"I mean in private."

Garrett glanced around the bare-lamp-lit room. "Private looks a might scarce. You'd best make good with what you got."

"I need to see Paulita."

"Paulita Maxwell?"

He nodded.

"You want me to send someone for her?"

"Pete won't never let her come. Take me over there."

He shook his head. "I don't know, Billy. We'd have to take Dave along."

"You mean you can't unhook us for an hour."

"That's right."

"Please, Pat. Alls I want to do is say a proper good-bye. Won't ya do it for old times' sake?"

"I don't want no part of goin' out in the cold," Rudabaugh said.

"Shut up, Dave," the Kid said.

"Don't you sass me, pup. I'll bash your head in with these here chains."

Garrett fired a warning glare. "Back off, Rudabaugh. You'll go if I say you will."

"So how 'bout it, Pat?"

Garrett rubbed his chin for a moment. "All right, Billy, on one condition."

"What's that?"

"You give me your word we'll have no trouble from you or your fragrant friend there on the way to Santa Fe."

"You got my word."

"How you figure the Kid here can give his word for me?"

Billy held up his shackles. "You ain't goin' nowhere without me."

Garrett smiled. "Same as you're goin' to Maxwell's with him. Kip, you and your ten-gauge keep an eye on Pickett and Wilson here while John and me take Billy and stinky here over to Maxwell's."

"You got quite a mouth on you, Garrett, when you got a man chained up."

Garrett wrinkled his nose at Rudabaugh. "The sooner we get you outside the better."

Garrett rapped on the door at the Maxwell house. Footsteps sounded inside. The door opened to Pete.

"Sheriff?" He looked puzzled. "I'll have the wagon for you in the morning."

"Thanks, Pete. That's not why we're here.

Billy asked to see your sister."

"Who is it, Pete?" Paulita emerged from the darkened hall behind her brother.

"It's Sheriff Garrett."

"And me, Paulita!"

"Billy!" She ran to the door and pushed past her brother. Garrett stood aside. "Where are your manners, Pete? Let them in." She led them into the lamp-lit room that served as a parlor, holding Billy's manacled hand. She examined the chains and looked into his eyes. She turned to Garrett and smiled sweetly.

"Might we have a few minutes by ourselves?"

"I'm afraid that won't be possible, ma'am."

She pulled a pout. Billy lifted his arms and encircled her in his cuffs. She rested her head on his chest.

"Aw, ain't that nice."

"Shut up, Rudabaugh," Garrett said. Poe rapped the outlaw in the back with the butt of his Henry.

Billy bent to her ear, gaining as much privacy as the situation allowed. "I was plannin' to quit, Paulita. I was hopin' you'd run off with me." She lifted her chin. Her eyes filled. A droplet spilled down one cheek. A second spilled down the other. He kissed them away. She kissed him. He held her.

"All right, Billy, time we get you back over to the hospital."

He let her go.

"Wait, Senor Sheriff!" The order echoed down the hall from the kitchen.

Garrett paused at the door. Deluvina padded down the hall clutching a warm blanket. She went to Billy.

"Here, my little boy, take this. It will keep you warm on your journey."

"Much obliged, Deluvina."

She stepped back beside Paulita and put her arm around the girl. They watched him go together.

Walking the prisoners back to the hospital Poe sidled up to Garrett. "You really think you can trust the Kid?"

Garrett's brow knit in question, an eye lit in moon reflected snow.

"About givin' us no trouble, I mean."

He lifted his chin to the Kid's back. "I can now."

TWENTY-SIX

Puerto de Luna
December 25, 1880

Dusk deepened past purple. Rumpled clouds opened a window to a halo around a cold moon. Warm light spilled from windows lining the frosted ruts up the central street. Light snow finished off a Christmas scene, somehow festive even as Garrett and his deputies drew their prisoners up at the town marshal's office. Garrett clumped up the boardwalk and drew his Colt self-cocker to oversee unloading the prisoners.

The office door opened to a thickset trunk of a man with a flushed round face and a bristling red mustache. "What do we have here?"

"Sherriff Pat Garrett out of Lincoln." He never took his eyes off his prisoners as Poe and McKinney helped the manacled men out of the wagon.

"Town Marshal Jethro Cumberland, Sheriff. What can I do for you?"

"We're takin' these boys up to Santa Fe. I was hopin' you might have a place we could lock 'em up for the night."

"Jail's kind a quiet on Christmas. I got room. Bring 'em along this way."

"Much obliged, Marshal."

McKinney and Poe herded the prisoners into the small office behind Cumberland. The office had a desk littered with wanted circulars, a gun rack beside the door and a small stove in the corner working hard against the cold. "Who might we have here?"

"The ugly one is Dave Rudabaugh. These two are a couple of his men and this one is William Bonney."

"Billy the Kid and Dirty Dave, that's a hell of a haul, Sheriff." He chuckled. "Wish I was sellin' rope up in Santa Fe."

The jail at the back of the office had two cells, both empty and both cold. Cumberland opened the first. The deputies ushered Pickett and Wilson in. The marshal locked the door and opened the second. "These boys been fed yet?"

"Not yet," Garrett said.

Poe prodded Rudabaugh and Billy into the cell.

"I'll order some supper for 'em then," Cumberland said.

Garrett waved Poe away from the Kid. "Not him, not yet."

Billy fixed Garrett with a piercing glare. "What, I don't get nothin' to eat on Christmas?"

"Not here. I'm takin' you out to supper."

Poe's jaw dropped. "You sure, Pat?"

Garrett nodded. "He ain't goin' nowhere, John. Unhook him from his partner there."

Billy cracked his crooked smile. "Why?"

"For old times' sake. Besides, I got your word. No trouble."

"Well I'll be . . ." Billy trailed off.

"Likely will," Poe said.

"John, you and Kip go on over to the hotel and get us rooms. Get some supper. I'll see you at the hotel later. Com'on, Billy."

He lifted his handcuffs. "What about these?"

"I'm in the Christmas spirit, Kid. I ain't lost my mind."

They found Katie's Kitchen a short walk up the street. A handful of candlelit tables stood covered in checked gingham cloth that matched the curtains. Katie must have had the green napkins out for Christmas. The proprietress raised a brow at the young man in handcuffs and the tall lawman. She showed them to a table near the window and explained the shepherd's pie special. Garrett ordered two whiskies and two orders of the special. They watched lacy snowflakes float lazily in the reflected window light until the drinks were served.

Billy lifted his glass, studying the amber glow. "Why, Pat?"

Garrett shrugged. "Like I said, for old times' sake." He took a swallow. "Look I'm sorry things ended up like this, Kid."

"No reason they needed to," he said and took a swallow. "All I ever wanted was a pardon like everyone else. You know that. Why me, Pat? Why am I the only one?"

"You killed a lawman. The law takes a hard liking to that kind of thing."

"Shit, Pat, I wasn't the only one behind that wall when Brady got shot. Who's to say it was even me who shot him?"

"Was it, Billy?"

"I'm feelin' honest, Pat. Like you said, I ain't lost my mind. I'm only askin', who's to say?"

"We'll never know. You didn't plead that case. You took to rustlin' and counterfeitin' and such."

"That was just makin' a livin' when there wasn't no other way. If I'd a got that pardon, I'd a rode out of Lincoln County and never been no trouble to nobody."

"Maybe so, Billy, but you didn't. It'll be hard to convince a jury of that now."

Billy tossed off the rest of his drink. Garrett signaled for two more. Bells jangled beyond the window. A sleigh passed, drawn by a flashy high-stepping long strider. The passengers bundled in heavy buffalo robes laughed clouds of steam at some silent joke.

"You know sometimes I think if I'd given up on the pardon and just lit out of the territory things might have turned out different."

Garrett thought some. "You might be right. I doubt I'd be sheriff if the Cattle Growers Association hadn't gotten all riled up. It was rustlin' that done that. Hell after the war, everybody was pretty much ready to let bygones be bygones."

Billy gazed out the window for a long moment. "Yeah, you takin' over the sheriff's office made a difference. You got Tom and Charlie. Charlie was gonna quit, you know."

"I didn't know that."

"I talked him into one last job. Now he's dead. I guess he won't be tellin' his grandkids them stories about ridin' with Billy the Kid after all." He shook his head. "I was fixin' to quit too. I told Paulita that. She might have run off with me if I'd a quit. Guess I sort a just run out of time."

"A lot of things would be different if we could undo the past."

Two steaming plates of shepherd's pie arrived. The Kid picked at his food. "So it comes down to you and me. Who would ever have guessed?"

"Not much left between us now. My work's done. The courts will finish things off." He thought some. "Like I said, I'm sorry things turned out the way they did, Billy. Maybe there's a better day out there somewhere."

"I hope so. I doubt it, but I hope so. Anyway, thanks for the supper and the talk. Merry Christmas, Pat." He tossed off his drink.

Las Vegas
December 27, 1880
Billy lay on his bunk staring into a cold gray ceiling. For all his wild ways he'd never spent much time in jail. There was the time Brady locked him up in Lincoln for stealing Mr. Tunstall's horses. Mr. Tunstall knew it wasn't true. Brady was just coverin' up for Dolan's boys. John Tunstall stood up for him. Not many ever did. He got him out, gave him a job and won his loyalty. That loyalty lived on long after Dolan's men gunned the man down. He remembered the

time Dolan had him locked up. Marshal Widenmann got him out that time, mostly because Deputy Ledger had been locked up with him. That was more of Dolan's dirty work. Governor Wallace had him held in protective custody while he waited to testify against Dolan. He should have done it. Maybe he'd have got his pardon. Then again, maybe not. He never could bring himself to trust Wallace. That was pretty much it for jail, though. Each time he had a way out. This time felt different. This time, out likely meant a trip to the gallows unless he could somehow manage an escape. Damn.

The office door rattled open beyond the cell block. Muffled voices announced the arrival of his keepers. The springs groaned in complaint as he sat on the bunk. Garrett came in followed by two men.

"That him?" the tall one with watery blue eyes and drooping mustache asked.

Garrett nodded. "Morning, Billy."

"Pat."

McKinney carried four bundles he passed through the bars. Each contained a new suit of clothes.

"Here put these on."

Billy held up his chains. "Not much dressing gonna happen until these come off."

"Uncuff 'em, Kip," Garrett said.

Once the chains were removed the prisoners set about changing clothes. The lawmen trooped out of the cell block. A mousy little fellow in a bowler hat and heavy tweed cloak came in. He wore thick spectacles, slipped off the bridge of a sparrow-like nose and felt gloves with the fingers cut off to allow for a pencil and notebook.

"Cyrus Wartz, *Las Vegas Gazzette.* I was hoping I might have a word with you gentlemen."

Rudabaugh shot the journalist a venomous glare. "Why don't you stuff your little pencil up your ass and go straight to hell."

"Com'on, Dave. That ain't no way to treat a visitor."

"And who might you be?"

"William Bonney."

"Billy the Kid, oh quite so. I must say I've heard a great deal about you."

He smiled. "Likely you ain't heard the half of it, Mr. Wartz."

"Then you won't mind answering a few questions for me."

"Do I have to listen to this shit?"

"Shut up, Dave."

"Your day's comin', pup. Don't say I didn't warn you."

"Yeah, right. What would you like to know,

Mr. Wartz?"

The journalist referred to his notes. "I understand you and your desperado associates are wanted for rustling, murder, counterfeiting and untold numbers of other such despicable acts."

"Pshaw, ain't nary a word of truth to it. I don't know about these boys, but I ain't part of no desperado gang. I'm just an honest gambler. I got caught up in all this on account of a snowstorm and John Chisum havin' a grudge over a debt he owes me. It's all a case of mistaken identity. It just goes to show, if you're a big enough man in this territory, you can have the law clean up your messes for you."

Wartz scratched at his pad. "So you're saying John Chisum is the cause of all your troubles?"

"Hell, yes. It'll all come out at the trial. I expect I'll be fully acquitted."

"My, my, that seems a most remarkable claim under the circumstances. What about the allegation of murder in regard to the death of Sheriff William Brady?"

"There was a dozen men behind the wall that day. Who's to say who shot Brady? Brady's the one who stepped in front of a duly swored posse servin' an arrest warrant. This'll all come out in the trial."

Wartz blinked behind his spectacles. He scratched his chin and shook his head. "Most extraordinary. So you claim you are not associated with these . . ." He groped for the proper word. "These other gentlemen."

"That's right, though I don't know as I'd call these owl hoots gentle anything. How could you possibly believe a man of my upstanding character would associate himself with the likes of these?"

"Shit." Rudabaugh farted noisily.

Wartz wrinkled his nose. "Yes, I see your point. Thank you for, ah, your time, Mr. Kid." He turned to the door.

Poe passed the hastily retreating reporter as he entered the cell block followed by McKinney. He opened the cell door. McKinney stepped in jangling manacles and leg irons.

"Is that really necessary?" Billy asked.

"Pat says so, Kid."

The deputy clamped a cuff on his wrist tight. Message sent. Message received. He cuffed the other wrist and chained his ankles.

"Get up."

Billy stood.

"All right, let's go."

Poe and McKinney herded the prisoners

into the outer office where Garrett waited. He led the way outside.

Out on the street, morning light brightened the chill. Garrett led the way along the boardwalk toward the depot. Billy shuffled along, dragging his chains beside Rudabaugh. Wilson and Pickett followed, trailed by Poe and McKinney.

A block from the depot Billy heard a low hum rising above the idling locomotive. When they turned the corner he saw a crowd gathered at the depot. A sour knot collected around the biscuit and coffee he had for breakfast. No sooner had they rounded the corner when somebody spotted them.

"Here they come," someone yelled.

The murmur rose, words lost in a garbled rumble. Garrett kept his pace, ramrod straight, eyes fixed ahead. He said nothing. The crowd filled the street and spilled up the station platform. They'd have to pass through it to get to the train. As they approached the station platform, angry voices became clear.

"That's them!"

"Murderin' rustlers!"

"Them sons of bitches don't need tryin'. They need hangin'."

"I got a rope." A burly man with a bushy

beard brandished a coil.

"Me too."

"Yeah!"

The crowd surged forward.

Garrett stopped. He reached for his gun. "Kip, get on up here," he said over his shoulder. McKinney clumped around the prisoners with his double-barreled 10-gauge. "Air that thing out to get their attention."

McKinney lifted the muzzle. The throaty roar of the heavy-gauge shotgun reverberated off the depot wall. The crowd melted back up the street. With one practiced motion, McKinney cracked the big shotgun open, extracted the spent shell, reloaded the chamber and snapped the gun closed.

Garrett didn't need any more opening. "Com'on." He set a brisk pace for the train, climbing the platform. He led the way to the first open passenger car and stood aside for his charges to board. "Kip, you stay with me."

"Much obliged, Pat," Billy said as he passed by.

"Just doin' my job, now get aboard." He nodded his unspoken order for Poe to follow the prisoners on board and keep an eye on them.

Garrett and McKinney faced down the

crowd. McKinney held the shotgun stock to his right hip, the muzzle pointing over the crowd's head, the threat enough to hold the angry mob at bay.

Poe stuffed his prisoners into passenger seats and sat down behind them. A nervous conductor hurried through the car. He stepped out onto the platform as the last of the freight was hastily loaded.

"All aboard!" He swung back into the coach.

The whistle shrieked. The engine chuffed. Couplings engaged with a clank, passing from one car to the next. Garrett swung into the car followed by McKinney, his scattergun still leveled at the crowd. The train slowly rolled away from the station, gathering speed.

Billy broke into his crooked grin. He waved to the howling crowd as the car passed the frustrated lynch mob.

TWENTY-SEVEN

Santa Fe
January 3, 1881
Cold light from a frost covered window barely lifted the shadows in the stark courtroom. The defendants sat on a wooden bench below the judge's massive desk. An American flag flanked the desk beside a portrait of President Hays. The jury box next to the window stood empty, occupied by a curtain of dust motes reserved for preliminary hearings. The prosecutor and a court appointed defense attorney made their obligatory appearance though they had little part in the proceedings.

Garrett sat behind the Kid, wearing his duster against the chill. The potbelly stove in the corner between the judge's desk and the jury box did little to warm the room. The Kid looked straight ahead, the gravity of his circumstance coming clear in the austere courtroom setting that in time would decide his fate.

The door to the judge's chambers opened with a bang. The bailiff stepped out. "All rise. District Court for the Fourth Circuit, New Mexico Territory, is now in session, the Honorable L. Bradford Prince presiding."

The black-robed jurist took his seat. His gavel cracked like a pistol shot. "The bailiff will read the charges."

"David Rudabaugh, William Wilson and Thomas Pickett also known as the Dodge City Gang, are charged with multiple counts of rustling, murder, trafficking in counterfeit currency and robbery."

"And how do the defendants plead?"

The defense attorney half left his seat. "Not guilty, Your Honor."

"Very well. Let the record show the defendants have entered a plea of not guilty. The defendants are hereby bound over for trial by this court. They shall be held in the Santa Fe jail without bail pending the outcome of their trials." Prince turned to the bailiff.

"William Bonney, also known as William Antrim and Billy the Kid, is charged with the murders of Andrew Buckshot Roberts and Sheriff William Brady. He is separately charged with multiple counts of rustling and trafficking in counterfeit currency."

"How does the defendant plead?"

The attorney serving as defense counsel half stood. "Not guilty, Your Honor."

"Let the record show the defendant has entered a plea of not guilty. The defendant will be transferred to Third District Court in La Mesilla to stand trial for the murders of Andrew Roberts and William Brady. He will be held in the Santa Fe jail until a trial date can be set."

The gavel cracked.

"All rise."

Billy struggled to his feet. His head felt light, his knees a little watery. Knowing what was coming and hearing it pronounced struck him as two different things.

January 10, 1881

Billy lay on his bunk, staring into ceiling shadows. It was daylight. You could tell. The stone walls and steel bars were gray during the day. At night the whole place went black. It was cold. That never changed. The gray hours got interrupted by metal trays of sometimes warm brown, green and white things. The pattern repeated itself at a maddeningly slow pace. Day by day hours whiled away, waiting. He was caught in the slow grinding wheels of justice that propelled him to some uncertain future. The cell block door clanked. Keys rattled.

"You got a visitor, Kid." The deputy raised a doubtful brow toward his shiny bald head. "He says he's your lawyer."

Billy sat up, squeaking the bunk springs. "That would be Mr. Leonard."

"Ira Leonard, Esquire, at your service." The scruffy barrister sniffed at the skeptical deputy and scratched the salt-and-pepper stubble on his chin. His rumpled suit and stained linen hadn't improved since he drafted the pardon letter for Billy back in White Oaks.

"William, I take it by these, ah circumstances, the pardon letter didn't work out for you."

"No, sir. Not so far."

"I'm sorry to hear that. It is one of the reasons we lawyers don't guarantee our work." He sniffed. "Deputy, get me a chair so I might confer with my client."

The jailer dragged a barrel backed chair into the cell block and set it beside Billy's cell.

"Now be a good fellow and excuse yourself."

"Crusty old bastard," the guard mumbled to no one in particular as he closed the office door.

"Crusty, indeed." Leonard took his seat. He set a pair of smudged spectacles on the bridge of his nose and fitted the wire bows behind his ears. He opened his case and withdrew a sheaf of papers. "Now, William, I understand the charges we face are those that were the subject of that letter I drafted for you last year." He consulted his notes. "You are charged with the murder of one Andrew Roberts more colorfully known as Buckshot and one Sheriff William Brady. Is that correct?"

"It is."

"I understand you entered a plea of not guilty at your preliminary hearing."

"I did. That's what the court lawyer told me to do."

"Sound advice absent a more considered view of the case." Leonard grimaced at a sudden gas pain and belched. "Shouldn't eat beans for lunch. The question is how do we go about proving that?"

"First off, I never shot Buckshot Roberts on account of he shot me first."

"Is there a witness who can corroborate that?"

"Co-robbery? Hell, I didn't steal nothin' that time."

"No, no, sorry. I mean a witness who will agree that's what happened."

"Sure, lots of 'em."

"Who should we call then?"

"Ain't none of 'em here 'cept me."

"Then I expect we'll have to put you on the stand."

"Well, I should hope so. Who else is gonna testify for me?"

"Now about Sheriff Brady. As I recall the circumstances surrounding that allegation are not quite so cut and dried. How is it that you assert your innocence in that case?"

"A bunch of us Regulators was behind the Torreon wall that day. We was duly swored deputy US marshals there to arrest Billy Mathews for the murder of John Tunstall. Brady drew his gun. That's when the shootin' started. Who's to say who actually killt him?"

"I see. Hmm." He fingered the stubble on his chin. "Are there any witnesses we can call to corrob . . . er, agree with your story? I mean witnesses we can call."

He thought. "Doc Scurlock, he's over in Texas somewheres."

"That narrows things down. Anyone else?"

He thought some more. "Tom is dead, Charlie is dead. McNab is dead." He shook his head. "Nope, just me."

Leonard sat back. The chair creaked. "Seems a rather hazardous lot you associated yourself with. We don't have much to work with here, William. If there were so many others with you, why are you the only one charged?"

Billy slammed his fist against the palm of his hand. "That's the point! It ain't fair! Never has been. Dolan and his Santa Fe pals make me out for an easy target."

"Santa Fe pals you say. You're sure?"

"Damn sure."

"That explains some."

"Some what?"

"Warren Bristol's presiding. William Rynerson is prosecuting."

"Bristol? Ain't there another judge in the whole of New Mexico Territory?"

"It wouldn't seem so by these proceedings. All we can do is our best."

January 27, 1881

He stared at the blank sheet of paper. The ink pot and pen threatened to write yet another letter to Governor Wallace. What good would one more do when all the others had failed? Likely not much, but it gave him something to fight the cold, gray, waiting monotony. It was cold all right. The stove in the outer office did precious little to heat the four cells back here. He'd been there long enough to get himself moved to

302

the cell closest to the office door for all the good it did, which wasn't much. The days drifted by from pale gray to brighter gray to black night. Each came with watery coffee and a biscuit followed sometime later by a not so warm plate of salt pork and beans. He'd lost track of them. The only relief came with the news they were fixin' to move him to Mesilla for trial. He got up and paced.

Likely they'd hang him. Murder was a hanging offense. It still riled him. Why just me? What about the rest of them sons a bitches? Hell, he'd been nicked early in the Buckshot Roberts scrap. He had nothing to do with gut shooting the old gunman. And the Brady killing? He was one of several men behind the Torreon wall that day. All the others got pardons. Not Billy Bonney, no pardon for him. Why? Because he called Brady out? Because Brady was a sheriff and somebody had to pay for his killing? Brady was no better than a murderer himself. Dolan's dirty sheriff set John Tunstall up for murder sure as if he pulled the trigger himself. The governor knows all that. It just ain't fair. Maybe the judge will see it ain't fair. He shook his head. Not likely. They was all looking for a reason to put him away. Badass Billy the Kid brought down by law and order comin' to New Mexico Territory. Someone needed a desperate outlaw done right. Sure as hell couldn't a been Dolan or one of his Santa Fe pals.

He sat down on the bunk beside the blank sheet of paper. No sense trying to explain all that away. The governor made a deal. I'd get a pardon if I testified against Dolan. I did my part just like I said, sorta. Now it's up to him to keep his part of the bargain. He picked up the pen and dipped it in the ink pot.

Governor Lew Wallace . . . Oh yeah, he reminded himself . . . *Honorable . . .*

Santa Fe
March 28, 1881
Sunlight crept into the cell from a barred window near the ceiling. Morning. So what? The Kid hadn't slept much that night. They were moving him to Mesilla today. He'd sleep on the train. His last faint hope for pardon passed with the announcement Governor Wallace had resigned. He'd never so much as answered even one of the letters. He'd be gone before long. President Garfield named some feller named Sheldon to replace him. This Sheldon feller was as likely to keep a promise Wallace wouldn't keep as a pig takin' flight. Sheldon wouldn't

know nothing more of William Bonney than what he read in the papers. He'd given his story to that newspaperman back in Las Vegas for all the good that did. The little weasel wrote a story that made him sound loco, seeing things the way he did.

His last tray came with its cup of thin coffee water and a hardtack biscuit. It took half the coffee to soften the biscuit. By the time he finished, keys sounded in the cell block door. Two men in cheap suits came in. They had the look of his new keepers. The tall, sad-eyed one with the thick mustache appeared to be in charge.

"Bonney? Deputy US Marshal Tony Neis, this here is Deputy Bob Olinger. We're to escort you to Mesilla for trial." He didn't sound like a lawman. He spoke the quiet bookish way of a preacher or a school teacher.

Olinger got the Kid's attention. A big thick man, he wore a black frock coat stretched over his girth. His bull neck denied a soiled linen collar its button. He had rough, knobby ham hocks for hands and small cruel eyes tucked in the fleshy folds of a puffy face. Olinger ogled him, threatening menace.

Neis inserted a key in the cell lock. The door clicked open. Olinger stepped inside.

"Gimme your wrists."

He snapped manacles on the Kid's extended wrists, tight enough to cut the skin. Billy held his expression blank while the big deputy shackled his ankles. Neis led the way to the outer office. Olinger gave him a shove from behind. Billy relaxed his wrists as soon as the bull deputy stepped behind him. The cuffs loosened. He took comfort. He could sure enough shuck them when the time came. The time would come. That much was certain. He'd had enough of jails. He had no thought of climbing a gallows. He'd make a break or go down in a hail of bullets. It was only a matter of choosing odds in his favor.

He got a second boost from a friendly face, waiting in the jail office.

"Mr. Leonard, what are you doin' here?"

"Good day to you, William. Am I not still representing you?"

"Sure you are. I just didn't expect . . ."

"Expect that I'd accompany you to La Mesilla? I have to get there somehow. This way I get to be certain you're treated properly along the way."

Neis raised an eyebrow. "Who might this be?"

"Ira Leonard, attorney at law, at your service. Marshal?"

"Neis, Deputy US Marshal Tony Neis, Mr. Leonard. Am I to assume you represent Bonney here?"

"As a matter of fact I do."

"And it is your intention to accompany us to La Mesilla?"

"It is indeed, Marshal. Very perceptive of you."

"You're perfectly free to ride any train you wish, Mr. Leonard, but let me remind you, Deputy Olinger and I are federal officers engaged in the discharge of official duties. Any attempt to interfere with those duties will be met by the full measure of the law."

"Thank you, Marshal. I am familiar with your position and your obligations. I assure you, I wouldn't dream of interfering with the legitimate duties of your office. I'm merely accompanying my client to ensure that at no time does the performance of those duties infringe on my client's legitimate rights."

Neis pulled a frown.

"What the hell did he say?" Olinger grumbled.

"Nothing, Bob," Neis said.

Billy smiled.

"Move the prisoner along, Bob."

TWENTY-EIGHT

La Mesilla
April 6, 1881

As courtrooms went, La Mesilla's Third Judicial District didn't offer much compared to Lincoln, let alone Santa Fe. It did have one thing in common with both of them. The long arm of the Santa Fe Ring rested firmly on the scales of justice in Judge Warren Bristol's court. Upon his arrival in Mesilla, the judge ordered that Billy should stand trial for the murder of Buckshot Roberts. The trial commenced with the judge's call to order the morning of April 6.

Leonard waited patiently for the proceedings to begin. The room fell silent.

"Your Honor, if I may address the court."

Bristol bunched bushy white brows. "Mr. Leonard?"

"Your Honor, with respect to the charge of murder in connection with the death of Andrew Roberts, my client wishes to move

308

for dismissal."

The courtroom erupted in a buzz. Bristol scowled. He banged his gavel. "Order! Order! This court will come to order." He let the hum fall silent. "Mr. Leonard, approach the bench if you please."

Leonard lowered his head to hide a half smirk as he shuffled from the defense table to the bench.

Bristol hunched forward, his voice confidential. "Mr. Leonard this is most irregular."

His head bobbed. "It is, Your Honor. But then so is the charge against my client, as I expect to prove."

Bristol chewed what felt like a mouthful of nails. "Proceed, Mr. Leonard. This better be good."

Leonard returned to the defense table with a twinkle in his eye. He composed himself and turned back to the judge.

"Your Honor, as you know, the events in question took place at Blazer's Mill, April the fourth, eighteen hundred and seventy-eight. A gunfight took place that day between one Andrew Roberts, also known as Buckshot Roberts and a posse of deputy US marshals seeking to serve an arrest warrant on Mr. Roberts."

Prosecutor William Rynerson bolted to the

full extent of his seven-foot frame. "Your Honor, I object. I fail to see the relevance of these assertions to a motion for dismissal." He glared at Leonard. "The prosecution will show, in the due course of these proceedings, that the alleged legal standing of this so-called posse is much in dispute."

"Your Honor, the defense is merely trying to establish the location, timing and circumstances of the charge in question."

Bristol shook his head in frustration. "Overruled, Mr. Rynerson. You may proceed, Mr. Leonard."

"My client was wounded by the initial shots fired, well before the fatal shooting that led to Mr. Roberts' demise."

"Objection, Your Honor! Is the defense moving to dismiss, or pleading its case?"

"Sustained. Mr. Leonard, if you have a point to make with respect to the validity of the charge against your client, I suggest you make it before I rule your motion out of order."

"Your Honor, with all due respect to this court, our motion to dismiss is quite simple. This court lacks jurisdiction in the matter."

The courtroom erupted again. Bristol answered, pounding his gavel. "This court damn well better come to order. Bailiff, call the sheriff! One more outburst and I'll have him clear the courtroom!" The crowd quieted.

"Now, Mr. Leonard, you've made an assertion prejudicial to the jurisdiction of this court. I suggest you back it up and be quick about it before I hold you and your motion in contempt."

"Your Honor, Blazer's Mill, the site of the alleged confrontation is part of the Mescalaro Apache Reservation. As such, it is a federal protectorate, beyond the jurisdiction of the territorial courts."

This time the courtroom held silent. Expectation hung thick in the air. Bristol sat back, absorbing Leonard's assertion. He cut his eyes to the prosecution, inviting some counterargument. Rynerson sat rooted in his chair. Bristol pursed his lips, his voice barely audible, but for the silence in the room.

"Very well, Mr. Leonard. Case dismissed." He rapped his gavel.

The court exploded. Bristol banged his gavel. Silence fell nearly as fast as the outburst broke out. Red in the face, jaw clenched, Bristol glared at Leonard. A vein throbbed at his temple. "The defendant is bound over for trial on the charge of murder in respect to the death of Lincoln County Sheriff William Brady. Court is adjourned!"

The gavel rang.

"I demand to see my client." Leonard hunched over the deputy's desk his whiskey reddened eyes aflame in the halo of lamplight.

The deputy braced in defiance. "Visiting hours is over."

"I don't give a damn about your hours! My client goes on trial for his life in the morning and I need to see him now. Get your ass out of that chair and open the door before I get the sheriff out of bed to do it for you."

The man blinked. The feisty old son of a bitch just might do it. If he dragged the sheriff down here in the middle of the night you could count on the fact he wouldn't be happy. Then again, what harm could it do? His chair creaked as he got to his feet. He took the keys down from their peg.

"This is again' my better judgment."

"At least you demonstrate judgment. I won't quibble as to the quality."

The guard pulled a frown.

"We'll need a lamp."

He found one beside the stove, fumbled for a lucifer, scratched a light and trimmed the wick.

Leonard tapped his foot impatiently. "I'll need a chair."

The deputy handed him the lamp and grabbed a wooden chair as though he'd as soon smash it over the old man's head. He fitted the key in the cell block door and stood aside allowing the lawyer to go in with the lamp.

"You got a visitor, Kid."

Lamplight spilled into the cell. Billy threw back a rough wool blanket. He rolled over the complaint of rusty springs and sat up, rubbing his eyes. Leonard took the chair from the guard and drew it up beside the cell.

"That will be all, thank you. I'll call when we're finished."

The guard shuffled out, plainly annoyed.

"What brings you by this time of night, Mr. Leonard?"

"I'm afraid I have some rather bad news, William. I returned to my hotel from supper this evening to find an order from Judge Bristol's court. It seems I've been removed from your case."

"What? How can he do that?"

"It is most irregular, to use the judge's favored term, but we all serve at the pleasure of the court."

"But, why?"

313

Leonard made a steeple of his bony fingers, his face a mask in the lamplight. "Hard to say. If I had to guess, I'd say our little motion for dismissal caught the good judge somewhat off guard. I suspect we offended the pleasure of the court by, shall we say, making him appear less than in control."

"Good judge, my ass! Now who's to defend me? Am I not entitled to a lawyer?"

"You are, William. In this case two. Judge Bristol has appointed one Albert J. Fountain and one John Bail to represent you."

"Who the hell are they? What do they know about my case? The damn trial starts tomorrow."

"The trial does start tomorrow and those are both good questions. I suspect we shall learn something of what is at play here by the opening of the proceedings."

Billy stared, gap-toothed. He shook his head. "I don't know what you're talkin' about."

"Well, under such circumstances, the proper course of action for your newly appointed representatives would be to move for a continuance for the purpose of familiarizing themselves with the particulars of your case."

"Move for a what?"

"Sorry, for a delay while they study the

charges and formulate a defense."

"But you don't think they will."

He shrugged. "I could be wrong. I hope so."

"So I got lawyers just so they can say I had lawyers." He got off the bunk and paced his cage. "So what do I do? How do I defend myself?"

"I'll attend the trial and keep track of the proceedings. I may be able to advise you on things you should say or ask your attorneys to say. Mind you I won't be able to take a hand in the actual trial, but if you are not given fair representation, perhaps we can build a case for appeal. I'm afraid that's the best I can do."

Billy hung his head. He had a bad feeling about this. Then he hadn't had a good feeling from the beginning. For some reason, powers beyond his understanding had their fingers on his case. It didn't much matter what he did.

April 8, 1881

Two sheriff's deputies led Billy into the courtroom the next morning. He took in the crowd and found a few familiar faces he hadn't expected. Pat Garrett sat at the end of the second row, bathed in morning light from one of the tall windows that lit the courtroom. Mr. Leonard sat in the first row behind the defense table. He favored Billy with a wink as he crossed the room. The first row behind the prosecution table proved more interesting. Billy Mathews and Jimmy Dolan himself sat behind the giant prosecutor Rynerson. Dolan arched an eye with a look of smug amusement. What the hell were they doing here? A panel of straight-faced sober jurors sat in rows along the far wall behind a low railing with a clear view of the judge's bench and the witness stand.

Two men in dark suits sat at the defense table. The slight one had slicked-back hair, a full mustache, dark eyes and a pasty smile. He introduced himself as Albert Fountain. The shorter man with a nervous habit of checking his pocket watch was introduced as John Bail.

Judge Bristol arrived to the usual fanfare and called the court to order. He wore the relaxed demeanor of one in complete control of the situation until he noticed Ira Leonard. He scowled at the defense attorney's presence, slowly coming to the realization he could do nothing about it for the moment. He glanced at the defense table. No one moved. He turned to the prosecution.

"Mr. Rynerson, you may proceed with your opening statement."

Billy leaned across Bail fiddling with his watch. "Hey," he whispered. Fountain gave him a sidelong glance. "Ain't you gonna move for one of them delays so you know my case?"

He shook his head. "No need."

"Your Honor, gentlemen of the jury," Rynerson intoned. "On the afternoon of April the fourth, eighteen hundred seventy-eight, the defendant William Bonney, more notoriously known as Billy the Kid, did, in the company of members of the vigilante group known as the Regulators, lay in ambush on the streets of Lincoln, New Mexico."

Billy leaned across the table again. "We wasn't vigilantes. We was duly swored deputy US marshals."

Fountain waved his objection aside and motioned for him to be quiet. Billy sat back, Ira Leonard's worst fears confirmed.

Rynerson continued. "That morning Lincoln County Sheriff William Brady, accompanied by deputies William Mathews and George Hindmann, walked eastward down the main street of Lincoln. His purpose was the serving of an arrest warrant for one Alexander McSween, the defendant's employer. On passing that portion of Lincoln's main street bordered by the Torreon wall, Sheriff Brady was accosted by the defendant, William Bonney, and his cut-throat associates. A gunfight ensued in which Sheriff Brady and Deputy Hindmann were killed. Deputy Mathews, who will appear before this court in due course, barely escaped with his life. Gentlemen of the jury, the prosecution will present evidence and testimony to this court sufficient to prove beyond the shadow of doubt that the defendant, William Bonney, did with malice aforethought, shoot and kill Sheriff William Brady in cold blood." Rynerson returned to his seat.

Bristol turned to the defense table. "Mr. Fountain, you may present your opening statement."

Fountain half rose from his seat. "We have nothing at this time, Your Honor."

Billy swiveled in his seat.

Leonard shook his head.

The Kid clenched his teeth. Murder clouded his eye.

Lady Justice stood motionless, her blindfold firmly in place.

"Mr. Rynerson, you may call your first witness."

"The prosecution calls William Mathews."

Twenty-Nine

The bailiff held the Bible. Mathews placed his hand upon it.

"Raise your right hand. Do you swear to tell the truth, the whole truth and nothing but the truth, so help you God?"

"I do."

"That'll be a first," the Kid said.

Bristol leveled his gavel at him. "That will be enough out of you."

Rynerson approached the witness stand and clasped his hands behind the tails of his long frock coat. "Now, Mr. Mathews, at the time of the murder, you were employed as a deputy sheriff in Lincoln County under Sheriff Brady. Is that correct?"

"It is."

Billy leaned across Bail. "He keeps sayin' murder, ain't he s'posed to prove that first?"

Fountain pursed his lips. "You'll have your say soon enough. Best be quiet now, son, before the judge holds you in contempt."

"Contempt. That about sums it up."

"Describe for this court if you will what took place on the morning in question."

"Well, sir, it's pretty much like you told it there a few minutes ago. Me and George was with Sheriff Brady on the way to arrest Mr. McSween. We got up to the Torreon Tower when Billy the Kid jumps up from behind the wall there."

"Billy the Kid, that would be the defendant would it not?"

"It was him all right."

"What happened next?"

"The Kid hollered somethin' and next thing you know he starts shootin'. Sheriff Brady and George go down. I run for cover dodgin' hot lead every step of the way."

"Then what happened?"

"Some boys come runnin' from the Murphy and Dolan Mercantile up the street. They come shootin'. The Kid and the rest of them fellers behind the wall lit out runnin'."

"No further questions, Your Honor."

"Mr. Fountain, you may cross-examine."

"No questions at this time, Your Honor."

"No questions!" Billy shouted. "What the hell you sons a bitches bein' paid for?"

"Mr. Fountain, I suggest you restrain your

client before I find it necessary to do it for you."

"Beggin' your pardon, Your Honor." He scowled at Billy.

The Kid hissed. "What's he gonna do, hang me? You two ain't doin' shit here. You call this a trial? You call this justice? This is a stinking pile of horse shit!"

"You may step down, Mr. Mathews. Mr. Rynerson, you may call your next witness."

"The prosecution calls James Dolan."

Dolan rose and strode toward the witness stand.

The Kid caught his eye. "I thought we had a treaty, Jimmy."

He glanced at the Kid. "I thought we did too, once."

"I kept my part."

"Your Honor, I object. The defendant is endeavoring to intimidate the witness," Rynerson said.

Dolan shook his head. "Don't worry, it'd take way more than him to intimidate Jimmy Dolan."

"You talk big, Dolan, when they got a man chained up."

Bristol banged his gavel. "Mr. Bonney, you open that mouth of yours once more out of turn and I'll have you gagged!"

■ ■ ■ ■

Billy had no more than returned to his cell when the jailer came in followed by Ira Leonard.

"You got a visitor, Kid. Visiting hours is over in thirty minutes. No exceptions this time." The cell block door banged closed.

"We'll have to be quick about things, William. I doubt I can force any leniency on the rules since I no longer represent you."

"Thanks for coming, Mr. Leonard."

"Were you able to gain any satisfaction from your lawyers after court recessed?"

"Do you mean are they actually gonna do any lawyerin' for me?"

"Yes, something like that."

"No. They's puttin' on a show, nothin' more than that. They said they'd put me on the stand if I like."

"Do you plan to let them?"

"I don't know. I might just as well take a piss on the judge's desk for all the good it would do. What do you think?"

Leonard rubbed the stubble on his chin. "There's no easy answer to that. If you take the stand, you get to tell your side of things. Make the point about all the other shooters behind that wall. Maybe you can create reasonable doubt that someone else could be the killer. That's all you need to do, you know. Create doubt, I mean. If you had true defense counsel to help, it would certainly be worth the gamble. Under these circumstances, unfortunately you can't count on Mr. Fountain for much of anything. You'd be out there on your own to face Rynerson's cross-examination. That man will cut you up for buzzard bait if you give him the chance."

"I figure I'm buzzard bait either way. At least if I testify, I get the satisfaction of somebody hearin' my side of things. It likely won't do no good, but sittin' there with my thumbs up my ass ain't doin' no good neither."

"Yes, well when you put it like that, I must say I couldn't agree more. Good luck, William. See you in court."

April 9, 1881

Morning sun slanted through the courtroom windows tinting the polished wood a tawny glow. Garrett wasn't in his seat of the day before. He'd moved over next to Mr. Leonard. Dolan and Mathews had moved toward the back of the room, not anticipating any turn of events which might recall them to the stand. The bailiffs led Billy to the defense table. Neither lawyer acknowledged his presence. He turned to the seats behind him.

"Morning, Mr. Leonard. Pat."

Leonard nodded.

"Billy," Garrett said.

"You enjoyin' the show, Pat?"

"Show?"

"Yeah, all this law and justice you swore to uphold."

Garrett returned a blank stare.

"Look at 'em." Billy lifted his chin to Mathews at the back of the room. "If I got blood on my hands at least it ain't innocent blood. It was Mathews killt Mr. Tunstall. He never done nothin' to nobody, 'cept maybe get in Dolan's way. There Dolan sits pious as a parson waitin' for Sunday services to begin. The only reason that son of a bitch don't have blood on his hands is 'cause he has the likes of Mathews to do his killin' for him. So here I am, fixin' to get sentenced to hang 'cause somebody toldt me I was a duly swored deputy just like you. They call this a trial? They take away my lawyer here 'cause he might get me a fair hearin'. Then they replace him with them two." He jerked his head over his shoulder. "They ain't worth a pinch a shit between 'em. Then there's them other boys behind the wall that day. Where are they? Some's dead. Where's the rest? Is any of them on trial? Nope. Just me."

"Some of them let it go, Billy."

Billy held Garrett's gaze. He understood the point Pat made at supper last Christmas. "You always was an honest bartender, Pat."

"All rise."

"Do you solemnly swear to tell the truth, the whole truth and nothing but the truth so help you God?"

"At least that'll make one of us."

Bristol clenched his jaw, his patience clearly still raw from the previous day's proceedings. "Bonney, you going to swear or would you rather step down?"

"I swear."

"Be seated. Mr. Fountain, you may proceed."

"Now, Mr. Bonney, you may tell the court in your own words what happened on the morning in question."

"I rode into Lincoln as part of a posse of deputy US marshals. We was there to arrest Billy Mathews for the murder of John Tunstall."

"Objection, Your Honor. The defense has yet to establish any legitimate legal authority for the band of vigilantes known as the Regulators."

"Objection sustained. The jury will disregard the assertion that Mr. Bonney acted under the authority of a sworn peace officer."

"Hold on a minute. Do I get to tell what happened or not?"

"Continue, Mr. Bonney."

"Like I was sayin', I rode into town with a posse under Deputy Marshal Frank McNab."

"Objection, Your Honor." Rynerson held out his hands to the judge in frustration.

"Mr. Bonney, unless you can prove the assertion that you were a legally sworn deputy, you will refrain from making such claims in your testimony."

"Well, Your Honor, sir, I was."

"Who swore you in?"

"Dick Brewer."

"Who is Dick Brewer?"

"Dick was foreman at the Flyin' H ranch where I worked for Mr. Tunstall."

"And this Dick Brewer was a US marshal."

"A deputy."

"And who swore him in?"

The Kid shrugged. "I don't know."

Bristol rubbed his temples. "Mr. Bonney, is there any witness you can call, such as Mr. Brewer who can back up the claim that you were deputized?"

"Buckshot Roberts killt Dick Brewer at Blazer's Mill."

"Is there anyone else you can call on?"

He thought for a minute, then shook his head. "No, sir. The rest of the boys in the posse was all deputized same as me. Some are dead. The rest are gone off with their pardons."

"I see. Then I'm afraid I must rule in favor of the prosecution's objection."

" 'Course you do."

"You may proceed."

"We waited at the Torreon Tower for Billy Wilson to come along."

"You were waiting for Deputy Wilson?" Bristol asked.

"He was the one we had a warrant for."

"Objection."

"Sustained."

"Do I get to say my piece or not?"

"Mr. Rynerson, I believe you've made your point. Perhaps if you defer some of your objections to cross-examination we might actually get through this. You may proceed, Mr. Bonney."

"We waited behind the Torreon wall until the sheriff and his deputies come up the street. When they got up to my end of the wall, I stood up and wished Sheriff Brady a good day. He went for his gun and the next thing you know everyone was shootin'. The sheriff went down, so did Deputy Hindmann. Mathews run off. Some of Dolan's gunnies come runnin' down the street from his store shootin' at anything that moved. That's when Frank McNab called us off. We went for our horses and lit out."

"Anything further you'd like to add, Mr. Bonney?" Fountain asked.

He thought a moment. "There was a half dozen men behind the Torreon wall that day. Any one of 'em could have killt the sheriff. Who's to say I'm the one killt him? We thought we was duly swored deputies. Even if the giant over there argues we wasn't. Brady drew his gun. That makes it self-defense."

"Your witness, Mr. Rynerson."

The prosecutor drew himself up to the full measure of his seven feet. He clasped his hands behind his back and dropped his chin to his chest as though in thought. He crossed to the witness stand, towering over the defendant. "Now, Mr. Bonney, or do you prefer Billy?"

"Billy does well enough for most."

"Very well then, Billy, you say that when the sheriff approached you stood up and wished him a good day. Is that right?"

"It is."

"So you were hiding behind the wall."

"We all was. We didn't want Mathews to know we'd come for him."

"So you waited in ambush."

"No, sir. We waited to arrest him."

"Arrest him. Haven't we been through that? You can't claim you represented the law unless you can prove it. So you stood up from your hiding place and in your words, bid Sheriff Brady a good day. And by that gesture you ask this jury to believe that the sheriff went for his gun?"

"That's what he done."

"He attempted to draw his gun in response to a greeting of good day."

"Yes, sir."

"Was your own weapon drawn when you jumped out of your hiding place?"

Billy glanced at Fountain. The lawyer held his seat. "I, I don't remember."

"You don't remember. Mr. Mathews recalled that it was."

"Billy Mathews is a lyin' murderer."

"Mr. Mathews isn't on trial for the murder of Sheriff Brady, Billy. You are. No further questions, Your Honor."

THIRTY

District Attorney William Rynerson gave the appearance of a fire-and-brimstone preacher in his black suit, stern expression and full beard. He fixed the jury box in a gaze that might penetrate each and every member's heart and soul. Slanting afternoon sun fell across the jurors, casting them in an other-worldly light. Twelve solid New Mexican citizens, sheepherders, ranchers, shopkeepers, a bank teller, a blacksmith, all of them cut from the stock of which statehood is made. They all knew the benefits of statehood would come only when the territory rid itself of the likes of Billy the Kid. They'd convict. Every last man jack of them knew the stakes. He'd made sure of that in seating them. All he had to do was summarize their thinking for them, and call for their decision.

He looked at the defense table, amused. Fountain and Bail had played their parts, or rather failed to play them, rather convincingly. For all the contribution Bail had added to the proceedings the court might well have saved the territory its money. That wasn't his problem. Hell, Fountain had even put the Kid on the stand. It had been child's play to destroy his credibility as a witness, let alone his feeble defense. Even the facts he got right could be tainted with question. Rynerson had little doubt of the verdict. He had only to take the stage and render his closing arguments. Newspaper reporters packed the back of the courtroom. This was his stage. From here, the powers in Santa Fe would propel his career forward. Who could tell where? The governor's office? He'd already come a long way. The irony amused him. Former gunman builds political fortune by prosecuting the most notorious gunman in New Mexico history.

"All rise. Third Judicial District Court is now in session, Judge Warren Bristol presiding."

The judge took his seat. "Be seated. Mr. Rynerson, you may enter your closing arguments."

"Thank you, Your Honor." He approached the jury box, careful to connect with each man in his turn. "Gentlemen, we stand here today, together charged with a sacred duty.

It is our duty to see justice carried out in a case of capital murder."

"That man!" His arm shot out to point at the defendant. "William Bonney, variously known as William Antrim and Billy the Kid, is a scourge on the good people of New Mexico." He turned back to the jury box, strode to the far end and leaned his hands on the rail. He cast his luming shadow across the jurors in the window light. "Here today, you will hold him to account for his most grievous crime, the cold-blooded murder of Sheriff William Brady. A murder committed whilst the sheriff was engaged in performing the duties of his office, an office whose purpose is to serve the decent, law-abiding citizens of New Mexico.

"Before we consider the weight of evidence presented here, I must ask you to be mindful of the solemnity of your duty. This is the trial of one notorious outlaw for the crime of capital murder. But it is more than that." He stepped away from the rail, letting the shaft of sunlight lend a dazzling brilliance to his features and mystical truth to his words. "This trial symbolizes a great and noble struggle by the people of New Mexico to assert law and order in this territory." He paced back and forth before the jury along the shaft of light, speaking as though personally to each man. "You gentlemen, by your deliberations here today, will tell our fellow citizens in this territory and in the states beyond that we New Mexicans stand for law and order. This territory will not tolerate the lawless likes of Billy the Kid or any other criminal. I have every confidence that each of you will faithfully discharge this, your sacred duty."

He clasped his hands behind his back and crossed to the defense table, drawing the jurors' attention to the Kid, slouched in sullen defiance. "William Bonney, by your own account, you assert you acted as part of a posse, lawfully engaged in the pursuit of accused suspects. I submit, gentlemen of the jury, that this so-called posse was in fact a vigilante mob, acting outside the law with no legitimate authority in the jurisdiction in question. On April the first, eighteen hundred seventy-eight, the defendant, by his own admission took part in the ambush of Sheriff William Brady and his deputies, George Hindmann and William Mathews as they walked the streets of Lincoln. The defendant claims that Deputy Mathews resisted arrest and that Sheriff Brady drew his gun in support of Deputy Mathews' resistance."

He returned to the jury box. "Gentlemen,

Sheriff Brady drew his gun in the line of duty to thwart the illegal actions of a vigilante mob. And further" — he pointed again — "that man, William Bonney, drew his gun and deliberately shot Sheriff Brady dead while he engaged in the performance of his duty in office. What claim on law and order have we the citizens of New Mexico if we tolerate the cold-blooded murder of peace officers engaged in carrying out the duties of their office?"

He let the import of the charge settle. "Then again, a mere three days later on April the fourth at Blazer's Mill and again by his own admission, the defendant took part in a gunfight that resulted in the murder of Andrew Roberts. While he is not on trial for that killing, once again the accused would have this court and the citizens of New Mexico believe these actions were the result of duly authorized law enforcement actions. Gentlemen, does it not strike you as odd that in every action taken by these so-called Regulators, the subjects of their alleged law enforcement were gunned down? In no case did the vigilante mob arrest any of the alleged accused or seek justice in a court of law. In the case before us and others for which the defendant does not now stand accused, the illegal actions of these Regulators resulted in cold-blooded killings. Gentlemen, Sheriff Brady was murdered. He died by the hand of that man, William Bonney. It is your sacred duty to find him guilty of capital murder."

April 13, 1881

A stone-faced jury filed into the courtroom to take their seats in the jury box as the clock ticked its way toward four o'clock. Billy slouched at the defense table, Fountain beside him. Bail had not seen fit to attend the sentencing. Leonard sat behind him, his wrinkled coat open, his hands folded across his paunch. His head rested on his chest eyes closed. Rynerson drummed his fingers on the prosecution table, unable to read anything from the jurors' expression.

"All rise."

Black robed Judge Warren Bristol strode to the bench and took his seat. He clapped his gavel. "Be seated. Gentlemen of the jury, have you reached a verdict?"

The foreman, a gnarled man in overalls rose. "We have, Your Honor."

"How do you find?"

"With respect to the charge of murder in the death of Sheriff William Brady, we the jury find the defendant guilty as charged."

The courtroom murmured.

The Kid slumped in his chair.

Rynerson closed his eyes, vindicated.

Leonard nodded to himself.

The foreman handed the verdict to the bailiff.

"The defendant will rise," Bristol said.

Billy looked to Fountain. The attorney stood. The Kid pulled himself up on the defense table, his legs heavy, unsteady.

"The defendant has heard the jury's verdict. Therefore, by the power vested in the Third District Court for the Territory of New Mexico, I hereby order that the defendant shall be transferred to Lincoln, New Mexico, where on the thirteenth of May, eighteen hundred eighty-one he shall be hanged by the neck until dead. May God have mercy upon your soul."

The Kid glared at Bristol. "Go to hell."

The judge banged his gavel. "Take him away!"

THIRTY-ONE

April 15, 1881

The jailer's keys jangled. He entered the cell block followed by two men. "Time to go, Kid. This here is Deputy J. W. Bell. I believe you know Deputy Olinger. They're here to take you to Lincoln." He fitted a key in the door and unlocked the cell.

Bell stepped in. A man of average height, the deputy had an easy manner about him. He had a full mustache, a twinkle in his eye and smile lines at the corners, hardly the demeanor of a hardened lawman. He manacled the Kid's wrists and feet. "This way, we got a prison wagon out front." He led the way toward the office. Olinger waited at the cell door.

Billy glanced at the big deputy as he passed. "Bob." He managed a crooked grin.

"That's Deputy Olinger to you, boy. You best remember my rules and fast, Kid, if you know what's good for you." His eyes and a cruel curl at the corner of his mustache filled in *or else.* He fell in behind the prisoner.

Spring could be dreary. A cold light rain fell from folded felt clouds, rendering muddy ruts still stiff with winter frost a slippery slime. The prison wagon matched the mood. It was a circus wagon for wild animals without the bright paint and gold leaf. Bell opened the cell on wheels and helped Billy hoist his heavily chained limbs inside. Seating consisted of rough wooden benches bolted to the floor. The wagon might hold as many as a dozen prisoners. Billy was the only passenger for this trip. The door clanged shut. Bell twisted the key in the heavy padlock.

He tied his saddle horse to the back of the cage and climbed up to the driver's box. Olinger put on a slicker to ward off the rain. He toed a stirrup and launched his bulk into the saddle of a sturdy bay. He nudged the horse up alongside the wagon and patted his rope.

"Enjoy the ride, Kid. It won't be long now."

"Hey up!" Bell called to the mule team. The wagon lurched forward, rocking its way over the muddy ruts.

The campfire snapped and popped sending showers of sparks into a cold black sky. Bell and Olinger sat beside the fire with plates of hardtack, jerky and beans. The circle of firelight illuminated the wagon beyond the comfort of its warmth. Billy huddled on a bench, cast in orange and black shadow bars. He shivered with the cold. The beans had gone cold on his tin plate by the second forkful.

"Hey, J. W., it's cold out here. How about lettin' me sit by the fire some?"

Bell glanced at Olinger. "He's all chained up, Bob. Don't seem like it'd do any harm."

Olinger scowled. "Get used to it, Kid. The only place you're goin' is to a cold grave. The next heat you see is likely to be in hell."

"Com'on, Bob," Bell said.

"Let him be." He turned toward the wagon. "You ever seen a hangin', Kid?"

No answer.

"Too bad if you haven't. It'd give you something to think about besides bein' cold. Me, I seen quite a few back in Fort Smith. The first thing the good people of Lincoln have to do is build you a gallows. One with a trap door that breaks clean. You cain't have a good hangin' without a clean drop. In Fort Smith they did enough hangin's, they had a permanent gallows. You always got a clean drop on that gallows. They had good hangmen too. No substitute for experience when it comes to a good hangin'. Those boys knew how to tie that noose proper. They knew where to put that big old knot for the best chance to break your neck. That's a good hangin', when they break your neck. If I was you I'd be most worried about the hangman. Don't expect they got that much experience up in Lincoln."

"All right, Bob, ain't that about enough?"

"Shut up, J. W. I'm just givin' the boy there somethin' to think about. It'll take his mind off the cold. Yeah, Kid, I'd be worried about gettin' a good hangin' in Lincoln. You don't see many bad hangin's in Fort Smith, but I heard about a few. See if your neck don't break, you choke to death. A lot of swingin' and kickin' goes into that. You piss your pants. Your face gets uglier than ordinary. The hood mostly hides that, but it must not feel too good. Sure looks ugly, though. Course that ain't the worst hangin'. A real bad one can take your head off. Imagine that. The body falls through the trapdoor. So does the head, unless a course it lands on the scaffold. Then it just sort a rolls around there, spillin' blood all over.

The noose just swings. Yup a bad hangin' is what I'd worry about. Some inexperienced hangman don't know how to do it proper. That'd worry me."

"Go to hell, Olinger."

"Maybe someday, Kid, but you'll be there long before me. Sleep well."

Fort Sumner
April 18, 1881

Dusk crowded the kitchen for light, not yet banished to the need of a lamp. The ashen-faced girl stood framed in the hallway entrance.

"They're fixin' to hang him, Deluvina." She rushed into the older girl's arms.

"There, there, muchacha."

"But they're gonna hang him. They're gonna hang my Billy."

"Who told you this?"

"It's all over town." She sobbed.

Boots sounded at the front door. Heels clicked along the hall. "I guess she heard," Pete said.

Deluvina nodded.

"I tried to tell her it wouldn't come to no good."

Paulita lifted her chin. She glared watery-eyed over her shoulder. "So you got what you wanted, Pete."

"No I didn't, Paulita. I didn't want you to get hurt."

"Well I am."

"I know. I'm sorry. I tried to warn you."

"That s'posed to make me feel better?"

He shook his head. "No, I don't s'pose so." He turned on his heel and clumped back down the hall to the front proch.

"He means well, muchacha."

"I know." She buried her head in Deluvina's shoulder. "He just don't have to be so damn right all the time."

Deluvina's gaze drifted over the girl's head, away to some far seen place. She turned a knowing vision over in her mind, unwilling to say anything unless it should be so. She closed her eyes. The vision grew stronger. A knowing grew firm in her heart.

"I do not see this hanging."

"I won't neither." The girl sobbed. "They say it'll be down in Lincoln next month. I couldn't bear the thought a watchin'."

The Navajo girl saw far. "I do not see this hanging."

Tularosa
April 19, 1881
The roadhouse amounted to little more than a rest stop on the stage road between La Mesilla and Lincoln. Lincoln County

didn't allow for lavish accommodations. Most nights they camped along the road. Bell and Olinger slept under the stars in good weather, under the wagon in bad. Other than an occasional concession to nature's call, they kept the Kid in his cage. At least this stop meant a hot meal that amounted to something more than fatback and beans.

As luck would have it, for good or ill, a stage pulled in shortly after they did. As was their custom in such situations, Olinger had the watch while Deputy Bell went inside to see about supper. The custom never left the Kid to himself.

The stage driver announced they'd stop for supper and to change teams. The passengers stepped down from the coach led by a man in dark suit and bowler hat. He looked a little unsteady on his feet as he helped a beautiful woman in a plum colored dress down. She accepted his help without looking any too pleased for the favor. Proper lady, Billy thought, bothered by a drunk drummer. Likely she'd be glad of a rest stop.

"Hey, who you got there?" the drummer called to Olinger.

Olinger glanced at the man annoyed. Most everything annoyed him.

"A prisoner," he said.

"I might never have guessed. Anybody famous?"

The sullen deputy ignored the question.

A stage hand came around the coach to unhitch the team. "That there's Billy the Kid," he said under his breath. "They's takin' him up to Lincoln to hang."

"You don't say." He turned to the woman who'd started into the roadhouse. "I say, Miss Bancroft, do you know who they have in that prison wagon?"

"I'm certain I do not."

Her curt reply confirmed Billy's suspicion. Undaunted the drummer pressed on.

"That there's Billy the Kid. I read about his trial. These officers are taking him up to Lincoln to hang."

"Oh, my!" She covered her mouth with a handkerchief filled hand.

"Com'on, let's go have a closer look. It isn't every day you see a notorious condemned desperado."

"You gonna let them make a spectacle out of me?" Billy asked.

"Shut up, Kid. You made a spectacle out of yourself the day you killed Sheriff Brady. For all I care the good citizens of New Mexico can make a sign post out of your worthless hide."

The drummer tried to take the woman's

344

arm. She shook him off, but followed him, her curiosity aroused.

Billy sat in gathering shadows as the curiosity seekers approached the wagon. The woman was quite pretty with delicate features, a porcelain complexion and dark violet eyes. They stopped a few steps from the wagon.

"Can't see much from here," the drummer said.

They moved closer.

Billy made a sudden lunge at the bars. "Boo!"

"Ahh!" She screamed and shrank back.

The drummer nearly jumped out of his skin.

Billy broke into peals of laughter. The laughter turned to a howl of pain when Olinger slammed his rifle barrel across his fingers where he gripped the bars. "What did you do that for, Bob? I was just funnin' the folks."

"Shut up, Kid."

The woman squared her shoulders. "Is it necessary to strike a defenseless prisoner like that? He certainly couldn't do us any real harm."

"You've had your look, ma'am. I suggest you move along."

She looked up into the wagon. "Does he

mistreat you like that often?"

"I'd rather not say."

"He does, then." She turned on Olinger. "I shall see this matter reported to your superior."

"This is a condemned murderer, lady. He don't get no special treatment. Now move along before I have you arrested for obstructing justice."

"You what? I declare, sir, your conduct is most unbecoming an officer of the law."

"What's goin' on here, Bob?" Bell asked.

"This man is abusing the prisoner," the woman said. "Are you his superior?"

"No, ma'am."

"Who is then?"

"Shut up, J. W.," Olinger said.

"You shut up, Bob. It's Sheriff Pat Garrett out of Lincoln."

"And who might you be?"

"Deputy J. W. Bell, ma'am."

"And this man?" She stuck her chin at Olinger.

"Don't pay her no mind, J. W."

"I'll take care of this, Bob."

"Ma'am, I assure you, I'll see to it the prisoner comes to no further trouble."

She seemed to settle some. "See that you do, though I'm still of a mind to report this man." She turned on her heel and marched into the roadhouse.

Olinger spat.

Bell handed him a plate of roast beef, biscuits and gravy. "Here you eat this out here. I'll get you a plate that's still hot, Billy."

"Don't coddle him, J. W."

"No need to abuse him, either."

"You handle a sidewinder your way you get bit. I'll handle him my way."

Lincoln
April 21, 1881

The prison wagon lumbered up the street to the courthouse under a warm spring sun and a chill northwest breeze. Bell hauled lines and drew the team up along the side entrance to the second-floor jail. He set the brake and wrapped the lines around the handle. He climbed down and set off for the sheriff's office. Olinger swung down from his saddle and looped a rein over the iron fence to the courthouse side yard. He wandered over to the wagon.

"Your new home, Kid, for a few days at least." He laughed.

Bouncing around in a box for most of a week had given him plenty of time to think. He didn't need bully Bob Olinger to remind him they planned to hang him. The way he had it figured he had three weeks to get the routine down and figure his opportunities. One thing was sure. He wanted no part of a rope. He'd bust out of this jail or die in the trying. Either way he'd be better off by his reckoning.

Bell bounced down the courthouse steps with a ring of keys. "Pat says put him up in number two." He unlocked the cage. "Com'on, Billy, let's get you settled."

He stood hunched over, and dragged his chains to the back of the wagon. Bell helped him down and led the way to the side door. Olinger came along with a rough shove that about knocked the Kid down. *Bust out or die trying.* Either way he promised himself, *he'd kill the son of a bitch Olinger.*

The side door to the former mercantile known as the House led to the sheriff's office and jail. A stairway from the first-floor office led to the second-floor jail. Billy followed Bell up the stairs to a landing. A corridor at the top of the stairs led past a closed door to a row of cells. The door caught his interest. Bell paused at the second cell. He unlocked the door.

"In here."

He stepped inside. Bell started to close the door. "Hey, what about these?" He held up his manacled hands.

The deputy paused. "I guess they can come off now."

Olinger arched a brow. "You sure, J. W.?"

That made it certain. "I'm sure, Bob." He removed the cuffs and locked the cell door. Olinger led the way out of the cell block. He went down to the office while Bell took the chains to the door Billy noticed at the head of the stairs. He unlocked it and stepped inside. Billy strained to get a glimpse of what was inside. He could just make the end of a rifle rack. *The armory.* He cracked his gap-toothed grin. He flexed his wrists where his cuffs had been. He was beginning to get a feel for this jail already.

Bell relocked the room and disappeared down the stairs. Billy stretched out on the bunk. Between the springs and a rickety wooden frame he guessed he might wake himself up if he rolled over. At least it stood still. He must have dozed off on account of waking up to sunlight slanting along the cells from some uncertain source and the tapping of boot heels coming his way. He rolled up on an elbow and brighted.

"Afternoon, Pat."

"Billy. I see they got you settled."

"I guess."

"Supper won't be along for a couple hours so I thought I'd come by and see if you need

349

anything."

"That's right decent of you. I could use a gun, a horse and the loan of your keys."

Garrett laughed. "I should have known you'd try to impose on my good nature. I don't think so, Kid. I was thinkin' more like a Bible or writing paper and pen for a last will and testament or such like that."

"Hell I wrote Governor Wallace enough letters some might get to thinkin' he's my adopted father. All I ever asked for was the pardon he agreed to give me if I testified against Dolan. If he'd a kept that bargain, I'd a rode off and never been no trouble to nobody. But no, the answer's always the same, no answer. The new governor ain't even took office yet. I cain't think of anyone else to write to."

"Well, there's the acting governor. He might not pardon you outright, but he might commute your sentence or grant a stay of execution."

He shook his head. "And get myself caged up for the rest of my days."

"You might get paroled sometime down the road when all the hot blood simmers down. Things like that have a way of happening."

"Maybe for some, but things like that don't hold much for me."

"Look, Billy, I know you want a pardon. You figure you deserve it like everybody else. I might even agree with you, but somehow you got yourself on the wrong side of the politics of this thing."

"What's politics got to do with it?"

"More than you might think. The governor ain't gonna pardon you unless the district attorney agrees. Rynerson ain't about to do that. You're a notorious outlaw. He's fixin' to ride your conviction all the way to higher office in Santa Fe."

"And for that, I hang. Who's the murderer here anyway?"

"All I'm sayin' is give the governor a chance. Plead for clemency. He may be willing to do that even if he won't pardon you. Then take your chances on parole. We'll get a minister to counsel you, attest to your repentance, your reformed character. With a little luck, you'll be out in a few years."

"A few years. I'll think about it."

Garrett turned. "Let me know if you need anything."

His footsteps died away in the fading light.

THIRTY-TWO

April 25, 1881
The plan started with being a model prisoner. Deputy Bell was the key. He was a decent man just doing his job. Olinger was a son of a bitch. You couldn't even talk to the bastard. No, Bell was the key. Billy heard him on the stairs, coming with his lunch tray. It was time to test the fit.

"Lunchtime, Billy."

"Oh, J. W., am I glad you're here. I was just about to call. I gotta go to the privy somethin' fierce."

Bell set down the tray. "I'll get the shackles."

Billy grabbed his gut and grimaced. "Don't know as I can wait, J. W. We don't need 'em. I won't be no trouble. I promise."

"I know you won't be no trouble, Kid, but I'm gonna wrap you up just the same."

"Then hurry, J. W., please." *Nuts, I thought that might a worked.*

The deputy fetched the shackles from the armory. He quickly opened the cell and snapped the cuffs and manacles in place. Billy headed for the stairs with Bell close behind. As he started down the stairs he noticed that in his haste, Bell failed to re-lock the armory door.

"Don't you go gettin' ahead of yourself," Bell said.

"Just keep up, J. W."

They clumped down the stairs to the of-fice side door.

"Hey where you goin' with him?" Olinger asked.

"Privy."

"What's the rush?"

"Urgent." Bell said as they scooted out the door.

Billy made it inside the outhouse, dropped his britches and sat on the rough two-hole bench. "Oh lord, J. W. You're a godsend you are." He smiled his crooked smile. It was as good as done. He just needed the right time. He finished his business and stepped out into the sunshine.

"Ah that's better. Com'on, J. W. Let's see what's for lunch."

Meek as a lamb he went back to his cage. Bell left the tray and went back downstairs.

"You hadn't ought to let that sidewinder

talk you into things like that, J. W. I'm tellin'
you he cain't be trusted."

"He weren't no trouble at all, Bob. Like
you said, you handle him your way and I'll
handle him mine."

April 28, 1881
Something was up. Billy couldn't hear
exactly what was said, but Garrett seemed
to be handing out more than the usual
instructions that morning. Could today be
the day? He had a hunch. His stomach told
him it was getting on to lunchtime when
the stairs announced someone coming.
He'd come to know the heavy clumps and
the stairs creaking under Olinger.

He stopped outside the cell with a tray
and slid it through a slit in the bars. "Lunch,
Bonney, come and get it."

Billy rolled off the bunk. He inspected the
tray — salt pork, hardtack and a cup of not
quite hot watery coffee. "My, my. Look at
this. Somebody forgot the apple pie."

"Pie's bein' served over at the Wortley,
where I'll be havin' lunch soon as I'm done
here. Don't worry though, Kid, I'll eat an
extra piece just for you."

"I'm sure you will, Bob. You didn't get
them impressive gut muscles pushin' away
from the table."

"Shut up, Kid. You'll run out of sass before too long. I expect to take great pleasure in draggin' your sorry ass up them scaffold steps. Your legs will be like lead weights. You'll probably shit your pants before they ever even get the noose around your neck. Just to keep things straight, the sheriff left for White Oaks this mornin' for a little business. That leaves me in charge, so you best watch your mouth or I'll fix it for you."

"Be sure to cuff me up first. I wouldn't want you to have an accident."

"Like I said, you'll run out of sass soon enough. The sheriff took the wagon up to White Oaks so he can haul back the lumber for your gallows. I just hope we can make that trap drop clean. Have a nice lunch."

"You too, Bob." He smiled. *This is it. The smart ass son of a bitch is about to get his.* He listened to the side door slam. He waited five minutes while he bolted his food.

"J. W.!" The Kid rattled his coffee cup on the bars.

"What?" The muffled voice echoed up the stairs.

"I'm done and I gotta piss."

Bell mumbled something to himself and clumped up the stairs. He rounded the landing to the armory and unlocked the door. He disappeared inside and came out moments later with the shackles in hand. He tugged the door behind him with a boot. The door stopped still ajar. Billy took it for a sign.

Bell fumbled for the key at the cell door, juggling the cuffs and chains. Billy considered jumping him before he put the chains on. No, better to be sure no one was left in the office downstairs. The door swung open. He held out his wrists.

"Please don't jam 'em like Olinger, J. W. The man likes to cut off the feelin's." The cuffs clasped to an easy fit.

"Turn around."

The deputy snapped the shackles around his ankles from behind. He backed out of the cell, allowing Billy to lead the way downstairs. The office was empty, *so far so good.* They stepped out the side door into a bright warm spring day. He filled his lungs with fresh air. He could almost taste freedom.

"Fine day ain't it, J. W.?"

"Fine day indeed."

"I figure to miss fine days like these."

They reached the privy. "I'll wait right here."

"Won't be but a minute," the Kid said.

The door banged shut. Shadowed light leaked between chinks in the rough cut plank walls. Urine replaced the sweet smell of fresh air. He managed his buttons and went about his business, finishing his plan to the telltale splatter in the black hole below. He stepped back outside with a smile.

"That's better. Much obliged, J. W."

"No trouble other than my lunch gettin' cold."

"Well let's get me locked back up right quick, so you can get back to them fine biscuits and gravy." He led off at a quick pace, fast enough to get ahead of Bell but not so fast as to seem a runaway. The deputy reached the side door as Billy turned up the stairs. He paused on the landing, his back to the stairs and slipped the handcuffs off his wrists. He balled a heavy iron cuff in his fist and glanced over his shoulder.

Bell climbed the last couple steps to the landing. "Move along there," he ordered.

The Kid spun, throwing the full measure of his weight behind an iron blow that gashed Bell's temple, stunning him. He sank to his knees, blood oozing from his temple into his eye. Billy's left hand snaked out, grabbed Bell's gun by the butt and yanked it from his holster. He cocked the gun and stepped away from the deputy.

Bell shook his head in a shower of blood, blinked and managed to find his feet. His eyes registered recognition at the muzzle of his gun. He turned and retreated down the steps to the office. The Kid leveled the gun and fired. The Colt spit fire. A deafening blast filled the small space in a cloud of acrid smoke. The bullet struck Bell in the back, exiting his chest. The stairwell wall exploded in a shower of adobe chips, splattered in blood. Bell twisted on a stair near the lower landing and fell back against the wall beside the bullet hole. White eyed in disbelief he fixed on the dark figure at the top of the stairs for an instant. He stumbled off the landing down the last steps to the office side entrance. He staggered out the door to the yard.

Sorry about that, J. W. Billy stuffed the gun in his belt and shuffled to the open armory. He found Olinger's 10-gauge Whitney in the first case. He grabbed the shotgun and a box of shells. He ducked down beside a corner window overlooking the side yard where Bell's body lay. He opened the window and smiled to himself in anticipation.

The shot woke old Godfrey Gauss from his nap on the porch of a small house in back of the courthouse. He pushed his bent frame out of his rocker and stepped off the porch, cautiously making his way toward the courthouse. The old German immigrant befriended the Kid while employed by John Tunstall as a cook. The sound of a gunshot coming from the courthouse meant trouble. Experience told the old man trouble in this case meant the Kid. As he reached the side door, Bell stumbled out and collapsed in his arms. Gauss lowered the lifeless body to the ground in shock.

The muffled shot stopped a forkful of roast beef halfway to Olinger's mouth. "What the hell was that?" He scraped back his chair, threw his napkin on the table and drew his gun. As he headed for the restaurant door, he glanced out the front window and saw Bell stumble out of the courthouse. He collapsed in Godfrey Gauss' arms. He knew the Kid had gotten loose. He dashed through the door, took the boardwalk in one long stride and ran across the street angling for the courthouse side door. He broke stride to see if Bell could tell him what had happened.

Gauss looked up from where he knelt beside the body. "Da Kid shot Bell, Bob."

Olinger cocked his gun and continued

toward the side door.

"Oh, Bob."

The familiar voice had a teasing lilt. Olinger looked up. Who could forget the gap-tooth grin in that window behind double-barreled black muzzles?

Both muzzles exploded. The double load of heavy-gauge buckshot shredded the big deputy's chest nearly decapitating him. The charge lifted his lifeless body off its feet and threw it back into the ditch at the side of the road.

Bob Olinger would have eternity to remember that crooked grin.

"Godfrey, saddle me a good horse," Billy called down. "I'll meet you at the stable."

Gauss left the fallen deputies and hurried to the stable in back of the courthouse. The best horse in the barn was an easy choice. It belonged to Sheriff Garrett.

Billy searched Bell's pockets for the key to his leg irons. He searched the office and then the armory. *What the hell happened to them?* The sun had begun its descent. People started milling around town as word of the jailbreak spread. Armed with the big shotgun and Bell's Colt, he didn't expect trouble. Still you never knew when some citizen might fancy himself a hero. He clanked down the alley behind the court-house to the stable, still shackled at the ankles. Too bad his feet weren't smaller.

He found Gauss in the stable lit like a sepia tintype in the slanting afternoon sun. He had a sturdy bay cross-tied and saddled. "He looks good, Godfrey."

"Best von here," the old German said. "Sheriff Pat vill miss dis von."

"Garrett's horse?" Billy laughed. "I like it."

"Not dat he vill do you much good chained up like dat."

"Can't find the damn key." He shuffled back to the tack room. Gauss followed and watched as he rummaged around.

"Vhat happened?"

Billy glanced at the old man. "I slipped my cuffs and jumped J. W. He ran. I had to shoot him. Too bad, he was decent to me."

"Bob vas not."

"That son of a bitch, I enjoyed blowin' his sorry ass to hell." He found an old prospector's pick and pushed past the old cook back into the stable. He dragged his chains to an anvil used to fit horseshoes. He stepped his left boot on top and set to work on the chain.

Time passed to the steady beat of ringing steel. Sweat poured down the Kid's face soaking his shirt. His arm ached with the effort. Progress came slow and grudging. He leaned the pick against the anvil and straightened the bunched muscles in his back.

"Godfrey, come take a few licks at this thing."

The old man hobbled over to the anvil. He picked up a misshapen link and turned it over in a watery gaze. "Ve might be here all night und not get you out of dese."

"Just get one link and I can ride."

"Ja." He placed the chain across the anvil and gripped the pick with two gnarled hands. He hit the damaged link a sharp blow with the pick's heavy flat edge. He turned the link over and inspected his work. He nodded, replaced the chain and positioned the link just so. He struck it again. He held it up to the late-afternoon light streaming through the open barn door.

"What the hell are you doin', old man? Are you gonna hit the damn thing or hope it falls off from rust."

He placed the link on the edge of anvil and struck a heavy blow. The link shattered with a plink. "Dere."

"Why didn't you tell me you knew what you was doin'?"

"You vouldn't haf believed me."

"Likely not. Now I gotta ride." He wound the loose chain around his right ankle. He stuffed the 10-gauge into the saddle boot and checked the cinch. The bay whickered as he released the cross ties and gathered the reins. He toed a stirrup and swung his heavy right leg across the saddle.

"Vhere you go now, Villy?"

He paused. "Good question, old man. One worth some serious thinkin'. Just now, I don't know and that's best for the road." He touched his hat brim and squeezed up a trot out of the barn. He wheeled north and booted up a gallop, trailing dust in the gathering gloom.

"Go mit Gott, Villy."

THIRTY-THREE

Lincoln
April 29, 1881

The heavily loaded wagon creaked and bumped up the street toward the courthouse. Garrett sat in the driver's box, hauling the lines on a matched mule team. He eyed the sun slant, wondering if they could get the lumber unloaded before dark. He reckoned not. It would keep until morning parked out back. They had two weeks to construct the gallows, so there was no rush. He drove past the courthouse and turned west, circling around back. He hauled a stop and set the brake. The climb down from the box felt good, first for the stretch and then for relief from the hard bench seat. He started for the side door, figuring to get Bell or Olinger to help him with the team.

"Guten abend, Sheriff."

Old Godfrey Gauss hobbled off the darkened porch of the small house off to his right.

"Good evening, Godfrey."

"Haf you heard da news?"

"What news?" Garrett tensed, his instinct alert.

"Da Kid escaped."

"What? How? Where's Bell?"

"Dead."

"Bob?"

"Him too."

Garrett felt his gut turn to water. How in hell? "When?"

"Yesterday."

"What happened?"

"Villy yumped Bell vhile Bob vas at lunch. Dey fought. Villy shot him. Bob come running from da Vortley. Villy shot him too. Den he escaped."

"How?"

"On your bay."

"Shit!" He rubbed his chin in disbelief, digesting the news. He looked at the loaded wagon. The Kid cheated the hangman, at least for now. He thought back to their conversation of a week ago, *so much for clemency.* He had two more murders added to his record and lawmen at that. He had balls. You had to give him that.

Where would he go? The talk they had

Christmas Eve over dinner played back in his mind. The Kid wasn't stupid. He was likely long gone to Mexico by now.

"Vhen vill you go after him, Sheriff?"

He tilted his chin, eyeing the old man beneath an arched brow. "I'll get up a posse and see if we can pick up his trail, Godfrey. He may turn up somewhere, but I got a strong hunch we've seen the last of Billy the Kid."

"Vhat vill you do vit dat?" The old man nodded to the wagon load of lumber.

He shrugged. "Maybe we can sell it and get the county's money back. The Kid won't be needin' it. Not now at least. Gimme a hand with the team will you?"

Stinking Springs
April 30, 1881

Billy sat with his back against the rough stone wall. Dim light played across the dirt floor. He felt chilled in spite of the warm spring day. Ghosts filled the shadows, Tom, Charlie. He could still smell smoke. He'd wrestled with himself most of the afternoon. Mexico made sense. Get long gone. Change your life. Find an honest job. Forget Lincoln. Forget the damn pardon. Let it go like the others. All that made sense. So what was he doing hiding out at Stinking Springs?

Stinking Springs made sense too. It was the last place he reckoned they'd look for him. But that wasn't all of it. Stinking Springs was less than a day's ride from the reason he wasn't on his way to Mexico. That long-gone new life with an honest job included Paulita Maxwell. He was in love. He couldn't get his mind around it any other way.

So what could he do about it? He had to see her. He had to know if she'd run off with him. Sure she would. Then again maybe not. What would a gal like that want with a passel of trouble like him? He'd have to see her to find out. That meant showing up at Pete's place. Could he trust Pete? Not likely. The man looked the other way, but he didn't much care for him hanging around his little sister. Garrett might look for him there too.

What would Pat do now? He'd left him two dead deputies. That made for unfinished business. If he got away clean, old Pat just might let him get gone, like they talked about that night in Puerto de Luna. Christmas wasn't it? Not that long ago, though it sure seemed like it now. With two dead deputies, you had to figure he'd try to hunt him down. Well one thing was sure, if old Pat or any other law dog found him, he'd go out in gun blazing glory. He'd gotten close enough to a hangman's noose to smell the hemp. He wanted no part of that. That's it. That's what it came down to, a new life with Paulita or one last gunfight. Life or death, kind of how he'd lived it all along. That made the decision. Hide out for a spell. Let the smoke clear. Then go see if she'd have him.

Old Fort Sumner
May 2, 1881

A soft spring breeze ruffled her thick black hair. She brushed a wisp away from her eyes. She couldn't think where to go or what to do. The peach orchard brought him close somehow. The light scent of blossoms matched her mood. He'd escaped. Shot his way out of the Lincoln jail and escaped. Her heart filled with relief, like a heavy weight had been lifted from her breathing. She wandered among the trees. The new spring grass felt soft beneath her feet. She paused beside a tree they used to favor in those first stolen moments together. She recalled the whispered words the night they took him away. He said he planned to quit. He wanted to take her away. Would he now? Would he come for her? She felt a flutter. A familiar ache gone quiet in these long last months tugged her to the soft earth. She sat, leaned her back against the tree and tucked her knees up to her chin. Sunshine filtered through newly burst leaves dappled the grass around her.

He would come. She knew it and smiled. When? Soon. As soon as it was safe. Then what? They'd run away. Where? Anywhere it was safe. Mexico maybe. Would it ever be safe? It would. They'd find a place where no one knew Billy the Kid. That Billy would disappear into thin air. Sooner or later they'd think he was dead. They'd be safe then, safe to live like normal people, without shootings and posses and jails and such horrid things. She refused to consider the notion of hanging. She let her mind drift on the breeze, safe to marry and have a family. Did he mean that? Did running away mean that? Sure it did. Her Billy might be too shy to say such things, but that's what he meant. She could feel it. Women knew these things. He'd come for her soon.

Late-afternoon sun let a chill creep out of the mountains. Paulita headed home in the slanting light. Pete would be home soon, looking for some supper. What would he do when she left? She couldn't think about that. He'd have Deluvina when the time

369

came. She wondered how it would all play out. Would Billy come for her in the night? Would Pete wake up one morning to find she was gone? Or would they take their time? Make careful plans and slip away? The possibilities excited her. How could they not? A new life with her Billy, what more could a girl want?

She crunched up the front walk and climbed the porch step. She let herself into the dimly lit parlor and down the long hall to the kitchen. She started at the pantry, selecting canned peaches and beans while eyeing a cured ham for slicing. The front door slammed. Heavy footfalls in the hall told her Pete was home. He appeared in the kitchen.

"I s'pose you heard."

"About Billy? I did." She carried her selections to the kitchen counter.

"You think he'll come here?" Pete asked.

"He might," she said.

"He might at that."

She whirled. "That ain't nothin' to you, Pete."

He raised his hands in mock surrender. "I didn't say it was. All I'm sayin' is if he does, he ain't welcome to hide out here. He's a wanted fugitive. This family don't want no part of bein' accomplice to him."

"Speak for yourself, Pete. He ain't here. He ain't been here, but if he comes, when he comes, he'll be welcome to me."

He shook his head. "Didn't you learn anything over all this?"

"Learn what?"

"The law catches up. The man was tried for murder, convicted and sentenced to hang. Sure he escaped, but he killed two men doin' it. He's a murderer, Paulita. They'll get him again and when they do, he'll hang."

She clenched her fists at her hips in defiance. "Not if we get away first."

"So you figure to run off with him and that'll make it all right."

"I do, if he'll have me. Now get out of my kitchen if you figure on havin' supper."

He shook his head, drew his pipe from his pocket and headed out to the porch.

Lincoln
May 5, 1881
Garrett folded his copy of the *Santa Fe New Mexican* and set it beside his coffee cup. The editorial page offered brutal indictments of the Kid and a governor whose resignation afforded him the opportunity to "move on" to some notion of a publishing career. The paper roundly criticized the

leadership vacuum Wallace left behind, pending the arrival of his replacement. Santa Fe wasn't happy about the Kid's escape. They wanted to make an example of him. The paper gave voice to the frustration of the unseen powers behind territorial government. In the end, all they could do in the absence of the governor was offer a reward for capturing or killing Billy the Kid.

Garrett didn't see it happening. He'd led a posse on a wide swing east toward the panhandle and southwest toward Mexico and Arizona. They'd found no trace of the Kid. His gut said Billy slipped through somewhere on the trail to Mexico. If the Kid was still in the area, the reward would give good reason to turn him in. Still he doubted it. For all his misdeeds, Billy had friends, a lot of them. He understood it. He'd counted the Kid a friend once himself. Deep down it would have pained him to see the Kid hang. If Billy had petitioned the governor for clemency, he'd have given the request his support. It might have worked. Then again, it might not. It sure looked like the powers up north had it in for the Kid. Governor Wallace might have been an improvement over Axtel and all his connections to the Santa Fe Ring, but in the end they were all politicians, driven by the winds of power and money. For now, those winds were driven by the promise of statehood. Bringing a notorious desperado like Billy the Kid to justice made a fine example for the appearance of law and order. He was a symbol, a trophy they could trumpet in the papers to prove New Mexicans did the right thing.

This jailbreak and the bodies he left behind put him beyond the prospect of clemency. If they caught him again, he'd hang. He doubted they'd catch him. The Kid was too smart to get caught again. If by some fool chance they did manage to corner him, it would end in gunplay sure as sunset. He'd never let them put him back in a cage, let alone swing him at the end of a rope. He might as well sell the lumber. One way or another, the Kid would cheat the gallows.

THIRTY-FOUR

South Spring
May 8, 1881

Ty let out his loop and tossed. The bawling yearling thrashed in the muck, mired to her belly. The calf jerked. The loop sailed past the outstretched neck. He missed. Sweat glistened on Deacon Swain's shiny broad face across the muddy splatter. His dark features split in a white toothy grin. He let out his loop as Ty reeled his in. Deac's loop dropped clean. He dallied the horn as his buckskin backed the line taught.

"Haul 'er out, Deac!" Ty called. "You got me this time."

The sturdy buckskin took his cues and backed the heifer to solid purchase at the shallow edge of the mire. She hauled herself up the rest of the way. Deac slacked his rope. She shook it off, lifted her tail and trotted across the valley floor to rejoin the herd.

"Rider comin'," Ty said as he wheeled the steel dust west.

"Looks like Mister Johnny's back."

Ty nodded. "He rode into Roswell this mornin'."

The rider veered south toward them waving.

"Yup, it's him all right."

Minutes later Roth drew rein. "Ty, Deac, afternoon boys."

"Johnny, how was Roswell?"

"Plenty of excitement in town. The Kid escaped."

"What?"

"Yup, busted out of jail up in Lincoln last week. Shot J. W. Bell and Bob Olinger to boot."

"Well I'll be, they was supposed to hang him next week. Any idea where he went?" Ty pulled off his hat and wiped his brow on his sleeve.

"Not a trace so far. They're talkin' up the reward for him again, but that's about all."

"That'll likely get some folks' attention."

"If I was still huntin' bounty it'd get my attention. It might even be worth checkin' out some of his Mexican friends to see if any of them is hidin' him."

"I doubt he'd stick around here with a price on his head and a hangman's noose waitin'."

"I expect you're right. Guess I'll just stick to ranchin'."

"Com'on, Deac, let's head home. Supper's waitin'."

Ty soaked up the last bit of gravy with a piece of biscuit and popped it in his mouth. "That was mighty good, honey."

Lucy smiled. "There's fresh apple pie for dessert."

"You do know how to spoil a man."

"Why don't you go on out to the porch and enjoy this fine spring evening. I'll clear up here and bring you a piece."

"Best offer I had all day." He scraped back his chair, gathered up his plate and took it to the washstand. They built a simple house that fall after the war. It had a front room that doubled as a kitchen on one end and a parlor with a stove on the other with one bedroom off the back. That's as far as they got before winter set in. The porch and a comfortable swing came the following spring. They planned to add on as time went by.

Outside the spring evening felt soft and pleasantly warm. The swing gave off a comfortable creak as Ty took a seat. The gentle sway relaxed him and Lucy whenever they found time to enjoy it. Further up the hill to the north and west, window lights winked at Johnny and Dawn Sky's house. Beyond that he could make out the lights from Chisum's hacienda. The scene made a comfortable feeling of home. He'd come a long way from that white house with the picket fence in Cheyenne and all the painful memories that went with it. It seemed a lifetime ago. In some ways it was. Two lifetimes really.

The door squeaked open. "Guess that hinge could use a little oil."

"Oh, I don't know, the front door to a home kind of owes you a welcome." She handed him a plate with a fork and a piece of apple pie.

He took a forkful. It crunched juicy sweet apple, flaky crust and a hint of cinnamon. "I'm spoiled."

"You are."

They ate their pie in silence. When he finished, Lucy stacked his plate with hers and set them on the porch beside the swing. She snuggled up close. Ty wrapped an arm around her, at peace with the early spring night sounds. Stars splashed across the black velvet sky. The light caught the dark pools Lucy turned up to him.

"Ty, are you planning to go after the Kid?"

He shook his head. "There's no federal warrant for him now."

"Good." She snuggled closer.

"Why, if a man didn't know no better he might get the idea you liked havin' him around."

She slapped his chest playfully at the tease. "Don't let it go to your head. I just think it's important."

"Important? I just thought you liked it. Why is it important?"

"I think it's important for a father to be close to his son."

"What?"

"You heard me."

"Lucy?"

"Yes."

He kissed her.

Up the hill the lights winked out.

Looks like we'll be addin' on.

Stinking Springs
May 13, 1881

Billy rolled out of his blanket. He sat up and stretched. His stomach growled. He was out of supplies. He'd drunk the last of his coffee the previous night. He hadn't had any whiskey in a week. The frijoles and tortillas his Mexican friends had staked him to, had run out. You could scarcely get

378

enough meat off a jack rabbit to flavor a watery stew. He had to do something, but first he needed a courtesy call on nature.

He got up and cracked open the door, the frame still bullet scarred from the shoot-out last winter. He stepped into the early morning light and sucked in a deep breath of fresh air. It held a hint of cool with the promise of another warm day. He went around the side of the cabin and unbuttoned his trousers. The sun crept over the hilltops to the east, painting the sky pink and gold.

He took another breath as his water ran out. Fresh air, free air, he buttoned his fly. Today was the day. May 13, he'd kept track of the days on the cabin wall. Today was the day he was supposed to hang. He smiled his crooked smile. Damn he felt good. Only one thing could make him feel better. She often smelled like fresh coffee. His mouth watered. His watered part felt something too. He had to do something.

It had been more than two weeks. Time enough for the smoke to clear. Time enough for Garrett to search Fort Sumner if he was of a mind to. It was time to go see if Paulita would have him. He'd rustle up some grub on the ride in. Then, tonight . . . He smiled again.

The Barlow kid came in handy. He could count on him to keep his mouth shut. He had a room with the Mexicans who lived in the old barracks up around the peach orchard. Barlow would put him up, take care of the bay and get him what he might need by way of whiskey and food. The Mexicans wouldn't say anything, either.

He let the evening wear on toward ten. Late enough old Pete should be running his sawmill. He slipped out the back of the barracks and made his way through the peach orchard to Roswell Road on the west end of the fort. It ran past the Maxwell place. It also gave him the least chance of being spotted. He walked down the road, thankful for a cloud cover that muted the moon.

The Maxwell house was dark. He crossed the yard toward the porch. He could hear Pete's snore coming from the front bedroom. He smiled. He slipped around the side of the house to her window. Hell of a lot nicer this time of year compared to them frosty winter nights. He tapped on the pane and waited. Nothing. He tapped again.

A ghost-like white shadow moved in the darkness. Dark eyes went wide with delight. A bright smile appeared. She pointed to the back door. He nodded and hurried around back. He could feel his heart thump. Excitement tightened his chest. Breath stuck in his throat. He'd missed her. The promise he'd have her told him how much.

She eased the door open. He stepped inside. She melted into his arms. He found her lips. They forged a kiss fueled in liquid fire. Time stood still. He ran his hand along the sleek curve of her back parted from his touch by a thin veil of nightdress.

"Oh, Billy, when I heard you escaped I wondered if you'd come."

"Wild horses couldn't keep me away, girl." He kissed her again.

"Not here," she said. "Come." She took him by the hand and led him through the darkened kitchen to her room. The door closed with a soft click. She buried her head in his chest.

"I was so scared after you left that night. Then there was that awful business about the trial. The papers said they was gonna hang you."

He lifted her chin. Tears glittered on her checks. "We're gonna make all that right between us this time. You'll see."

She smiled up at him. "Good. Let's talk about that later." Her fingers found his buttons.

■ ■ ■ ■

"He's back, ain't he?" A clearly annoyed Pete leveled the accusation. Early morning light filled the kitchen as Paulita poured his coffee. "I ain't seen you with a spring in your step since the last time he was here. Tell me the truth, Paulita."

"What business is it of yours?"

"It's my house and you're my sister."

"You may own the house, but you don't own me."

He ground his teeth in frustration. "Look, Paulita, can't you see what you're doing? The man is a condemned murderer. If the law gets hold of him, he'll be dead. You could get caught in the middle of a shoot-out and die yourself. What are you thinking, girl?"

"I love him. Nothing you can say is about to change that. Now leave us be. We'll figure it out."

"You'll figure it out. Go figure where you'll be when he's swingin' from the end of a rope."

Thirty-Five

June 10, 1881
A gentle evening breeze blew through the open window. Moonlight played the tender curves of her tawny body sprawled against his pale side. Her hair spilled across his chest, a tangled curtain drawn across her face.

"Paulita, are you awake?"

She purred somewhere in the back of her throat.

"I, I come back to ask you somethin'."

She lifted her chin and brushed the hair from her eyes.

"I been thinkin'. It's time to go away."

She pulled a pout. Tears welled in her eyes.

"No, no, not like that." He wrapped his arm around her and stroked the silken planes of her back. "I mean for us to go away. Start a new life, an honest life somewhere. Somewhere where they don't know Billy the Kid. Somewhere safe, where guns are for huntin'."

She lay her head on his chest and let loose a flood of hot tears.

He lifted her chin. "That's nothin' to cry about. Paulita, I'm tryin' to tell you, I love you. I'm tryin' to ask if you'll run off and marry me. I'm askin' if you'll have me and make us a new life."

A bright white smile parted crystal tears. "Yes, Billy, oh yes."

He kissed the tears from her cheeks.

He buttoned his shirt in the gray light just before dawn. She lay in the rumpled sheets, misty eyes following his every move.

"We'll need some things. A wagon, a couple of mules. You think Pete might help us?"

She bit her lip pretty sure she knew the answer to that. Then again, maybe, just maybe . . . "He might. You know he don't approve."

"I know. So you don't think he'll help?"

She thought a bit. "Maybe, if I tell him I'm in a family way."

"You are?" He sat down on the bed and took her hand.

She shook her head. "No, I'll just tell him that. It's worth a try."

"See what you can do. I got a little stake

hid away from my bad days. It ain't much, but it'll give us a start."

"You talk like the bad days are over."

He kissed her fingers. "After the war, all I ever wanted was a pardon like everybody else. Pat says I got crosswise with the politics somehow."

"Pat?"

"Sheriff Garrett. Maybe he's right, I don't know. All I know is that there's no pardon for Billy Bonney. If Pat's right about the politics, I don't know what I done. If I don't know how I done it, I sure as hell don't know how to undone it. It's time to move on. Someplace nobody knows us. Someplace we can start over fresh." He stood.

She slid off the bed and kissed him. "I'll see what I can do about Pete."

June 20, 1881

Pete pushed back from the supper table. "That was mighty good, Paulita. Roast chicken and it ain't even Sunday."

She lowered her eyes as she struck a match to light a lamp against purple dusk. She added coffee to Pete's cup and poured some for herself. She sat back down at the table and folded her hands in her lap.

"All right, what is it?"

She looked up. "Don't be mad."

He didn't like the sound of this. "Don't be mad at what?"

"We're gonna get married."

"You're gonna what?"

"You heard me. We're gonna get married and move away, someplace we can start over fresh."

"You don't need to start over fresh, Paulita. Billy might like to, but he's a condemned murderer."

"Don't say that no more! He's gonna be my husband."

"Why, Paulita? Don't you see what a terrible mistake that would be?"

"Why? We love each other. Can't you see that after all this time?"

"But there are so many other good, decent men you could love and marry."

"None of them that's the father of my child."

Pete sat back. He shook his head and rubbed his face in his hands, helpless. "I see. Guess I'm not surprised. I should have seen this comin'. Maybe I did and just didn't want to believe it."

"We need your help, Pete. We need a wagon and a mule team."

"You think they're gonna just let you ride off into the sunset never to be heard from again? You'll both be lookin' over your shoulder every day for the rest of your lives, wondering. Is today the day they come for us?"

"We won't have to look back if nobody knows where we went or who we become."

He shook his head. "There are powerful people who want Billy to hang for his crimes."

"Billy explained that to me, about the pardon and all. It's time to give it up. It's time to move on. That's what we're gonna do, Pete. Will you help?"

"You're about to make the biggest mistake of your life and you want me to help."

"Not just for me, Pete. Do it for the baby."

Deluvina chided herself for listening. She couldn't help it. She cared for the girl. She cared for the outlaw boy. Maybe they should have their chance. Her visions had been right. He'd escaped hanging. He'd come back. Now he meant to take her away. She was determined plain enough. Pete couldn't see it. She knew.

She heard Pete scrape back his chair. His footsteps died away down the hall. She stepped into the kitchen as the girl began to clear the dishes away. Paulita paused and met her eyes.

"You heard?"

She nodded.

"Then you know."

She arched a brow at the girl. "Deluvina knows."

Paulita's cheeks darkened.

"Deluvina knows you do not have a baby."

She pulled a scowl. She balled her fists on her hips. "How? How do you know?"

Her black eyes twinkled. She shrugged. "These things women know."

"You're not going to tell Pete are you?"

"Come, muchacha, let us wash these dishes."

Lincoln
July 10, 1881
Lunchtime, Garrett pushed back from his desk. He adjusted the Colt on his hip and left the office by the side door. Summer gripped the town like standing too close to a smithy's forge. Hot wind blew sage balls and a passing dust devil. Heat waves shimmered past the Torreon Tower where Lincoln's only street made a gentle bend west. A dark rider resolved out of the haze, jogging purposefully toward him. Garrett paused, waiting to cross the street.

He recognized John Poe. What would bring him down from White Oaks? He'd taken the sheriff's job up there after they gunned down Jim Carlyle. Poe eased his mount over to the courthouse and stepped down.

"Afternoon, John."

"Pat."

"What brings you to Lincoln?"

"Maybe the Kid, I'll leave it to you to decide."

"I was just headed over to the Wortley for some lunch. Come along, we can talk there."

The Wortley dining room was quiet at midday with only a light local crowd. Garrett took his usual table in the corner by the window where he could keep an eye on the street. Poe slid into a chair across from him. Both ordered the ham and bean special.

"So what's this about the Kid?"

"A few days ago a man I know by casual acquaintance came to see me. He claims to have overheard two men talking in a stable where he was sleeping. They mentioned the Kid. The man took what they said to mean the Kid is hiding out around Old Fort Sumner."

"Do you believe him?"

"No reason not to. Is the information accurate? That's the question. I have a hard time believing the Kid would be fool enough to stay in the area, facing a death sentence with a bounty on his head."

"I agree. I swear he lit out for Mexico."

"That's why I thought I'd leave it for you to decide."

The plates came. They occupied their thoughts with slabs of hot ham and beans, soaking up the juices with fresh baked bread. "For all the dubious quality of the information, I don't think we can ignore it," Garrett said after a time. "Most any other place in the county I'd be real doubtful, but he does have a history of favorin' Old Sumner."

"That's why I rode down here to let you decide. So what do we do?"

"I'll wire Kip McKinney up from Roswell. Then head on up to Fort Sumner and have a look around. I got a bunk for you in the jail. We can head out when Kip gets here."

Arroyo Taiban
July 13, 1881
McKinney agreed to accompany Garrett and Poe, though he too doubted the likelihood of the Kid having stayed in the country. They rode west out of Lincoln to disguise their purpose before turning north to Fort Sumner. They rode as far as the sand hills four miles south of the fort where they made camp around midnight. They awoke

with the sun the morning of the fourteenth and made their plan over coffee.

"John, you're not well known in town," Garrett said. "Ride in and have a look around. See what you can find out. Kip and I will wait here out of sight. If you find out anything, meet us in the peach orchard northwest of town after dark. Do you know it?"

"I do."

"If nothing turns up in town, ride out to Milnor Rudulph's place. Milnor is an old friend. If the Kid is in the area, he may know somethin'. Either way, he'll put us up for the night. If you don't meet us in the peach orchard, we'll meet you there later. I'll give you a letter to introduce you to him."

Poe tossed the dregs of his coffee and stood. "I'll saddle up and be on my way."

"Don't make it too obvious askin' about the Kid in town. He's got a lot of friends there. If he gets a sniff of us lookin' for him he'll get gone in a hurry."

"What about Rudulph?"

"I don't make Milnor any special friend of the Kid's. I'll write you a note while you saddle your horse."

Ten minutes later Poe wheeled away and rode into town.

THIRTY-SIX

Fort Sumner
July 14, 1881

Poe reached the old fort at midmorning. The settlement was populated by Mexicans, Indians and a few hard-bitten white men. Most were sympathetic to the Kid. All of them were suspicious of strangers. He drew rein at the rail in front of Beaver Smith's saloon. It was early in the day for such things but a lubricated tongue might be his best source of information. He noticed the young man lounging in the shadow of the porch almost immediately. He came up out of the barrel-backed chair he had tipped back against the saloon wall. For a moment in the muted light of the porch Poe thought it might be the Kid. He carried a similar slope-shouldered frame. Poe stepped onto the boardwalk.

"Howdy, stranger." The young man eyed him with interest.

"Howdy," Poe said. "You know where a fella might find a good meal hereabouts?"

"Bob Hargrove's over yonder on Stinking Springs Road."

He had a boyish look about him, something like the Kid in that way too, except for a darker skin and rough shave that had some whisker to it. "Much obliged."

"What brings you to Fort Sumner?"

Two men of surly disposition eased their way out of the batwings onto the porch. They cocked their ears to the young man's question.

"I'm a cattle buyer out of White Oaks, passin' through on my way to the panhandle." That seemed to satisfy them. "Guess I'll chase some trail dust out a my throat before I get somethin' to eat. Care to join me?" The prospect of whiskey sealed a guarded acceptance.

The young man extended his hand. "Billy Barlow."

"John Temple." Even the name almost fit. Barlow led the way inside. Poe signaled the bartender. "What'll it be?" Barlow and his friends ordered whiskey. Poe ordered a beer.

Two rounds later, he finished his beer and bid his farewells. The subject of the Kid never came up, though a wary air of suspicion lingered over his sudden arrival. He felt a hostile tension like these men were waiting for unknown events to unfold. He still had doubts about the accuracy of his informant's information. It could be these men were just naturally suspicious. Then again, maybe they had something to hide.

Poe took his time wandering over to Hargrove's. He stopped into the general store to pick up a few things, exchanging pleasantries with the shopkeeper and a customer or two. He checked out the stock at the old corral, but saw no sign of Garrett's bay. Lunch at Hargrove's uncovered nothing more than another helping of suspicion brought on by being a stranger. He collected his horse after lunch and rode east out of town before turning north seven miles to the Rudulph place.

Rudulph Ranch
Sunnyside

Old Rudulph had a rugged angular frame hardened by work. He seemed every bit as wary of Poe as the townsfolk had been until he read Garrett's letter. After that he made Poe welcome and invited him to supper, though he remained noticeably uneasy.

"So you say Pat'll be along tonight?" he said around a mouthful of mutton.

"He will, unless I ride in to meet him."

"What brings you boys all the way up here?"

"I'm sure you've heard Billy the Kid escaped jail down in Lincoln."

Something clouded the old man's eye. "I did hear somethin' about that. Few weeks back wasn't it?"

"End of April it was. Hasn't been no sign of him since. We got a report he might be hidin' out in or about Fort Sumner."

The old man blinked nervously. "You hear rumors like that. I find it hard to believe."

"Sheriff Garrett thought you might have heard somethin' more than rumor, Mr. Rudulph. That's why he sent me up here. We'd be much obliged for anything you can tell us."

"Pshaw, don't believe none of it. He ain't stupid. A man like that with a price on his head and a death sentence waitin'. Who'd be fool enough to stay around parts he was well known?"

The old man lifted his fork. His hand trembled. Poe guessed he knew more than he was letting on. He was plainly afraid. That usually meant a man had something to be afraid of. That tended to confirm the information they had. It was as close to the truth as they were likely to get unless they encountered the Kid. He folded his napkin and pushed away from the table.

"Mr. Rudulph, I thank you for your hospitality."

"Does that mean you'll not be stayin' the night?"

"No, sir. I believe I best go back to town and meet Sheriff Garrett there." The old man's shoulders sagged. You could see the tension drain out of him. He was afraid all right. There had to be a reason.

Fort Sumner

"The wagon needs a little work, but the mules are as fine a pair as I've seen in years. You have much experience with mules, Billy?"

He shook his head across his coffee cup as they sat at the supper table. Pete's attitude softened some once he agreed to help. He still didn't approve of what his sister was about to do, but plain enough he wasn't going to change her mind either.

Paulita began clearing away the supper dishes, leaving the men to their talk.

"Mules ain't really stubborn the way you hear. A good one is as willing as any horse. Some can be opinionated over things a man asks them to do, but if you treat 'em right they'll come round to your way of thinkin'."

"I'll keep that in mind. When will the

396

wagon be ready?"

"A couple of days I reckon. You figured out where you're headed yet?"

"I got a notion."

He cocked an eyebrow for more.

"Best nobody knows for everybody's sake, including yours, Pete. Me and Paulita appreciate your help. We do. We'll let you know when we're settled, but that's all I can promise."

"Probably best we get you on your way then."

"The longer we stay around, the more likely somebody finds out I'm here. You and I both know there's folks hereabouts who know I'm here."

"You got a lot of friends in these parts, Billy."

"Yeah, and likely an enemy or two, it only takes one of them."

Pete nodded. "I'll get the wagon fixed up quick as I can." He scraped back his chair, yawned and stretched. "It's been a long day. Reckon I'll turn in."

Paulita kissed him on the cheek. "Good night, Pete. And thanks."

He held her eyes for a time. He shook his head, favored her with a concerned smile and ambled down the dark hall to his room. He found Deluvina beside the door.

"You mean to help them?" she whispered.

He shrugged and nodded. "What more can I do?"

"Deluvina is afraid for her."

"I am too."

"Then why do you help them?"

"She's already in a family way."

The girl shook her head.

Punta de la Glorieta

Poe circled west of the old fort as he rode south. Night fell under a rumpled blanket of low running cloud. Little light found its way through breaks in the clouds. Four miles north of the old fort he came to the end of a ridgeline. He brought his horse down to a walk. A bright moonlit break in the clouds revealed two riders headed his way. A moment later they disappeared again under the cover of darkness. He drew rein and waited, uneasy, his hand rested on the gun butt holstered at his hip. Two shadows resolved out of the darkness. Garrett and McKinney he thought more in hope than recognition. He waited.

"Easy, John, it's us."

Tension drained away in the quiet greeting.

Garrett and McKinney drew rein. The three men stepped down.

"Did you learn anything?" Garrett asked.

"Nothin' you could hang your hat on, but my gut tells me he's somewhere hereabout. Folks in town are on edge. Your friend Rudulph didn't want to talk about the Kid. He was nervous as a cat the whole time I was there. When I asked about the Kid he acted afraid plain enough. A man's not frightened like that unless there's somethin' to be frightened of. That's why I came in."

Garrett scratched his chin. "Hereabout could be anywhere. If I was to bet though, I'd bet he'd come sniffin' around Pete Maxwell's sister. The Kid had it bad for her at least at one time. We can keep an eye on Pete's place from the peach orchard without much chance of bein' seen." He glanced up at a break in the clouds. His eyes followed a splash of moonlight to a dark grove of trees. "It looks like those clouds are clearin' out. It'll be bright as broad day before you know it. Let's ride on in. We can hide our horses in the trees and keep an eye on things. Mount up."

Thirty-Seven

July 14, 1881
9:00 p.m.

They rode into the orchard from the north, keeping the shadows between the settlement and the moonlit hills behind them. They tethered their horses in the trees and loosened their cinches. Here and there splashes of moonlight filtered through the trees, rendering the grove an eerie maze of light and shadow. They moved, keeping as much to the shadows as possible. Ahead, flickers of lamplight pricked the ragged silhouettes assembled in the orderly ranks of the old military settlement. They took positions in the shadows where they could plainly see Pete Maxwell's place by the light of the moon. Time passed. Now and then someone came or left Beaver Smith's place down the block. Mexican voices drifted on the night air, coming from the old barracks east of the orchard. Nothing moved near the Maxwell place. Two hours later, Garrett grew restless.

"He ain't comin'. I was afraid this was a wild-goose chase. Let's slip on out of here. If no one knows we're on the hunt for him, maybe somethin' will turn up later."

Poe's earlier doubts had turned into gut conviction. The Kid was somewhere nearby. He could feel it. "Pat, I'm tellin' you, somethin's goin' on here. You know Pete Maxwell. If the Kid is seein' his sister, he's as likely as anyone to know where he is. I think we should at least go down there and have a word with him."

"Hell it's the middle of the night, John."

"It's Billy the Kid, Pat."

"All right, let's have a look." He led them through the trees, past the old barracks east of the orchard. Garrett led the way south on Roswell Road to the Maxwell place. The former officer's barracks stood close to the road behind a small fenced yard. A pillared porch wrapped around the front and side. The house was dark, the porch in deep shadow. The front door stood open, a concession to the evening heat. Garrett paused at the gate.

"You boys stay here," he said in a low voice. He let himself in and crossed to the porch. He disappeared in the dark passageway.

McKinney moved off down the fence toward the side of the house. Poe drifted a short way past the gate under cover of the porch.

It was hot. Barlow couldn't sleep. He left the stuffy room he shared with the Mexican and sat on the porch, his back propped against the still warm adobe. The wind blew hot and dry, moonlight washed sand and scrub a frosty white.

Que pasa? Something moved in the trees at the edge of the orchard. He came suddenly alert. The tall stranger he'd seen earlier in the day curiously jumped to mind. Cattle buyer he said. He caught a glimpse. Three men, little more than dark shadows, emerged from the orchard. He didn't recognize any of them in the distant mottle of moonlight and shadow. They crossed Stinking Springs Road and disappeared down Roswell. Could be headed for Beaver Smith's. Late to start drinking. What the hell were they doing in the orchard? They weren't talking. He'd have heard them. He didn't have a good angle to see where they went. Billy was with Paulita sure as anything. He didn't like the smell of this. It might be nothing. Then again, it might be trouble.

He slipped back inside the small room, the air thick and hot in his throat. He stepped over a snoring Mexican and found his gun belt. He pulled the long-barrel .44 from the holster and jammed it in his waistband. He didn't bother with his boots. He bumped the slumbering Mexican as he picked his way to the door, his snoring barely interrupted by a grunt. He crossed the street, turned west to Roswell and started down the road toward the Maxwell place. The street appeared deserted. He shook his head. Nothing. The men were likely down at Smith's having a drink. He thought about giving it up. Shit he was wide awake now. Maybe he'd throw down a drink at Beaver's to put him mindful of sleep.

Wait a minute. Something, someone moved in the shadows in front of Pete's house. That didn't make sense at this hour. One of his men come in from the ranch? Maybe, or was it one of the men he'd seen? A feeling of alarm crawled up the back of his throat. He grabbed the butt of his gun and picked up his pace.

Garrett stepped into the dark passage. Off to his left, heavy snoring came from what must be a front bedroom. He stepped into a room partially illuminated by moonlight streaming through a single window. The open window provided little relief from the heat. He moved into a dark corner beside the bed and shook the mattress gently.

"Pete, is that you?"

Poe saw a man coming down the street. *Who's out at this time of night?* He had his hand at his waist as though buttoning his pants. No boots either, likely someone out to answer nature's call. The man headed for Maxwell's like he belonged there. It could be Maxwell or a guest of his. Kind of slope-shouldered though. Poe shrugged it off. The man started up the porch. He paused to glance at Poe in the shadow of a porch post. Suddenly he turned, a gun leveled.

"Quien es?" *Who is it?* He backed toward the door.

Poe stepped away from the post into the moonlight and showed his hands. "It's me, John Poe. No trouble, I mean you no harm."

The man backed through the doorway and disappeared. A moment later his head re-appeared.

"Quien es?" He disappeared again without waiting for an answer.

■ ■ ■ ■

It was dark inside. Barlow looked around allowing his eyes to adjust to the lack of light. He felt more than saw a large room on his right, likely the parlor. A dark passage disappeared ahead. To the left, pale light, spilling through the open door behind him painted another doorway. He heard hushed voices as he approached.

"Pete, who are those men outside?" he hissed.

Garrett stood beside the bed. Someone or something moved in the hall.

"Pete, who's this?" he whispered as he eased the .41 self-cocker out of his holster. A slope-shouldered silhouette appeared in the doorway.

"Quien es?"

"It's him," Maxwell said.

Garrett's gun exploded in a blinding flash. The concussion thundered off the walls in the tiny room. The force of the blast buffeted his ears. The intruder stumbled. Blinded by the muzzle flash, Garrett dove to the floor and fired again. The intruder groaned in the darkness. Something heavy thumped a dull slap against the earthen floor.

Maxwell jumped from his bed and bolted for the door. Garrett scrambled to his feet behind him.

Poe drew his gun and started for the door at the sound of the first shot. The second shot filled the doorway in white light, illuminating the crouched shooter. Poe flattened himself to the door frame, unsure who the shooter might be. The acrid smell of gun smoke drifted out of the ringing silence. Somewhere in the dark passage, someone gasped, a telltale gurgle sounded death's rattle.

Poe risked a look around the door frame. A body lay in a pool of moonlight, gunmetal glint beside it. Suddenly a dark figure burst from the bedroom running toward him. He ducked out of the doorway. A second man followed the first. Poe leveled his gun. Garrett brushed it aside.

"Don't shoot, Maxwell. That was the Kid, come in there on me. I believe I got him."

"Are you sure?"

"I heard him fall."

"No. Are you sure it's him?"

"Sure it's him. I know his voice too well to be mistaken."

"Pat." Maxwell gasped. He shook his head, confused. He never finished the thought.

The first shot jerked Paulita back from the gauzy veils of sleep that enfolded her in the echoes of pleasure. Billy sat up straight, his eyes wide white in moonlight. He stifled her scream at the second shot and covered her with his body. The shooting fell silent. She heard muffled movement in the hall. Fear flooded her as she made sense out of their peril. She wriggled out from under Billy and hopped out of bed. She circled the foot of the bed, a copper sprite bathed in pale light. She gathered Billy's clothes. He climbed out of bed and drew his gun. She shoved his clothes at him.

"Get dressed and get under the bed," she whispered. "I'll see what's going on." She fumbled for her nightdress and drew it on.

The shooting drew a crowd. Late-night drinkers and gamblers stumbled out of Beaver Smith's down the street. Others rousted from their beds piled out of the barracks along Stinking Springs Road. Many were friends of the Kid. Someone recognized Garrett. Another jumped to the conclusion they'd cornered the Kid. Word spread. They'd shot Billy the Kid.

Garrett read the mood of the crowd. "John, you and Kip keep watch while me and Pete clean this up."

Maxwell led the way back inside. Moments later he appeared in the passageway holding a single candle. Poe made out a body sprawled on its back, a gun in the right hand. A butcher knife lay at his side. Garrett kicked the door shut. Poe turned back to the crowd.

"Pete, what's going on?" Paulita whispered through a crack in her bedroom door.

"Get back inside, Paulita. Let me handle this."

The candlelight fell on the fallen man's death mask. Garrett stood at his feet. Realization dawned. "It ain't him, Pete." His voice barely rose above a whisper. "This ain't the Kid. You said it was him. Who is it?"

"Name's Billy Barlow, he's a friend of the Kid."

"What's he doin' here?"

Pete shrugged.

"It was dark. I thought sure it was him."

"I thought so too. He kind of looks like the Kid, the way he's built and all. He had a gun."

"No excuse for killin' the wrong man, Pete. What have I done?"

Maxwell's mind raced over the circumstances, begging an anwer to Garrett's question. The notion dawned. "He could be the Kid."

Garrett stared at the body in disbelief. "I killed the wrong man, Pete. What are you sayin'?"

"Nobody knows who that is except you and me."

"You're sayin' we bury this Barlow boy and say it's the Kid?"

"That's what I'm sayin'. Look, Pat, you and I both know Billy got a raw deal after the war. All he ever wanted was the pardon all the rest of 'em got."

"He's said as much to me more than once. But why would you stick up for him?"

"Billy and my sister Paulita are in love."

"I heard that. I also heard you say you was against it."

"I am against it. Maybe this way I can do something about it. If Billy was dead, he'd get away clean. Nobody looks for a dead man. You'd be famous. You wouldn't have to explain how you killed an innocent man. Probably you could use that reward too."

Get away clean, his mind drifted on the thought, smoothing his mustache in the web of his thumb and forefinger. "He might get away at that. I don't know, Pete. We'll need a coroner's report, probably an inquest too."

"Leave that part to me. First thing we've got a do is get the body out of here. The fewer people see it the better. Who you got outside?"

"John Poe and Kip McKinney."

"Either of 'em know the Kid?"

"Yeah. They was both with me when we captured him."

"I'll get someone who can help us."

Garrett furrowed his brows as though still undecided.

"Look, Pat, that crowd out there already thinks you shot the Kid. The story's half told. Tellin' the other half'll be way easier than explainin' how you shot the wrong man. Now give me a few minutes and I'll be out to get you."

Garrett stepped outside. Pete closed the door. Poe and McKinney had stationed themselves in the yard blocking the gate against the gathering crowd. Most folks in Fort Sumner considered the Kid a friend. As word of his shooting spread, the mood of the crowd turned hostile.

"What's goin' on in there?" McKinney asked.

"Pete's got some womenfolk to calm down

while we figure out what to do with the body."

"You got him? You shot the Kid?"

Garrett cocked an eye to the moon, coming to his conclusion. "Yeah, I did."

Someone nearby overheard him. Word spread through the crowd like wildfire. At that some started to drift away while others murmured among themselves.

THIRTY-EIGHT

Pete knocked on Paulita's door. "You can come out now, but be quick and be quiet."

Billy came out followed by Paulita. "What the hell happened?"

"Garrett's here. He came lookin' for you. Barlow showed up. That's him there." He jerked his head down the hall toward the body.

Paulita covered her mouth with a hand. Billy shook his head. "Likely come to warn me."

"That's the way I figure it. Garrett mistook him for you and shot him."

"Damn."

"Stroke of luck as I see it," Pete said.

"Luck?"

"Sure. I can fix it so everyone thinks it's you. You can disappear. Nobody will follow a dead man."

"Pat will never go along with it."

"Sure he will. He killed an innocent man.

If it's you that's dead, he's a hero. Now com'on let's get you out of here."

A tear welled in Paulita's eye. "What about me?"

"You need to stay here and grieve over your loss," Pete said.

Billy took her in his arms. "I'll come back for you as soon as things settle down."

"That's it," Pete said. "Let's go. We got work to do."

She held him stubbornly. "Promise, Billy?"

"I promise."

"Get back in your room, Paulita, and have a good cry. Come on, Kid, let's get you out of here."

Billy stepped past Pete to have a look at the body. "Poor bastard, all he ever wanted was to be like me. Looks like he got his wish, just in time to give me mine." He bent down and picked up the long Colt. "Ain't my style, but maybe I can put it to some use for him." He kissed Paulita. "I'll be back."

She stepped into her room and closed the door.

"Hurry," Pete said. He led the way down the hall to the kitchen. Billy followed. At the back of the kitchen he pointed to a hallway. "That leads to the armory. Where's your horse?"

"Stabled at Paco's."

"There's a crowd gathering out front. The commotion should keep people busy for a time. Slip out the back, get your horse and get lost."

Billy cocked his chin. "Why you doin' this for me, Pete?"

"Because you're gonna ride out of here and never come back."

"What about Paulita? I promised her."

"You heard me, Kid. You're never comin' back."

"But I love her. What about the baby?"

"There ain't no baby. Deluvina told me." He locked the Kid's eyes. "It's over, Billy. You're dead, you live. She's free. That's the deal. You ever show your face near her again, I'll have every lawman in the territory trackin' you until they do kill you."

The Kid knew dead serious when he saw it. He disappeared down the darkened passage.

Pete waited until the footsteps died away. He turned on his heel and hurried back to the front of the house. He stepped over the body to the front door. Out on the porch he spotted a man he could trust. Manuel Abreau was not only a friend of the Kid, he spoke only Spanish.

"Manuel." He motioned for him to come

in. Poe glanced over his shoulder.

"Let him in," Garrett said. "We need his help."

Abreau climbed the porch. Pete spoke in Spanish.

"We need you to help move the Kid's body. Remember it's the Kid's body." He fixed the man's eyes.

Abreau nodded without understanding.

"All right, Sheriff, let's get on with it."

Pete led the way inside. Manuel cut his eyes from Garrett to the body. He understood.

Poe glanced over his shoulder at the body beyond the open door. Something struck him as odd. He couldn't put his finger on it for a moment. Then it hit him. *The gun, what happened to the gun?*

Maxwell kicked the door closed. "We can put him in the carpenter's shop while I figure out the coroner parts." He stepped over the body toward the hallway, holding the candle. Pale light spilled over the swarthy face with a rough shave, contorted in death to a gap-tooth grin.

"Follow me," Maxwell said.

Garrett picked the body up by the shoulders. Abreau grabbed the boots. They carried the body down the dark passageway following the candle glow.

415

They reached the kitchen and turned down another hall to a room at the back of the old officer's quarters. Maxwell opened the door and set the candle on a table. The room smelled of sawdust. He cleared a hammer and chisel away from the top of a workbench against the far wall.

"Put him there till we can figure out what to do about buryin' him."

They hoisted the body up on the bench. Abreau and Garrett stepped away. The wound still oozed blood, leaving a trail across the carpenter shop floor to the bench. Maxwell closed the eyes and turned the face to face the wall. He picked up the candle and led the way back to the hall. He handed the candle to Garrett and locked the door. *Habit,* Garrett thought. *This one ain't goin' nowhere.*

Pete led the way back to the front of the house. He showed Abreau to the door. "Remember, amigo, on your sainted mother's head, Billy the Kid is dead. Tell no one anything more."

Manuel nodded and left.

Garrett paced the parlor still uncomfortable with what they were doing. "All right, Pete, what do we do about a coroner's report?"

Maxwell stroked his mustache. "We'll appoint a jury to hold an inquest."

"We'll appoint them? Ain't that somewhat unusual?"

"We'll appoint 'em and have Alejandro Segura sign off. He's justice of the peace. That'll make it official."

"When do we get him?"

"That can wait until we're done."

"You sure he'll sign off after it's all over?"

"Couldn't be helped. We had to move fast on account of that angry mob out there. Yeah, that's it."

"What do we do about an inquest?"

"I'll send for Milnor Rudulph in the mornin'. He's postmaster up here. He can foreman the inquest. He's a respected civic official. That should look all right."

"What do we do about jurors?"

"Leave that to me. All we have to do is get Milnor to sign off on the verdict."

"How are you fixin' to do that?"

"We'll show him the body. You tell him it's the Kid. Then we'll show him the coroner's report."

"What coroner's report?"

"The one I'm fixin' to write soon as we're done jawin' here. Then I'll have him sign the verdict. It'll match the coroner's report and already have the signatures of a couple of jurors."

"How you gonna manage that?"

Pete smiled.

"Won't he think that's odd?"

"Maybe. We'll just tell him things is movin' fast on account of the crowd and the popularity of the deceased. Might scare him some. Fright makes for easy persuasion."

"You got it all figured out ain't you, Pete?"

"You'll see."

July 15, 1881

Morning sun slanted through the kitchen window. A fresh pot of Arbuckle's bubbled on the stove. Pete hunched over the table scratching out his coroner's report. Garrett poured two cups of coffee. He carried them out to the parlor and handed one to Poe.

"Much obliged, Pat." He blew on the cup and took a sip.

Garrett took the second cup to McKinney out on the porch. The crowd had thinned, though a goodly number remained. He handed McKinney the cup.

"Everything all right, Kip?"

"Quiet now."

"Good. Keep an eye on things." He went back inside.

Poe looked up. "What did you do with the body?"

"Locked it in the carpenter's shop."

Locked? Poe knit his brow. "You gonna put it on display?"

The question stopped Garrett for an instant. That was the way things were done with high profile cases. Most often photographs were taken to prove reward claims. "No, I don't figure we best do that. Not with that mob out there."

Poe shook his head as the sheriff returned to the kitchen.

Pete set down his pencil. He handed the coroner's report to Garrett.

William Bonney, also called Billy the Kid, was killed by a gunshot wound to the left breast, fired by Sheriff Patrick F. Garrett.

It was signed Pete Maxwell in the absence of a coroner. "Sign it on the witness line, Pat."

Garrett smoothed his mustache. "You think that'll stand up, Pete? I mean me witnessing a report of my own actions."

"It'll have to. We ain't got no other witness."

"What about one of my deputies?"

"Let me try again. We ain't got no other witnesses who won't ask no questions."

Garrett bent over the table and scratched

his signature. "What are we gonna do about a coroner's inquest?"

"I sent for Milnor Rudulph early this morning. I told him Justice of the Peace Segura wanted him. He'll act as foreman. I'll write a verdict to match the findings of the coroner's report. All he'll have to do is sign it."

"What about jurors?"

"Give me a minute." He poured another cup of coffee and went back to writing with a fresh sheet of paper. Maxwell printed a list of names, Jose Silva, Antonio Savedra, Pedro Antonio Lucero, Lorenzo Jaramillo and Sabal Gutierres. "There." He put down the pencil. "Justice Segura can send for them soon as we get done with Milnor. I'll get their signatures later."

"I thought you were going to wait on Justice Segura until we was done."

"He decided it'd be easier to get the others on his say-so."

"When did he come by?"

"Early this morning."

"It is early this morning."

Pete smiled. "You just missed him."

Garrett shook his head. "While you're writin', add something about me getting the reward." Maxwell went back to writing. Garrett watched over his shoulder. Moments later, Pete handed him the coroner's inquest verdict.

William Bonney was killed by a gunshot wound to the left breast, fired by Sheriff Patrick F. Garrett. We the jury find Sheriff Garrett acted in the performance of his official duties and in self-defense in the face of an armed adversary. We are unanimous in the belief that the gratitude of the whole territory is due Sheriff Garrett as is the reward for the death of this dangerous desperado.

Garrett handed it back. "Good." He scratched his chin. "You really think this'll work Pete?"

"Who's gonna complain? You? The Kid? New Mexico is rid of a notorious killer, case closed."

Poe squinted into a blazing midday sun. Overhead bright blue sky faded to pale light. He watched a buckboard rumble past the peach orchard, making its way south on Roswell Road. A sturdy black horse jogged in the traces. Milnor Rudulph drew rein at Maxwell's gate. He stepped down. Poe remembered the angular frame awkward as a scarecrow. He glanced nervously at the crowd. Poe stepped off the porch and opened the gate, eyeing the crowd to make way and not give the man any trouble.

Rudulph greeted the deputy with a grateful nod and continued up the walk to the porch. Maxwell greeted him at the door.

"Pete."

"Milner. Thanks for coming. I think you know Sheriff Garrett."

"Sheriff." He glanced around. "Where's Alejandro?"

"He couldn't stay," Maxwell said.

"What can I do to help?"

"We're conducting a coroner's inquest into the death of the outlaw Billy the Kid," Garrett said. "We need someone to serve as foreman. Pete says you're a respected civic servant and just the man for the job."

"I ain't so sure."

"I'd say you're just the man we need."

"I think we should get started right away," Pete said. "For all his banditry and mayhem the Kid was well thought of in these parts. The mood of that crowd outside is cause for some concern."

"I noticed driving in. I agree. Let's get on with it. What do I need to do?"

"First you need to identify the body."

"I'm not sure I can. I've never seen Billy the Kid before."

"Pete and I have already identified the

body. It's all here in the coroner's report." Garrett handed him the report.

"I didn't know you were coroner, Pete."

"I'm not officially. Alejandro only has me acting coroner on account of we don't have one."

Rudulph nodded. "I see."

"All you have to do is view the deceased and confirm the coroner's report. Now if you'll just follow me." Maxwell led the way down a dimly lit hall to the carpenter's shop. He unlocked the door and stepped inside. He lit a lamp in the windowless room. Garrett and the postmaster followed. He held the lamp near the door. The halo of light reached through the gloom to illuminate the body atop a bench on the far wall.

Garrett crossed the room to the bench. Rudulph followed. The body lay on its back, the face turned to the wall in shadow. "That's him, Mr. Rudulph, the notorious outlaw Billy the Kid."

"Well, I'll be. Sure don't look like much does he?"

"He's no longer a threat to the good people of New Mexico."

He nodded. "You're to be congratulated, Sheriff."

"Thank you, sir. Have you seen enough?"

"I have. What's next?"

"You need to sign the inquest verdict."

They left the carpenter's shop. Maxwell snuffed out the lamp and locked the door. He led the way back to the parlor.

"What must the inquest do then?"

"Basically you have to decide if Sheriff Garrett acted in the line of duty," Maxwell said. "If you agree, all you have to do is sign the verdict as foreman."

"Given the identity of the victim that seems rather cut and dried."

"It is. In fact the inquest is something of a formality for the record," Garrett said.

Maxwell handed the postmaster the verdict. "Here is what you need to certify."

He read.

Rudulph wrinkled his brow. "Don't we need to convene as a jury to come to a verdict?"

"Normally, yes," Garrett said. He nodded to the crowd noise outside. "In this case, for reasons of keeping the peace, there isn't time. We are moving as quickly as possible to bury the remains."

"I see." He seemed skeptical.

"As you said, it's pretty cut and dried. If you agree, all you need to do is sign."

He thought a minute. "It seems a bit irregular. Then again, under the circumstances, I understand your concern."

Maxwell produced a pencil. Rudulph signed and handed Pete the pencil and paper.

"Thank you, Milnor. Sheriff Garrett will see the documents are properly filed at the courthouse. You have fulfilled your duties."

"If there is nothing further you require, I shall be on my way. I must say I don't like the look of that crowd, either."

Garrett showed the postmaster out. Poe escorted him to his buckboard. He climbed aboard, clucked to his horse, wheeled around and picked up a trot up the street toward home. Poe watched him go. *This is an inquest? Damnedest thing I ever seen.*

"What about the rest of the jurors, Pete?"

"I'll take care of it. I've got the carpenter working on a coffin. The next order of business is to get a grave dug."

"Won't the other jurors need to see the body?"

"I seen it." Moments later he handed Garrett the verdict, complete with the marks of all five jurors. "How's that?"

He shook his head. "Are you sure, Pete?"

"Course I'm sure. Them signatures is marked with an X. The fewer people know about this the better. That crowd out there believes the Kid is dead. They believe you killed him. We got sworn statements. Who's gonna question any of this?"

"We can't display the body."

"We got a hostile crowd out there."

"We don't have a daguerreotype."

"You see anybody with the equipment? It's too hot to lug the body to Las Vegas or Lincoln. Quick burial is the only option."

"That's the way you see it."

"It is. Good to hear you see it the same way."

Thirty-Nine

South Spring
July 18, 1881

Ty strolled up the path to Roth's house. His Saturday-night bath and Sunday shirt with the black ribbon tie wouldn't stay fresh long in the heat of an intense late afternoon sun. Roth waved from his porch and stepped down to join him. He swung through the gate in stride beside his partner.

"Afternoon, Ty."

"Johnny."

They continued up the hill toward the hacienda. Lucy and Dawn Sky had gone ahead to fix Sunday dinner at John's. The weekly family gathering was intended to make up for the fact Roth had spirited away the closest thing Chisum had to family when he married Dawn Sky.

"I can almost taste roast beef," Johnny said.

Ty nodded.

They clumped up the hacienda porch. Roth rapped on the massive oak door.

"It's open." Chisum's invitation consisted of a muffled shout from the parlor. The boys let themselves in and hung their hats on the coat tree beside the door. The house was filled with pleasant cooking smells, fresh bread, roast beef, a touch of cinnamon from a cooling apple pie and a hint of mesquite.

"It sure smells good in here," Roth said, loud enough for the compliment to carry to the women busy in the kitchen. He led the way into the parlor. Chisum sat in his favorite stuffed chair beside a large adobe fireplace, quiet now in the heat of summer.

"Glad you boys are here." He smiled. "I wasn't sure we'd get a drink before dinner."

"I'll get it," Johnny said.

"The bottle and glasses are on the sideboard in the dining room."

Roth chuckled. "Same as last week. I'll find 'em."

"How was your trip to Roswell?" Ty asked.

"Interesting news." Chisum gestured to a copy of the *Santa Fe New Mexican* on the table beside the settee. The headline caught Ty's attention.

Sheriff Kills Billy the Kid
Notorious Outlaw Dead After Fort Sumner Shoot-out

Ty snatched up the paper and read.

Lincoln County Sheriff Pat Garrett, accompanied by deputies John Poe and Thomas McKinney, cornered William Bonney, better known as the outlaw Billy the Kid, in the home of Fort Sumner rancher Pete Maxwell on the night of July 14th. A gunfight ensued in which Bonney was fatally shot.

Acting on a tip that the Kid might be hiding in or about Fort Sumner, Sheriff Garrett and his deputies arrived in the area earlier in the day. Their initial inquiry revealed no trace of the outlaw. While preparing to end the investigation and return to Lincoln, Sheriff Garrett called at the home of prominent Fort Sumner rancher Pete Maxwell. As the sheriff was preparing to leave, the Kid appeared out of the night with his gun drawn. Sheriff Garrett drew his gun and fired twice, striking the outlaw in the left breast and killing him.

Following a coroner's inquest, the Kid's remains were interred in Fort Sumner. The coroner's inquest found that Sheriff Garrett acted in the line of duty in regard to the shooting.

News of the Kid's death was greeted in Santa Fe with high praise for Sheriff Garrett's work. "Billy the Kid has been a scourge on the ranchers and good citizens of New Mexico for too long," said Attorny General William Breeden, speaking on behalf of Governor Sheldon. Breeden went on to herald the accomplishment as "An important milestone on the road to bringing law and order to New Mexico. Law and order that lays the cornerstone for statehood." The governor's office had previously offered a 500-dollar bounty for the killing or capture of Billy the Kid, making the Kid the most wanted desparado in the territory.

Roth returned with glasses and the bottle. He poured stout measures and handed one to Chisum and one to Ty.

"What's all the quiet about?"

Ty handed him the paper.

Johnny read the story and set the paper back on the table. He picked up his drink. "Well, I'll be. They finally got the Kid. Sure looks like the Cattle Growers Association picked the right man when they got behind Garrett."

Chisum nodded with a satisfied smile.

"Sure does doesn't it?" That backing had mostly come on his say-so, a fact that would no doubt further his already considerable standing in the association. He lifted his glass. "Here's to Sheriff Garrett."

Ty lifted his glass and took a swallow. He shook his head. "Funny how things work out sometimes. The law's been after the Kid for most of two years. Couldn't keep him locked up the one time they did catch him. Then all of a sudden, out of the clear blue, he stumbles into Garrett and gets himself killed. How do you figure?"

Santa Fe
August 20, 1881
Thomas B. (T. B.) Catron opened a prosperous law practice in Santa Fe after serving as US attorney for New Mexico Territory. Politically savvy, he cultivated favor with the powers behind the so-called Santa Fe Ring that in turn propelled him to success early in his career. That is until he found it more lucrative to parlay his influence and connections into a private law practice. Pat Garrett's claim on the reward offered for Billy the Kid was simple fare for a man of his stature.

As far as Garrett was concerned, access to the governor's office was worth Catron's

431

fee. Lew Wallace offered the reward while he was governor. He'd since been replaced by President Garfield's appointee, Lionel Sheldon. Garrett didn't know Sheldon. Catron knew that while Sheldon held the governor's office, the real power was in the hands of Attorney General William Breeden.

Garrett arrived at Catron's office the morning of the twentieth. The place smelled of wood polish and power. Bright rugs of traditional Navajo design covered the tile floor. White hot sunlight poured through tall windows in the outer office. A neat young law clerk in a dark suit and paper collar showed him into the lawyer's spacious office.

"T. B., good to see you again."

"Sheriff Garrett, my pleasure as well." They shook hands. The lawyer offered a guest chair drawn up in front of a massive polished desk. "Would you care for a cup of coffee?"

"No, thank you. I've had my limit this morning and please, call me Pat."

"All right then." He nodded to the clerk. "That will be all, Kennedy. Let's get down to business." He took his seat in a leather covered desk chair and opened the single folder occupying the blotter on top of his desk. "We have a little over an hour before we are to see the attorney general."

"Thank you for arranging that. I expect this will all go much better with your assistance."

"No trouble at all. Why don't we begin by you telling me about the events of" — he picked up a pen and checked his notes — "July fourteenth. Yes, tell me what happened."

"I got a tip the Kid might be hiding out in or about Fort Sumner. Actually I'd been hearing rumors for some time, just nothing real solid."

"What made this tip different?"

"It came from a rancher I know in the area. I rode up there with John Poe and Kip McKinney. We got to the orchard northwest of town around nine o'clock the night of the fourteenth. We took up a watch on the Maxwell place thinking the Kid might show up there."

"What made you think that?"

"Pete Maxwell complained about the Kid courtin' his younger sister. Anyway things were pretty quiet other than the usual comin's and goin's at the saloons and some Mexicans squatted out at an old barracks near the orchard. Around eleven o'clock somebody left the barracks and headed down to Maxwell's place. That's when I decided to investigate. We left the orchard and went down the street to Pete's house. It looked pretty quiet. I left Poe and McKinney on watch outside and went in. I heard someone sleepin' in the front bedroom. I figured it was Pete and went in to speak with him. While we was talkin' quiet like I heard someone in the hall speak in Spanish."

"Could you make out what was said?"

"Quien es? You know, who is it? Then I heard it again. This time he's talkin' to Pete. Right then I knew it was the Kid. All at once he comes through the bedroom door with his gun drawn. I fired and heard him grunt. I couldn't see nothin' on account a the muzzle flash. I dove for cover and fired again. Pete jumped out a bed and ran for the front door. I ran after him and got there just in time to keep Poe from shootin' him in the confusion."

"And you knew you'd shot the Kid in the dark?"

"Sure. I knew his voice. I'd a recognized it anywhere."

"Then what happened?"

"The shooting woke up half the town. People come runnin' from every direction. Most of 'em considered the Kid a friend. They knew he was around. Some guessed what happened when the ruckus come from Maxwell's place. Me and my deputies took watch over the body until we could convene a coroner's inquest the next morning."

"So a formal inquest was held."

"It was."

"That would have been the morning of the fifteenth."

"That's right. Alejandro Segura called it. He's justice of the peace in Fort Sumner."

"Do you have a coroner's report or a copy of the inquest verdict?"

"Not with me, they're on file in Lincoln. Milnor Rudulph served as foreman. I didn't know none of the others. Pete Maxwell seemed to know them, though."

"And what did the jury find?"

"They said I shot Billy the Kid in the line of duty. The words is fancier than that, but it was pretty cut and dried."

"Then what happened?"

"We buried him."

"Did you have a public showing of the body?"

He shook his head. "Like I said the shootin' drew a crowd. The Kid had a lot of friends in the area. They was none too happy about what happened. We did our business and got out of there as fast as we could."

"Did you at least have a photograph taken?"

"We didn't have anyone to do it and it was too hot to take the body somewhere they could."

"I see. Then we base our claim on the verdict of the coroner's inquest."

"That and the witnesses. Pete Maxwell saw the whole thing. John Poe was there. So was Kip McKinney."

Catron fished a gold watch out of his vest pocket. He popped the lid and snapped it closed in a smooth practiced motion. "Time to leave for the attorney general's office, Pat."

"What do we do with him?"

"Tell him the story just like you told it to me. I may ask a few questions to help you along. After that, I'll write out a formal claim and take it from there."

September 5, 1881

William Breeden studied the reward claim filed by T. B. Catron on behalf of Sheriff Pat Garrett in regard to the death of Billy the Kid. It seemed routine really, based on the account the sheriff gave him during their meeting. The sheriff was an honorable man, highly respected by powerful men in the territory. The powers that be clearly wanted to be done with the Kid. They'd plainly decided to make an example of the young gunman. All he had to do was rubber-stamp the desired outcome and move on. What could be easier? Still 500 dollars was not an inconsiderable sum. Acting on behalf of the governor he felt a special obligation to his stewardship of the office. He didn't want to wave his hand over something that might come back to fault him later. He drummed his fingers on the page, conflicted with knowing the right way to proceed.

The claim rested on the coroner's inquest verdict for lack of any other substantiation, that and the testimony of a handful of witnesses. Sheriff Garrett hadn't presented the verdict at the time of their meeting. The very least he should do is have the verdict verified. It might be good to talk to some of the people who were there, as much for the sheriff's benefit as for his. He saw no harm in taking a little time to make sure things got done right. Garrett may not see it that way, but he should if he were to think about it.

"Sullivan!"

His assistant appeared at the office door. "Yes, sir?"

"Come in, please."

The young man crossed the tile floor.

"Have a seat." He passed Garrett's claim across the desk. "Please advise T. B. Catron that this office will conduct an inquiry into the claim and advise him and his client of the results. We do not authorize payment of the reward at this time."

"Yes, sir. Is there anything else, sir?"

"Yes. Send for Marshal Sherman. I'd like to see him."

September 7, 1881

The assistant showed US Marshal John Sherman into Breeden's office.

"You wanted to see me, sir?"

Breeden stroked his beard as he scanned the paper in front of him before turning his attention to the next meeting. He looked up.

"Oh, Marshal Sherman, why yes, please come in. Have a seat won't you."

Sherman crossed the office and took the offered wing chair. "What can I do for you?"

He ruffled through a stack of papers pushed to the side of his desk. He found the claim filed by T. B. Catron. He passed it across the desk to the marshal.

"Sheriff Garrett down in Lincoln has claimed the reward for Billy the Kid. Would you have one of your men check it out? It's routine of course, but before we pay out a sum like that we should at least verify the official records."

Sherman ran his eyes down the page. "I don't recall reading anything about a public viewing of the body. Come to think of it there weren't any pictographs in the papers, either." He handed the letter back to Breeden.

"That's right. The claim rests on the verdict of the coroner's inquest. We need to verify those records. I believe they are on file at the courthouse in Lincoln. It might be good if we interviewed some of the witnesses too. Just so we have a bit more verification than the sheriff's word on it. I'm sure it's all in order, but it seems worth an inquiry considering the amount of money involved, don't you agree?"

"I do, sir. We'll take care of it. Will there be anything else sir?"

Breeden smiled. "No, John, that will be all."

FORTY

South Spring
September 12, 1881

Lucy stretched. Her back ached with the weight of the child. The kitchen glowed soft gold in late afternoon light. Outside a freshened wind blew out of the northwest. The sky turned dark smoky blue. It was time for a change. You could feel it in the air. Autumn was coming. The time had come for canning and putting up for the winter. These were busy days with much to be done before decent weather ran out. She placed another stack of tomato jars on the pantry shelves. She sighed, the chore done for the day. Ty would be home for supper directly. She took a stick of kindling from the wood box, opened the grate and stirred the ashes. She felt heat rise and added a bit of kindling. She coaxed it to a flame. A few more sticks and she had the start of a fire. She closed the grate to the sound of approaching hoofbeats.

Early for Ty by the color of the sky, she glanced out the window. No mistaking the big black man loping down from the hacienda. She smiled, wiping her hands on her apron. She opened the door and stepped out on the porch. The swing creaked in the wind. The breeze ruffled her hair. Deac drew rein. He touched the brim of his slouch hat with a broad white smile.

"Afternoon, Miss Lucy. How's dat baby comin' along?"

"Just fine, Deac, though I must say he's a little heavy today."

"My mama used to say when dey gets heavy like dat a woman's gotta sit down and rest herself some for both a dem."

"Sounds like a wise woman, but then who'd fix Ty's supper?"

"He fix for himself on the trail. Just don't tell him I said so." He laughed that deep throaty laugh that came from somewhere in his barrel chest.

"What brings you by, Deac?"

"Mister John sent me into Roswell today. Dey had a letter for Mister Ty, looks kind a impotant." He handed Lucy an envelope stamped *US Marshal's Office, Santa Fe.*

She bit her lip. Sherman's office usually meant some assignment that would take him away. "Much obliged, Deac. I'll see he gets it first thing."

Swain smiled and touched the brim of his hat. "You take care of dat baby now, Miss Lucy. You hear?"

"I will, Deac." She smiled and waved as he wheeled away and loped back up the hill. Back inside she closed the door and set the envelope beside Ty's chair. She added wood to the fire and set about supper.

An hour later Ty's boots clumped the porch step. She greeted him with a smile as he opened the door.

"Sure smells good in here. I'm so hungry I could eat a bear."

"Sorry, no bear tonight, just fatback and greens."

"You can't fool me. I smell fresh bread."

"Well, maybe some. There's a letter for you on the chair. Deac brought it from town. Looks like it's from Marshal Sherman."

He tore it open and read by the lamplight.

"What's he want?"

"Garrett's claimed the reward for killin' the Kid. The attorney general wants the claim verified before he pays out the money. Looks like I'll have to ride up to Lincoln and talk with Pat."

"How long will you be gone?"

"It shouldn't take more than a few days to check things out. I won't go until we have the stock in winter pasture next month."

Lincoln
October 1881

Winter wasn't far off. Old Man Frost laid his hoary breath on the land that morning, dusting juniper and pine dotted hillsides a frosty green. Silver light glistened across a yucca studded tapestry of golden autumn sage patched in red rock and rust. A hot cup of coffee took some of the chill off for the ride into Lincoln. They didn't find occasion to visit Lincoln as often now with Roswell nearby. Still the main street with its gentle curve, the Torreon Tower, the mercantile Ty still thought of as Tunstall's store and the Wortley Hotel all held memories. He drew up in front of the courthouse. The former Murphy and Dolan store known as the House was now the seat of law and order in the county. *Times change. Or do they?*

Ty slipped down from the saddle and looped a rein over the side yard fence. He trudged up the front step. Most of the events that led to the Kid's death swirled around this place the way a stream eddies around a rock. The war, the murders, even the Kid's escape from justice flowed from this building and the things it stood for. Those things had changed with the passing of time, but the House still stood. The Kid couldn't stand against it. None of the rest of them could either. It was done now. He was about to help write the final chapter. He felt a sense of history as he stuck his head in the sheriff's office. Garrett wasn't there. He crossed the hall to the county clerk's office.

Ben Curtis, the pinched county clerk, wore a green eyeshade. He glanced up from a pile of papers on his cluttered desk and blinked behind spectacles, his eyes lost in reflected window light. His shirtsleeves bloused over garters above the elbow. "Afternoon, Ty. What can I do for you?"

"Afternoon, Ben. I'm lookin' for Sheriff Garrett."

"He rode up to White Oaks yesterday. I expect he'll be back later today."

"Maybe you can help me then. I've been asked to verify Pat's claim on the reward for Billy the Kid. I'd like to have a look at the coroner's report and the verdict from the coroner's inquest."

"So this is official business then?"

Ty nodded. "Attorney general's orders by

way of the US marshal's office."

"Sure thing, I'll just be a minute." The clerk hoisted himself out of his chair and shuffled to the back of the office. He paused before a long cabinet filled with drawers. He selected one, drew it open and thumbed through the contents. "Let's see here, Bonney, Bonney, here we are." He drew out a sheet of paper and moved on to another drawer. He ran through the contents, paused and scratched the stubble on his chin. He tried another drawer, closed it with a puzzled look and returned to the counter.

He slid the sheet of paper across the counter. "Here's the inquest verdict."

Ty picked up the paper and read. The verdict was terse. Garrett shot the Kid in the line of duty about covered it. The jury further felt obliged to suggest Sheriff Garrett worthy of the reward. That struck him as something beyond what one would expect from such a proceeding. Several of the jurors signed with their mark, witnessed by Pete Maxwell. He slid the paper back across the counter.

"What about the coroner's report?"

Curtis lifted his eyeshade and wiped his brow on his sleeve. He shook his head. "Damnedest thing, I cain't find it. It should be here. I don't exactly recollect filin' it, but

I must have." He shrugged. "I s'pose it could be misfiled. I don't fancy myself given to such things, but it happens."

"Take another look, Ben. It could be important. I'll check back with you before I leave town."

There was something wrong with the notion of a cold dust devil, but there it was, blowing down the street in blue shadows just before nightfall. Ty watched it out the window of his small room at the Wortley. A lone horseman riding in from the northwest told him his wait was over. The rider wheeled his horse behind the courthouse. Ty expected he'd find Sheriff Garrett, putting his horse up at the stable. With luck, he could wrap up this assignment over a pleasant supper.

He trudged across the street through the gloom behind the looming courthouse. Lantern light beckoned beyond the open stable door. Garrett hauled the saddle off the back of a sturdy chestnut and carried it to a rack along the back wall. He turned back to his horse, curry brush in hand when he noticed Ledger and broke into a broad grin.

"Ty." He extended his hand. "Haven't seen you in a spell."

He returned the smile. "Pat, it has been a while."

"What brings you to Lincoln?"

"Orders from Santa Fe."

"That sounds official."

"Officially routine, but reason enough to have a drink and some supper if you've got the time."

"After a long ride, that's the best offer I've had all day."

"I'm stayin' at the Wortley. What say we head over there?"

"Suits me fine. Give me a minute to run a brush over this big fella."

"He's a good-lookin' animal."

"I needed one after the Kid run off with my bay last summer."

"He took your horse to boot. No wonder you shot him."

"Cain't say that entered into my thinkin' at the time. What brings you to Lincoln?"

"Your bounty claim on the Kid."

"Does that mean I have to buy supper?"

"Not yet, we'll let the marshal's service do the honors for now."

"Well if you're buyin', let's get to it."

Garrett turned the chestnut into his stall, blew out the lantern and closed the barn door. They ambled back across the street to the Wortley, each absorbed in his thoughts.

They found a corner table in the nearly deserted dining room and ordered whiskey. The waiter brought glasses and a bottle. They ordered steaks. Ty poured. He lifted his glass.

"Congratulations, Pat. Takin' on the Kid and livin' to tell about it is no small accomplishment."

Garrett returned the toast and tossed off his drink. "So what's on Marshal Sherman's mind?"

Ty refilled their glasses. "He just wants to make sure of the details before they send you your money."

"All right, how can I help?"

"Tell me what happened for a starter. The inquest verdict is kind a short on detail."

He chuckled. "I s'pose it is." He took a swallow of his drink. "We got a tip the Kid was hidin' out around Fort Sumner. I picked up John Poe and Kip McKinney and rode up there to have a look around. We holed up south of the fort on the thirteenth. I sent Poe into town the next morning to have a look around. He wasn't well known up that way so he wouldn't tip our hand if the Kid was in the area. We agreed to meet north of the fort that night.

"Kip and I rode in and met John around nine o'clock. Poe didn't have any word of the Kid, but he had a strong suspicion Billy was in the area. I'd heard sometime back the Kid was seein' Pete Maxwell's younger sister, so we decided to keep an eye on the Maxwell place. We watched a couple hours or so. I'd had enough by then, and was ready to pull out. That's when we spotted someone leave the old barracks headed for the Maxwell place. I decided to follow him and investigate.

"We went down to Pete's house. I left John and Kip on watch outside and went in. Pete was in bed. I went to his room and woke him up. Just about then we heard someone in the hall. He must have seen us 'cause he asked Pete who we was. He spoke Spanish. I recognized the Kid's voice. Pete said it was him just before the Kid come through the bedroom door with his gun drawn. I drew and fired. I hit him good. You couldn't miss at such close range. The shot didn't put him down right away. I couldn't see too good after the muzzle flash in the dark, but I heard him. I got off another shot. Turned out I didn't need it. The Kid was dead."

The waiter arrived with their steaks, mashed potatoes and beans. They settled in to a few bites of supper.

"Then what happened?"

"Not much more to tell really. We convened a cororner's inquest the next day and buried the body once it was over."

"You didn't display the body?"

He shook his head. "The Kid had a lot of friends in Fort Sumner. The shooting drew a crowd. They was in kind of an unfriendly mood."

"Well, at least the jurors must have been glad to be rid of the Kid. They as much as awarded you the bounty with their verdict."

A puzzled look crossed Garrett's eyes. "I guess so. Never thought about it really. How's your steak?"

"Best I've had in a while."

"How about another drink?"

"Don't mind if I do."

They finished off supper with apple pie and coffee.

"So when do you figure to head back south?" Garrett asked.

"I should wrap this up tomorrow I reckon. One last question."

"Sure."

"Any idea why Ben Curtis can't find the coroner's report?"

Garrett's eyes turned flat. He shrugged. "No, why?"

"He couldn't find it today. He thought it might be misfiled. He said he'd look some more. Who's the coroner up Fort Sumner way?"

"I don't know as they have one officially."

"Who signed the report then?"

Garrett met his gaze. "Pete Maxwell acted as coroner that day."

Ty nodded. *Pete Maxwell had had a busy day.*

FORTY-ONE

Fort Sumner

Ben Curtis couldn't find the coroner's report the next day either. Two days later Ty rode into the old fort. He'd been fighting with himself most of the way. Pat killed the Kid. It was as simple as that. The coroner's jurors had said as much. Something didn't feel right though, the missing coroner's report for starters. There could be a hundred explanations for that. Then you had Pete Maxwell. The Kid was shot in his bedroom. What was he doing there in the middle of the night? All right, figure he was seeing Pete's sister. How did Pete wind up acting coroner? For a report gone missing? Why was Pete witnessing signatures on the inquest verdict? It left him no choice. He'd rather be goin' home. Instead, he rode up to Fort Sumner to have a talk with Maxwell.

He rode into town past Beaver Smith's. He continued north along the west end of the old military quadrangle to the peach orchard. He drew rein and wheeled the steel dust around. He pictured the scene as Garrett had described it. Late afternoon sun had faded into purple shadow. The curtain fell on early evening. Not yet dark, but close enough for his purposes. From this vantage point he could see the front of the buildings, lining Roswell Road. The first building, a long single story, ran off to the east on the north side of Stinking Springs Road. It appeared inhabited by Mexicans, chickens and goats. He guessed the third, a more impressive structure than the rest for the Maxwell place. It had a fenced yard and a covered porch on two sides. He couldn't draw much from that observation. He rode back to the home with the fenced yard and stepped down at the gate. He swung the gate open and made his way up the path to the porch. Shadows amplified the darkness. He rapped on the door.

Footsteps within answered his summons. The door opened to a thickset man with a drooping mustache.

"Yeah?"

Ty took off his hat. "Evenin'. I'm Deputy US Marshal Ty Ledger. I'm lookin' for Pete Maxwell."

"You found him. What can I do for you,

Marshal?"

"I've been asked to look into Sheriff Garrett's claim on the bounty for Billy the Kid. I'd like to ask you a few questions."

"Sure. Com'on in. I was just clearin' up supper. There's coffee if you'd care for a cup."

"That'd go mighty good about now."

"Take the chill out." He led the way down a dark hall to a lamp-lit kitchen at the back of the house. "Have a seat." He gestured to the kitchen table. He cleared away the last few dishes and poured two steaming cups of coffee.

Ty's stomach rumbled at the suggestion of food. He'd had a long day on the trail and no supper.

"You out of Lincoln, Marshal?"

He shook his head. "Roswell when I work for the marshal's service."

"You're a long way from home, then. What can I do for you?"

He took a sip of coffee. "If you don't mind, you can start by tellin' me what happened that night?"

"I was asleep."

"Where?"

"Front bedroom, just right of the door. Sheriff Garrett woke me."

"What time was that?"

"I don't know, a little past eleven I reckon."

"How well do you know Sheriff Garrett?"

He chuckled. "Well, some better after that night."

"How well did you know him at the time?"

"We was acquainted."

"Were you surprised to find him in your bedroom?"

"In the middle of the night, hell yes, wouldn't you be? I didn't have long to think on it though. Right about the time he woke me we heard the Kid in the hall."

"Did you know it was the Kid?"

"No, just someone askin' who those men were outside."

"Do you remember exactly what was said?"

He thought. "Quien es, that's it. He spoke Spanish."

"What happened next?"

"Sheriff Garrett asked who it was."

"What did you tell him?"

"I didn't have a chance to answer. The Kid come through the door and asked who was out there."

"In Spanish?"

"Yeah. That's when Sheriff Garrett recognized him. He drew his gun and shot him."

"Did the Kid have a gun?"

"He did."

"Was it drawn?"

"I didn't see it, until after we got some light on the body."

"When was that?"

"The Kid stumbled. The sheriff went after him. It was dark. You couldn't see anything after the first muzzle flash. The sheriff fired again."

"Then what happened?"

"I jumped out of bed and got the hell out of there. The sheriff's deputies come a runnin'. I practically run into one of 'em on the porch. He had his gun drawn. Lucky for me the sheriff was right behind me. He called the man off."

"Then what happened?"

"We all kind of caught our breath. I went back inside and lit a candle."

"Is that when you recognized it was the Kid?"

He nodded.

"Did Sheriff Garrett inspect the body?"

"He did."

"Did anyone else?"

"Deputy Poe saw the body. Manuel Abreau helped us move it to the carpenter's shop. Say you sure got a lot of questions, Marshal."

"There's a lot of money involved. The attorney general wants to make sure we've got the facts right."

Maxwell pulled an annoyed half scowl. "We put the body in the carpenter's shop until we could call a coroner's inquest."

"I see." He decided to pass over the inquest for the moment. "Where's the carpenter's shop?"

"Down the hall there."

"Mind showin' it to me?"

"Suit yourself." Maxwell picked up the lamp from the kitchen table and led the way down a long hall running south from the kitchen. The carpenter shop door opened onto a windowless room. Maxwell stood aside to admit Ty. The room was dark. It smelled of sawdust and oil.

"Where did you put the body?"

"On the bench there." He pointed his chin to the shadows on the far wall.

Ty crossed the room. The lamplight barely penetrated the shadows at the bench. "Mind bringin' that lamp a mite closer?" Maxwell stepped up behind him. Yellow glow spilled over the scarred bench top. Dark brown stains marked the spot where the body must have bled out. "How long was the body here?"

"Until the next afternoon when we buried him."

"After the coroner's inquest."

"That's right."

"Thanks, Mr. Maxwell. I've seen enough here."

Maxwell led the way back to the kitchen. "More coffee?"

"A little. Thanks."

He poured what was left of the pot and returned to his seat.

"Now about the coroner's inquest, I saw the verdict on file at the courthouse in Lincoln. Things seem pretty cut and dried."

"That's the way we saw it. Say are we about done here, Marshal?"

"Just a couple more questions, Mr. Maxwell. Who is the coroner up here?"

He shuffled his feet. "We don't exactly have one, officially that is. It's a small town. Some of us wear whatever hats need wearin' from time to time."

"Who wore the coroner's hat for the Kid's inquest?"

He fixed Ty with a cool gaze. "I did."

"So you wrote the coroner's report then."

"I did."

"That seems a little irregular, don't it? I mean the man was killed in your bedroom."

"I was here. I could identify the deceased and I can write."

"What became of the report?"

"I gave it to the sheriff to file."

"The county clerk couldn't find it."

"I wouldn't know nothin' 'bout that."

"How did your coroner's report compare to the findings of the inquest?"

"They was pretty much the same. Like you said, things was pretty cut and dried."

"Did your coroner's report recommend Sheriff Garrett for the reward?"

He shook his head. "No, that part come later."

"The jury foreman was Milnor Rudulph."

"That's right."

"Where can I find Mr. Rudulph?"

"Milnor's the postmaster hereabouts when we need one. He's got a small place just north of town. Are we about done?"

"Just one last question, Mr. Maxwell. What was Billy the Kid doin' in your house that night?"

Maxwell let the question hang in the air. "He was, ah, he was seein' my sister Paulita."

"He was seein' your sister."

"Yeah, you know, callin' on her."

"Was he a friend of yours?"

"Me? Hell, no. I was again' it. I tried to talk her out of it. She wouldn't listen."

"Is your sister here? I'd like to talk to her."

"She's not here."

"When will she be back?"

"I don't know. She was pretty broke up after the Kid's death. She went back East to visit family."

Sunnyside

Ty rode into the Rudulph place at mid morning. *Cut and dried,* it might seem so on the surface, but the deeper he picked at the stories the more questions kept getting in the way. Small and run-down might have been a better description of Rudulph's place. He found Milnor Rudulph balancing a new buckboard wheel in a shed that passed for his barn. Rudulph stepped back from his work. He greeted the stranger in the cordial way folks often did in rough country, with a leveled Winchester.

"Mr. Rudulph?"

"I am. State your business."

"Ty Ledger, Deputy US Marshal. I'd like to ask you a few questions."

"About what?"

"The coroner's inquest into the death of Billy the Kid."

Rudulph knit his bushy brows and set the Winchester aside. He wiped sweat from his brow. "Step on down. Care for a cup of cider?"

"That'd go real good about now."

"Com'on we can sit on the porch."

Rudulph disappeared inside the cabin. He returned moments later with two cups of cider. He set himself down in an old rocking chair.

"Sorry I ain't got but one chair. I reckon a young fella like you can sit on the step."

Ty smiled and took a sip of his cider. "That's mighty good. The step will be fine."

The rocker creaked.

"Mr. Rudulph, you acted as jury foreman for the coroner's inquest. Is that correct?"

"It is."

"When did you arrive on the scene?"

He scratched the gray stubble on his chin. "Mid mornin' I'd say, right about now."

"Did you inspect the body?"

"I did."

"Where was it?"

"They had it laid out in the carpenter's shop in back of the Maxwell place."

"Were you able to identify the body?"

"Good as I could. I didn't exactly know him. I seen a wanted poster. Seemed like a good likeness, but it was pretty dark."

"It was dark in the carpenter's shop?"

"That's right."

"Was there anything unusual about the body?"

He wrinkled his brow, then shook his

461

head. "Nope, like I said it was pretty dark."

"But you still saw a good likeness, to the wanted poster I mean."

"Sure, I guess."

"Who were the other jurors?"

"I never saw the rest of 'em."

Ty sat up. "You never actually saw the jurors?"

"That's right."

"So you never really convened as a jury."

"No."

"Didn't that strike you as odd?"

"Sort of, but look we done things kind a quick. The Kid had friends in Fort Sumner. They was none too pleased about his bein' shot. Pete and Sheriff Garrett thought it best to get the proceedin's over with."

"Then how did you reach a verdict?"

He shrugged. "It was pretty cut and dried. The Kid was dead. The coroner's report said so. The sheriff and Pete was there. They said so."

"Did you write the jury verdict?"

"No. It was written by the time I got there."

"Who wrote it then?"

"I don't know, Alejandro Segura, the justice of the peace called me. Maybe he done it."

"Did you see Justice Segura that morning?"

"No, he left before I got there."

"Didn't that strike you as odd?"

"Well maybe it should a, but like I said with the crowd, all we was thinkin' was get the business over."

"Who gave you the verdict?"

"Pete. He was kind a runnin' things."

"Pete was runnin' things. Not the sheriff?"

"No."

"Did the verdict Pete gave you recommend Sheriff Garrett be rewarded for killin' the Kid?"

"I believe it did. I know we didn't change nothin'."

"Did you sign the verdict?"

"I did."

"Were you the first to sign it?"

"I was."

"Thanks for the cider, Mr. Rudulph. And thanks for your help."

FORTY-TWO

Ty stared at the circle of firelight, wrapped in a blanket against the night chill. *Cut and dried,* he turned the words over in his mind. Lawmen killed notorious outlaws in the line of duty all the time. Witnesses came forward. Bodies were identified. Official inquiries took place. Proceedings like that were routine. Nobody questioned the findings. For some reason, this case didn't add up.

He tossed another log on the fire, sending a shower of sparks into the night sky. *Why?* He didn't know Pete Maxwell, but the man sure showed up in the middle of things. He knew the Kid plain enough. If he disapproved of Billy seeing his sister, he wouldn't shed any tears over the killing. So why would he take charge of the proceedings? Why would he write the coroner's report? Why was the report missing? Maybe it was never filed. Why? Pat Garrett was an honorable man by every account he knew.

Then there was the matter of the inquest itself. According to Rudulph, the jurors never actually convened. They'd simply signed on to a predetermined verdict. Predetermined by whom? A justice of the peace Rudulph never saw? Or could Maxwell have written the inquest verdict too? Pete "was kind a runnin' things," Rudulph had said. Maxwell himself said the part about Garrett deserving a reward "come later." Why? Ty wasn't a lawyer, but common sense said that the proceedings couldn't be legal.

The burial seemed hasty. Bodies were always displayed publicly in high profile cases. Pictographs were taken of the body and those responsible for bringing the desperado to justice. Not in this case. Rudulph blamed it on a hostile crowd.

All of it left him with a thorny question. What was he going to report to Marshal Sherman? What were they going to tell the attorney general? Is Garrett's claim cut and dried? That was the easy answer. Anybody who'd read a newspaper account knew Pat Garrett killed Billy the Kid. Why did they do things the way they did? Could it all be blamed on the crowd? Men like Garrett, Poe and McKinney handled crowds all the time. In fact they did in this case, all through the night and into the next afternoon. It occurred to him, he might never know all the answers. He banked the fire against the night chill and rolled up in his blanket. He had another stop to make. After that, he had to figure out what it all meant, if he could.

White Oaks

A rumpled blanket of gray cloud laden with the scent of early snow poured out of the mountains. Even after a long day's ride the steel dust had the breeze in his nose and a lively step to his gait. The town had gotten around to building a sheriff's office Ty noticed as the steel dust pranced down the rutted central street. Smoke curling from the stovepipe and a light in the window promised some relief from the cold. He drew rein and eased himself down, stiff with the cold. He looped a rein over the hitch rack and climbed the boardwalk step.

John Poe sat at his desk haloed in lamplight. He glanced up at the sound of the door and broke into a broad grin. He stood and extended his hand.

"Ty, what brings you up here? Don't you know it's fixin' to turn winter on us?"

"Sure feels like it out there, John."

"It must be an official visit. A man

466

wouldn't ride up here from South Spring this time of year unless he had to."

"It is official. The attorney general asked us to verify Pat's claim on the bounty for the Kid. I understand you were with Pat that night."

"I was."

"Mind tellin' me about it?"

His eyes drifted over Ty's shoulder in thought. "Let's talk. How about a drink and some supper to go with it?"

"Sounds good. I'm hungry enough to eat fence posts."

"White Oaks may not have all the comforts of Lincoln, but I believe we can do better than fence posts for supper."

Ty put the steel dust up at the White Oaks livery just down the street from the Alhambra. Most of the saloons in town served food. The Alhambra had the best food according to Poe and an actual menu to boot. They found a back corner table away from the piano and the gamblers. The bartender brought glasses and a bottle. He offered the menu. Poe recommended the fried chicken with biscuits and gravy. The bartender went off with orders for two. Ty poured them each a drink. Poe took a swallow.

"So how is your investigation goin'?"

The question took Ty back a bit. Poe asked as though he might already know the answer. "Seems like it should be pretty cut and dried."

"Seems like it should, but it's not, is it?"

Ty met his eyes. "No it ain't. Mind tellin' me your side of it?"

"Who have you talked to?"

"I started with Pat. Then I rode up to Fort Sumner to see Pete Maxwell. After that I talked to Milnor Rudulph."

"Good. You've likely uncovered some pieces that don't quite add up."

"That's why I'm here."

Poe tossed off his drink. Ty refilled his glass.

"Pat sent me into Fort Sumner the morning of the fourteenth to scout out the place. I played cattle buyer on a buying trip so as not to give us away. I hung around town, talked to folks, had some lunch and rode out to see Rudulph. He's a friend of Pat's. My gut told me the Kid was somewhere in the area. A couple of boys I met in town was real suspicious. I figured them for friends of his. Nobody said anything about him, but it sure seemed like they had something to hide or had reason to expect trouble. That was all just a feelin' until I got to Rudulph's place. Pat gave me a letter to introduce me to the man. He knew who we was. I told him we had information the Kid was hidin' out around Fort Sumner. That made him real uncomfortable. Afraid I thought. A man ain't fearful unless there's somethin' to be afraid of."

The bartender came along with two steaming plates of fried chicken. Poe ordered a beer. Ty did the same.

"I met Pat and Kip at the peach orchard that night accordin' to plan. We kept watch on the Maxwell place 'til around eleven o'clock. By then Pat had pretty well decided the Kid wasn't gonna show. He was ready to pull out. I figured we'd spent the best part of the night watchin' the Maxwell place on account of knowin' the Kid called there. It didn't make sense to ride back to Lincoln without even talkin' to Maxwell. Pat agreed when I pressed it. We went down to the Maxwell house. Pat told me and McKinney to wait outside while he went in. He wasn't in there very long when a feller come down the street from the direction of the peach orchard."

Ty paused a forkful of chicken halfway to his mouth. "Pat said you followed a man who came out of the Mexican barracks while you were still in the orchard."

Poe shook his head. "That feller came

469

along after Pat was inside with Maxwell. He spotted me and Kip when he came into Maxwell's yard. He said somethin' in Spanish."

"Quien es?"

Poe shrugged. "Might a been, I don't speak the lingo."

"It means who is it? What did this feller look like?"

"Not real big, kind a slope-shouldered. It was dark under the porch shadow. We never got too close. Anyway he goes inside. Next thing you know we hear gunshots. Me and Kip draw our guns and run to the door. I get there first just as Maxwell comes runnin' out. I damn near shot him in all the commotion. Fortunately Pat come out and says it's Maxwell. Then he says he shot the Kid. Maxwell goes back inside to get a candle. He comes out and tells Pat he better come inside and take a look."

"Did you see the Kid's body?"

"I saw a body. I couldn't really see too well. It was still pretty dark with the shadows. Pat and Maxwell said it was him."

"Do you think it was him?"

"I took them at their word at first. Now, I'm not so sure."

"Why?"

"I don't know. Things happened kind a

strange."

"What do you mean, strange?"

"They hid the body in a carpenter shop and locked it up. Hell, a notorious desperado like that, you put him on display, take pictures, make yourself out a hero. They didn't do none of that. Buried him so fast the body likely wasn't even cold."

"Milnor Rudulph says they worked fast because the Kid's friends in town were angry. They felt threatened."

"Yeah there were some folks hangin' around. Me and Kip kept guard of 'em. Some of 'em was angry. Some was curious. I didn't make it out to be all that bad. Kip's big old shotgun has a way with crowds. Even if the crowd was ugly, that don't explain everything they done."

"Like what?"

"They never held a coroner's inquest. They brought Rudulph in and next thing you know they've got a verdict."

"I saw the verdict. It makes Garrett out the hero. If they didn't hold an inquest, where did the verdict and the signatures come from?"

"I don't know. The only one I saw come and go was Rudulph."

"Rudulph says he was appointed by Justice Segura. He says he never saw him because

Segura couldn't stay around."

Poe shrugged. "I never saw any justice."

"The verdict had five signatures."

"Maybe so, but me and McKinney stood guard on that house until they buried the body."

"Are you saying those signatures were forged?"

"I'm sayin' I didn't see anybody but Rudulph, Maxwell, Garrett and a Mexican fella that helped 'em move the body. Maxwell wrote the coroner's report. A few juror signatures ain't askin' much after that."

"The county clerk in Lincoln can't find the coroner's report."

"Likely says the same thing as the inquest verdict."

"Why would Maxwell do that?"

He shrugged. "Like a lot of things, it don't make sense, unless there was some other reason to get things done quick."

"Like what?"

"Like mistaken identity."

"You sayin' it wasn't the Kid?"

"I'm sayin' I don't know. It was dark."

"But why would Maxwell help Garrett cover it up if he killed the wrong man?"

"Folks say the Kid was seein' Pete's younger sister. They say the Kid was in love with her."

"Pete claims he was against that. How would that explain Maxwell helpin' Garrett?"

Poe shrugged. "Like I said things got strange the minute the shootin' stopped."

"If the body wasn't the Kid, then who was it?"

Poe shrugged. "I purely don't know. The Kid had a lot of friends. The man who went into the house spoke Spanish. He might a been Mexican. He kind of fit the Kid's description. If I had to guess, I'd say it might a been one of his friends."

"So you think Garrett killed the wrong man and that he and Maxwell covered it up."

"I can't prove it, but it sure smells that way."

"Then what happened to the Kid?"

"Good question."

South Spring

Fire crackled, releasing a shower of sparks up the chimney. A soft glow spread across the hearth, warming the cozy parlor against the swirling snow outside. Roth and Ledger sat before the fire. Lucy and Dawn Sky worked at cleaning up the supper dishes. Dawn insisted on doing most of the work while her friend rested in the advanced days of her pregnancy.

"So what are you going to tell Marshal Sherman?" Roth's question hung on the soft scent of mesquite. What to tell Sherman indeed.

Ty shook his head. "Damned if I know. I had plenty of questions before I talked to Poe. He flat don't think the man Garrett killed was the Kid. If he's right, who the hell was it? If Garrett killed the wrong man, that could be murder. You can't charge a man with that unless you've got proof. You take what Poe says along with Rudulph and Maxwell's parts and you know that coroner's inquest was faked. You don't have a legal record that shows the Kid is even dead, let alone Garrett killed him. You got Garrett's word and Maxwell's word. Maxwell's word ain't worth much given all he was doin' at the time."

"That still leaves you with the question. What do you say about the bounty?"

"Well he sure don't have a clean claim."

"True, but does anyone want to hear that?" Roth said.

"What do you mean?"

"Everybody thinks Garrett killed the Kid. He's a hero in Santa Fe. The governor thinks he struck a blow for law and order. The statehood crowd will beat that drum all the way to Washington. Nobody wants to hear it ain't true."

"May not be true, but I cain't prove it ain't true either."

"All I'm sayin' is most folks believe Pat killed him and that's what they want to believe."

"Are you sayin' I should just go along? That ain't truthful."

"I'm not sayin' that, Ty. All I'm sayin' is whatever you say, you need to understand somebody ain't gonna want to hear it."

"Shit!"

"Smells like that too don't it?"

"All right, Johnny, you were a bounty hunter. What do I tell Marshal Sherman that won't get a man paid a bounty he may not deserve?"

Roth threw another log on the fire. The delay didn't render the question any easier. He returned to his chair and stroked his chin. "It's really about proof ain't it? One way or the other, he either did or he didn't."

"I can't prove either."

"There's your answer."

"What? Tell Marshal Sherman I spent the best part of three weeks traipsin' halfway across the territory and back to prove a notorious outlaw was killed and couldn't do it."

"I wouldn't advise puttin' it quite like that."

"How would you put it then?"

"Simple truth is you need more proof."

"So who do I call a liar?"

"Nobody. You tell Sherman the coroner's report is not on file at the county courthouse. Your investigation revealed certain irregularities in the conduct of the coroner's inquest. The irregularities are acknowledged by all parties as necessary owing to a concern for civil unrest among the Kid's sympathizers in the area. You're concerned that the irregularities may mean the inquest verdict ain't legal. You put the burden of proof back on Garrett."

"The coroner's report is missing. I don't expect it'd be worth any more than the inquest verdict, but that's my opinion. The fact is it is an official confirmation of death we don't have. You may be on to something here, Johnny."

"If Garrett has a legitimate claim on that bounty, let him come forward and prove it. As far as your report is concerned the Kid's death isn't in question, you just need more proof."

Ty cocked an eyebrow at his friend. "You ever think about goin' into politics, Johnny?"

"Me? Hell, I got enough trouble figurin' out the cattle business."

FORTY-THREE

Las Vegas
September 2010

Great-grandpa Ty's story ended there. Rick glanced at the unopened envelope. Golden light slanted across the pool, making its way toward sunset. He stood and stretched. There was more to the story. That's where his research took over. He left the office and made his way down a short hallway to the kitchen, his boot heels tapping a hollow trail along the tile floor. He opened the refrigerator, grabbed a can of diet cola and cracked the pop-top. He took a swallow. *Aluminum* just wasn't the same as those frosty little green bottles. Maybe it was progress, but like a lot of things that claimed progress, it wasn't always for the best. He made his way back to the office and folded his frame into the desk chair. The envelope lay undisturbed. He took another swallow.

The contents of that envelope might be

another form of progress that some wouldn't take for the best. A lot of history and legend had grown up around the story. Pat Garrett killed Billy the Kid. Did anybody but a few historical hobbyists care that might not be the case? They'd been through it all before. There were those, like Great-grandpa Ty and John Poe, who doubted Garrett's story at the time. Then there was the flap in the thirties over Brushy Bill Roberts. His claim on the Kid's identity had proven a hoax, which only served to confirm the accepted historical account and all the legendary exploits that went with it. Hell, they made a movie out of the Roberts claim in the eighties. The Kid's legend in death had grown bigger than he'd ever have dreamed. Billy the Kid was a tourism bonanza in New Mexico. A lot of folks stood to be unhappy about the John Miller story if it turned out to be true. It didn't end in New Mexico. It began there. John Miller it seems appeared on the face of the earth the day he married Isadora right here in Las Vegas. No record of him exists before that day less than a month after Pat Garrett shot a man in Pete Maxwell's bedroom.

Las Vegas, New Mexico Territory
August 8, 1881

The wagon plodded up the dusty street through the center of town. A slope-shouldered young man dressed in trail-stained britches, a plain spun shirt and slouch hat held the lines to a sturdy mule team. A dark-skinned Mexican girl sat in the driver's box beside him. She wore a simple calico dress and bonnet, battered by gusts of hot summer wind. Nothing distinguished them from the other dirt poor, save the long-barreled Colt slung in a holster at the young man's hip.

He drew the team to a halt before the small white church at the head of the street. He climbed down from the box and held out a hand to help the young woman down. She glanced anxiously at the church.

"We must find a padre at the mission," she said in Spanish.

He shook his head. "The minister can marry us all the same. We ain't got time for all the padre's questions."

She took his arm and let him lead her up a low rise to the church steps. He pulled open the heavy wooden door and led her inside. The church smelled of oil soap and candle wax. Golden light suffused the orderly rows of pews arranged before the pulpit. A thin older man with a white fringed bald pate hunched over a stack of hymn books near the front of the church. He stood up and smiled as though he sensed their presence.

"Good afternoon. May I help you?"

The young man pulled off his hat and led the girl down the center aisle. "We come to see about gettin' married."

He smiled again. He met them at the head of the aisle and extended his hand. "Why then you've come to the right place. Parson Gaylord's my name."

"John Miller," he said. "This here's Isadora."

"Isadora, that's a lovely name."

She smiled.

"She don't speak English."

"I see. She does know she's getting married?"

He smiled a crooked smile. "Sure she does."

"When were you planning these nuptials?"

"We kind of thought maybe today."

"Today?"

"Yes, sir, Reverend, sir. See we're just passin' through on our way West. We don't have much time and we don't figure on seein' a church anytime soon after this one."

"Say, you're not running away are you?

Her parents do know she's getting married don't they?"

"Her parents is dead."

"I'm sorry to hear that."

"Her older brother give us his blessin'."

"I see. I suppose that'll be all right then."

He gave a gap-toothed grin. "So, how 'bout it, can we get to it then?"

The Parson wiped his hands on his pants. "We'll need a witness. Let me get my wife from the parsonage. Have a seat. We'll be with you in a few minutes."

Twenty minutes later, they marched down the center aisle to the chords of an organ tune played by Parson Gaylord's wife. The parson met them at the foot of the sanctuary. His wife finished the last note and hurried up the aisle to stand behind them.

"Dearly beloved, we are gathered here today to join this man, John Miller, and this woman, Isadora . . ."

"Martinez," the young man said.

"Isadora Martinez in holy matrimony. If there are any present . . ." He raised a brow over their heads. "I guess we can skip over that part. Do you, John, take this woman to be your lawful wedded wife, for better or worse, for richer or poorer, in sickness and in health until death do you part?"

He looked into her dark liquid eyes. "I do."

"Do you, Isadora . . . does she understand?"

She nodded, blushed and averted her eyes.

The parson glanced at his wife. She smiled and shrugged. "Do you, Isadora, take this man to be your lawful wedded husband, for better or worse, for richer for poorer, in sickness and in health until death do you part?"

"Si." She smiled a little smile.

"Then by the powers vested in me before almighty God, I pronounce you man and wife. You may kiss the bride."

He did.

"That'll be two dollars."

Ramah, New Mexico Territory
1890

Isadora chased her husband John and Noah Fitch away from the table, waving her hands as though shooing a fly. She and Millie would clean up the supper dishes and clear the table for their customary game of Parcheesi.

The men repaired to the parlor as ordered. John took a seat in his favorite rocking chair beside an old trunk. His guest took a place on the settee. Noah rolled a smoke while

John packed his pipe. They'd been friends going on seven years now as the Millers carved a working ranch out of rough country the way Noah's father had done two decades before. Hard men, they'd formed a bond, each knowing he had a neighbor nearby if ever he needed help. A three-mile ride qualified as nearby in these parts. Their smokes came to light.

Miller was a good man with a yarn. Fitch had come to appreciate his stories. He had, it seemed, limitless insights into the infamous Lincoln County War and the exploits of the notorious outlaw known as Billy the Kid. Fitch marveled at his knowledge and conviction about the Kid. John brooked no argument when it came to the way things happened those long years ago, no matter the conflicting stories or wild accusations that continued to attend the events of the war and the Kid's life. John knew the Kid. That much he admitted. He knew the Kid's story so well Fitch couldn't help but wonder if his friend might in fact be the Kid. Enough stories had circulated, calling to question Sheriff Garrett's claim on the Kid's life, for some folks to wonder if Billy might actually have survived that night back in '81. He'd confronted John with the question once or twice. Miller only smiled and shook his head. Millie had gotten a different answer from Isadora on more than one occasion. That comported with a general wariness about John's demeanor and the fact he never left himself far away from the long Colt he wore.

He was easy to engage in conversation about the old days or to invite into some demonstration of marksmanship skills with that gun. As he listened to the women wash the dishes in the kitchen he decided to pass the time with a story.

"You know, John, I've listened to your stories about how the Kid broke out of the Lincoln County jail. I know he shot his way out, but how in hell did he pull that off while he was chained and under armed guard?"

Miller tamped the tobacco in his pipe and puffed a fragrant cloud of blue smoke. He smiled. "Weren't really that much to it, Noah." His eyes glazed behind the smoke, seeing a day in time past. "The sheriff had gone up to White Oaks. They said he went to buy lumber to build a gallows for the Kid. Olinger brought the Kid his noon meal and went on over to the Wortley for lunch. That left J. W. Bell in charge. Bell was all right, maybe too nice for his own good. The Kid figured this might be his best chance to escape. He called Bell to take him to the privy. Bell made a mistake when he came upstairs to get the cell keys. He left the armory door unlocked, but that part came later. Bell took him out to the privy."

"Some say old Gauss hid a gun in the privy."

Miller shook his head. "Some thought so. They figured the only way the Kid could have pulled it off is if he was armed. Old Godfrey was easy to blame for that notion. He lived behind the courthouse and he was an old friend of Billy's from their days workin' for Mr. Tunstall. He didn't do it, though. The Kid wasn't armed when he come out of the privy. On the way back to his cell he got ahead of Bell a little bit. He got to the top of the stairs and waited for Bell. He jumped him when he come off the stairs."

"That's the part I never understood. The Kid was chained wasn't he?"

Miller nodded.

"Then how the hell did he get a jump on Bell before he could draw his gun?"

Miller shrugged as though there was nothing to it. "He shucked his cuffs."

"He shucked his cuffs. Just tossed 'em away?"

John shook his head. "Nah, he hit Bell

with 'em."

"He got 'em off, though."

"Yup."

"How'd he do that?"

"Just somethin' the Kid could do."

Now Fitch shook his head. "John, I don't ever question you when you talk about the Kid or the war, but that's one I have a real hard time believin'."

Miller shrugged. "Don't know why. Here, I'll show you." He went out back of the kitchen and came back with a length of rope. "Here, tie my hands behind my back."

"What?"

"Tie my hands."

"You don't need to do this, John."

"Com'on, do like I say."

Fitch came around behind him and tied his wrists.

"Tie 'em good and tight."

"I'm workin' on it."

"That's better. Good and tight?"

Fitch inspected his work. "Any tighter your hands'll turn blue."

"Now go on back to your chair and sit down."

Fitch took three strides to his chair and turned to sit down. Miller stood, unmoved from the spot he'd left him, rubbing his wrists. The rope lay on the floor at his feet.

He sat down in the rocker and scratched a match to relight his pipe.

"How'd you do that?"

He shrugged. "Same way the Kid done. He shucked his cuffs."

"Yeah, but how?"

"Small hands. You know the rest of the story. He jumped Bell and got his gun. J. W. made a run for it. Too bad really. No choice but to shoot him. He was a real decent feller. Nothin' like Olinger. That sumbitch deserved what he got."

"You boys ready to play?"

"Sure 'nuf, Millie." John smiled. He started for the kitchen.

Noah glanced at the rope on the floor. The knots were still tied.

Ramah, New Mexico
June 1938

It was a warm sunny day. Noah Fitch sat in a rocking chair on his porch overlooking a sloping hill that fell away into a deep arroyo. He wore a jacket in spite of the heat and had his legs wrapped in a gray wool blanket. Even warm days gave chills to the thin blood that came to a man north of eighty. Still it felt damn good to breathe clean air.

A dust cloud on the road below the ranch

caught his eye. They didn't get much traffic out this way, even fewer visitors. He watched an olive green sedan of indeterminate make climb the winding road, switching back and forth to make the climb. Sunlight flashed on the windscreen and chrome trim as the car came level with the drive into the ranch. The car slowed. It made the turn like a great green beetle and continued to climb the rutted single lane. *Company coming.* To what did he owe the pleasure? More likely it wouldn't be any pleasure at all. He didn't recognize the car. In the old days he would have been reaching for a rifle or a shotgun at the sight of a strange rider coming. No more. These days folks were civilized. They came wearing suits, with cases full of papers about taxes and such. Time was when things were a whole lot simpler.

The car braked to a stop at the end of the drive. The dust cloud trailing behind caught up and billowed around the driver as the door opened. The young man in a fedora wore a brown suit. It didn't look like it'd show the dust much. Still he expected city folk felt obliged to keep such things clean. It'd likely cost him a pretty penny to have it cleaned and pressed. He smiled. It felt like a small revenge for whatever trouble he might be totin' in that brown leather case of his. He came up the stone walk.

"Mr. Fitch?"

He nodded. "I am."

"Harvey Westbrook. I represent the Prescott Arizona Probate Court." He held out his hand.

Noah took it in spite of his best judgment. "Prescott, you're a long way from Arizona young man."

"We're trying to settle the estate of one John Miller. I believe you were acquainted with Mr. Miller."

"Sure, I knew John. His estate you say, sorry to hear that. I didn't know he passed."

"I'm sorry to be the bearer of bad news. Mr. Miller passed away late last year at the Pioneer Nursing Home in Prescott. We are trying to locate his rightful heirs to receive his personal effects."

"Afraid I can't help. The Millers never had any children of their own. They had one adopted son. Last I knew he went missing in the war. Anything of value?"

"Not really, personal effects, an old trunk, that's about it."

"The old trunk, we always wondered about that, me and Millie."

"Wondered about that, what do you mean?"

"Some of us wondered what it might tell

490

us about John's past. John wouldn't talk about it, except to say it was just some old stuff. 'Memories of the old days,' he said. Didn't sound important enough to keep it locked all the time. Do you know what's in it?"

"I do. Why?"

"Well John had a past. He didn't talk about it directly, but he was full of stories."

"Stories?"

"About Billy the Kid. He seemed to know most everything about the Kid. Things almost no one would know. Some of us thought he might really be the Kid. One time when he'd had a little too much to drink he admitted it. Later when he sobered up he went back to denyin' it, but I never quite believed that. John always was a straight shooter. I think the whiskey just loosened his tongue. Isadora said he was the Kid too."

"Isadora?"

"His wife. She told Millie, my wife, more than once that John was Billy."

"You know, Mr. Fitch, I wondered about the contents of that trunk. We don't usually go to these lengths to find rightful owners when it comes to personal effects, unless there's a substantial amount of money involved. But in this case, I decided to make an exception. I wondered about that trunk."

"Mind if I ask what's in it?"

Westbrook tipped his hat back on his head. "I guess it can't hurt under the circumstances. There's an old sombrero, newspaper clippings about the Lincoln County War. There's more clippings about Billy the Kid and an old tintype of a young man armed to the teeth, wearing a battered old top hat. It's the picture they say is the Kid."

"Is that all?"

"No. There's an old forty-one Colt, Thunderer model."

"The Kid's gun."

"I guess it could be."

AFTERWORD

Las Vegas, New Mexico
September 23, 2010

Rick Ledger stared at the envelope, sensing the culmination of a quest begun as a boy. The DNA results he held in his hand would not be conclusive. They would not establish the Kid's identity. Nevertheless they could make a powerful addition to the circumstantial evidence surrounding the case.

No record of John Miller had ever been found prior to his marriage to the woman called Isadora. Physically, Miller resembled the Kid. He had buck teeth, sloped shoulders, prominent ears and the scars of multiple gunshot wounds on his body. While he never made a public claim that he was Billy the Kid, he did confide the claim to a few trusted friends, who regarded him as a straightforward man of his word. Isadora confirmed more than once that her husband was in fact, Billy the Kid. The infamous trunk went missing in the custody of the State of Arizona when the rightful heirs could not be found.

Garrett's account states that Alcalde Segura convened the coroner's inquest formaned by Milnor Rudulph. Alejandro Segura's official records of the period make no mention of the death of the Kid or the coroner's inquest. Other sources claimed Pete Maxwell wrote the coroner's report and the inquest verdict. The coroner's report, entrusted to Garrett, was never officially recorded. The original coroner's inquest verdict has never been found, though a photostatic copy was found some fifty years later. According to that document, the inquest concluded that Garrett killed the Kid in the line of duty and that he deserved the reward. The language that ascribes "the gratitude of the whole territory is due Sheriff Garrett as is the reward for the death of this dangerous desperado" seems odd for the verdict of such a proceeding rendered in a community known to be friendly to the Kid.

Deputy Poe, who originally supported Garrett's account of the events, later changed his story, offering his own version of the events of July 14, 1881. He joined Paco Anaya and several others in stating that a proper inquest never took place and that the jurors who signed the verdict never saw the body. Misspellings on some of the juror signatures suggested they may have been forged.

Parts of Ty's story were confirmed by other accounts. The body was not displayed publicly as was the custom with high profile outlaws in those days. No photograph was taken of the body or Garrett with the body, as was also the custom in high profile cases. Instead, according to Deputy Poe, the body was closed in the carpenter's shop. The body was buried July 15, a short time after the hastily convened coroner's inquest.

Critics of a conspiracy allegation point to inconsistencies in Miller's story as he told it on different occasions. The same could be said of Garrett's account in his book. Parts of his story have been disproved or come into question under close examination. Garrett claimed, for example, that the Kid had a gun. No gun was ever found. Critics of the Miller story point out that his Colt did not match the Kid's preferred .41 Thunderer model. It is doubtful either inconsistency should be taken as conclusive. If Miller was Billy the Kid, inconsistencies in his story might be explained by the fact that he had reason to lie. Inconsistencies and inaccuracies in Garrett's story similarly suggest the possibility he lied.

Rick fingered the bone-handled knife he used as a letter opener resting beside the envelope. After all these years he found himself left with many of the same questions concerning Garrett's actions following the shooting that confounded his great-grandpa. If Garrett killed the Kid, why hide the body? Why not take public credit for bringing down one of the West's most notorious outlaws? Why the hastily trumped-up coroner's inquest and the rush to burial? How do you explain the missing coroner's report? Was it ever filed in the first place? And perhaps the most interesting question of all, why didn't Garrett assert his claim on the bounty more aggressively?

The widely discredited "kangaroo" coroner's inquest, hasty burial and lack of public viewing of the body or photographic evidence all suggest a cover-up. The language in the verdict — *the gratitude of the whole territory is due Sheriff Garrett as is the reward* — seems a purely self-serving reach, beyond the purview of such a proceeding. Garrett never aggressively pursued the bounty after his initial claim came into question. Why? Did he simply settle for the notoriety of having killed the Kid, knowing his reward claim could not withstand serious scrutiny? He did receive cash awards from grateful citizens groups across New Mexico Territory. The following year the New Mexico Legislature did authorize payment of the reward, without rigorous examination of the validity of the claim. Is it possible that putting the Kid's death to rest suited some political purpose?

Ledger stared at the envelope. The results would not conclusively end the controversy. Added to the circumstantial evidence, they might be enough to persuade a court to grant access to the remains of Mary Antrim, the Kid's mother. Her DNA might bring an end to the controversy once and for all. Then again, 129 years after the events of that July night, the Kid's legend lives on larger than life. Disputes over the circumstances of the Kid's death may be more about the tourist dollars at stake than the truth. He picked up the knife and wondered. *Would truth ever end the controversy, or was it lost to a legend undeniably worth more?*

AUTHOR'S NOTE

Another theory on the events of July 14, 1881, holds that Pat Garrett shot Billy the Kid but did not kill him. Some proponents of this scenario suggest the Kid played dead and that Garrett never knew he survived. That assertion does not explain Garrett's behavior after the shooting. He is clearly implicated in the irregularities surrounding the coroner's report and the coroner's inquest. For purposes of this story, the author concludes Garrett's actions strongly suggest he was party to a cover-up. The question then is why? Friendship for an outlaw who killed two of his deputies doesn't seem worth the personal risk in such a high profile case. In fact Garrett's friendship with the Kid was casual at best. Killing the wrong man is a much stronger motive for a cover-up.

History tells us that Paulita Maxwell was not the woman known as Isadora Miller.

Paulita and the Kid were romantically involved. In fact the relationship is thought to have deepened in the weeks following his escape from jail. Pete Maxwell's motive for participating in a cover-up might well have been to get the Kid out of Paulita's life once and for all.

The suggestion that Billy was in Paulita's bedroom that night is speculation. It fits the romantic story and is more entertaining than the accepted account which holds that the victim was there to get a slice of beef. That said, the speculation is intriguing for more substantive reasons. According to Deputy Poe, the victim reached the Maxwell front porch that night and discovered strangers skulking about. If you were Billy the Kid, a wanted desperado with a death sentence hanging over your head, do you go inside to find out who they are, or do you scoot back to your hidey-hole? By Garrett's own account the Kid was too smart to take such a risk. If, by contrast, you are Billy Barlow or some other friend of the Kid, you have no reason to fear the unidentified strangers. If your friend is hiding nearby, your instinct is to warn him of potential danger. You might go inside to find out the identity of the strangers. Someone went into Pete Maxwell's house that night and very likely died. Was it to get a slice of meat, or to warn the Kid?

If the Kid was hiding in the area when the shooting occurred, he probably got word of his "death" pretty quickly. In a "Mark Twain moment," he could easily have decided that an exaggerated report of his death was better than a pardon. It is possible he escaped and later assumed the identity of John Miller.

There are those who vigorously defend the accepted historical account of these events, largely as told by Garrett in his 1882 book, *The Authentic Life of Billy the Kid.* There is little doubt Pat Garrett authored that history. The printed word of the time surely had that effect. For confirmation, one need only consider Libbie Custer's biographical creation of her husband's legend. Apart from money, which Garrett denied was his motive in writing the book, the publication seems self-serving in other respects. The power of the pen firmly established his claim of having killed Billy the Kid. In the book, he suggests Poe and McKinney questioned the identity of the victim at the time of the shooting. He then goes on to refute the allegation. Initially Poe supported Garrett's version of the events. He changed his opinion later. Garrett's recounting of the events in his book more than a year later seems a convenient response to Poe's later suspicion.

This story is based on John Poe's version of those events, circumstantial evidence, unanswered questions and a little old-fashioned deduction. It contradicts Garrett's account and the historical record that follows from it. The story poses a plausible version of events that speculates answers to many disputed aspects of the case. Did Pat Garrett kill Billy the Kid July 14, 1881, or did he kill the wrong man and cover it up? Did Billy the Kid live out the remainder of his days as John Miller? Historians have their verdict. History has its legend. Pat Garrett claimed he killed the Kid. John Poe, a respected figure in his time, and others who were there question that claim. Both cases are circumstantial. Neither case can be proven beyond the shadow of doubt.

Most of the characters and events recounted here are based in historical fact. The author has taken creative liberty in characterizing individuals and describing events. The roles of John Poe and Kip McKinney have been expanded to limit the number of characters presented to the reader. Other deputies for example, rode with Garrett when the Kid was captured at

Stinking Springs. The parts played by Poe and McKinney as portrayed in the events of July 14 are consistent with Poe's account. The Kid's relationship with Paulita Maxwell has been embellished as previously disclosed. William Rynerson, a district attorney of the time, did not personally prosecute the Kid. Ty Ledger, Johnny Roth and a few others are fictional characters.

Researching historical events invariably uncovers inconsistencies which contribute to creative interpretation. No story could be more fraught with such controversies than the events surrounding the death of Billy the Kid. Where there is conflict between historical fact and the author's portrayal, it is the author's intent to present a fictional account for the enjoyment of the reader.

Paul Colt

SELECTED SOURCES

BOOKS

Garrett, Pat F. *The Authentic Life of Billy the Kid.* New York: Sky Horse Publishing, 2011.

Nolan, Frederick. *The Lincoln County War, A Documentary History.* Santa Fe: Sunstone Press, 2009.

Poe, John William. *The Death of Billy the Kid.* Santa Fe: Sunstone Press, 2006.

WEB SITES

McCarty, Nick. "Chronology of the Life of Billy the Kid and the Lincoln County War." April 26, 2012. http://www.angelfire.com/mi2/billythekid/chronology.html.

ABOUT THE AUTHOR

Paul Colt creates historical fiction that crackles with authenticity. His analytical insight, investigative research and genuine horse sense bring history to life. His characters walk off the pages of history into the reader's imagination in a style that blends Jeff Shaara's historical dramatizations with Robert B. Parker's gritty dialogue.

Paul's first book, *Grasshoppers in Summer,* received Finalist recognition in the Western Writers of America 2009 Spur Awards. *Boots and Saddles: A Call to Glory* received the Marilyn Brown Novel Award, presented by Utah Valley University for excellence in unpublished work, prior to being accepted for publication by Five Star Publishing.

To learn more visit www.paulcolt.com.